For the Love of Martha

MARIA MURPHY

POOLBEG

This novel is entirely a work of fiction. The names,
characters and incidents portrayed in it are the work of the
author's imagination. Any resemblance to actual persons,
living or dead, events or localities is entirely coincidental.

Published 2015
by Poolbeg Press Ltd.
123 Grange Hill, Baldoyle,
Dublin 13, Ireland
Email: poolbeg@poolbeg.com

1

A catalogue record for this book is available from the British Library.

ISBN 978-1-78199-911-0

Printed by CPI Group (UK) Ltd, Croydon, CR0 4YY

www.poolbeg.com

About the Author

Maria Murphy, poet and author, lives in County Kildare with her husband and two sons. Lured by her passion for the sea, she often returns to her home county of Cork.

Acknowledgements

A truly heartfelt thank-you to:

Kieran, Sam and Luke for your love and support.

To my parents for all those prayers!

To Alison Maxwell for running that first creative writing course – I'm glad that I chose it over the flower-arranging class!

To the Kildare County Council Library and Arts Service for awarding me the Tyrone Guthrie Residency Bursary Award to stay in the Tyrone Guthrie Centre at Annaghmakerrig, where this novel was begun.

To the members of the Naas Harbour Writers for your help and wisdom, and especially to Margaret Scott for her friendship, input and advice, and for never letting me give up.

To Theresa Murray O'Meara for proofreading the manuscript before submission.

To Neil Donnelly, who encouraged the initial spark and kept it burning, for always being there for advice and guidance.

To Vanessa O'Loughlin of The Inkwell Group, without whose help this book would still be an unpublished novella!

To those who saw, and believed in, the artist in me – especially Aedín, Philip, Clare, Noel, Martina, Niall, and Julia.

To my cousin, Caroline Sheehan, who was with me the day I got the news that my dream was going to come true, and who celebrated it magnificently with me in the wild and beautiful surroundings of West Cork and the sea.

A huge thank-you to all at Poolbeg, especially Paula Campbell, and my editor Gaye Shortland who made the editing painless!

And finally, grateful thanks to you, the readers.

For Julia

It is only with the heart that one can see rightly;
What is essential is invisible to the eye.

The Little Prince, by Antoine De Saint-Exupéry

Prologue

All was still as Juliet made her way across the courtyard in the fog and around by the orchard wall. The iron bars of the gate were cold to her touch. She stood for a long moment. The nearby trees looked lifeless in the dull grey light, while those far off were mere shadows where the fog was thickest.

A beep from the phone in her pocket seemed totally out of place, like an insult to the orchard's silence. She switched it off.

Her natural curiosity fought with a feeling of unease, and won, compelling her to push the gate open and step inside. She turned left, as though not of her own volition, and followed the pebbled path. The musty scent of the old, lichen-covered branches hung in the air. The wall ahead turned right, as did the path. Juliet followed it for a few feet and then stopped abruptly. There in front of her was the exact scene she had dreamed – the same group of trees standing on their own section of grass near the wall and to the left of them an old stone bench.

'How can you dream of a place you've never seen before?' she muttered, unnerved.

The sadness she'd felt on waking that morning was back, like a physical weight, while echoes of the sobbing she'd heard in her dream swirled around her. The recall was so vivid that for a moment she thought she could actually hear it. Her eyes darted around, searching for any movement, but there was none. There was no one there.

'Is it you, Martha?' she asked, her breath disturbing the fog. 'Is it your sadness I'm feeling? If so, what made you so sad and why am I the one to feel it now?'

Her words went unanswered, and it got colder. She shivered. With relief she heard a car door close in the yard and she quickly left the orchard.

Chapter 1

Berkshire, England, 1888

In hindsight it amazed me that the moment could have carried such insignificance, considering all that was to follow . . .

I picked up another ribbon, held it against my bonnet and examined the contrast in the mirror on the counter. The colour clashed with my auburn hair.

'What about this yellow one, Martha?' Mrs. Beckett the shopkeeper said, laying it next to the others.

As I reached for it, I was distracted by the raised voice of another customer and the excitement in her tone.

'There he is now,' she exclaimed, as she and two other ladies moved closer to the window, their bustles bobbing and twitching as they leant forward, jostling for position.

I got a fleeting glimpse of a horse and rider passing on the street, leaving me with the impression of height and broad shoulders in a dark frock coat and hat. But I did not see the face.

I turned back to Mrs. Beckett, my eyebrows raised in question at the fuss.

'That's the new doctor,' she informed me. 'And I must say he is a wonder, especially for one so young. Easy on the eyes too, I don't mind saying. For twenty years, old Doc Johnson couldn't give me any relief for these aching knees of mine. But Dr. Adams there, he gave me an ointment that eased them straight away. Mind you, he told me that if I lost a little weight that would make them even better. "Not likely," I told him, "and I married to the best baker in all of Berkshire!"'

She guffawed, her hands resting on her ample waist. Her mirth was contagious and I laughed too.

'It's a long time since I had a slim figure like yours,' she said.

'Thank you,' I smiled, then held up another ribbon.

'Ah, there you go,' she said. 'That colour is perfect. Pretty as a picture!'

Was I pretty, I wondered, looking at the familiar reflection. Well, my father had always said that I had eyes that were alive with laughter. They were sober now, and the same blue as the ribbon I held. My nose was straight, my cheekbones high, and my chin neither too sharp nor too round. I ended this contemplation with a shrug, turned from the mirror and took some coins from the purse hanging from my wrist.

'I'll take it,' I said.

Mrs Beckett nodded her approval and wrapped the ribbon in paper.

'Give my regards to Mrs Pershaw,' she said, handing it across to me.

'I will. Thank you and good day.'

Stepping out into the bright August sunshine, I waited for two carts to pass before crossing Main Street.

As it happened I had to walk by the new doctor's house and surgery. The memory of another doctor, only months before, telling me that my father was dying was fresh in my mind, so I had no desire to meet this one or any other member of the medical profession either.

Leaving the village I walked along the lane, trying to ignore the familiar pain of my father's absence. Although I missed him every day, I was determined to keep my spirits up. It was what he, who had been a great lover of life, would have wanted.

Twenty minutes later I walked through the gates of View Manor and headed up the driveway, still marvelling at my good fortune to be living in such a grand mansion, in such beautiful parkland.

Yes, I was very fortunate. On that pleasant thought, I gave a little skip as I rounded the corner of the west wing, and came upon my cousin, Helena Pershaw, sitting at a table on the terrace outside the open doors to the drawing room.

'Martha,' she called as the maid put down a tray in front of her, 'you are just in time for lemonade!'

'I was on my way to the nursery,' I said.

'Sit for a moment. Lily will bring Beatrice down shortly.' Ice tinkled against glass as she lifted the jug.

I sat near her, wishing that day dresses with high collars and long sleeves had never been invented. After removing my bonnet, I took a welcome sip of the chilled drink.

'Did you purchase anything?' she asked.

Before I could reply Beatrice appeared, her tiny hand gripping the maid's. Letting go, she ran into Helena's arms. There was a great likeness between mother and daughter, their two blonde heads pressed close together, one neatly coiffed with a pleat at her neck and the other covered in bouncing curls.

'Thank you, Lily.' Helena dismissed the maid with a smile.

'Did you have a nice nap, Beatrice?' I asked.

She nodded, jumped down from her mother's lap, ran to me for a hug, and then began a hopping game around the cracks in the paving.

'You are so good with her,' Helena said.

'She is very bright for three and a half,' I said.

Helena smiled at the compliment.

'You have become a good friend to me, Martha. I hope you are happy.'

'Oh yes, Cousin, very happy,' I rushed to reassure her. 'Having no other living relatives but you, I shudder at the thought of what might have become of me after Father's death if you had not invited me to live with you as Beatrice's governess. I cannot thank you enough.'

Helena smiled, reached out, and gave my hand a gentle squeeze. 'Your home is with us now.'

I relaxed in quiet contentment. A bee droned past, the scent of roses lingered on the warm air.

Beatrice soon grew bored with her game and wandered over to a low wall where she sat to watch a spider make a web. I was only eighteen and yet the simple freedoms of childhood seemed a very long time ago.

'My throat is sore.' Beatrice's voice broke into my thoughts.

Concerned, I went and hunkered down in front of her. My hand went to her forehead, but to my relief it was cool to the touch.

'Can I see where it hurts?' I asked, tilting up her chin.

Obligingly she opened her mouth and pointed into it with a small finger.

Helena was now beside us. 'Well?' she asked anxiously.

'It is a little red,' I told her, 'but she doesn't have a fever.'

'Good,' Helena said. 'Keep a watchful eye on her for the rest of the day, Martha.'

'Of course.'

I led Beatrice over to my chair.

'How about sucking on a little bit of ice?' I suggested.

Her curls bounced as she nodded.

The ice seemed to soothe her and within minutes she was off my lap and jumping again. After a while I took her down into the garden while Helena did some sewing.

In the nursery, a few hours later, Beatrice refused to eat her supper, saying again that her throat was sore. Her forehead was now warmer.

'All right,' I said, in a mock stern voice. 'I will let you go to bed tonight without supper, but just this once. Now, into your nightgown!'

She laughed but it turned into a cough and, lacking her usual spirit, she let me get her ready for bed. Seeing a faint rash on her chest, I fetched Helena. She came to Beatrice's room already dressed for dinner in a sapphire-blue gown. The diamonds at her neck shimmered in the evening light as she leaned over her daughter.

'Her fever is still not very high but a rash should never be ignored,' she said. 'I think we should send for the doctor.'

'Best to be safe,' I agreed.

'Oh, I wish James was back from Italy!'

So I was going to meet the new doctor after all, I thought as I went downstairs to send one of the servants to fetch him from the village. I hoped he was worthy of the praises Mrs. Becket had showered on him earlier that day.

Chapter 2

London 2010

Juliet pushed the door shut with her elbow before bending at the knees to shrug off the shoulder-strap of her camera-equipment bag onto the floor. She slung the tote bag down beside it before continuing into the open-plan living space. Sighing with the pleasure of being home, she just stood for a moment to admire the apartment, the clean lines of steel and wood in the kitchen area, the polished wooden floor and glass coffee table in the living area. Some people thought it a bit severe, even sterile, but she needed its simplicity to soothe her after the busyness and unpredictability of life on an assignment.

Her one concession to cosiness was a deep crimson armchair which her mother had bought her as a housewarming gift the previous year. The sight of it made her smile and, after making a cup of coffee, she settled into it with a sigh, curling her long legs under her. She dialled her mother's number and fiddled with the ends of her short blonde hair while waiting for her to answer.

Frances Holmes picked up after three rings.

'Hello?'

'Hi, Mum, it's me.'

'Hello, love. How are you? How was your trip?'

'Amazing –'

'That's great, pet,' Frances cut in. 'I've been waiting for you to ring. I need to ask you a favour.'

Juliet was surprised at the interruption. Her mother was usually anxious to hear every detail of her trips.

Frances continued. 'Can you house-sit an apartment in Florence for two weeks, starting Saturday?'

'What? But I'm just home! I can't go travelling again so soon.'

'That was work, dear – this would be a lovely holiday for you. You work too hard and don't take enough time for yourself.'

'I'm taking time for myself right now,' Juliet replied, smiling and pressing further back into the comfort of the chair. She could hear the hum of London traffic from across the park below her window, and found it soothing.

Using the pause as an opportunity to press her case, Frances continued. 'I can't get away from the practice at the moment because our other paediatrician went into labour two months early. I simply can't leave them in the lurch here. But I promised a friend of mine that I'd be in Italy on Saturday to mind her apartment, and I don't want to let her down.'

'But it's Wednesday already. I'll have the debriefing at work and other stuff, not to mention unpacking and laundry,' Juliet protested.

'Black combats and white T-shirts are not exactly what you wear when on holiday in Italy. You won't be needing them.'

Juliet glanced over at her discarded bags. 'So why does your friend need someone to house-sit her apartment in Verona anyway?'

'Florence,' her mother corrected, 'and her name is Elizabeth,

9

Elizabeth Pershaw. She used to be in my book club up to five years ago before she moved to live permanently in Florence. We've kept up the friendship since. But now she's going to America for a month and she doesn't like to leave the apartment empty. So she insisted I would be doing her a favour if I stayed there for two weeks to keep an eye on the place, water her plants etc.'

'Why can't Dad go instead?'

'Work on the new orthopaedic wing has gone to tender at last and he has to be around to oversee that.'

'If she's going away for a month, why does she need me for only two weeks?'

'Apparently her son is going to spend the second fortnight there.' She paused. 'Come on, think about it – Italy in June – the wine, the food, all that lush vegetation. It will be completely different from the dry heat of Africa.'

Juliet was immediately transported back. 'Oh, Mum, I got some fabulous shots. There was this magnificent lioness and her cubs and we got up so close. I took some beauties of them. They'll definitely be in next month's issue.'

Juliet felt the thrill again as she spent the next few minutes filling her mother in on her latest photo shoot.

'The sunsets there are everything people say they are – absolutely magnificent!' she enthused.

'I'm sure, but I worry constantly about you when you're away working. It'll be a relief to know you're in such a civilised spot as Florence for a change.'

She was successfully reeling Juliet in.

'I don't think Rob has a new assignment lined up for me for a few weeks. I suppose I could ask for a couple of weeks off. I hadn't even thought of holiday plans.'

'Thanks, love. I'll call Elizabeth straight away and then I'll change the name for the flight. I'll email you details.' There was a pause. 'I suppose you could take Russell with you.'

'I'm not seeing him any more. I finished it before I left for Africa. It just wasn't working.'

'Of course it wasn't working. You weren't suited at all.'

'I thought you liked him.'

'I did but there was no magic between you.'

'You always say that.'

'Well, there wasn't. Your eyes didn't light up when he came into the room.'

'Like with you and Dad.'

'Still,' her mother sighed contentedly. 'After all these years.'

Juliet pictured them as she had often seen them – her father grabbing her mother in the kitchen and dancing her around to a slow song on the radio, she with her apron on and some cooking utensil in her hand. She would pretend to bat him away at first, saying the dinner would be ruined, but then she would snuggle in close and they would be lost in their own world until the song finished.

Juliet came back to the present as Frances spoke again.

'Don't settle for anything less than magic, my love.'

'You must be the only mother in the world who doesn't mention ticking clocks to their unmarried twenty-nine-year-old daughters.'

'There's still plenty of time, don't worry. Just don't fall for some Italian who will want you to live over there with him and his *mamma*. Seriously, you'll have a lovely time. I'm so disappointed I can't go.'

'Maybe it's what I need. It'll be good to travel without the team for a change. It's been a while since I've taken any photographs simply as a tourist.'

'Great, that's settled. Now go pack some girly clothes and

11

don't forget to check your emails later for all the details.'

'Wait! Don't do anything until I fix things at work. I'll text you.'

They hung up.

Juliet continued to sit, watching the trees moving in a squally shower. Even though it was the beginning of June, it looked like a day in October. English summers seemed to be getting worse each year, she thought, so a couple of sunny weeks in Italy might be very nice indeed. She began to feel that familiar kick of excitement at the thought of going to a new place, but this time without the accompanying rush of adrenaline at the possible dangers that would be encountered. Yes, an uneventful two weeks was definitely gaining in appeal.

She pressed the speed dial on her mobile for her editor at the wildlife magazine she worked for.

'You did good, Juliet. The photos you sent through are wonderful, and I've seen the outline of Jack's article. It's going to make a very good feature.'

'Sorry they were a couple of days late. We had trouble with the sat phone.'

'No problem.'

'Well, while you're in such a great mood, will you give me two weeks off?'

'Starting when?'

'I need to travel on Saturday.'

'Okay, well, if we bring the meeting forward to Friday morning, work through the day, and if we can all agree on which pics work best, then, yes, you can have your two weeks.'

'That's great, Rob, thanks. See you Friday.'

Well, it seems that's decided then, Juliet thought, hanging up. A quick text to her mother confirmed that she would go.

She went to the bedroom and threw open her wardrobe doors.

There was nothing suitable there. It had been a few years since she had taken a real holiday and she didn't have anything pretty in there, certainly nothing suitable for a stylish city like Florence. Obviously she was going to have to fit a bit of shopping into the next two days too.

'I'll think about it tomorrow,' she said out loud and, suddenly overcome with fatigue, she got ready for bed.

Chapter 3

Berkshire, England, 1888

It was midnight and still the doctor had not arrived. The message had come back several hours earlier that he was attending a birth and that he could not come straight away. Beatrice lay flushed against the pillow, coughing every now and then. Helena and I were keeping vigil on either side of the bed. I too had changed into a dinner gown, a dress of pale peach, because Mother Pershaw, Helena's mother-in-law, had insisted we join her for dinner while Lily watched over Beatrice. Since the child was not very sick, Helena had meekly complied.

The house was quiet, the staff having been sent to bed earlier – going reluctantly, concerned about the little girl as she was much loved. Helena had been firm, assuring the butler that I would let the doctor in, knowing that I would not let her sit up alone or be able to sleep when my charge was unwell.

Another hour passed and, restless, I got up, crossed the wooden floorboards and pushed up the sash window. The room had grown stuffy and a fresh waft of air, scented with late summer flowers, caressed my cheeks. My eyes slid shut and I inhaled deeply, my fingers playing absently with the pearls at my throat.

'Those pearls are pretty,' Helena commented, stretching her back. 'I remember seeing your mother wearing them when I was a child.'

'Yes, my father gave them to her as a wedding gift.'

We lapsed into silence again, the hissing of the lamp by the bed the only sound.

Tedium brought Helena to her feet also, setting her pacing the room for a while before resuming her seat.

I returned to Beatrice and, squeezing out a cloth in a bowl of cool water, I pressed it to her forehead.

It was nearly two in the morning when we heard a horse approaching.

'Thank the Lord,' Helena exclaimed. 'Martha, run down and let him in.'

Taking a lamp, I descended the curved staircase. The light momentarily lit up each portrait of the Pershaw ancestors as I passed, my shoes echoing against the stone steps in the hush of night. I hurried across the expanse of black and white tiles in the entrance hall to place the lamp on the round table in its centre. I needed both hands to draw back the large bolt, and to pull open the heavy front door.

I watched a tall figure taking the front steps two at a time, a medical bag in his right hand. He stepped inside. I had to tilt my head to look up into his face. Neither of us spoke.

For a moment my breath was stolen. I had never seen him before and yet it was as if part of me recognised him. He studied me with serious brown eyes, a slight frown between his brows.

'I am Dr. Adams. I think you were expecting me.'

'Yes, yes, we were,' I said, closing the door firmly behind him. Then I stood to take the leather gloves he had just removed.

15

They were warm in my palm.

I placed them on the table as he removed his hat. His black hair fell across his forehead and at the back was a little longer than was fashionable, falling over his collar. The style suited him, emphasising the cheekbones on a lean face above a cravat slightly loosened, but still properly tied. My impression of his height earlier that day had been correct, for I now thought him to be at least six foot two.

He shrugged off his light riding coat and, taking it from him, I swiftly laid it on the velvet button-back chair by the door. A pleasant mixture of night air, leather and horse emanated from it.

Picking up the lamp, I led the way up the staircase, my skirts rustling in the silence.

'How is the child?' he asked.

I noted his consideration for the sleeping household by his lowered voice.

'Her throat is sore but her fever is mild. However, we are concerned about a rash on her body.' I pushed open the bedroom door.

Helena rushed over. 'Doctor,' she said, holding out her hand, 'I'm Mrs Helena Pershaw. Thank you for coming to see Beatrice. I am sorry for troubling you at this late hour.'

The doctor took her hand and gave a slight bow over it. 'Dr. Adams,' he murmured, his eyes already moving to the child.

Helena led him over, and I moved to stand at the foot of the bed.

Beatrice was awake and looked up at the doctor, her eyes wide in her flushed face, her blonde curls damp against her forehead.

'Hello, Beatrice.' His voice was gentle, while his eyes scrutinised her face intently.

When she did not reply, he gave her a soft smile and took her wrist between his long fingers. Watching him, I wondered what those fingers would feel like on my skin. Heat immediately rushed to my cheeks when I realised what I was thinking. I took a step back into the shadows, grateful for their concealment.

'Who is this?' he asked, nodding at a doll half hidden under the sheet but held in a firm grip by Beatrice's other hand.

'Vicky,' Beatrice croaked.

'Hello, Vicky,' he said, shaking the tiny hand of the doll. 'My name is Dr. Edward Adams, and I am going to make Beatrice better so she can play with you again very soon.'

I watched, mesmerised, as his gentle words brought a smile to Beatrice's lips.

'How old are you, Beatrice?'

'Three,' she replied.

'My goodness, you are practically all grown up.'

The smile widened to a grin.

'Now, do you think you can let me look at that sore throat?'

She nodded, and I moved forward to hold the lamp aloft for him. Taking a small mirror from his bag, he angled it to catch the light and shone it into Beatrice's mouth.

'Thank you,' he murmured when he was done.

I replaced the lamp and he continued his examination.

'Good girl,' he praised Beatrice when he was finished. 'It was lovely to meet you. And you too, Vicky.' He smiled at the doll.

Beatrice giggled despite her sore throat.

Helena lovingly brushed the hair back from the child's forehead before looking up at the doctor expectantly.

'Her throat is very inflamed, but her chest sounds clear. The rash is merely a heat rash brought on by the fever.' Reaching into his black bag, he took out a small brown bottle. 'Give her one spoon of this elixir now and one again in the morning. I shall come back in the afternoon to check on her. Meanwhile give her

17

small, but regular, drinks of water. Sponge her body completely with tepid water every hour to keep her fever down.'

His words, though quiet, were authoritative and reassuring.

'Thank you so much, Dr. Adams.' Helena smiled at him and then looked closer. 'Why, you are pale with tiredness yourself!' She turned to me. 'Martha, take Dr. Adams down to the kitchen and make him a strong cup of tea before he goes home.' She addressed him again. 'Cook has gone to bed but Martha will find you something to eat, sir, if you are hungry.'

'That's very kind of you, Mrs. Pershaw, thank you,' he said as he closed his medical bag.

He bid Helena and Beatrice goodnight.

My hands, which were clasped behind my back, tightened their grip at the thought of being alone with him for a while.

I once more took the lamp and led him down the main stairs and then the back stairs to the basement, all the while unable to think of anything to say.

Pushing open the kitchen door, we were immediately enveloped in the warmth from the stove which had been carefully banked up for the night.

Cook's domain was pristine. The flagstones were scrubbed and the long wooden table was already laid for the servants' breakfast. The doctor took the lamp from me, placing it at one end of the table while I went to put a small kettle onto the hottest part of the stove. Reaching for the tea caddy, I glanced over at the window where his eyes met mine in the reflection on the glass. My hands went still. Our eyes held for a long moment. The silence began to hurt my ears and I blinked.

'Do you take milk? I shall get some,' I blurted.

Without waiting for his reply, I hurried into the pantry. Returning with a cloth-covered jug and some butter, I saw him pulling out two chairs, facing each other across the table before two of the already set places. Then I fetched some bread and cheese, and the remains of a joint of ham.

'You must have tea also, Miss . . .?

'White,' I said as I went to get a breadknife and a carving knife from the dresser.

'Miss White. It has been a long night for all of us. Here, let me help you with that.'

Taking the carving knife from my hand, he began to slice the ham. Behind his back, I glanced at the window again to see if my hair was neat. I patted the back of my head, making sure the combs were still in place, and ran my hand over the front of my dress, then twitched the bustle into place before turning to attend to the boiling kettle. He stood by the table until I brought the steaming teapot over, then held my chair for me as I sat down.

Such manners at nearly three in the morning, I thought, and smiled.

'Something amusing you, Miss White?' he asked, amusement lighting his own eyes.

'It just seems strange to be having tea in the middle of the night. I have never known the house so quiet.'

The house creaked just then and we both laughed.

'It seems the house might have an opinion of its own,' he said.

We laughed again and the nervousness I had been feeling lifted. He seemed different now that the formality of his work was over – more relaxed and at ease.

'Is there a new baby to be celebrated in Mirrow tonight?' I asked, pouring the tea through the strainer.

'Yes, a fine boy, born to Mr. and Mrs. Peters out at Wren Farm.' His eyes shone as he spoke.

As I began to cut the bread, I noticed the way he picked up his cup and cradled it in his long fingers.

'That is good news,' I said. 'Please help yourself. It must be a while since you have eaten.'

He looked towards the ceiling as though trying to recall his last meal. His jaw, with a shadow of growth, tilted upwards and he moved his knuckles over it making a rasping noise. I liked the sound of it.

'I think breakfast was the last time I ate.'

'My goodness!' Heat once more came into my cheeks. 'How can you expect to race around the country taking care of people if you do not feed yourself properly?' I cut more bread with rapid strokes.

My hand was covered by his as he stopped my agitated movements. 'I see you have a fine temper for such a petite person, Miss White. But I have done all my doctoring for one night, I hope, so please do not cut a finger off on my account.'

His hand slid from mine, leaving it burning where his touch had been. I placed my hand in my lap and straightened my spine even more.

'Well, doctors are in short supply,' I said, 'so you cannot afford to get ill.' I tilted my chin, defying him to think I cared about him personally.

'You are absolutely right,' he said, reaching for the bread and butter.

His stomach rumbled as he prepared his sandwich. He smiled and, forgetting my self-consciousness, I smiled back at him.

'So, Miss White, are you family?' His eyes flicked briefly to my peach dinner gown which was evidence enough that I was not a servant.

'Distant family. My father was Helena's – Mrs. Pershaw's – third cousin.'

'Ah, you are visiting?'

'No, I live here now since my father's death four months ago.

Cousin Helena gave me the position of Beatrice's governess.'

'I see. My condolences.'

'This is actually Mrs. Pershaw Senior's house,' I continued and, to distract myself from the grief that was always close, I babbled on, 'but she was quite agreeable to me coming to stay. I think she would like them to continue to live here but Helena and James plan on building their own house some day. He is a merchant and travels the world, but I dare say they will get around to it soon. For Mrs. Pershaw Senior,' I lowered my voice to a whisper, 'is quite a formidable lady and I think Helena would like to be mistress of her own home.' I stopped and pressed my fingers to my mouth, realising I had been talking too much. 'Oh dear, I fear I am being indiscreet. I must blame it on the unusually late hour.'

'Nonsense, Mrs. Pershaw Senior's reputation is so well known in the town that even I have learnt of it already. Please go on,' he urged. 'What about your mother?'

'Mother died when I was fifteen.'

'Brothers and sisters?'

Shaking my head, I stared at him, daring him to feel pity for me. His eyes narrowed slightly before he reached for some more bread.

'Do you like it here?'

'Oh yes. The Pershaws are wonderful and I love this countryside.'

'You enjoy walking?'

'Yes.'

'As do I.'

I held my breath, thinking he was going to ask me to walk with him sometime but instead he asked if he might have some more tea. I exhaled and enquired if he had been doctoring long.

'You must be no more than six and twenty,' I said, his easy

manner allowing me to ask the question without feeling impertinent.

'I am eight and twenty and qualified a year and a half ago.'

'Where did you train?'

'St. Guy's Hospital in London. Do you know it?'

'Yes, I visited an aunt there once. Did you stay on there after you qualified?'

'Yes, I interned there for a year and then went to Cornwall for six months to work with my uncle, a wonderful man. While he practised standard medicine, he also used a lot of herbal remedies which were passed on to him from his mother. He very kindly shared a lot of his knowledge with me.'

I was surprised at this, as most doctors shunned traditional medicine, but I felt it would be impertinent to ask about that. 'Do you like being a doctor?' I asked instead.

'I love it,' he replied, leaning towards me, his eyes alive and passionate. A lock of black hair fell onto his forehead, and I longed to touch it. 'Figuring out what is wrong with people,' he continued, 'and making them better when I can is a privilege, and tonight, helping to bring new life into the world – that will never cease to fill me with wonder.'

His eyes shone. I felt very drawn to this vibrant man.

'Your heart is very obviously in what you do. I have no doubt you are a wonderful doctor, Dr. Adams,' I said, remembering how he had won Beatrice over.

'Edward,' he said, looking at me intently. 'My name is Edward.'

'Edward,' I barely whispered it. 'Then you must call me Martha.'

There in the silent, warm kitchen, an intimacy settled over us.

Lifting his hand, he caressed my cheek with a fingertip.

'Martha,' he said softly.

I could not pull my eyes away from his. 'Helena will be wondering where I am,' I said, flustered.

'Yes, of course,' he said.

But neither of us stood up. He trailed his finger down my cheek once more. His eyes fell to my lips then met mine again.

'Thank you for the tea,' he said, breaking contact and pushing his chair back in order to stand up.

Relief and disappointment warred within me.

'I'll see you out.'

Back upstairs in the hall, I opened the front door as he put on his coat. He pulled on his gloves as he walked towards me.

'I'll be back to see Beatrice tomorrow,' he said, picking up his bag.

'Today,' I corrected as he stepped down one step.

Turning, his face now level with mine, he gave a slight bow.

'It is still not soon enough,' he said softly, his eyes warm with promise. He ran down the steps, mounted his horse, and waved before taking off down the driveway.

I thanked God for the bright moon to light his way, and hurried back up to Helena and Beatrice, with the peculiar feeling that I had just met the other half of myself, a half I had not known was missing.

Chapter 4

Florence, Italy, 2010

So much for two weeks of quiet, Juliet thought, hiding a smile when the taxi driver hurled a string of what she presumed to be curses at another driver the moment he pulled away from the kerb at Peretola Airport. The driver was reckless but, instead of being nervous, she found his passion exhilarating.

Elizabeth Pershaw's apartment was located in the old town part of the city and the taxi drove through crowded streets to get there. The late afternoon was warm and she was glad she was wearing new crop trousers and a sleeveless top.

While they were stopped at some traffic lights on the edge of a piazza, Juliet's attention was caught by a scene at a sidewalk café. She whipped out her Leica with the 50mm lens. Leaning through the open window of the taxi, she focused on two small children sitting on a low wall in front of the tables, sharing a huge ice cream, one watching intently while the other took a lick. Juliet clicked, then checked the screen for the quality of the photo. Pleased with it, she looked over at the children again, but

24

this time she noticed a man sitting alone at a table behind them, whose eyes were boring into hers. It sent a peculiar jolt through her. He was in his mid-thirties, with an interesting face, bordering on handsome, neatly cut dark hair and broad shoulders. He was wearing an open-neck white summer shirt and chinos. Her photographer's eye took in the details in a split second, while at the same time she was surprised at how he was frowning at her.

She forgot him a moment later when the taxi drove into a narrow cobbled street, called Via Martino, which was lined on either side by three-storey buildings with balconies of various shapes and sizes dotted along the walls. The driver stopped at the third door on the right. Having put Juliet's luggage down on the cobbles, he accepted his payment and drove off with a screech of tires.

Juliet stood outside a large wooden door with three doorbells to the left of it. She saw that *E. Pershaw* was the third bell but, following the instructions in the email from her mother, she pressed bell one and waited for a Signora Padelli to open the door.

'Signora Padelli?' Juliet asked when a small round woman appeared.

'*Sì?*' the woman replied.

'*Buongiorno*, I'm Juliet Holmes.'

'*Ah sì, sì. Benvenuto!*' the woman said with a huge smile before launching into a spate of incomprehensible Italian, while gesturing to Juliet to enter.

Inside was a large stone hallway with two doors off it, one of which was open. Reaching inside it, Signora Padelli took a bunch of keys from a hook and indicated that Juliet should follow her up a flight of stone stairs with a very decorative metal banister. This led to a landing with two doors leading from it.

Signora Padelli passed them both and led her up another flight to the top landing which had one door at its centre.

'Have a nice holiday,' she said, with her strong accent, and, putting the keys into Juliet's palm, she left.

Unlocking the door, Juliet was surprised at first to find the room she entered was in darkness but, as her eyes adjusted, she realised that the shutters were closed, presumably to keep out the heat of the day. Instead of searching for a light switch, she carefully made her way across the large living room, around various pieces of furniture.

After fiddling for a moment with an old-fashioned clasp, she pulled open a set of floor-to-ceiling windows then pushed wide the shutters which revealed a flower-bedecked balcony. It was large enough for a table with two chairs. Potted rose bushes stood on the left, and a row of herbs on the right. She recognised tarragon, thyme, basil and mint. Bougainvillea wove in around the railing with its distinctive perfume. The balcony was at the back of the building and overlooked a courtyard with an array of hanging baskets and a trail of sweet pea up the opposite wall. Voices and sounds came from the apartments below. The rich aroma of freshly baked bread wafted up, making Juliet inhale deeply.

Lifting the camera that was around her neck, she took a few shots before going back inside. Now that there was sufficient light, she could see that the room held a lot of antique furniture, not exactly to her taste, but which had an elegant charm. Her eye was drawn to the large settee in the centre of the room, which faced the balcony and had a bright yellow throw draped across the back. She ran her fingers over the throw.

'Silk no less,' she murmured. 'You have style, Elizabeth Pershaw.'

She wandered through a door on her right in search of a

bedroom but found herself in what looked like a study. Books lined one wall and a desk and chair stood in the corner. This wasn't so dark, as the shutters hadn't been closed properly and a chink of light was getting through. On the desk there were piles of papers and files beside an open laptop.

'You're obviously a busy woman who doesn't tidy up before you go on holidays,' she murmured.

As she moved towards the window to open the shutters fully, her camera beeped. She paused in front of the desk and held it up to check the battery.

Then she heard a sound in the apartment and froze.

'Who are you and who are you working for?' a low, angry English voice said behind her.

Juliet whirled around.

A man loomed large in the doorway. She immediately recognised him as the man at the café and the dangerous edge she heard in his voice had her heart pounding hard. The fact that he had followed her there rendered her speechless with fear.

He took a step forward and stopped. She stepped back, bringing her up against the desk. He looked angry and he was well built. Juliet knew he could easily overpower her. She felt around behind her back for something on the desk to defend herself with, but couldn't find anything.

Her eyes darted to the window.

'We're three storeys up, so don't even think about it,' he warned. 'Now answer me! Why are you following me and why are you photographing me and my work?'

'*You* followed *me* here!'

'Don't mess with me. I know it was you in the taxi and now you've broken in here.'

'I didn't break in! I used a key.'

'Where did you get it?' he demanded, his eyes cold.

'The concierge gave –'

'You're lying.' He cut her off, his words clipped and, if possible, he seemed even angrier. He took another step towards her.

Seeing her chance, she pulled a file from behind her and flicked it and its contents into his face, before trying to dart around him.

Although it distracted him momentarily, he moved fast and managed to grab her arm and swing her around. She drove her elbow hard into his stomach. Grunting, he loosened his grip – just enough for Juliet to break free. She dashed for the door but again he caught her, turned her to face him and held her by her upper arms.

His face was very close to hers and she thought she could see fear now as well as anger in it.

'I got the key from the concierge!' she gasped. 'This is a misunderstanding. I'm a professional photographer, but today I was just a tourist taking holiday snaps. That's all! I swear I'm not spying on you or anyone else.'

She glared at him, smelling coffee on his warm breath. She ploughed on.

'I'm here to house-sit this apartment for the owner, Elizabeth Pershaw, so please take your hands off me and tell me who the hell *you* are, and what *you're* doing here.' Her voice had grown firm, despite the fact that she was shaking inside.

His hands moved off her so abruptly that she nearly lost her balance.

'Oh my God. I'm so sorry. You must be Frances Holmes. But my mother said you weren't coming.' As he spoke he moved quickly to the window and threw open the shutters, allowing him to get a better look at her.

Discovering he was Elizabeth's son just about conquered her

need to run for the door and scream for Signora Padelli. But still she edged towards the living room, her eyes fixed on him, unsure if he was still a threat. He stayed by the window.

'Frances is my mother,' she said gruffly, rubbing her upper arms where he had gripped them. 'And you're correct, she couldn't come, but she asked me to be here instead, which I now seriously regret agreeing to.'

He had paled. 'I've hurt you. I'm so sorry. It's my work, you see.' He waved a hand over the desk. 'I've been consumed by it and I thought . . .' he grimaced, 'well, you know what I thought.'

Moving hesitantly around the desk, he came to stand in front of her.

'I think we should start again. I'm Logan Pershaw, Elizabeth's son.'

He put his hand out to her. She glanced at it warily, then back at his face. When she didn't reach out, he let his hand fall to his side.

'Do you have a name?' he prompted.

'Juliet,' she replied.

'When I spoke to Mum a few days ago,' he said, 'she mustn't have known that you were taking Frances' place. I was due here in a couple of weeks anyway and, since I'd finished my fieldwork a little early, I thought I'd mind the place for her for the whole month while I finished writing up my research.'

A strained silence fell but, knowing his story matched what her mother had told her, Juliet realised he was telling the truth.

'Look,' he said, 'I'm really sorry for threatening you like that. Please let me get you a glass of water or something. Shall we go to the kitchen?'

His politeness had the tension in Juliet's shoulders loosening a fraction.

She followed him back through the living room and into a

small but beautifully rustic kitchen, full of earthenware dishes and pots. One shelf was laden with spices, herbs and homemade jams and, Juliet estimated, at least a dozen cookery books. Normal things, she reassured herself, in what had become an anything-but-normal situation.

When he indicated a chair at the small wooden table, she sat down gratefully as her knees seemed to have turned to water.

'Perhaps you'd prefer tea,' he said, holding up a teapot. 'Mum might have left England five years ago, but she never left that habit behind.'

'Actually, I would prefer coffee, if that's okay,' Juliet said, noting a trace of something other than English in his accent, but not recognising it.

'Sure,' he replied.

While the kitchen was filled with the noise of coffee beans being ground, she tried to think straight. She couldn't stay here now. Not with a stranger.

'I'll find a hotel and move in there, then change my flights tomorrow.' She only realised she'd spoken out loud when he looked over at her and shook his head.

'No, I'll leave,' he said. 'Mum would have a fit if you left. I can hear her now, saying how she thought she'd raised a gentleman.'

A slight flush tinged his cheeks and she knew he was remembering the scene in the study. He looked at her and grimaced. She couldn't help smiling, and the tension between them eased another notch.

Putting two aromatic cups of coffee down, he sat across from her. Now that the storm had left his eyes, they seemed to be a softer blue, and she could see a hint of green near the pupils. His jaw was strong with a slight cleft in his chin. He looked over at her, dark eyebrows drawn together in a frown.

'The least I can do is to take you out to dinner. It will be easier to figure things out on a full stomach.'

Juliet wasn't sure if that was a good idea.

When she didn't say anything he continued. 'Have you been to Florence before?'

'No.'

'Well then, now that I have succeeded in ruining your first day in this magnificent city, allow me to make amends by ensuring that your first evening leaves a better impression. Let me show you a little of Florence and introduce you to some wonderful food.'

I've faced lions and snakes, and even a mad walrus once, she thought. Surely an evening with Logan Pershaw couldn't be that dangerous? To give herself a moment to think, she sipped slowly at the coffee before answering. A pang of hunger helped her to make up her mind.

'Okay, I'll let you be my tour guide, but I must warn you I'll be using my camera.' She softened the barb with a smirk.

'Ha ha!' he said, beating his breast in mock atonement, but also looking relieved at her humour. 'If you don't mind me asking, why couldn't your mother come over?'

'Mum's a GP and something came up at the practice so she just couldn't get away. Dad's a doctor too,' she added, 'an orthopaedic surgeon.'

He nodded and they finished their coffee in silence. He got up and led the way back into the living room.

'You might need a jacket or cardigan, or something. There can be a cool breeze in the evenings this time of the year.'

They both looked over at Juliet's bags, where they stood inside the door.

'I'll just put your things into Mum's room and you can freshen up or whatever,' he said, avoiding eye contact, before going over to fetch them.

Juliet found his slight awkwardness very sweet. She followed him down a little hallway, past what must have been his room, as she could see a shirt lying on the bed. The next room was more spacious and more feminine. The bed was covered in a beautiful white bedspread with tiny blue rosebuds embroidered on to it, with matching cushions on a long window seat.

Logan opened the shutters for her before leaving, closing the door after him.

She sank down on to the soft bed. She couldn't think straight. She didn't know why she had accepted the invitation to dinner. She really should have insisted on finding a hotel immediately where she could forget all about this apartment and the paranoid man in the room next door, and try to salvage a little bit of this trip to Florence.

But instead here she was at six thirty in the evening, heading out to dinner with him, and why? Because a part of her felt she had a right to be here and that he was correct: he should be the one to leave. On the other hand, he was Elizabeth's son. Well, they could just battle it out over dinner.

She took a quick shower in the en-suite bathroom before changing into a pair of navy pants and a turquoise top. Just below the sleeves of her top she saw red marks where his fingers had gripped her. She knew she would be bruised the following day. Picking a light cardigan out of her bag, she put it on to hide the marks, then slung her camera bag over her shoulder before returning to the living room.

He wasn't there and, while she waited for him, her eye was caught by some photographs on the wall above the piano. One was of a much younger Logan in graduation robes with a scroll in his hands. At least he definitely was who he said he was. That was reassuring. Another was an old sepia photograph of a family in front of a large country house in clothes Juliet guessed to be from around the end of the 19th century. Another was a coloured photograph of the same house but with a man and a woman holding a baby in front of it, dressed in more modern clothes, and the last was of a boy of about eight sitting up on a tractor in a field of wheat. Juliet leant in close, trying to figure out if that was Logan too.

'I loved that tractor.' His voice spoke from behind her and a pleasant shiver ran down her spine.

'It was an old battered David Brown, and I loved everything about it – its oily smell, the clacking of the gear stick and the sound of the engine. They say you never forget your first love, and that tractor was mine.'

She smiled at the warmth in his voice for the old tractor.

'And this is your graduation?'

He nodded.

'From where?' she asked.

'Cambridge University, at the ripe old age of twenty-two.'

'And is this Elizabeth and your father?' she asked, pointing to the group of three in the other photograph.

'Yes, that's Mum, Dad and me.'

'That's a big house.' She looked at the house in the background of his family photograph and in the old sepia photograph.

'It's Carissima, where I grew up. It was built by my great-grandfather, James Pershaw, in the 1880s. It's in Ireland – County Monaghan to be precise.'

'Ah, that explains your accent. But why an Italian name for a house in Monaghan?'

'I'm not sure, but my great-grandfather was a merchant who travelled the world for his wares – perhaps he was particularly fond of Italy.'

'Can't say I blame him.'

Before she could ask about the people in the old sepia photograph her mobile rang.

33

'Oh, hi, Mum.' Juliet met Logan's eyes. 'Yes, safe and sound.'

Logan rolled his eyes in self-mockery and left the room.

'The apartment is beautiful. Yes, I'm settling in fine.' She crossed her fingers for the lie. 'I'm just going out for something to eat. I'm starving. So why don't I call you later? Okay? Love you too. Bye.'

Logan came back in. 'You didn't tell her?'

'No.' When he continued to look at her, she shrugged. 'Mothers worry. And there isn't any need for her to worry, is there?' She looked him straight in the eye.

He met the challenge in them with a smile. 'Absolutely none,' he agreed. 'It's bad enough that my own mum would kill me if anything happened to you, without drawing Frances on me too.'

She grinned back at him. 'Let's go eat.'

'After you,' he said, holding the front door open.

Downstairs they met Signora Padelli. '*Signore Logan!*' she exclaimed and embraced him, kissing both cheeks. 'I did not expect you for another two weeks!'

She looked from him to Juliet with raised eyebrows, smiled at Logan and pinched his cheek, murmuring something about '*amore*', before going back into her own apartment, chuckling.

Logan just rolled his eyes and smiled.

Chapter 5

Berkshire, England, 1888

Having slept for only a few hours I awoke with a start. I dressed quickly, putting on a light cotton dress over my corset and bustle petticoat, and since the day looked to be warm I did not bother with a shawl. Anxious about Beatrice, I hurried into her room. Lily, the housemaid, was with her and she was still asleep. Helena and I had taken turns to sit up with her during the night and, when Helena had come to relieve me at five, Beatrice's fever had just broken. At that point I happily went to my own bed.

'How is she?' I now asked Lily, placing a hand on the child's forehead to reassure myself that her fever had not returned.

'She's much improved, miss. She went into a good sleep about two hours ago. Mrs Pershaw went to bed then too and she said you were to go for a walk, if you wish, before you start duties for the day. I'm to stay with Beatrice 'til you come back.'

I was only too glad to comply as I felt the house was not big enough to contain me and the strange new excitement that was filling me that morning.

Wearing my light summer coat and blue bonnet, I took the path through the gardens and out into the woods beyond. Raising my arms to the sky, I gave a little skip. The conversation of the previous night had filled me with the hope of a new friendship and, yes, even the possibility of love. Flowers seemed more vivid and the birdsong sweeter. I could not remember ever feeling so light in spirit or being so alive with such a wondrous energy. I did not have much experience of men, although my father had introduced me to a few in the months before his death. But I had not found anything special in them and a second invitation had not been issued to any of them.

I felt Edward Adams was different. My reaction to him had been immediate. He fascinated me in so many ways: his looks, his intelligence, his gentleness. I hoped he had seen something interesting in me also and that he was as keen as I to continue the acquaintance. He certainly seemed to have hinted at it on his departure. I hugged myself in delight.

Returning to the house less than an hour later, I stopped by the kitchen, collected a breakfast tray and took it up to Beatrice's room, relieving Lily.

Beatrice was awake.

'I brought you some nice soft porridge for your breakfast. Do you think you could eat some?'

She shook her head. 'My throat is sore.'

'I know, sweetheart, but Cook made it very milky and it will slip right down. Just try one little spoonful.'

Despite a lot of coaxing, I only managed to get her to eat four spoonfuls.

Exhausted after her disturbed night, she fell asleep again very quickly.

Helena came to check on her and, satisfied that she was doing well, left to talk to Cook.

Sitting in a chair near the bed, the lack of sleep caught up with me and I dozed for a little while. Beatrice slept on and off for the rest of the morning which seemed to pass very slowly.

In the afternoon, as the time drew closer for the doctor's second visit, I fidgeted around Beatrice's room. Helena came in with some sewing and sat next to the bed. I knew I would have a good view of the avenue from the chair by the window, so I sat there pretending to read.

'Is there something the matter?' Helena asked. 'That is the third time you have sighed in the last ten minutes.'

'No, no, I'm fine. Just daydreaming,' I replied, bending my head over my book to hide the blush I could feel staining my cheeks. I was grateful that Beatrice chose that moment to ask for a drink of water, which took Helena's attention away from me.

The sound of trotting hooves drew my eyes back to the avenue and I saw him emerging from the trees on his chestnut horse. My palms grew damp and I felt hot and cold all at once.

Within minutes Higgins, the butler, was showing Dr Adams into the bedroom. He looked just as handsome in daylight, his shoulders broad beneath his frock coat and his eyes bright with enquiry. The pleasure of seeing him again made me smile. However, without looking my way, he walked straight to the bed and addressed Helena.

'Good day, Mrs. Pershaw. I trust you are well?' he said solemnly. He nodded in my direction but did not make eye contact. 'And how are you today, young lady?' he asked Beatrice.

She gave him a shy smile.

'She is brighter,' Helena said. 'Her fever is not as high and she took some broth at lunchtime.'

'Excellent.'

They continued to discuss her condition as he examined her throat, but I did not hear a word of what passed between them, my disappointment was so immense. Where was the good-humoured person who had talked easily to me in the still of the night? But then I began to realise he was being professional and was remaining properly formal. I had new hope that when I showed him out he would once more talk amiably with me.

Coming out of my speculation, I heard him tell Helena that Beatrice should not need another visit from him, but she was not to hesitate to call him if she was worried about anything. Helena thanked him and asked me to show him down to the door.

'Please do not disturb yourself, Miss White,' he said, closing his bag and still not looking at me. 'I can see myself out. Good day to you both.'

And he was gone.

I did not understand. I had not imagined the intimacy of the previous night. But was my lack of sleep making more of it than it had been?

I leant against the windowsill, watching him mount his horse. He looked up and directly at me for a moment. I held my breath as hope began to rise, only to be quashed again as he pulled on the reins and rode away without saluting.

But I did not feel sorry for myself for long. Oh no. My temper saved me from that. I chose anger instead – anger at him for being so cool and distant, then anger at myself for being a fool.

I went about my duties for the rest of the day, keeping my feelings hidden, and was relieved at last to be able to escape for some air when Beatrice was asleep and Lily was watching her again.

Crossing the hall, I was delayed by Mrs. Pershaw Senior. She was a large woman who walked proudly despite the need for a cane, which she thumped imperiously with each step she took. Dressed entirely in black, from head to toe, except for a pearl choker necklace, she stood looking down her nose at me.

'Well, Martha,' she boomed, 'what did the doctor have to say?'

'He . . . I . . .'

'Come along, girl,' she snapped. 'Is the child improving?'

'Oh yes, yes, indeed,' I replied, pulling myself together. 'He said she is doing very well. As a matter of fact, he will not need to come to see her again.' My voice caught on the last words.

'Good, good.' She nodded her approval then peered more closely at me. 'You, however, are looking a bit wan. Careful you do not fall ill as well.' She managed to make it sound like an order rather than an expression of concern. 'Go out and get some fresh air.'

That was a definite order and, since it was my intention anyway, I was through the door and outside before she had closed the drawing-room door behind her.

Instead of going left down the avenue, I went around the side of the house to the gardens.

In the balmy evening I walked up and down the paths, trying to make sense of what had happened. I knew I had not imagined the promise in his words: '*It is still not soon enough.*' So what changed in the few hours between meetings? Did I appear unappealing in the daylight?

Walking to the pond in a corner of the garden, I peered down at my reflection. I turned my head this way and that, checking for flaws, coming to the conclusion that I just was not to his taste.

I whirled away from the pond in disgust at being so superficial. While I admired his good looks and black hair, it was his passion and spirit that had attracted me the night before, so why should I accuse him of judging me on looks alone? And yet if that was what had happened, then was I not better off without him?

I groaned in frustration, for the image of him sitting at the kitchen table in the soft lamplight floated before me again, bringing back the warmth and softness of our encounter, and I really did not want to think ill of him. I touched my cheek where his finger had lingered.

Life had been so simple the day before, and now it was nothing but confusion. But one thing was sure: the Pershaws had been wonderful to take me into their home and I was not about to go around with a long face, as if I was not appreciative. I did not want to give them any cause for concern. Surely I could easily forget a person in whose company I had, after all, spent only a few minutes? With firm resolve I returned to the house.

Two days later I was on an errand in the village and had stopped to speak with the vicar's wife. Over her shoulder, the street was reflected in the butcher's window. In it a movement caught my eye and I saw it was Edward coming across the street. My heart beat quickened. But when he got to our side of the street, he walked right past us without stopping to speak to us.

As I walked home I seethed at his rudeness and promised myself I would not give him another thought.

Chapter 6

In the following days I threw myself into my duties with extra vigour, inventing new games to entertain Beatrice, who was regaining her strength rapidly, and to distract myself. We played dress-up in the nursery – she the princess and I the dragon. The game would always end with me grabbing her, pretending to blow fire, until she dissolved into a fit of giggles. Then I would calm her down by singing nursery rhymes.

The hardest time for me was when she was drawing. It gave me too much time to think and to puzzle over what had happened. But, unable to come up with an explanation, I would ruthlessly thrust all thoughts of the doctor from my mind again.

One fine afternoon, when Beatrice was fully better, Cousin Helena came into the nursery. Beatrice threw herself at her, hugging her around the knees.

'Hello, my darling,' Helena said, scooping her up.

Beatrice put her little arms around her mother's neck, then

41

leant back to put her hands on her cheeks, encouraging her mother to make funny faces.

'Mummy, can we have a picnic?' She pressed her nose against Helena's.

'Have you been a good girl for Martha?'

'Yes, I have. Have I not, Martha?' Beatrice looked at me with a smile impossible to resist.

'The very best,' I replied.

'A picnic it is then,' said Helena, putting Beatrice down. 'Martha, will you ask Cook to prepare a basket for the three of us?'

'Can we have cake, Mummy?' Beatrice asked, already gathering together the dolls she wanted to bring along with her.

'Why don't we let Cook surprise us?' Helena suggested, picking up the child's shawl.

It was a merry party that left the house twenty minutes later. Helena was carrying a blanket and I a small basket. We both carried parasols.

'Where do you want to go?' Helena asked Beatrice who was skipping down the front steps.

'The hill, the hill!' Beatrice sang as she jumped off the bottom step.

'The hill it is.' Helena smiled at me.

The hill was really only a small mound beyond the gardens at the back of the house.

It took us half an hour to get there, with Beatrice constantly stopping to examine flowers and stones, and anything else that caught her eye. I was more relaxed than I had been in days and enjoyed her chatter.

When we got to the top of the mound, Beatrice ran around with her arms spread wide.

'I love this place, Mummy, because I can see the whole world!'

Helena and I laughed, but to her it must have seemed that way. From where we were standing, we could see to the village in one direction and across meadows and woodland in the other. Indeed it was a lovely spot to have a picnic. Helena spread the blanket on the ground.

Beatrice played with her dolls a few feet away from us. The afternoon had become quite warm and we were glad of our parasols, and Cook's lemonade to quench our thirst. I wished I could undo the button at my throat. Instead, I fanned my face with a napkin.

After a while Beatrice came over and ate her fill of sandwiches and cake. I was wiping crumbs from her face when she pointed to a horse coming along the bridle path which ran around the base of the little hill.

Shielding my eyes from the sun, I saw a chestnut horse coming our way. I recognised the rider instantly.

'I believe it is Dr. Adams, Beatrice,' Helena said.

Without the restraint of adult inhibitions, Beatrice called to him at the top of her voice.

'*Hello, hello!*' She waved down at him.

The doctor looked up, reined in and dismounted.

Having secured his horse to a nearby log, he strode up the hill. Beatrice went to meet him. Helena and I stood.

'Good afternoon, young lady. You are looking very well indeed.'

'Mummy says you made me all better,' Beatrice replied, taking his hand and leading him towards us.

'Good afternoon, Dr. Adams,' we said simultaneously.

Edward removed his hat and bowed slightly towards Helena. 'Good afternoon, Mrs. Pershaw.' Turning to me, he again inclined his head. 'Good afternoon, Miss White.' This time he looked me in the eye, but I did not see any warmth there, just politeness. 'I hope I am not disturbing your picnic.'

'Not at all,' Helena said, as we resumed our places on the blanket. 'Would you care for a cool glass of lemonade, Doctor?'

'You are very kind.' Edward sat on the grass and accepted the proffered drink. 'It is exceedingly warm for the end of August, is it not?'

'Indeed,' Helena agreed. 'We are glad Beatrice suggested the picnic. It will be autumn before we know it, and it would be a shame to be indoors today.'

Out of the corner of my eye I could see him tilt his head and drain his glass in one go. There was something very male in the action, and almost intimate, seeing his Adam's apple move with each swallow. I looked in the direction of the village, but turned again to watch as Beatrice picked up her doll and knelt down next to Edward.

'Vicky has a sore arm. Can you make her better too?' she asked, her face very serious.

'Well, now,' he replied, 'may I take a look?'

She solemnly handed over the doll, pointing to its left arm.

A little of my annoyance at Edward melted as he took the doll gently and laid it on his outstretched knee, saying: 'Nice to meet you again, Vicky.'

Beatrice giggled.

He examined the arm. 'Oh dear! How did it happen? Did she fall off her horse?'

Beatrice shook her head, her ringlets bouncing furiously. 'She was chased by a dragon, and fell down a big hill.' She moved closer to Edward and climbed up unto his lap.

He wrapped his arm around her as Helena smiled at them.

'That sounds frightening,' he said. 'Did the dragon catch her?'

'No, I saved her,' she said proudly.

'I see.'

'Can you fix her?' she asked.

44

'I shall certainly try,' Edward said, reaching into his pocket and pulling out his handkerchief, which he skilfully wrapped around the doll's arm, tying it off with a neat knot. 'There you are. That should have her better in no time.' He gave the doll back to the child.

Beatrice hugged it to her cheek then turned and hugged Edward. He laughed softly, putting his arms around her, and I knew I was in danger of losing my heart to him, while also knowing how futile that seemed to be.

'The vicar had a very nasty cough last Sunday, Doctor Adams,' Helena said as Beatrice scampered off to have a private conversation with her mended doll. 'I hope he has not had reason to become a patient of yours this week?'

'No, indeed, I met him this morning and he is very well. Apparently his wife, Mrs. Wallis, gave him some concoction with honey in it which, he says, cured him. I must find out what it is.'

I plucked at a blade of grass, surprised again that there was a curious rather than censorious note in his voice. I guessed that Edward would always have an avid hunger to learn more and more about healing.

'Did you not tell me, Cousin Helena, that Mrs. Wallis's mother used to be the village midwife?' I asked, speaking for the first time since Edward had joined us. 'Perhaps she passed on some of her own remedies to Mrs. Wallis which might be useful to you.'

The latter I addressed to Edward forgetting, in my enthusiasm for his skills, that it would draw his eyes towards me, and I saw again the light that burned in them for his profession, as it had on the night in the kitchen. I lowered my gaze to the blade of grass as he replied.

'Mrs Wallis never mentioned it,' he said. 'Perhaps she was afraid to. Alas, some doctors do not take kindly to other people giving them advice, which is a great shame indeed, as some old and very sound cures get lost forever.'

'I am sure Mrs. Wallis would be very happy to tell you what she knows,' Helena assured him. 'She is a very good friend of mine. I shall have a word with her.'

'Thank you. I would appreciate that,' he said.

'Rest assured it will be done.'

A moment later he stood up. 'Unfortunately, ladies, loathe though I am to leave this restful scene, I must get on, if you will excuse me? Thank you again for the lemonade, Mrs. Pershaw. Good day to you.'

'Good day, Doctor.'

'Good day, Miss White.'

'Good day, Dr. Adams,' I said, flicking a quick look at him, only to be speared by the intensity of his, before he turned to Beatrice with a smile.

'Take good care of Vicky now,' he instructed.

She nodded enthusiastically, her curls bouncing.

'Goodbye!' she called after him as he returned to his horse.

He waved up at her from the bottom of the hill and rode off.

'He is a pleasant young man. Such a change from the last doctor we had, who was very grumpy and quite likely to lose his temper if you did not follow his advice. Dr. Adams is so gentle, and so good with Beatrice, do you not agree?'

'He is a fine doctor,' I replied.

We stayed there for the afternoon, playing games with Beatrice and making up stories with Vicky and even more dragons in them.

'I suppose we had better go home,' Helena sighed, checking the time. 'We have stayed longer than I intended, but it is so lovely here today.' She stood and gathered up the blanket. 'Come along, Beatrice,' she called.

Despite her words, we took our time strolling back, unwilling to bring the afternoon to a close. We spoke very little. My thoughts were fully occupied once again with Dr. Adams, how his hair shone in the sun, looking silky to the touch, and how gentle and attentive he had been with Beatrice. I could not fault his pleasant air and manners, but I wondered at his final glance which I felt was in contrast to his earlier indifference. Added to my annoyance now was confusion, and disappointment at myself for still finding him attractive despite his aloofness.

Higgins was at the door when we got back and he took the basket and blanket.

'Mr. Pershaw has arrived home, madam,' he said.

Before Helena could comment, Mother Pershaw's voice came booming across the hall.

'You have been gone long enough and your husband home this past hour with no one here to greet him.'

You are here, are you not? I thought, feeling sorry for Helena as she readied herself to receive yet another scolding from her mother-in-law who stood there with both hands resting on top of her walking stick, glaring at us.

'It was such a lovely afternoon –'

'James is upstairs changing,' Mother Pershaw cut across her. 'I have had to speak to Cook about dinner since you are so late. Poor James is exhausted from his travelling and should go straight to bed, but he insists on joining us for dinner.'

'I shall go up to him right away, Mother.'

'Yes, that would be best.' She looked at Beatrice who was hopping around the tiles on one foot. 'Martha, Beatrice should have a bath to quieten her down and settle her for the night. Please see to it.'

She marched off into the parlour. Helena and I looked at each other with blank faces, both unprepared to show our true feelings lest we be caught in that indiscretion.

Helena hurried up the stairs.

'Beatrice, time for your bath,' I said, holding out my hand to her.

I was furious on Helena's behalf. She was perfectly capable of issuing instructions about her daughter's care without interference from Mother Pershaw but, since she was living in her house, she had to keep silent. James Pershaw would not countenance a bad word being said to his mother.

He appeared at the top of the stairs just then, twirling one of the ends of his long black moustache. In a fawn topcoat of fine material, and wearing a silk cravat, he looked every inch the prosperous merchant that he was. Although taller than Helena, he was only about five foot nine but, like his mother, he had an arrogant stance that made him seem taller.

His steely grey eyes, which I thought must have many times helped to close a deal in his favour, glowered down at us now.

'I have been home this past hour, Helena,' he said. Although his voice did not boom, I could not believe how similar his scolding tone was to that of his mother's.

'Hello, James,' Helena said quietly, going up the stairs. 'Welcome home. It was a beautiful day so we took Beatrice for a picnic. If I had known it was today you were coming back I would not have gone, of course.' She was respectful, but firm.

'Yes, of course,' he said, his tone gentling while he circled his shoulders as if to rid himself of some discomfort. 'I was just disappointed not to see you here, that is all.' He put his arm around her waist when she reached him. 'I have a lot to tell you, dearest,' I heard him say as they disappeared from view.

Although I was halfway up the stairs with Beatrice, he did not acknowledge our presence. Beatrice began to run ahead but the sound of their door closing made her stop. Turning towards me, her bottom lip began to tremble.

'If we are quick with your bath, you will have time to talk to your father before bed,' I reassured her. I went to chase her, which brought the smile back to her face.

I was annoyed that he had ignored her. I could understand his slight to me. I was, after all, Helena's cousin, not his, and while she treated me as a member of the family, he was more reserved and saw me as a servant. But there was no excuse for ignoring his daughter.

He came to the nursery after Beatrice's bath. She ran into his arms. He gave her a warm hug before addressing me.

'I have asked Cook to send up a tray for you tonight so that you may eat with Beatrice this evening, as I have some business I want to discuss over dinner with Helena and Mother.'

'Of course,' I mumbled, a little surprised as this had not happened before. But I was also pleased that I would not have to sit through dinner with them.

James spent a few minutes listening to Beatrice's chatter before excusing himself. Supper arrived shortly afterwards and was over quickly. Beatrice willingly climbed into bed, tired after all the afternoon's activity. I read her a story, brushed her hair away from her forehead and kissed her goodnight. She asked me to kiss her doll goodnight too. I picked it up and did as she bid, brushing my thumb over Edward's handkerchief before tucking the doll in beside her.

'Goodnight, sweetheart,' I said.

I went to my own room and sat on the window seat, watching the evening sun slipping down the sky, and going back over each moment of the afternoon.

The next morning I took Beatrice out walking. Just before we left, she insisted on us going back upstairs for her doll.

'Come along now,' I said as she hugged Vicky. 'We want to get back before the rain comes.'

She scampered down the stairs by my side, the doll swinging wildly from one hand as she gripped my hand with the other.

'I see her arm must be improving if you can wave her about like that.'

'The bandage is making it better,' she said, beaming at me.

The route I had chosen was short: down the driveway, out the gates and along the lane to the crossroads. Throwing a critical eye at the sky, I believed we would have enough time before it rained.

Near the crossroads there was a field of haystacks.

'Can we go in and play?' Beatrice asked. 'Please, Martha?' She tugged at my hand.

I looked around and saw no one. 'All right, but just for a few minutes.'

I helped her over the fence and then climbed over after her. She immediately started running, darting in and out behind the haystacks. I chased her, never quite catching up. Then she took a turn chasing me. There was a lot of shouting and laughter.

When I thought it time to go, I let her catch up with me and pretended to stumble onto a pile of hay. She threw herself on top of me. Grabbing her, I started tickling her and we both rolled around laughing, until we were out of breath. We lay there for a moment, the warm smell of hay in our nostrils.

Sitting up, I straightened my bonnet and pulled pieces of hay from my hair. Turning to do the same for Beatrice, a movement on the road caught my eye and I saw Edward astride his horse, watching us. I blushed at the thought that he had seen me in such an unguarded moment, and did not know what I would say to him.

But there was not to be any conversation. He pulled at the reins, the horse having taken the opportunity to nibble at the grass verge, and with the briefest salute he rode away.

My cheeks grew hot with indignation. So you are going to continue to ignore me, I thought. It was all right to stop and talk yesterday when Helena was there, but not when I am on my own with Beatrice. Well, you have made your indifference quite clear once again, sir, to the point of being rude!

To confirm my opinion, Beatrice asked: 'Why did the doctor not stay? He should have looked at Vicky's arm.'

I heard myself defending him, not for his sake, but for hers.

'There must be someone else who is very sick that he has to go and see. And he knows you are taking very good care of Vicky. Now come along, we must get back – those clouds are moving in.'

I brushed the rest of the hay from her clothing and she plucked some from the back of my dress, before we climbed back out over the fence.

Beatrice chattered as we walked, blissfully unaware that I was not saying much in response. It would have been a perfect opportunity for him to talk to me again as he had in the kitchen that night, with no one but Beatrice around. I did not imagine his tenderness, I insisted to myself. So what game was he playing with me? My anger at his behaviour took on a new intensity.

'Look,' Beatrice exclaimed, 'a horseshoe. May I keep it, Martha?' She bent down and picked it up. 'Mummy says finding one a horsey lost is lucky.'

'Of course you may bring it home. We will shine it up and keep it in the nursery.'

I thanked God for Beatrice and her distractions.

The first raindrops started to fall as we approached the house.

James and Helena were in the hall when we arrived, but they stopped talking when we came in and it was blatantly obvious that they did not want us to hear what they were discussing. Helena started to fuss about him, passing him his riding crop and gloves after he shrugged into his coat.

'It is beginning to rain,' I said to cover the awkward silence.

'Still, I must be on my way,' James said, addressing himself to Helena. 'My meeting in London will not wait.'

Beatrice ran over to him. 'I found a shoe,' she said. 'Look, Father!'

'Yes, very nice, dear,' he said, patting her on the head without even looking at the horseshoe.

'Look, Mummy.'

Helena sank down to her level and took the proffered treasure from her hands.

'This will bring us great luck.' She hugged Beatrice to her.

'I shall be off then,' James said. 'I should be back the day after tomorrow.'

He kissed Helena briefly on the cheek and patted Beatrice on the head again.

Inclining his head slightly in my direction, he muttered 'Martha', then he took a second glance, frowned, rolled his eyes to heaven, and passed through the open door, out to the groom waiting with his mount.

I turned and looked at myself in the mirror, seeing immediately what he had seen, a piece of hay sticking out from above my left ear. I hastily pulled it out and suppressed a smile.

'Let's go and find something to polish that shoe with.' I took Beatrice by the hand and led her towards the kitchen, giving Helena a smile as I passed.

'Martha,' she called after me, 'Mother Pershaw is out today, visiting. I thought we might have a picnic lunch in the conservatory because it is too wet to have one outside.'

Beatrice and I beamed at her. We both loved her sense of fun which, unsurprisingly, was more evident in the absence of husband and mother-in-law!

We spent a delightful hour, sitting on a blanket in the

conservatory, eating a picnic among the trailing plants and scented flowers, inventing stories about adventures in the jungle. I mused that while Beatrice might not receive much affection from her father, she had it in abundance from her sweet-natured mother. I could not help wishing for her sake that James would hurry up and build them their own house, so that she would be away from the oppressive presence of Mrs. Pershaw Senior. The distance, I thought, might also improve James' attitude.

It was a tired Beatrice I put to bed that night. As I tucked her in she was already half asleep, but she put her arms around my neck and hugged me tight.

'I love you, Martha,' she murmured as her arms dropped away and she slid into full sleep.

I looked down at her for a moment, thinking how wonderfully simple a child's life could be, where a game of chasing in a hayfield was enough to make her happy.

I, too, wanted to be happy, and decided that giving up any daydreams I'd had about Edward was going to be the first step. I was going to put all thoughts of him out of my mind and forget him completely. With a sigh, for I knew my task would not be easy, I extinguished Beatrice's light, kissed her on the forehead and left the room.

Chapter 7

Florence, Italy, 2010

The subtle taste of Parma ham made Juliet's eyes close involuntarily for a moment in pleasure.

'It's delicious!'

An array of meats, olives and breads was spread out on the table between them.

'And this is just the starter. One could easily become very fat here.' Logan laughed as he helped himself to another olive. 'It amazes me when I visit Mum how she can still be so slim when she is surrounded by all this.' He waved his hand over the table.

Juliet agreed. They were sitting at one of three tables outside a tiny restaurant in a small narrow street. There was room for only about eight tables inside but the place was buzzing with the passionate voices of several Italian families enjoying good food and company. The air was balmy and still as the light began to fade.

Logan had explained the different dishes, and to her delight he didn't try to influence her decision. Arrogant men who thought they knew what other people liked and ordered it for them were one of her pet hates.

'This is a little bit off the beaten track,' Logan said, 'but you can be guaranteed the food is good when the Italians eat here themselves. Just leave some room for the stew,' he warned as Juliet popped another piece of bread drizzled with olive oil into her mouth.

It was good advice. The beef stew that followed was delicious, the meat tender and rich with fresh herbs. Juliet finished every last morsel on her plate, washing it down with a very nice Montepulciano.

During the meal Logan had told her a bit about Florence, the best things to see and do during her stay, but now over coffee and a lemon liqueur which the proprietor had served with a flourish and a description of his own lemon groves, they moved on to more personal subjects.

'So,' Logan asked, 'are you a doctor too, like your parents?'

Juliet looked up at him. The lean, sharp angles of his face were more obvious in the fading light, but his full lips softened the lines. His wide solid shoulders were relaxed and his fingers played idly with a teaspoon. He certainly had a very strong physical presence, she thought, wondering what he did for a living. Her guess, considering his build and light tan, was that it was something outdoors.

Watching the candlelight dance in his eyes, she felt like a moth drawn to a flame. But getting burned had not been part of the plan for this holiday. She dropped her gaze to her coffee cup and answered his question.

'No, medicine never really did it for me. I'm a photographer for *Wild Nature*, a wildlife magazine.'

'Impressive. It's a classy magazine. I often buy it. I'll note the photographer's name in future.'

His words were warm and friendly, rather than flirtatious. Juliet was relieved.

'So you travel a lot?' he asked.

She nodded. 'I've been to all five continents, each more interesting than the last.'

'What was your favourite shoot?' He leant his elbows on the table, intently interested in her answer.

Juliet smiled. 'That's easy! Killer whales in the Gulf of Alaska.'

Now she too leaned forward, transported back to the trip. 'It was one of my first assignments, and it was wonderful. I wasn't even supposed to be on that trip, but the assistant photographer broke a leg and I was asked to fill in even though I was just a rookie at that point. I knew I'd be a general dogsbody, lugging bags on and off the boats and taking care of the equipment etc, and that the main photographer would be getting all the good shots, but I didn't care. I knew it would be the trip of a lifetime and it was. Oh Logan, you should see it when one of those magnificent whales breaks free of the water close to your boat, then crashes back down into the ocean, splashing water high into the air, its white and black skin glistening in the sun. It's just indescribably beautiful.'

'I think you describe it very well,' he said softly, looking at her intently. 'I feel I'm standing on the deck beside you.'

Juliet blinked, and laughed at herself. 'I'm sorry. I get a bit carried away when I talk about my work.'

'I can understand that kind of passion – I feel the same about mine.'

Now that he had given her an opening she jumped at it.

'So what do you do?'

'I'm a professor of plant science at Cambridge University.'

Juliet's eyebrows shot up. Could she have been more wrong?

'I know what you're thinking: so, why all the cloak-and-dagger stuff?' he said.

Juliet shrugged, palms upwards. 'Well yes, actually.'

'I've been on sabbatical for the past year, doing research for a paper on biodiversity for the UN. With the frightening trend towards genetic modification, it has become vitally important that food and plant sovereignty be preserved.'

'I've heard the term *food sovereignty*. Doesn't it mean the right to grow and harvest your own native crops?'

'That's right. I would describe it as people having the right to healthy food which is appropriate to their culture, produced ecologically and sustainably, and having the right to define their own agricultural practices.'

Juliet nodded slowly. 'In Africa I saw where outsiders had come in and put thousands of acres of land under roses etc, therefore not allowing the local people to grow the crops they need to feed themselves and their families, depriving them of the means to be independent.'

'That's exactly what I'm talking about.' He smiled at her, seeming genuinely pleased that she understood. He leaned closer and lowered his voice. 'In the course of my research I've become particularly interested in the humble apple, which botanists believe had its origins in Central Asia – Kazakhstan, to be precise. That's where I've just been, collecting information.' He paused for a moment. 'Whales might be your passion, but the apple is mine.'

'So you thought I was stealing some of your research for someone on the genetic-modification side, someone who is not interested in preserving heritage and original species?'

'Yes.'

'In that case you're forgiven,' she said quite seriously. 'If I thought someone was going to mess with my work I would defend it too.'

Acknowledgment and understanding of the other's passion for their work passed between them in a lingering look.

Logan spoke first. 'In the vernacular of my students, it's nice when someone "gets" you.' He reached out and took her hand where it lay on the tablecloth. The rightness of it shook her to the core and she couldn't speak.

After a moment his eyes became very serious. 'I really am sorry that I frightened you today,' he said.

She tried to find the words to reassure him but for a moment all she could hear in her head was her mother's voice from the phone call in London, saying the word 'magic'. She shook her head to rid herself of the word, blaming the wine and the city for such nonsense.

'I'm fine – no permanent damage.'

He released her hand and, placing his napkin on the table, signalled for the bill.

'Are you ready to move on?'

At her nod he continued, 'You can't let your first evening in Florence pass without tasting their gelato. You do eat ice cream, I hope?'

'Yes, of course, but I couldn't eat another thing.'

'Let's walk then so you can work up an appetite.'

'If you insist!' She groaned but got to her feet with a smile.

'Do you want me to take that for you?' he asked, indicating her camera bag.

'No thanks, I hardly know I'm carrying it. It's a part of me at this stage.'

Juliet couldn't remember ever having such a relaxing evening, one edged with laughter and full of entertaining conversation. As they wandered along by the Arno River, she and Logan talked some more about their work and the different places they'd been. Juliet was struck by how gentle the exchange of stories was.

Neither of them rushed, nor tried to outdo the other. She enjoyed the content of Logan's stories and loved listening to his lilting voice, and he listened well when she spoke of her travels.

When up ahead the famous Ponte Vecchio, the oldest bridge in Florence, came into view, Juliet paused in mid-sentence to take it in. It was like a linear village floating above the water. The top of the well-known covered corridor across the bridge was caught in the last rays of the sun. She took the camera from her bag and started snapping.

Logan spoke close to her ear. 'Stop looking at it through a lens and just experience it,' he teased.

Taking her hand, he led her towards the bridge, where they mingled with the crowd, pausing now and then at the various stalls and shops lined along the interior of the bridge. When they arrived at a statue, whose nameplate read *Benvenuto Cellini*, Juliet noticed padlocks of all shapes and sizes locked to parts of the bridge around the statue.

'What's the significance of those, do you know?' she asked Logan.

'It's an old tradition, where lovers lock the padlock onto the bridge and then throw the key into the river, symbolising their unity for all eternity. However, there have been so many over the years they are regularly cleared away to avoid damaging the bridge, and now it's against the law to put them here.'

'Well, some lovers are still determined to keep with tradition obviously,' Juliet commented, touching with a fingertip one tiny lock, the size of her thumbnail.

'True love will always win out, I suppose,' Logan said quietly.

Juliet looked up, expecting to see a teasing look on his face, but he was gazing into the river with a small frown between his brows. She gave his hand a little squeeze and brought back his attention to her.

'I thought once that my parents had it,' he said, 'but sometimes other things are stronger.' His face cleared as he drew her further along the bridge, ensuring she was not jostled by the crowds. 'It's a pity you didn't meet my mum before she left for America. She's an amazing woman. She had a degree in botany and, after she divorced Dad, got a job in a garden centre back in England, steadily worked her way up to manager and eventually went out on her own as a consultant garden designer. She found something she loved and made her dream come true.'

'So that's where you got your interest in plants?'

He nodded.

'And your mother?' Juliet continued. 'Does she not miss having a garden now?'

'No – that surprised me too. When she retired, she decided she wanted to live in Florence, surrounded by life and vitality of a different kind. Mind you, having said that, I think she spends a lot of time in the parks and she is a member of a walking group that explores the Tuscany countryside most weekends.'

'Mum said Elizabeth was a very active woman for her age. She sounds like good fun.'

Logan nodded again. 'Now, surely you're ready for that ice cream?'

Still holding her hand, he led her through some more streets to a well-lit square, with cafés, bars and restaurants dotted around its edge. In the far corner was a *gelateria* with a huge display of ice creams. After some deliberation, Juliet went for a scoop of pistachio. She watched Logan ponder on the options, sticking out his bottom lip a tiny bit in concentration. There was something unconsciously sensual about it and it softened his face, making him look vulnerable and attractive all at once. After a while he chose one scoop of chocolate and one scoop of kiwi.

Sitting on a park bench beside a fountain they ate in

companionable silence, Juliet aware that she had never felt so comfortable with someone in such a short space of time.

She scraped the last bit of ice cream from the little carton and got up to throw it into a nearby bin, returning to the bench thinking the subject of their accommodation had to be broached.

Looking straight ahead at the bubbling water, she made up her mind.

'I don't think you should go to the expense of staying at a hotel tonight,' she said.

Out of the corner of her eye she could see his spoon pause fleetingly before continuing to his mouth.

'The apartment has two bedrooms and it's getting late. We can sort things out tomorrow.' Her tone was matter of fact.

'You're very trusting of someone you just met.'

She leant forward, placing a hand on either side of her knees on the bench, and turning her head to look back at him. 'It doesn't feel like that though, does it?'

His eyes widened at her honesty, then crinkled at the corners in a smile. Then in that lovely soft accent, he said quietly, 'No, no, it doesn't.'

'Besides,' she said with cheeky grin, 'I'm sure there's a sturdy lock on my bedroom door,' she paused for effect, 'and on the study.'

'You're never going to let me forget, are you?'

She looked again towards the fountain, amazed at the jolt of pleasure the word 'never' had given her. It had a nice long-term ring to it.

'I suppose that's agreed, then,' he said, 'as long, of course, as there's a lock on my door, too. I'd hate to have to tell our respective mothers that the romantic city of Florence got the better of you and you took advantage of me.'

She burst out laughing. He joined in with a soft chuckle of his own.

Getting to his feet, he held out his hand and pulled her up. 'Come on, let's get back. It's been a long and, eh, eventful day.'

They strolled through the balmy evening, the sounds of Italy all around them, mopeds zipping up and down the streets, Italian voices raised in heated discussion, children playing ball down a narrow lane.

After a while they turned into their own street. When they let themselves into the building Signora Padelli was nowhere to be seen, although a television could be heard blaring behind her door.

'I'm glad we're on the second floor,' Logan whispered as they went past.

As soon as they were inside the apartment, Logan walked towards the study, but then stopped and turned around. 'I'll let you get some rest. I hope you sleep well.'

Across the room, Juliet rested her hands on the back of the sofa and smiled at him.

'I had a very enjoyable evening, thanks. You succeeded.' At his raised eyebrow, she clarified. 'My first day in Florence has left a good impression.'

He nodded and smiled back. 'Goodnight, Juliet,' he said softly before going into the study and closing the door behind him.

It was the first time he had used her name, and it sounded great in those liquid honeyed tones of his. She swivelled on one foot and went to her room. She leant against the inside of the door for a moment before silently turning the key, even though she felt stupid doing so.

At least there was an en-suite bathroom behind one of the doors, so there wouldn't be any awkward meetings in the corridor in the middle of the night or a queue for the shower in the morning.

Juliet slowly got ready for bed, trying to analyse the warm glow she was feeling. There was something tender and caring about Logan that she was drawn to and he had certainly been attentive to her all evening in a very discreet way. The independent streak in her would have rebelled at anything more overt. An old-fashioned word popped into her head and she gave a funny strangled laugh as she realised it totally described what she was feeling. He had made her feel *cherished*. She laughed again, deciding that this wonderful city was making her fanciful. Another old-fashioned word, she thought, shaking her head at herself and turning out the light.

Chapter 8

Berkshire, England, 1888

I could not forget him. The days rolled on and Edward was there
in everything I did and saw. Even the joy was gone from my
walking because I felt I should be walking with him, sharing
with him the sound of the cuckoo, or watching the house
martins dipping and diving at dusk. Nature was still beautiful but
it was painfully beautiful now. I wondered how I could have been
so content with life before I knew him, and how in a few brief
meetings he had filled me up so completely that his absence now
left me empty.

I wished Beatrice had not required a doctor and I had not
met him at all.

One morning, Mrs. Pershaw Senior and Helena took Beatrice
visiting to a neighbour's house. James Pershaw was still away in
Europe on business. I had the afternoon to myself and, since the
weather had brightened up after a morning of rain, I set out for
a long walk which would take me out through the woods and

home across the fields. I had only been walking about ten minutes when I came to the first kissing gate. I was closing it behind me when a sound from the right caught my attention and there was Edward coming around the bend of the bridle path on foot. He stopped abruptly when he saw me.

Removing his hat, he resumed walking and I braced myself to hear some lame excuse for his behaviour. Realising I was still holding the kissing gate, I let it slam shut.

He stopped and smiled.

'Something amusing you?' I snapped.

'No, it is not amusement. It is admiration . . . for your temper. For, Miss White, where there is temper, there is fire, and where there is fire, there is passion.'

As he spoke he came closer, his eyes locked with mine. My body weakened but my anger increased at the nerve of the man to talk easily as if he had not ignored me on two previous occasions.

'Miss White now, is it?' I questioned. 'Well, good day, *Edward*,' I said sarcastically. 'If you do not have the grace to be true to our conversation of the night we met, I do not have to follow suit. Are you one person in the shadows of night and another in the sunlight, *Dr. Adams*?'

I knew I was breaking all the rules of propriety but I was hurting and, God forgive me, I wanted to hurt back.

'I will not be party to your games,' I continued crossly, 'where you are all congeniality one moment and a stranger the next. My heart cannot take it.' The words rushed out in anger and I regretted them instantly, for I had exposed my feelings. I went through the kissing gate, not waiting to see the scorn or pity in his eyes.

I had not gone two steps on the other side when I heard it bang again and then two hands were catching my shoulders and turning me around.

'Martha,' he said, before pulling me into his arms and kissing me hard.

I was stunned, emotions going berserk inside me. He looked at me for a long moment and then very, very slowly lowered his head and brushed his lips against mine, this time with infinite gentleness. It was more wonderful than I could ever have imagined. I melted against him and he gathered me even closer, the kiss deepening. This is where I belong, I thought, as a tear rolled down my cheek.

He lifted his head and his face was so filled with tenderness when he saw the tear that another escaped immediately in its wake. He brushed them away.

'Martha, I am so sorry. I can see I have hurt you badly when that was the very thing I was trying to avoid.'

My pride was gone now, so I blurted out the question that had been burning inside me. 'Why were you different the next day, Edward? I thought there was something between us that night?'

'Of course there was – the moment I saw you it was as if I recognised you, as if I had known you all my life. I cannot describe the relief I felt when I realised you were not Mrs. Pershaw. But, you see . . .' his hands dropped from my shoulders and he stepped back, turning his empty palms towards the sky, 'I have nothing to offer you. I have been a doctor for just over a year. My inheritance went on my education. It will take me a few years yet before I can provide for a wife and family. So I have no right to court you, as I had no right to be so informal with you that night.'

He reached for a twig and snapped it in two, before looking back at me.

He gasped. 'Oh my God, you are radiant!'

I do not know what he saw, but I knew I was smiling while

at the same time my eyes were wet with tears. I wanted to cry with relief that he had cared about me all along and I wanted to laugh with the sheer joy of it.

I closed the distance between us. 'My first impression of you was correct – you are decent and true.' I laid my hand on his cheek. 'But, Edward, we have only just met – no one is talking about marriage and providing for a family. Can we not take it one day at a time?'

He took my hands in his and held them between us, close to his heart.

'It is no use, Martha. I already love you with every breath I take and I already know that, if I am to take a wife, I want it to be you. But I cannot ask you to wait another few years until I have saved enough to provide for you.'

'Yes, you can,' I whispered. 'Edward, I am only eighteen. There is no hurry. I could not leave Helena yet after all her kindness. I owe her a great debt for giving me a home these past few months and I want to repay that. Besides, when she asked me to be Beatrice's governess, she insisted that I would have to stay for a few years with Beatrice to give her stability. So we would have to court indefinitely anyway.'

'Are you sure?'

'Yes. You see, the last governess to Beatrice was with her from the time she was newborn until she was two and a half years old. At that point the governess received a substantial inheritance from an aunt of hers. Beatrice had become very attached to her, but the governess left immediately upon receiving the news of her inheritance and did not give Beatrice any time to get used to the idea. Helena said Beatrice woke crying every night for months afterwards. That's why she was insisting that stability was important for Beatrice now. I was only too happy to commit to staying indefinitely as I too needed stability after losing my father and escaping a bleak future on my own. I have to stay with them for now.' I touched his face. 'I can wait because I love you too.'

He threw back his head and laughed, before catching me around the waist, lifting me off the ground and twirling me around and around until we were both dizzy, my skirt tangling about his legs.

He put me down and kissed me again.

'I was drawn to you the moment I saw you,' he said, his eyes moving over my face. 'And though I tried to convince myself that I could not love you after one brief conversation in a kitchen in the dead of night, I failed. For when I heard you laughing in the field that day, and saw your smile as you sat there with hay in your hair, so natural and so relaxed, I knew I could never love anyone more. I had to leave quickly, as I was afraid you would see it written on my face.'

I touched that wonderful face and pressed my lips to his.

'Let's walk,' he said, taking my hand and tucking it into the crook of his arm.

We walked a little way and I felt I was walking on air, but all too soon some practical considerations impinged on my blissful state of mind.

I stopped and turned to him.

'Edward, we shall have to be careful not to be seen together. People would talk and the Pershaws would be shocked to think I was with a man without a chaperone.'

'You are quite right, my dear,' he said. 'We must protect your reputation at all costs.'

'And theirs.'

'Indeed.' He frowned. 'So . . . should we make a public announcement of betrothal?'

'Oh, Edward, for the reasons I've just given you about stability for Beatrice, I cannot be betrothed. I don't want Helena to think now that there is any threat to that stability, and she might if we were to become engaged. Besides, Helena and James are in effect my guardians and it is James, I suppose, you would have to approach to ask for my hand – if only as a courtesy. Can you imagine how he would react at this point? He would think you – and I – quite mad!'

Edward smiled. 'I see I am marrying a woman of sense as well as sensibility.'

'I should hope so!' I laughed. An idea had come to me. 'Edward, there is an old disused cottage not far from the woods, down by the river and still on Pershaw land – we could go there. It has an overgrown garden that will hide us from view.'

'That sounds perfect.'

The cottage was only a few minutes' walk away. The garden was at the back, on the river side of the cottage. Edward had to pull back the branches of an overgrown climbing rose bush to allow us in through a gap which once must have had a wooden gate.

Inside the garden walls was a profusion of summer colour, with yellow climbing roses covering the back of the old cottage, and tall trees and bushes giving us seclusion. There was a stone bench in the middle of the garden and Edward pulled back shrubs so we could walk to it and sit down. Here we spent nearly an hour, learning about each other's childhoods and families, and our views on different things. We discovered we both had a great love of French and carried on some of our conversation in that wonderfully romantic language. We kissed a lot and at times we just looked at each other and grinned like two children with a secret.

And we had a secret, for we had discussed the matter further and decided that no one should know yet about our courtship.

Chapter 9

Many wonderful days followed. I would go to the cottage garden each evening after Beatrice was in bed and, if Edward's work permitted, he would be there waiting for me.

When the evenings began to draw in earlier, we met as often as we could in the afternoons when Beatrice was napping and the housemaid was keeping an eye on her.

At the end of the first month, when Edward did not arrive at our meeting place two days running, I was not concerned, for the pattern of his work was unpredictable. I used the time to sit in the sun and remember our conversations.

On the third day he was there before me and swept me off my feet in a warm embrace. Setting me back down, he held my gaze solemnly for a long moment before slowly lowering his head and kissing me. At the back of his neck my fingers slid up into his hair, applying the slightest pressure, but enough to invite him to deepen the kiss. We were both breathless when we finally drew apart.

He pressed his lips to my temple before we sat down on the stone bench. I asked him about the cases he had treated that day.

'Perhaps you should have studied medicine too,' he said, after telling me about them. 'You have a great understanding and ask some very sound questions.'

'I love discussing your work with you. I am fascinated by it, but it also allows me to be part of the hours you are away from me.'

He squeezed my hand tighter and happily answered more of my questions, before asking me some of his own.

Our days took on a pattern of sorts, and on occasion we would have a chance meeting in the village. If people were within earshot, we would greet each other politely and discuss the weather. But Edward would always manage to whisper an endearment as he took leave of me.

Back in the Pershaws' house I behaved as usual and all was the same on the outside, but I was constantly smiling on the inside. My affection for Beatrice was even greater for bringing Edward and myself together.

Life went on for the Pershaws also, with the two ladies holding tea parties and Helena involved in good works in the parish. James continued to come and go on his travels.

'Martha, come and look at this cloth!' Helena called to me across the haberdasher's shop. She was standing with the assistant, admiring a dark material.

It was several weeks after Edward and I had started meeting secretly.

'Look,' she said as I joined them, 'this is a strong, warm material. It will make a fine dress for Beatrice for − for the winter.'

I would not have noticed the hesitation if it had not been followed by a slight blush on her cheeks, and I wondered at it.

'Yes,' she continued in a bit of a fluster, 'this will do her very well for winter.'

She pushed the bolt of material towards the assistant and ordered a couple of yards of it.

'What do you think of this lace?' she said then. 'It is very pretty. I think I shall take some of this too.'

I did not know what had got into her. She had seemed overexcited all morning, full of chat and admiration for the 'heavenly weather' and the 'beautiful sky' on our way to the village. James had returned from another trip the previous evening and I supposed she was just pleased to have him home. I smiled indulgently at her.

Beatrice was getting bored so I took her out to the street to watch some children play. I was hoping to catch a glimpse of Edward for he had not been at our meeting place for the previous three days. But I did not see him.

Helena soon joined us and I took the parcel of purchases from her. She took Beatrice's hand and linked my arm as well as we walked towards our carriage.

Leaning conspiratorially towards me, she said quietly: 'I just heard that Dr. Adams is engaged. Is that not wonderful news? He is such a nice man, and will make a wonderful husband and father, I am sure.'

An icy hand seemed to seize my stomach and, though I forbade the words to rise in my throat, they defied me.

'To whom?' I blurted out and gave a small cough to disguise the gruffness of my question.

She did not answer for a moment but helped Beatrice up into the carriage and got in herself. I climbed in after her, forcing myself not to repeat the question.

'I do not know her name,' she answered at last, after helping me to settle the packages at our feet. 'Apparently she lives in London and he has been up there recently to visit her family. The haberdasher's wife heard it from the merchant who delivers their materials. She is the daughter of a wealthy London merchant, apparently. Oh dear, I am gossiping, am I not? But I am happy for him.'

Fortunately for me, Beatrice and her mother talked constantly to one another on the short journey home and neither seemed to notice that I did not say a word. I believed that there must be some mistake, that Edward would not deceive me that way. But it was true that he had not shown up three days in a row.

'Martha?'

The carriage had pulled up in front of the house and the others had already alighted. I quickly stood and followed them, not meeting Helena's quizzical glance.

The rest of the morning seemed endless. I longed to be alone with my thoughts and finally, when Beatrice went for her nap, I escaped into the garden and on to the woods beyond.

When I came to a small clearing, I paced back and forth. It started to rain but I hardly noticed.

'I will not cry,' I muttered fiercely. 'I was a fool to think a penniless governess would be a worthy wife for him. I cannot blame him for making a more suitable match.'

But I could blame him for letting me love him and for letting the hope of a future together grow inside me. I could feel that hope slowly being strangled to death under my ribs.

Stopping abruptly, I sank to the ground in a puff of skirts, despairing at my own foolishness. I now saw the lonely life of a dependent, spinster governess stretching out before me. The rain was soaking through my clothes but I did not care.

'Oh Edward, if only I had been a rich heiress, and had something to offer a struggling doctor!'

Eventually the chill seeped into my bones and I realised the afternoon was moving on. I needed to return to the nursery. Standing up, I brushed bits of twigs and grass from my skirt, which was clinging wetly to my legs. My eyes burned with unshed tears and I shivered with cold.

I slipped in the back door, and washed my face in the scullery. Cook saw me and tut-tutted at the state of my clothes.

'Go up and change out of those wet things straight away before you catch your death. Young girls these days, no sense at all,' she muttered as she went about her business.

Tiptoeing so as not to leave a trail of wet footprints through the house, I hurried upstairs. My teeth chattered while I awkwardly put on a dry gown with numb fingers.

On reaching the nursery, I dismissed Lily and began instructing Beatrice on her colours. When she got a name correct, I drew a star over it and she would colour it in. Every now and then I hugged her close as if the warmth of her little body could assuage the chill in my bones and in my heart. But it was in vain.

Despite wearing two shawls, I was still shivering with cold when Helena came in to spend some time with Beatrice before her bedtime.

'Why, Martha, you are very flushed. Are you unwell?'

She came over to me as I replied through chattering teeth: 'I g-got c-c-caught in the rain t-today. M-my t-throat is s-sore.'

Helena put a hand on my forehead. 'Oh my goodness, you are burning up!'

She pushed me gently into a chair, and I did not resist. She rang the bell for the maid.

'Lily,' she said when she arrived, 'help me get Martha to bed.

She has a fever. Beatrice, you run along to Grandmama and tell her that I need to stay with Martha for a while.'

Beatrice stood where she was, clutching her doll.

Helena swooped down and gave her a hug. 'Run along, there's a good girl,' she said softly. 'Lily and I will make Martha all better.'

I tried to smile at Beatrice but I was too tired and was relieved when she ran out of the room. I slumped even more in the chair, my eyes drifting shut.

I was vaguely aware of Helena and Lily urging me to my feet and supporting me as they led me to my room. I sank gratefully onto the bed and allowed them to undress me and put me in my nightclothes as if I was Beatrice's age. I lay down, and gave a little moan as every bone ached. Helena pulled a sheet up over me.

'Cold,' I muttered, clasping my hands together over my chest, trying to pull myself into a tighter shape to get warm.

'I know, my dear,' Helena said, 'but I cannot cover you with blankets as you are already so hot.' She turned to Lily who was hovering at my feet. 'Lily, get some tepid water and cloths. We must bathe her to reduce the fever.'

A few moments later I whimpered as the cool water made me shiver even more. Helena murmured soothingly all the time. Her voice faded in and out as they worked and eventually they dried me, put a fresh nightgown on me, and tucked a sheet around me again. Helena sat by the bed, every now and then laying her hand on my forehead. I had no idea how much time had passed when I heard her speak to Lily again.

'Lily, the fever seems to be getting worse. Send for the doctor to come as soon as possible.'

When I heard this instruction I tried to protest, but it was impossible to rise up through the foggy waves which seemed to be pressing me into the bed. All that came out was another moan. I knew I did not want to see him but my head was too woolly to remember why. I rolled it from side to side in agitation.

A soothingly cool cloth was placed on my forehead and I drifted off into sleep. The fever continued to burn and I thought I saw Beatrice's doll standing by my bed, the same size as a human. She unwound the bandage from her arm and tried to cover my mouth with it. I thrashed around in the bed until I heard Helena's voice reaching through the fog, calming me with her words and making the frightening image disappear. A glass of water was pressed to my lips. I managed a small sip. I drifted off again, only to be woken by a fit of coughing that sent pain shooting through my chest. Again Helena gave me a drink and once more I sank into a restless blackness.

Chapter 10

I stirred and mumbled. It was dark, with a single lamp flickering on the bedside table. My burning eyes darted around the room. I was alone. I was shivering again, my nightgown drenched with sweat. My mouth was uncomfortably dry.

The door opened. Helena came in, carrying a candle. There was a man behind her. As he stepped into the light, I saw who it was. I was sure I said his name, but no sound came out. I wondered why he was here, and why Helena was allowing him to be here.

It was so good to see him, but he did not look happy. His forehead was creased with a frown. I wondered what could have happened to make him look so pale and worried.

Leaning nearer, he put his hand on my forehead. I tried again to say his name.

'Edward.' It came out in the barest whisper. His hand felt so good, so cool. I wanted it to stay there forever. My eyes slid shut, only to open again in disappointment when he took his hand away. I felt bereft. My eyes locked on to his, his burned into mine, hotter than any fever.

He turned to Helena. 'Mrs Pershaw, we need lots of ice. She is overheating dangerously. It seems she has a more severe dose of the infection Beatrice had.'

While Helena was giving instructions to Lily he turned back to me, leaned closer, stroked my cheek, and murmured my name.

'Martha, I will make you well again, I promise.'

I turned my head slightly to press against his hand. Too soon it was gone again.

Helena approached the bed while Edward examined my throat.

'Very inflamed,' he said before straightening up. 'This nightgown is soaked with sweat. It must be changed. Then we will cover her with a fresh sheet and pack it with ice. We must get her temperature down.'

From under heavy lids, I watched him remove his jacket and roll up his sleeves. Lily had come back into the room and he turned away while Helena and Lily changed my nightgown. They might as well have been changing the clothes on a rag doll I was so limp and completely unable to do anything for myself.

'She is ready, Doctor,' Helena said.

There was a knock at the door and suddenly the room seemed full of people moving in the shadows, bringing bucket after bucket of ice.

Edward leant over me again, his face close to mine.

'Martha, we are going to put ice all around you to bring down your temperature.'

I stared at him. 'But I am already so cold,' I mumbled.

'I know that is what you are feeling, but your body is very warm and we must cool it down. Will you trust me?'

Trust him? Why did that suddenly make me feel peculiar? I

did trust him, did I not? There was something I needed to remember, but I was just too tired to struggle with any thoughts.

He was still waiting for my answer. I nodded, which sent a pain down my spine, causing me to moan a little.

I saw Edward turn and signal. Lily and Helena came forward and very gently the three of them started to cover the sheet with ice.

Within moments my teeth were chattering and I whimpered in discomfort.

Edward's face came close again. 'It will not be for long, my dear. Just bear with it another short while.'

He had called me his 'dear' and in front of Helena. He should not have done that, I thought, our secret will be out. I rolled my head from side to side again in agitation.

Edward's cool strong hand once again returned to my forehead and quieted me. I began muttering words that made no sense but, after a few minutes, a lethargy came over me and I fell asleep.

I woke to the sound of ice moving on ice, and a weight being lifted off me. The sheet and ice were being removed. My head was clearer. Edward was not in the room. A candle had burned low on the table to my left. Helena and Lily efficiently stripped off my damp gown, towelled me dry and put on a fresh one.

I was exhausted from the effort of sitting up even though they supported me all the time, speaking comforting words. I was relieved when they lay me back down.

There was a tap on the door as Helena tucked a blanket up under my chin. I felt warm for the first time in hours. She called 'Come in!' and Edward entered, coming over to stand by the bed.

When he saw me awake his face relaxed into a smile.

However, I did not return it. My fever was gone, but my

senses had returned and, with them, the memory of his betrayal.

His formality had also returned, though his tone was gentle as he prompted me to open my mouth so he could examine my throat.

'Miss White, your fever has broken, but your throat is still inflamed. I am leaving this medicine for you with Mrs. Pershaw.' He placed a brown bottle beside the lamp. 'You need to rest for a couple of days.' Taking my wrist between his fingers, he checked my pulse.

Helena sat on the other side of the bed and held my hand. My eyes never left Edward's face.

As he put away his pocket watch he lowered my hand back down on the blanket.

'You hurt me,' I whispered, tears starting to my eyes.

A puzzled frown creased Edward's forehead and his hand jerked out as if he would wipe away my tears, but propriety stopped him.

'The doctor had to put ice on you, Martha dear, to break the fever,' Helena rushed to his defence, misinterpreting the source of my hurt, 'and now you are on the mend.' She patted my hand.

Before Edward could say or do anything she stood up.

'But you are exhausted and now you need to rest, is that not so, Doctor?' Turning to Edward, she continued before he could answer. 'And I dare say you do too, Doctor. It's getting very late. Lily will show you out. Thank you so much for your help.'

Edward had no choice but to go, but he looked at me for a long moment.

'I shall call in to see you tomorrow,' he said softly.

The tears continued to slip from my eyes.

Helena had turned her back to go around the foot of the bed in order to see him to the door. Edward quickly reached out a hand and caressed my cheek. This time I turned away.

I heard him but did not see him take his leave of Helena.

The door closed behind him and my sobs broke the silence in the room. Helena hurried over and took me in her arms, soothing me, murmuring all the while that I would be well again soon. I pressed my face into her shoulder and wept, wishing I could tell her about the searing pain of loving someone so fiercely who did not love me in return.

Chapter 11

Florence, Italy, 2010

Juliet lay in bed, looking at ceiling. Although it was only seven she was wide awake and her mind was busy. She'd had a wonderful evening with Logan but this was a new day and she needed to decide what to do next. She knew she couldn't stay there for the two weeks, because he had said that he had come there to work and she did not want to be in the way. One option was to go straight back to London, but that didn't appeal.

Being a creature of habit she threw back the duvet and moved to the space in front of the window where she did half an hour of yoga and then fifteen minutes of meditation.

By the time she had showered and was dressed in a yellow sundress and sandals, her mind was quiet and her decision was made. She was going to find an inexpensive hotel and move out later that day.

The marks he had left on her arms had left a slight bruising so she put on a light cardigan with three-quarter-length sleeves to cover them.

Because it was still early she was surprised to be greeted by the aroma of coffee when she opened her bedroom door. Logan was in the living room, sitting in an armchair, focused on some document in his hand. A coffee pot, two mugs and a plate of pastries were on the coffee table in front of him. Juliet frowned at the sudden jolt in her stomach at the sight of his damp hair. God, he looked great first thing in the morning!

She gave a little cough and said, 'Good morning'.

He glanced up. 'Good morning. I hope you're hungry because these are still hot from the oven and delicious.'

She moved closer and sat on the couch.

'You baked?' she asked incredulously, her eyes flicking to her watch.

He laughed. 'No, I just happened to jog past the best patisserie in Florence on my morning run. The smell is impossible to resist. You were up early yourself. I think I heard you moving around before I went out.'

'I like to do a bit of yoga.'

'Do you? I've never tried it.'

'I love it and I find it great when I'm away on a shoot. I'm with people all day long, so it's good to get some quiet time – you know, head space – before I step out of my tent, or hotel room, or wherever.'

'I'm impressed,' said Logan, reaching for the second mug to pour her a coffee. 'I'm sure that takes a bit of discipline.'

'I'd miss it now if I didn't do it,' Juliet said.

'That explains why you're such a calm person.'

'Not always!' Juliet laughed.

The balcony doors stood open to the morning air.

'The room is beautiful in this light,' Juliet said. 'I didn't really appreciate it last night. Your mother has some lovely things.' The sun shone in the windows and the scene seemed so cheerful and natural that she was aware of a deep disappointment that she couldn't stay there for the rest of her holiday.

Logan looked around, as if he hadn't looked at it properly in a while. 'Yeah, Mum loves antiques. It's what she missed most about leaving Carissima.'

Juliet looked over at the photographs on the wall. 'Last night you didn't get a chance to say who is in that old sepia photograph. They are outside the same house, aren't they?'

Logan looked up at the photograph. 'Yeah, that's Carissima too and that is my Great-grandfather James Pershaw, my Great-grandmother Helena, and their daughter, my Great-aunt Beatrice.'

He turned back to his coffee.

'And the fourth person?' Juliet asked, looking at the young woman standing next to the others, albeit with a fraction of a distance between her and them.

'Oh, that's Martha,' he replied, holding out the plate of pastries to her. She took one and he chose one for himself. He took a bite.

Juliet expected him to say more when he had swallowed, but he didn't. She prompted him again.

'Another relation?'

'I've no idea. On the back of the photograph it says: *James, Helena and Beatrice Pershaw, and Martha, 1889*.'

'This is delicious,' Juliet said, biting into her pastry again. She studied the photograph. 'Her clothes are a little plainer than those of your great-grandmother.'

Logan looked at the photograph again. 'I suppose you're right. I hadn't noticed that before.'

'You said your mother left Carissima?'

The question made Logan frown. 'She divorced my father when I was fifteen and took me with her to England.'

The strain that had crept into his voice made Juliet feel guilty for prying and she changed the subject.

'This is your mother's apartment so you have every right to be here and you need to complete your work in peace, so I'll be moving into a hotel today as soon as I find one.'

Logan blinked at the sudden change in topic and looked intently at her. 'But that's crazy. Why should you go to that expense when you were supposed to holiday here?' He paused, his eyes still fixed on her face. 'It worked out okay last night – why don't we both stay here?'

'But your work?'

He smiled. 'I presume you won't be throwing rave parties every night, and I will be closeted away in there most of the time,' he nodded towards the study, 'so I won't be in your way either.'

'Okay, if you're sure . . .'

'That's decided then,' he said. 'I'd better get to work. Will you have another one of these?' He pointed at the remaining pastries.

'No thanks, but they were delicious. Thanks for getting them.'

Logan got up and took his mug and their empty plates to the kitchen. He called back to her: 'I'll do my boring work while you go off and enjoy being a tourist.'

'You could always mitch?' The words of invitation were out of her mouth before she could stop them.

He reappeared in the doorway and leant against it, looking at her. 'Now that's tempting, but unfortunately I have a deadline I must meet.' His soft accent poured over her and, despite the rejection, his eyes held a flicker of promise.

Shrugging, she picked up her mug and the plate with the remaining pastries and moved towards the kitchen door and him.

'Well, maybe another time,' she said.

He continued to block the doorway, reaching out to take the mug and pastries from her. Their fingers touched and her eyes flashed up to his. A spark shot between them and she stepped back quickly in case she swayed towards those inviting lips and made a fool of herself. She definitely did not want to give him the impression that her gratitude for the free accommodation would come with benefits!

Turning towards her room, she offered a breezy 'See you later then.'

'See you, Juliet,' he said softly behind her, a hint of laughter in his tone.

When she came out of her room a few minutes later with her bag over her shoulder, the study door was shut.

At the nearest piazza to the apartment Juliet sat on a bench to plan her day, pulling out the guidebook she'd bought at the airport. The skies were clear blue and it was pleasantly warm.

She was reading about the gardens and parks when her mobile rang. Her mother's number appeared on the screen. Juliet made a guilty grimace and answered.

'Hi, Mum. I'm really sorry I didn't ring back last night. I got distracted.' Grimacing again she mentally kicked herself, knowing she had opened the door to a quizzing.

'Good morning to you too. Distracted? Now that's an interesting word.'

The hint of laughter in her tone made Juliet suspicious. A moped whizzed by and she put her hand up to block her other ear. 'Well, if you already know, you don't need me to tell you, do you?' She played along, humour coming into her own voice.

'Okay, okay – Elizabeth rang me late last night to apologise for the mix-up. Logan had just phoned her to explain that he had arrived early. She assured me that you would be safe with him, so I thought it okay to wait until this morning to ring you.'

'Mum, you're impossible!' Juliet laughed.

'So what happened?'

'I was only in the apartment a few minutes when he arrived and we cleared everything up quickly.' Juliet had no intention of telling her mother what had actually happened.

'So? What now?'

'Well, the apartment is huge and he's insisting that I won't be in his way while he works and that I should stay and continue my holiday.'

'Wonderful!' Frances exclaimed.

'I hope you're not matchmaking in that scheming head of yours,' Juliet warned.

'Of course I'm not. Love either happens or it doesn't. You can't force it. But I've seen photographs of Logan. Not only is he good-looking in that dark brooding kind of way, but he also sounds like a very interesting man. Elizabeth is very proud of him. And he's unattached!'

'Mum!' Juliet warned again but this time she couldn't help laughing. 'We're just in the same place at the same time, so don't get any ideas.'

'Yes, but maybe it's the right place at the right time.'

'I'm going sightseeing now, Mum,' Juliet said, refusing to take her seriously. 'Talk to you soon. Love you – bye.'

'Love you too.'

Juliet heard her mother's chuckle before she disconnected.

Strolling down the street, she imagined the phone call between the two mothers the previous evening, and their delight at the turn of events which had brought their offspring together in Florence – a city which Juliet had to admit was quite romantic. Maybe they were right, maybe a little holiday romance would do her good and, after all, they were both returning to

England at some stage, so if it got serious, well, that would be okay.

Having read about a sixteenth-century park called Boboli Gardens which had once been owed by the Medici family, Juliet decided that that might be a good place to spend the morning. However, the gardens were so spectacular, with so much to see, that she spent the whole day there.

That evening, pleasantly tired and hungry and still across the city from the apartment, Juliet decided to eat somewhere near the gardens. Wandering down Via de' Michelozzi, she heard music coming from a restaurant and went inside. There was a quartet in the corner, made up of two guitars, a violin and a clarinet. Juliet was shown to a table and sank into a chair, glad to be able to rest her aching feet.

She ordered the house special of linguine with sautéed courgette and onion, cooked in a Marsala wine sauce, with a side salad. When it was served, she once again marvelled at how such simple food could be so delicious.

Mellow tunes formed a quiet background sound to Juliet's meal and she lingered over a coffee afterwards.

Because it was dark when she came out, she ordered a taxi to take her to the apartment.

Logan was standing in the open door of the balcony on his phone when she got in. He was frowning and gave a nod in her direction. Since it sounded like a business call, Juliet left him to it, got a drink of water from the kitchen, and waved a goodnight as she passed back through on the way to her bedroom.

Ten minutes later, she was sitting up in bed connecting her camera to her laptop when she heard a tap on her door.

'It's open,' she said.

Logan's head appeared and, pushing the door a little wider, he leant against the door jamb. 'Sorry to disturb you,' he said. 'I was just wondering if you were okay. I was starting to get worried when you were so late coming back. I thought you might have got lost – a new city and all that.'

'That's sweet of you, but I was at the other side of the city when I got hungry for dinner, so ate over there.'

'I hope you got a taxi home? Florence does have its seedier side, you know – you can't be too careful.'

'Who made you mother hen all of a sudden?' she asked jokingly. 'It's not my first time away from home, you know.'

'Sorry.' He looked a little awkward for a moment. 'Eh, your mother rang about an hour ago, and I don't think she was very impressed that I didn't know where you were at ten o'clock at night.'

'Oh, for goodness sake!' Now it was her turn to be embarrassed. 'Pay no attention to her. She's just trying to bring out your protective side and throw us together or something. You're baby-sitting your mother's apartment, Logan, not me. I'm well able to look after myself, and she knows it. I'll call her tomorrow and tell her to back off.'

To her relief, Logan laughed. 'Well, I'm afraid there's a pair of them in it. My mother also phoned today and insisted that I take you for a drive into the mountains. She said, and I quote: "That girl is not to go back to England without seeing those beautiful hills, or you'll answer to me, my boy!" Isn't it funny how, no matter how old you are, you still have to obey your mother?'

Juliet's eyes were wide. 'No, you don't! You have work to do – I'm sure she'll understand.'

'She also left me in no doubt that you're not seeing anyone. Now, I wonder why she told me that?' he smirked.

'Mothers! Mine shared the same information with me about you. That pair are scheming, you know that?'

'I know.'

She was glad he seemed to be unfazed by it.

'The thing is,' he said, 'the idea of spending the day in the mountains with you is very appealing and, to tell you the truth, my head is a bit wrecked so I could do with a day away from work tomorrow. So what do you say?'

Juliet felt a sudden curl of excitement in her stomach.

'Honestly?' She gave him a dubious look.

'Honestly.' He straightened up. 'So?'

'Sounds great.'

'We can set off at ten, if that suits you.'

'Sure.'

'Well, goodnight then.'

'Goodnight.'

'Sweet dreams, fair Juliet,' he said softly, pulling the door closed behind him.

Juliet tapped a forefinger thoughtfully against her camera. 'This is getting interesting,' she murmured, before forcing her attention back to her laptop.

Chapter 12

Berkshire, England, 1888

The next morning I lay with my face turned towards the window, watching the clouds move across the sky. The burning in my throat had eased. Lily was fussing around my bed, straightening the blankets and chattering about the scare I had given them all and how Cook and the others downstairs were asking after me. I was too tired to reply and only managed the barest smile of thanks when she was finished tidying.

As she left she said the doctor would be coming to see me later. I needed no reminder, but the words still sent a twisting pain to my gut.

The curtains billowed gently in the breeze. My fever was completely gone, but I was drained of energy. I did not want to see Edward again and had told Helena earlier that I was fine and did not need him to come. But I only succeeded in wasting my breath as she would not hear of cancelling his visit. I was grateful for the great care she was taking of me, and felt very foolish for putting everyone to such trouble. I lay there dreading his arrival.

Within an hour I heard his horse approach and the sound of his voice drifted up through the open window as he handed his mount over to one of the stable boys. I took a deep breath and waited.

Too soon the door opened to admit him and Helena. I could not stop my head swivelling in their direction. He looked so well in his morning coat and waistcoat, and inside me the need for him warred with anger.

He crossed the room.

'She is looking brighter, is she not, Doctor?' Helena asked, smiling warmly at me. 'There is no trace of fever today. But she is terribly weak.'

'Good morning, Miss White,' Edward said. 'How are you feeling?'

I almost laughed at the question. Would not he and Helena be surprised if I replied regarding my emotional rather than my physical health? Their faces would be comical if I said, "My heart is broken, thank you, Doctor, and how are you?"

But bitterness took too much energy. Coldly I told him: 'Much better, thank you.'

'How is your throat this morning?' he asked, passing a professional eye over my face.

'Improved.'

'May I take a look, please?'

Reluctantly I opened my mouth and he leaned close to look in.

'Yes, much improved but still some inflammation there. Any pain in your ears or back?

'No.' My fingers fiddled with a loose thread on the blanket and I kept my eyes on it, for fear he and Helena would see the real pain lurking there.

'Good. Well, then, for now you need to take a few days' rest until the infection leaves your system and you regain your strength. But, Miss White,' the authority in his voice commanded me to look at him, 'you must not allow yourself to get caught in the rain like that again, for next time it could be much worse. Getting chilled like that leaves you very vulnerable to whatever infections are going around.'

Despite his sure tone, there was a puzzled look in his eyes. I turned my head away.

'You must stay in bed for a few days to regain your strength. Now I would like to take your pulse.'

He took out his pocket watch and, before circling my wrist with his warm fingers, he slipped a tightly folded piece of paper into my palm without drawing Helena's notice. He flipped the pocket watch open. My heart had started to race as instinctively my fingers curled around what I presumed was a letter.

'A little fast,' he murmured. He put the watch away and let go of my wrist. 'Mrs Pershaw, I shall drop by again tomorrow.'

'Surely there is no need,' I protested. 'Will I not be much better by then?'

'I will expect an answer to that . . . tomorrow,' he said meaningfully.

I pressed the letter further into my palm.

'I am sure the answer will be yes, my dear,' Helena joined in, oblivious to the double conversation taking place, 'as long as you rest.'

After he left, Helena lingered for a while, putting a book within reach and refilling a glass of water for me. My knuckles grew white as I gripped the letter. I longed for her to leave. But she seemed intent on reassuring herself that I did not want for anything.

'I think I shall sleep a little now,' I said.

'Of course, my dear. The doctor said that you need plenty of that. Lily will look after Beatrice for the next few days. So you just rest as much as you need. I will look in on you in a while.'

I turned my head on the pillows and watched her go to the door. 'Thank you for all your kindness, Helena,' I called after her.

She turned and smiled. 'You just get yourself well, my dear.'

As soon as the door closed behind her, I unfolded Edward's letter.

My Darling Martha,

Why do you look at me with such angry eyes? What have I done to hurt you so, my love?

I am sorry I was not able to meet you in the days before your illness; I had to make an unexpected trip to London and was unable to get a message to you. You cannot imagine my distress when I was summoned to attend you on the day of my return and found you so ill. I wished everyone in the room miles away so that I could whisper words of love to you to help you heal. Having to walk out of your room was the hardest thing I have ever had to do.

Please tell me what is wrong, my love, so that I can put it right.

Until tomorrow,

With all my love,

Edward

I let the letter fall against my chest. Helena must have heard incorrectly, was my first thought. A man just engaged to one woman would surely not write such words of love to another. And they were beautiful, wonderful words of love. I dared hope for a moment but then my second thought was that perhaps he was continuing the same game, and trifling with my affections despite his commitment elsewhere. But that seemed so against his character that I found it hard to believe it of him. And yet Helena had said he was engaged. My thoughts went around in circles until my head ached.

I put the letter between the pages of the book by my bedside, and fell into a restless sleep.

I stirred an hour later when Helena crept in to check on me. I needed to reply to Edward's letter but I could not ask her for a pen and paper because my tired mind could not think of any excuse as to why I might need it. She only stayed a few minutes, saying she would send Lily up shortly with a cup of tea.

I began to compose a reply in my head.

Soon Lily arrived and placed the tea on the table, put extra pillows behind me and helped me to sit up. When I asked for the pen and paper from my desk she did not question it. She merely told me how much Beatrice was looking forward to seeing me.

When she left I began writing.

Edward,

How I long to believe your words of love, but how can I when they come from a man who has just become engaged to another? If you felt my anger on your visit here then it was an outward reflection of the pain you have caused me. I would have understood, despite the pain, if you had changed your mind, deciding after all that you needed to make a good match, ended our association and then went to seek a wife. But to still declare love to me when you already had an agreement with another! To lead me on like that is unforgiveable.

As I doubt we shall ever speak again, the question that will burn forever in my heart will be 'Why?'

Martha

I folded the letter and pushed it under my pillow. The tea had gone cold and I fell back exhausted on the pillows. I slept on and off for the rest of the day and, during my waking hours, anxiety at the impending visit increased.

Chapter 13

'I hope that girl does not become a liability.' James Pershaw's irritated tones sounded from the corridor through the open door.

Lily was bringing in my breakfast tray and, before she closed the door, I saw Helena's embarrassed glance as she ushered her husband along. Lily's blush showed that she had also heard James' comment. I hated him for thinking I was some charity case who was not earning her keep.

Lily chatted too brightly, throwing open the curtains. I only listened with half an ear, already anticipating Edward's visit. But something caught my attention.

'What was that you said?' I asked, as she placed the tray in my lap.

'Higgins was complaining about his back, after hauling the trunks out of the attic.'

'Why was he doing that?'

'I don't know. But when the master got home last night he

told Higgins to get them out and dusted off. Where do you think Mr. and Mrs. Pershaw might be going?' A dreamy look came over her face.

'I have no idea, Lily, but it would be wrong of us to speculate,' I said gently.

'Of course, miss,' she said, snapping out of it and pouring my tea from a small silver pot, 'but it must be nice to see other parts of the world, don't you think?'

'Yes, Lily, but England suits me fine. I have no desire to travel.' Fool that I was, I still wanted to be in the same country as that man despite what he had done.

I wondered if they were actually going away on a trip and if they intended to take Beatrice, and therefore me, with them. The alternative would be grim, being alone here in the house with Mother Pershaw.

Lily returned shortly after I had finished my breakfast. I did not have much appetite but, remembering James' words, I had eaten determinedly. Lily removed the tray.

'Can you pass my brush and combs, please, and I shall fix my hair?'

Lily looked at me in surprise. 'You are to stay in bed all day by Mrs. Pershaw's instructions.'

'Eh, yes, of course, but I think it would help me to feel better if my hair was neat.'

Lily shrugged and I sighed with relief that she had not continued to argue. I needed to do something to help me prepare for my final meeting with Edward. My arms fell to the bed with the pain of that thought.

'Here, let me do it,' Lily said in a no-nonsense voice. 'That fever really took it out of you, miss.' In a few minutes she had my hair neatly brushed and held up with combs. 'There,' she said. 'That's better.'

She left the room and I fixed the neck of my nightgown and straightened the sheet across my chest. I was ready. But I had no idea what time of the day Edward would come. Although I was annoyed at how tired I was after doing so little I gave in to the lethargy, settled into the pillows and dozed for a while.

I was awoken by voices in the corridor — one that of an excited little girl. The door opened and Helena poked her head in.

'Come in,' I said. 'I am awake and I would love a visit from Beatrice.'

Helena and I smiled at each other as the little girl darted from behind her mother's skirts and ran to the bed.

'Gently now,' Helena warned when Beatrice climbed up onto the bed.

'Are you feeling better?' Beatrice asked me solemnly.

'Much better,' I assured her. 'I shall be up soon to play with you again.'

'The doctor fixed you just like me and Vicky.'

A lump formed in my throat at her innocent words and I had to swallow hard to avoid crying.

Unawares, she smiled and threw her arms around me.

'That's enough for now,' Helena said, putting out her hand and tugging Beatrice from the bed. 'Lily has a glass of milk for you in the nursery. Run along.'

Beatrice waved from the door and scampered off.

Helena turned back to me. 'You look much improved today.' Then, one eyebrow raised slightly, she commented, 'Your hair is nice.'

'Lily helped me.' I put a self-conscious hand to my hair. 'I think I shall get up now.'

'Nonsense! You shall stay in bed until the doctor says you are rested enough.' She paused. 'I know you must have heard James this morning. But you must pay him no mind. He returned very late last night and he is always testy after his business trips. You know he and I would be lost without your help with Beatrice. It is so much better to have family looking after her than some stranger.' She patted my hand. 'Besides, Lily is very much enjoying her temporary duties in the nursery. It gets her away from Cook for a bit. You rest now.' She smiled and left the room.

After about an hour I checked again that my letter to Edward was under my pillow. I had just reread it and replaced it when I heard a horse cantering up outside.

It must be him.

Taking the letter out again, I folded it and hid it in my palm. I could not believe my luck when Lily showed him in, saying that the two Mrs. Pershaws were gone to the village with Beatrice.

Lily hovered at the other end of the room while Edward walked forward to me. With his back to Lily, he blocked her view of me. This time I met his eyes. The solemnity in mine killed the smile in his. A frown creased his brow.

'Good morning, Miss White. How are you this morning?'

Mindful of Lily's presence, I answered his question. 'I am much improved, thank you, Doctor. I hope to get up today.'

He reached out to take my pulse. I slipped him the note. His smile returned as he unfolded it, but quickly faded again. As he read it through, his eyes opened wide as if in disbelief or amazement, and then his nostrils flared as if he was trying to suppress his anger.

He cleared his throat. 'I recommend you stay where you are and then you can sit out for a while tomorrow. You should be well on the way to recovery by then.'

His voice was strained and I feared that Lily might notice. His hands had clenched into fists and he threw a quick look in her direction as if to check whether he could speak without her hearing him. But of course it was impossible.

I lifted my chin and looked steadily at him. 'Then this can be your last visit, Doctor. Thank you. Good day. Lily, please see Dr. Adams out.'

Edward looked enraged at my cold dismissal, and continued to stand there. I just wished he would go as I could not keep up the charade of indifference for much longer.

Thankfully, the sound of Lily opening the bedroom door snapped him to attention and, snatching up his medical bag, he gave a curt 'Good day', turned on his heel and left.

I sagged back against the pillows and let the tears come. I was exhausted and could only come to the conclusion that his anger at having been caught out was all the evidence I needed. Any lingering hope died.

Chapter 14

I was physically well within a few days and back to my duties. As far as Helena was concerned, the hollows beneath my eyes and my lack of energy were due to the severity of the chill. I resumed my walks and passed through the kissing gate each day, determined to move on with my life despite the pain. I had my pride to help me. Edward had not attempted to reply to my note, which further assured me of his guilt.

Three days later it was raining in the afternoon, so while Beatrice napped I took a book to the conservatory and sat on a window seat, enveloped in the rich fragrance of the various plants, and listening to the rain on the glass roof. I was there a few minutes when I heard Helena and Mother Pershaw coming in. It was a large room and I was hidden from view behind a pillar. About to stand up and make them aware of my presence, I realised that Mother Pershaw was chastising Helena. I shrank back further on the seat, hoping to remain hidden so as not to embarrass her.

'When you moved in here as James' wife,' Mother Pershaw was saying, 'I believed it important that I hand over some duties to you, so you could practise the responsibilities of running a home and be a good wife to James — so you would be accomplished when the time came to run your own house.'

I heard a basket being placed on the table inside the door and stems being snipped by a secateurs.

Mother Pershaw was obviously standing still next to Helena as the thumping of her walking stick had stopped.

She continued her lecture. 'I do not think I overtaxed you by asking you to oversee the purchasing of food and discussing menus with Cook. But, honestly, Helena, last night's dinner simply did not meet my usual standards. Any cook is only as good as the instructions she gets and the ingredients she works with.' One thump of the stick accompanied this last. Her temper was obviously up.

'What in particular disappointed you about the meal, Mother?'

I could hear Helena's barely suppressed impatience.

I wished I had jumped up when they came in. I was hardly breathing now, so as not to give myself away.

'Those pears were not ripe enough for a start, and the beef was gristly.'

'I chose the pears myself and believed they would be ripe for tonight's dinner, but, remember, Mother, you insisted on changing the menus around which resulted in us having that particular dessert last night and not tonight. I told you the pears would not be ripe enough, but you insisted.'

'Do not be impertinent, girl, implying I am unreasonable.' Another thump of the stick. 'That dessert is good for the digestion and I will ask for it when it suits me.'

Poor Helena, I thought, she could not win. She seemed to think so too, for her reply was resigned.

'Yes, Mother, I'm sorry.'

I seethed on her behalf. She did not even bother to defend the meat, which I recollected as being perfect.

Mother Pershaw was not finished.

'James has been raised to expect a certain standard and as yet it seems to me you are not capable of providing it. It is just as well you are living with me and can learn from me, although it is proving to be a harder task than I had expected.'

I nearly gasped out loud, clamping my lips together at the last instant.

'Just make sure there is a vast improvement and that there is no fault with tonight's meal.'

With this parting remark Mother Pershaw left, her stick banging loudly on the tiles. The sound receded in the distance and a door closed. I heard Helena grunt, and the secateurs banged onto a table.

Then she walked deeper into the conservatory and saw me.

Jumping up, I opened my mouth to apologise for eavesdropping, but she launched into a frustrated tirade before I could speak.

'She is insufferable!' Pulling off her gardening gloves, she twisted them round and round. 'And an – an interfering busybody! I wish she would just let me do things my own way. She says she handed over duties to me, but she does not stop meddling, as though I am her puppet.'

This was quite an impassioned speech from the normally placid Helena, but I knew it marked her regard for me, to be so open about her feelings. She did not seem to mind at all that I had heard the discussion.

'Oh Martha!' She sat down on the seat I had vacated, her temper deflating with the movement. She continued in a calmer, if still frustrated tone. 'How I wish I had my own house to run!

If only James would hurry and sort things out.' Breathing deeply, she pulled herself together.

'The day will come before you know it,' I reassured her, hoping my words were true.

She suddenly smiled her sweet smile at me. 'Yes, it will, Martha, and we shall all be much happier there. We shall picnic when we like, create our own wonderful menus and there will be much laughter.' With this positive declaration she got up, returned to her basket, gathered it and the secateurs and left the conservatory with her head held high.

Sitting again, I opened my book but could not concentrate on the words. I could not help but contrast our futures. Yes, we would move to the same house, but Helena was looking forward to a home with her husband and child, maybe even more children, while I would still be alone while among them.

I indulged myself in the memory of that first night in the kitchen, where I believed I had a glimpse of Edward's true character, and where foolishly I had allowed the seed of a dream to develop, in which he was part of my future. When I remembered him there in the candlelight, I just could not believe it of him that he would deceive anyone. Doubt over my actions with the letter I gave him crept into my mind. Perhaps I should have given him time to explain the order of events in his own words.

I found myself making excuses for him – maybe he'd had no choice but to enter into the engagement with this merchant's daughter – maybe it was some family-honour issue, a promise to his dying father perhaps. My letter was so dismissive, and had condemned him outright without giving him any opportunity to explain.

But my temper began to build as soon as these thoughts surfaced. I stood and paced, huffing indignantly at the momentary weakness. I would not fall into the trap of blaming myself for any of this. Edward should have made it his business to explain himself. The fact that he had not only reinforced my opinion of him being a cad. I'd had a lot of time to think things over while I was still in my sick bed, and had come to the conclusion that the only way to move forward was to kill all feeling for him, and behave like we had never been anything but casual acquaintances.

I smiled wryly, for the first time understanding the satisfaction Mother Pershaw seemed to get from thumping her cane. If I had a cane at that moment I would have thumped it too, in equal measures of frustration and determination.

Chapter 15

Florence, Italy, 2010

Juliet sat in Elizabeth's small white Fiat out on the street, waiting for Logan who had gone back up to the apartment because he had forgotten his mobile phone. A column of schoolchildren, dressed in neat maroon uniforms, were led up the street by a teacher, while another brought up the rear. Both women were very smartly dressed. The clothes of all the other passers-by were also very chic, and Juliet made a mental note to put shopping on her itinerary.

As it was only ten, the street was still in shadow, but the day was already warm and Juliet rolled the window down.

A moped sped past, the driver in a white T-shirt and blue jeans, and the passenger who clung to him wore a mini-dress above long tanned legs.

Logan came out of the building and went around to the driver's side of the car. Juliet laughed as he gingerly folded his large frame into the seat.

'Not exactly built for a runabout, are you?' she asked.

'Well, it's cosy, if nothing else,' he commented, his shoulder pressed against hers inside the little car, his face very close when he clipped in his seat belt. His eyes met hers, dropped to her mouth for a second before rising again, twinkling with a roguish smile.

'Definitely designed for close friends.'

Sensation darted through Juliet's stomach. She broke the eye contact to fasten her own seat belt.

Logan switched on the ignition and pulled out with a lurch.

'Just give me a minute to get used to this – it's a left-hand drive and it's tricky driving with my knees up around my chin.'

Juliet chuckled. She felt comfortable and very alive in his presence and just knew it was going to be a good day.

Despite his unfamiliarity with the car and the fact that the Italians were lunatics on the road, Logan managed to get them out of the city unscathed.

Before long they were driving through beautiful green countryside, with vineyards and olive groves all around them.

'So where are you taking me?' Juliet asked, as the road began to climb up into the hills.

'We are aiming for a place called Fiesole, up in the hills. Archaeologically, it's very interesting and has wonderful views. It's not far, so we'll take a roundabout route so you can see a bit of the countryside. And we'll stop for morning coffee at a small village I know. I think it's important that I allow the circulation to return to my legs at regular intervals today!'

Juliet was thoroughly enjoying herself. She loved the feel of Logan's arm against hers, the sweet summer air coming in through the window and the breathtaking scenery.

Half an hour into the journey Logan turned off the main road and drove a few more kilometres to a very pretty village named Villaggio-Sulla-Diga.

'Village on the weir,' Logan translated, before turning into a small parking area beside a river.

'It's very pretty,' Juliet exclaimed, getting out and looking around her.

The village was built on either side of a weir, the two halves joined by a very old stone bridge. Across from where they stood was a house in typical Italian style with stone balconies and a tiled roof, with a garden that sloped down to a low wall by the river. In the shade of a Cypress tree, a small gate was inset into the wall, and outside it was a wooden jetty with a boat tied to it.

'Look at that. It's just what I imagined an Italian country house would look like,' Juliet said, pulling out her camera. 'Do you mind if I take a few photographs while we're here?'

'Of course not.'

As unobtrusive as she was skilful and swift, Juliet snapped away as Logan took her around the village, pointing out things of interest, like the old stone church that dated back hundreds of years, and two swans drifting backwards towards the weir, but who would every now and then nonchalantly move their powerful feet, to move them back up out of harm's way.

It was quiet, with only a few tourists passing them by.

'It'll be a different story by the afternoon, when the bus tours arrive,' Logan commented. 'It's much nicer to be here in the morning and practically have it to ourselves.'

'Yes, it's lovely. Thanks for putting it on the itinerary.'

They looked in one or two small shops full of trinkets. Juliet bought a fridge magnet of a village scene for her mother.

'Are you ready for coffee?' he asked when they stepped back out into the sunshine.

At her affirmative reply he led the way down a few steps between a craft shop and a candle-making shop, to a café at the end of the little cul-de-sac. Going through it and out the other side, Juliet found they were on a balcony suspended above the weir.

'Oh, Logan, what a great spot!'

'Pershaw Tours is all about satisfying the customer. We're so glad the lady is pleased.' He gave a formal bow and Juliet laughed at him.

They ordered cappuccinos and watched the swans.

'So how many other women have you brought here?' Juliet asked, her eyes full of mischief.

'Oh well, let me see.' He started ticking his fingers. 'There was April, Rita, Jessica, Nina, Sandra . . .'

Juliet laughed. 'Wow, that many – great memory you have there.'

He grinned.

'Seriously,' she prompted.

'Okay. Seriously, one. Her name was actually Sandra. We came out to visit Mum about a year ago. But we're not seeing each other any more.'

'Is that good or bad?'

'It's definitely good. It would never have worked.' He paused.

'Go on,' Juliet urged.

'I thought we were well matched – we were both in academia. However, she wanted me to move to a university I didn't like, in a city I didn't want to live in, in order to progress my career. I loved Cambridge and loved what I was doing there. We argued it back and forth. Then, at one point, when I was trying to convince her of the pros of staying where we were, I said that Cambridge was a nice place to bring up kids.'

He paused again and shrugged, but Juliet could see sadness in his eyes as he continued.

'She left me in no doubt that children were nowhere in her plans. Having a family eventually is important to me, so that was that. We parted company and I've heard that she thought I'd lost

109

the plot entirely when I took a sabbatical and was heading to Central Asia.'

'How long were you together?'

'Over two years.'

'Did she break your heart?'

'No, bruised it a little maybe, but it was the right decision.'

'And has there been anyone since?'

'A few dates here and there before I started travelling but, to tell you the truth, my work has taken over for the last while. Now, enough about me! What about you? Anyone back in England pining for your return?'

Juliet shook her head. 'No, I broke up with someone just before my last assignment. It was just a casual thing and wasn't going anywhere, so . . .' She trailed off, remembering her last date with Russell and how she had realised over dessert that she was bored. So out of fairness to him and herself, she had let him down gently by the time the coffee was served.

She couldn't help comparing it with how she was feeling now in Logan's company. Boredom was definitely not the word she would use to describe it. With a little bit of a jolt she realised that she would use the word *exhilarating*.

She looked up to find him watching her.

'So no broken heart for you either?'

'No, completely intact,' she quipped.

A duck quacking noisily on the water distracted them. Juliet snapped a picture of it.

'Can I have that for a moment?' Logan asked, indicating the camera.

She handed it over.

'Your eyes are a magnificent green in this light,' he said, pointing the camera at her. 'They should be captured for posterity.'

'No way. I prefer to be on one side of the camera only,' she said, putting her hand out, laughing, but Logan had already pressed the button a couple of times, leaning back out of her reach.

Giving up, she turned away to face the river, trying to ignore him while he took a few more shots of her profile.

'Well, at least you'll have proof you were in Italy,' he said, handing the camera back, and she put it around her neck.

He checked his watch and they got up to go. He placed a gentle hand on her back as they returned to the car.

Logan drove further into the hills, stopping a few times on the way to allow Juliet to enjoy the view back down the valley to Florence in the distance.

'I'm running out of adjectives to describe it,' she laughed, getting back into the car on one occasion. 'I had heard Tuscany was beautiful and always wanted to see it. Thank you for showing some of it to me, Logan.'

'My pleasure.' His knuckles grazed her knee as he put the car in first gear and pulled out onto the road.

Fiesole was very impressive. They spent an hour there, wandering around the ancient Roman ruins. Juliet asked Logan to pose for a photograph in the middle of an amphitheatre. He did a few gladiator impressions, which made it hard for Juliet to keep the camera steady because she was laughing so much. Although she didn't say it out loud, she was thinking that, with a build like his, he would pass for a gladiator any day.

Shortly afterwards, when he was standing looking at the distant hills through an old Roman arched window, unbeknownst to him Juliet, a few metres away, caught him on camera – his unguarded expression, the laughter lines around his eyes, his firm lips softened by the merest hint of a smile.

Juliet slowly lowered the camera, wanting to drink in with

her own eyes what she was seeing. There was no denying all that she found attractive about this man: his serious side and his humorous side, both appealing, his witty conversation, the tenderness in his tone when he spoke of his mother, and his strength when he spoke of his work, and of course the way he looked.

He became aware of her standing there watching him, and turned those deep blue eyes on her, one eyebrow raised in question.

'Juliet?' he queried softly.

At the same moment he began to slowly close the distance between them, but just then a bunch of tourists came around the corner, crossing his path, and the moment was gone.

Juliet, relieved at the sudden interruption, moved away. Steady, girl, you're moving way too fast here. You've only just met the guy, she warned herself.

When he caught up with her, she passed several comments about the ruins to divert him from the strangeness of the moment back at the arch.

'Is there a place where I can buy you lunch as a thank-you for this wonderful day out?'

'You don't have to do that.'

'I'd really like to.'

'Okay then, thank you, that would be great and I know just the place – Giovanni Ricci's vineyard and restaurant, not far from here. It's run by a friend of my mother's so we'll get a warm welcome. Giovanni is a genius in the kitchen.'

'Sounds perfect.'

Chapter 16

Logan drove them away from Fiesole, along winding back roads until they got to the vineyard.

The car park was almost full and two tour buses were parked awkwardly, but Logan found a spot in the shade of some Cypress trees.

Going through an arch, he led her into a courtyard and up some steps of what looked like an old stone farmhouse. Despite the fact that the stone was yellow and crumbling, the building had an elegant charm. Climbing roses bloomed around the door they passed through. They were in a small reception area. A bell sat on top of the desk and Logan pressed it.

'*Buongiorno, buongiorno!*' came a booming voice.

A tall man, in his sixties, came through a door, wiping his hands on a tea towel. When he saw Logan there, his face lit up.

'Logan Pershaw! It's wonderful to see you. It has been too long!'

He came around the counter and the two men embraced warmly.

'How is your mother enjoying America?'

'She's having a great time, thank you. Giovanni, this is a friend of mine – Juliet.'

The man looked her up and down, then kissed the tips of his fingers. '*Bella!*' he exclaimed. 'It is a pleasure to meet you!' He kissed Juliet on each cheek, before shaking her hand vigorously.

'I hope you are here for lunch, Logan.'

'Yes, please, if you have a table.'

'Always a table for Elizabeth's boy. Come, come.'

He put an arm around each of them and guided them down a hallway, through an empty dining room and out onto a large wooden balcony, where other customers were enjoying lunch in the warm air. The tables were covered in bright red-and-white gingham tablecloths, and shaded by large white umbrellas. There was a hum of conversation as most of the tables were full. Giovanni led them to the front of the balcony to a table for two.

The hillside fell away below them with row after row of vines stretching away into the distance.

'Giovanni, this view is magnificent,' Juliet said.

He beamed. 'It is my passion – that and cooking, of course.' He gave a booming laugh. 'I recommend the cold meat platter, and our selection of breads. And a *bella rosato*, fresh and cool, to wash it down. *Sì?*'

Logan looked to Juliet.

'Wonderful, thank you,' she said.

When Giovanni had poured them each a glass of water, he left to get their order.

'This holiday is certainly turning out to be way more than I expected. Thank you, Logan, for all this.' She waved her arm to take in the balcony and then the view.

'Well, you do know I'll have to give a written report to my mother that all went well, so I'm glad you're enjoying it.' He grinned at her and touched his glass against hers.

The food was all Logan had told her it would be and Juliet enjoyed two glasses of the *rosato* with it.

'I feel bad that you have to restrict yourself to one glass because of the driving,' she said.

'Don't. It doesn't bother me. Enjoy it.'

She did.

When he was serving them coffee, Giovanni wanted to know if they were doing the tour of his vineyard.

'Yes, please,' Juliet replied.

'Then I will give it to you myself.'

They passed another group just finishing a tour as they headed out. Giovanni called some instruction in Italian to the tour guide, before taking a wide-brimmed leather hat from a hook inside a shed door.

'Juliet, do you like the opera?' he asked as they walked but, before she could reply, he continued. 'My daughter is performing the lead role in Verdi's *Aida* this evening in the village hall only a few kilometres away. Here are two tickets.' He pulled them from his pocket and pressed them into her hand. 'She is *magnifica*! You will enjoy it.'

Looking every inch the proud father, he beamed at them, and Juliet, catching a look from Logan, knew they had no choice but to go.

She thanked him and he began the tour. His passion for his vines was very obvious and Juliet found it and the subsequent visit to the winery itself fascinating.

When they came back up out of the basement the smell of the old oak barrels was still in her nostrils and her skin was chilled. The heat of the sun was welcome. Giovanni and Logan were a few steps behind. Their shared interest in growing plants had them deep in conversation.

Seeing a bench under a tree, Juliet told Logan she would wait for him there. The afternoon had gathered heat and all of Juliet's senses were tired from what they had experienced already that day. Closing her eyes, she tilted her head back until it rested against the tree trunk and listened to her own breathing, slowly relaxing every muscle in her body.

Next thing she knew, she was waking up and her head was resting on Logan's chest and his arm was around her shoulders.

She gave a self-conscious laugh, straightening up. 'I fell asleep. It must've been the wine.'

'Giovanni has taken another tour around, but he apologised for boring you.'

Juliet looked horrified for a millisecond, until she noticed the teasing gleam in his eyes.

'Actually,' Logan continued, 'he was rather proud that his mellow *rosato* had helped you to relax. It's very Italian of you to take a siesta.'

'Was I asleep for long?'

'About half an hour. Eh, I hope you like opera?'

'Not really. You?'

'Nope, never could get into it, but it would break his heart if we didn't go.'

'Of course. Who knows, maybe it'll change our opinion?'

'We have some time to kill, so let's take a drive and swing back to the opera for six thirty.'

'That was . . . interesting,' Juliet announced when they were driving back towards Florence later that evening after the opera. 'Better than I thought it would be. They did a good job, considering the space they had in that hall. It must be an amazing production in some place like the Arena in Verona. Having said that, though, I'm afraid it's still not my thing. I can appreciate it, but I don't love it. Do you know what I mean?'

'Pleb!' Logan feigned mock horror. 'I can see the finer things in life are wasted on you.' He heaved a dramatic sigh. 'You know it's now impossible that you continue to stay on at the apartment. You'll just lower the tone.'

Juliet laughed. 'You nodded off at one point, so don't give me that!'

'Ah, rumbled! Maybe it was the fact that it was in Italian and I couldn't understand a word that did it.'

She laughed.

'What music do you like?' Logan asked.

'Jazz, blues, easy listening, that kind of thing. You?'

'A bit of everything really, except opera of course. I suppose if I had to choose my favourite artist, it would have to be Leonard Cohen. I was at his concert in London in 2008 and it just blew me away.'

'I was at that too!'

Logan glanced across at her, smiling. 'What a small world!'

'It was my mother who wanted to see him. She'd always raved about his music, but I didn't know it at all. But when we went to the concert I fell in love with that raspy, husky voice of his, and the lyrics of his songs are genius.'

'Have you read any of his poetry?'

'No.'

'I think you'd like that too.'

They drove on in companionable silence. Dusk was falling in the valley below and the first lights were coming on in Florence.

'This has been a wonderful day, Logan. Thank you so much.'

'Don't thank me, thank my mother. She made me bring you,' he teased.

Juliet raised her hand to thump him playfully on the arm but, with a lightning move, he caught it in his, bringing their hands down to rest on his knee.

His tone was warm when he said, 'I had a lovely day too. I'll be thanking Mum for the suggestion.' Taking his eyes off the road briefly, he sent an equally warm look her way, before quickly returning them to the narrow mountain road.

Juliet liked the pressure of his hand on hers.

'I can cook us some dinner if you like, when we get back?' Her suggestion was followed by a huge yawn. 'Oh excuse me, I think my senses are overloaded after today, and four acts of opera are exhausting.'

'You're too tired to cook. Beside which, I'm afraid I'm going to have to make up a bit of time this evening with work. So I suggest we order in some pizza, and I know it's very rude of me after our lovely day but I'll have to eat mine at the desk. Will that be okay?'

'Of course. You gave me a great day and I'm grateful for it.'

Back at the apartment the intimate atmosphere of the day lingered as they argued good-humouredly over the toppings on the pizza they were to order.

When it arrived, Logan divided it up.

Wishing he didn't have to work, Juliet poured herself a glass of mineral water, while he took his plate to the study.

'Hey, Juliet?' he called softly from the doorway.

She looked up, her stomach turning to liquid gold at his low voice.

'I really enjoyed today, thank you. Sorry about this.' He nodded his head towards his work.

Before she could reply he turned away, but then turned back again. 'I'll probably be working late, so I'll see you in the morning.' With that he went into the study and closed the door.

She thought how different he had looked standing there just then, like a gentle giant, compared to the angry threatening intruder she had thought him to be on her first day. Deciding she was starting to like him very much, she took her plate and camera out onto the balcony and relived the day by looking back through the photographs, taking her time over the ones of Logan. When she came across the ones he had taken of her, she was impressed with his eye. She wasn't surprised to see that she looked happy in them.

Chapter 17

Berkshire, England, 1888

There was a distinctive autumn chill in the air a few days after my illness as Helena and I walked past the shops in Mirrow village.

'I dislike it when the summer comes to an end,' I sighed. 'Look, those leaves are already starting to turn.' I pointed at the horse-chestnut trees on the edge of the green. 'More layers to wear, more rain, fewer walks. The summer is so much less complicated.'

'You sound a bit melancholic this morning, dear,' Helena remarked, glancing at me. 'I love the summer myself, but the autumn brings its own charms – cosy fires, blackberry pies, morning mist on the lawns . . .'

'Of course,' I smiled at her, and joined in. 'Gathering chestnuts, all the wonderful colours in the woods . . .'

'Exactly. There, you see?' she cajoled. 'Each season brings its own compensations.'

I smiled again. It was difficult to remain glum in her presence.

Her sunny disposition was a tonic in itself. She needed every ounce of it to share a house with Mother Pershaw, who had been very cantankerous since the altercation in the conservatory.

We stopped to look in the milliner's window. Helena admired a royal-blue bonnet, while for me the image of walking beneath a canopy of autumn leaves with Edward began to form in my head. I immediately stamped it out, and imagined him walking there instead with his fiancée. Today I imagined her to be tall, thin and talkative. The day before I had imagined her short, fat and silent – I even sometimes imagined her beautiful and kind. It was a game I had played in the few days since that awful last meeting, a game which quashed my own feelings and which I believed would prepare me for the inevitable day when I would see them together for the first time there on that very street or in church on Sunday mornings. I pretended to myself that the process was helping me forwards towards utter indifference to him.

No sooner had the thought entered my head when he rounded the corner near us at a brisk pace, medical bag swinging from his hand. Looking magnificent in his topcoat and hat, he stopped in front of us.

'Ladies.' Touching his hat, he bowed. 'Mrs Pershaw, I trust you are well?'

'Yes, thank you, Doctor.'

'Miss White?' He turned to me and, beneath the brim of his hat, his brown eyes were searching. Concern flashed across his face and I knew he was taking in the pallor of my skin and the hollows beneath my eyes. Just as quickly a polite mask concealed his concern. 'Are you fully recovered from your chill?' he enquired.

'Yes, completely, thank you.' My voice sounded strange to my own ears.

'She says she is, Dr. Adams,' Helena said, 'but I think she still lacks energy. Is there some elixir you could recommend to renew her strength?'

'Yes, of course. I shall get the apothecary to make one up and arrange for it to be delivered to you this afternoon.'

'Thank you, Doctor. Good day,' Helena said.

He bowed to us again and we moved on.

Helena chattered away, but I did not hear a word.

I could never be indifferent to him! I still loved him. Dear God, what was I to do? Was I going to feel this aching longing for him whenever I saw him? He might be marrying someone else, and he might have broken my heart, but I still longed for him to hold me and tell me that I was the one he wanted. I felt such a fool at my lack of pride. Even so, as Helena and I moved on, I was so aware of his presence behind us in the street.

Beatrice had spent the morning at the vicarage, playing with the vicar's daughter. As we made our way there, I suddenly remembered the travel trunks and longed to ask if Helena was planning to take us all on a trip. Now I wanted to get as far away as possible from Mirrow. I did not want to be here when Edward brought home his wife, for now I knew I could not bear to see them together. But, remembering my place, I held my tongue, knowing I would have to wait to be told.

The vicar's wife invited us in for tea and ushered us into her cosy front parlour. A tea tray sat ready on a small table in front of the fire. She offered us her famous fruit scones. I declined, having no appetite whatsoever, but gratefully accepted a cup of tea. Helena and she were good friends, and I excused myself, allowing them to chat, and wandered over to where the children were squabbling over a jigsaw.

Half an hour later I was thankful to see Helena getting up to leave. I was weary and wanted to get back home.

The morning had tired Beatrice too and she was cranky and difficult. By the time I had got her to eat her lunch and to settle for her nap, I felt I could nap also. I went to my room and lay on the bed but, despite being bone-tired, my mind would not shut down. After about ten minutes I got back up, deciding that a walk might soothe my restlessness. After telling Lily I was going out, I put on my coat and slipped through the kitchen door.

I did a turn or two of the garden but, feeling too hemmed in, I went into the woods. Just after passing through the kissing gate a slight breeze rustled the leaves overhead. When it caressed my face I stopped, closed my eyes, and breathed deeply. I finally began to relax. My shoulders sank down as I let the tension go from my body. But upon hearing a sound it returned. My eyes flew open and I saw Edward coming towards me on the path, but with his head down, so he had not yet seen me. When he did, he stopped.

I turned and rushed back towards the gate.

'Martha, wait! Please.'

It was the humility in the last word that had me turning back to him. I stood, holding my head high, and let him approach.

Stopping a few feet away from me, he searched my face before speaking. 'I owe you an apology,' he said. 'I have behaved like a petulant child, and my indignation prevented me from apprising you of the facts.'

He paused. I waited. Lifting my chin a little more, I braced myself to hear about his engagement in his own words.

He continued. 'I was angry at your accusation of my betraying you, for I felt the betrayal lay in your rushing to believe gossip.'

I blinked. This was not an apology. '*You* were angry at *me*?' With my nails pressing into the palms of my hands, I turned away.

With a lightning movement, he stepped forward and took hold of my arm, turning me back. I glared up into his face.

'Yes, I was angry!' His eyes blazed. 'After all we had said to each other, you were very quick to believe ill of me, to believe I would treat you like that.'

I shook his hand off my arm. 'Because you did treat me like that!'

We stood glaring at each other, each breathing very hard.

Then his face softened and he shook his head slightly.

'Martha, I am not engaged.'

My anger deflated so suddenly I felt lightheaded.

'What? What are you saying?'

'It was gossip.'

'But it was my own cousin who told me you were engaged to a merchant's daughter.'

'Still, it was an unfounded rumour. The merchant you mentioned wanted it to be fact. He and my father had been good friends, and his daughter Victoria and I had been childhood friends. It was the wish of both fathers that our engagement would come to pass and, in this instance, it seems her father was premature in speaking of this hope to some colleagues. She and I have great affection for each other, but more as brother and sister. She has no desire to become engaged to me either. Yes, I was in London, and obviously was seen visiting the house,' he snorted, 'but I was there so Victoria and I could, together, tell her father that we had no intention of marrying. I could not get back here fast enough to be with you again. You can imagine my shock and fear when, only back an hour, I was called to tend to you at your sick bed, my love.'

I drew in a quick breath at the endearment.

'You looked so ill. I knew I would do everything in my power to make you well again. And when you looked at me with

124

such hurt in your eyes, I thought it was because I had not been able to meet you while I was in London. I thought my letter would take that hurt look away. When I visited you the next morning, I was so relieved to see you improved, but was shocked and confused to see that the hurt had turned to coldness.'

'And we know the reaction your letter drew from me,' I said.

'Yes, your reply was very clear.'

He looked away as a muscle in his jaw tensed at the memory. I took his hand in mine.

'Do not go back to that now, Edward,' I said. 'It was all a terrible misunderstanding and we are both at fault for our behaviour, our thoughts, and pride. Please forgive me for my part in it.'

He pulled me gently into his arms. 'I too jumped to conclusions, believing you did not love me if you could so easily believe that I would betray you. But when I saw your face in town this morning, I knew you were not happy. I began to hope and I realised what a fool I had been to let you continue to believe a false rumour. It is I who ask for forgiveness.'

My muffled laugh against his shoulder had him pulling back to look into my face.

'What fools we both have been,' I murmured.

He smiled, then sobered. 'I love you, Martha. You are the one I want to be with.'

'I love you too,' I said.

He bent his head and kissed me gently on the lips, then on both eyelids. His lips trailed back to mine, which he captured in a burning kiss. His arms tightened their grip and my body melted against his. We were both breathless when eventually I pulled back in the circle of his arms.

'I must get home,' I said. Going up on my toes I pressed a quick kiss to his mouth, allowing my palms to linger on the lapels of his coat.

Once again he pulled me close and we got lost in another embrace.

When he released me, his eyes were warm and alive as he told me he would meet me at the cottage the following day.

I had taken only a few steps when he called after me.

'Martha, your elixir,' he said, taking a brown bottle from his pocket. 'I was on my way to the house with it.'

'I will not need that now,' I laughed lightly. 'I have never felt better in all my life.'

I ran off with the sound of his laughter in my ears and in my heart.

Chapter 18

The day after we had set things right between us, we met in the garden of the cottage once again. Despite the sun, it was cooler than on previous days. He put his arm around my shoulders and pulled me into the warmth of his side where we sat on the stone bench.

'Tell me a little more about your family,' he said.

'My father had a small estate near Brighton. He loved the land and had a huge interest in growing crops. He and his farm manager were always experimenting with different strains. My mother would often tease him, saying he should spend more time producing quantity, instead of rare species of wheat. It was not a very profitable estate. But she was very content with her lot, and loved him deeply.'

I sighed, missing them both terribly. Edward's fingers squeezed my shoulder.

'They knew and understood each other so well,' I continued. 'My father's heart was broken when she died. He had loved her with such intensity that he began to fade away himself when she was gone and he passed away two years later.'

I turned until I was facing Edward, both his arms around me now.

'I love with the same intensity,' I said, looking solemnly into his eyes. 'And if you cannot handle that, Dr. Edward Adams, perhaps you should walk away from me this minute and not look back.'

Holding my gaze, he caressed my cheek.

'I would expect and demand nothing less,' he murmured, 'as that is how I love you.' Lowering his head he moved his lips against mine, further kindling the fire that our words had already ignited.

Minutes later, I laid my forehead against his chest and tried to steady my breathing.

'Martha,' he whispered, his breath on my ear sending further rivers of sensation over my skin. 'Loving you is not the challenge. Refraining from eloping with you this minute is!'

I gave a breathless laugh, wondering how we would manage to keep our passion for each other in check for two years. It seemed like an eternity.

Leaning back in his arms, I looked up into his eyes. 'We shall have the rest of our lives to be together, and think of how wonderful it will be after all the . . .' I hesitated briefly, searching for the right word, 'anticipation,' I finished, blushing.

Edward laughed out loud, a booming sound that sent some crows into flight from high in the nearby trees. 'Martha, you are wonderful,' he said, pulling me to standing, then swinging me off my feet in a huge hug. 'But now I must take you back, for my sanity's sake!'

We set off.

'I wish we could marry sooner, though,' he said after a minute or two.

'So do I, but it is nice to have this time to dream and plan too.'

'A couple of years' dreaming is a long time, Martha.'

'I know but maybe after the first year we can make our engagement public, and step out more together.'

'We could do that now.'

'No, Edward, we have already discussed this. I owe Helena too much and you know the situation with Beatrice.'

He sighed. 'I do understand your feelings on the matter. You are so unselfish, my love – and I suppose I would love you less if it were not so. But I want to walk down Main Street with you on my arm and show you off.'

Smiling, I squeezed his hand. 'It is best that we keep it secret for now.'

We arrived at the kissing gate, where we needed to part company.

Edward pulled out his pocket watch and grimaced. 'It is time for you to go back to Beatrice, and Mr. Jones' bunions await me!'

The old oak we were standing under was stirred by a sudden breeze and a shower of leaves floated down. As we looked up, each leaf was caught in the sunlight and gleamed bright gold. We smiled and lowered our gazes until our eyes locked.

My breath caught at the wealth of love I saw there. A smile of pure happiness tugged at my lips, which he slowly lowered his head to kiss.

'Until tomorrow,' he murmured.

I returned to the house, kicking my feet through some fallen leaves, as gleefully as a carefree child.

Lily already had Beatrice up when I got to the nursery and the little girl came running over to me.

'Can I go out and kick leaves too?'

When I looked at Lily with raised eyebrows, she told me they had watched me through the window.

I would have to be more careful, I thought, of my displays of joy, or old Mother Pershaw might start asking questions if she saw me. I knew she would have a weakness if she thought I was meeting a young man unchaperoned! Though I had not said so to Edward, that was another reason I did not want anyone to know about us. If our relationship was out in the open, we might actually end up seeing less of each other, and might never be allowed to meet alone. They would surely become very suspicious of my daily outings, and might forbid me to go.

I dressed Beatrice in a coat and we went outside, where we stamped through the leaves under the trees at the edge of the garden, and threw great handfuls of them up into the air.

From where we were playing I could see Helena and James sitting on a bench outside the morning-room windows. Deep in conversation, they seemed oblivious to our antics. I saw Helena dab at her eyes with a handkerchief and James patted the hand that lay in her lap.

I wondered if Mother Pershaw had said something to upset her again. But before I could dwell on it further, Beatrice showered me with more leaves and ran off so I could give chase.

When we had had enough we went in through the scullery because of our dirty boots. While standing there, taking bits of leaves from Beatrice's hair, I overheard Higgins talking to Cook in the kitchen.

'A waste of time it was. Now I have to drag the blooming things back up to the attic again. And I had 'em all polished and lovely too. Now they'll just gather dust again.'

'It's not our place to question their whims, Mr. Higgins. Get young Robin to give you a hand, so you don't hurt that back of yours.'

The trunks! They were discussing the trunks. I had forgotten about them. It would seem that whatever trip had been planned was now cancelled. I sighed with relief. I certainly did not want to leave Mirrow now!

We left the scullery and were half across the main hall when we heard a horse thundering up the driveway. Higgins passed us quickly and pulled open the front door. On seeing Robin, the groom, dismounting, Higgins rushed out to him. Beatrice and I followed as far as the door.

'Good Lord, boy,' Higgins shouted. 'What's all this? Why have you not taken her around to the stable?'

'Where's the master?' Robin asked.

'I am here,' James replied, having come around the side of the house with Helena to see what was going on.

Robin thrust the reins at Higgins and hurried towards him.

'The church is on fire. I was just bringing the horse back from the smithy when the alarm was raised.'

My immediate thought was of Edward and his safety. He would surely be there helping to put out the fire.

James was already climbing onto Robin's mount. 'Go over to the farmyard and tell all the hands to go to the church at once. Higgins, you stay here with the ladies.'

'We are coming too,' Helena said, looking at me.

I nodded.

James began to protest but Helena cut him off. 'They'll need our help too,' she continued, 'if anyone is injured.'

Dread clutched my heart at her words.

James held her look for a moment, then, giving one swift nod, tugged on the reins and galloped off.

Helena called after Robin, 'Bring the carriage around!'

He touched his cap without slowing his pace.

By now Cook and Lily had appeared at the top of the pantry

131

stairs, curious about the fuss. I entrusted Beatrice to Lily, but not before giving her a reassuring hug. Her bottom lip had begun to tremble.

'Your father and the other men will put that fire out in no time,' I assured her, and ran down to fetch my boots.

Retying the ribbon of my bonnet with shaking hands, I rushed out to the carriage and climbed in beside Helena. Neither of us spoke in the few minutes it took for us to get to the village.

Chapter 19

Smoke was churning up into a dusky sky. As Robin drove the horses quickly down a deserted Main Street, we could hear the roar of the fire before we saw it. Coming out by the green, the church loomed up before us, the sight of its interior bright with flames making us gasp simultaneously.

In front of it, people were dashing about trying to help. The men, shouting to each other above the noise, had organised themselves into chains, passing buckets back and forth in two lines, one from the duck pond and the other from the water pump beside the green.

I could not see Edward among them. Helena was also craning her neck this way and that to find James.

Robin stopped the carriage and we jumped down just as the vicar's wife came running towards the crowd.

'Where's Henry? Where's Henry? Is he still in there? Oh God, is he still in there?'

She pushed her way towards the door. Helena grabbed her

arm and pulled her back.

'You cannot go in,' she shouted.

'But Henry . . .'

Helena nodded at me and I came and put my arm around Mrs. Wallis. Helena shouted a question at the men nearby.

'Yes, ma'am. They've gone in to get him out. I think your husband was one of them.'

Helena turned back to us, wide-eyed, but immediately tried to reassure Mrs. Wallis. 'James is going to get him out,' she shouted, squeezing her friend's hand. Her eyes, large with fear, met mine.

I still had not seen Edward, and I was afraid he was also inside. A loud crash sounded and we jumped. We continued to wait for what seemed like an age, until, to our relief, two men came out with the vicar being dragged between them, an arm around each of their necks. Collapsing onto their knees, they laid him on his back.

One of the men was James, the other I did not recognise. I looked beyond them into the smoke, but still could not see Edward.

I approached James. 'Is Edward in there?' I asked, tugging at his sleeve. He looked at me blankly. 'Dr. Adams,' I corrected myself. 'Is he in there?'

'I did not see him,' James replied. 'And he is needed urgently – the vicar's head is bleeding.' In his concern, my use of Edward's Christian name went unnoticed.

'I shall look for him.'

Rushing from group to group asking if they knew where the doctor was, I became more frantic with each shake of a head.

James was on his knees beside the vicar when I returned weak with fear.

'I cannot find Dr. Adams!' I shouted, trying to suppress my

panic. 'He must be still inside. You have to go back in and get him.' I tried to pull him to his feet.

'Here he is now,' James said, looking beyond me.

I whirled around. Helena was leading Edward over to us, his bag in his hand. I sagged with relief, swaying against James who quickly supported me.

'Martha, are you all right?' he said.

I pulled myself together and stood up straight. 'Yes, yes, of course. Sorry.'

Helena and Edward had reached us by then, Edward flicking me a quick look before kneeling down.

Helena stood beside me. 'They are turning the schoolhouse into a makeshift surgery. The doctor was there.'

I just nodded and kept my eyes on Edward.

Mrs Wallis was crying silently now, holding the vicar's hand.

Taking a white handkerchief from his pocket and pressing it to the wound on the vicar's head, Edward instructed Mrs. Wallis to keep pressure on it. Quickly scanning down the vicar's body he found a nasty burn on the back of his right leg. He held smelling salts under the vicar's nose until he started coughing and taking rasping breaths.

'We need to get him to the schoolhouse.'

'We can put him in the carriage,' I said, recovered now, and wanting to do what I could to help. 'I shall fetch it.'

He nodded.

As I rushed off I heard Helena bringing Edward's attention to James and his companion. 'Their hands have been hurt,' she said.

I returned with Robin and the carriage to where the vicar lay. Robin soothed the horses and tried to keep them steady. The vicar was lifted in and Mrs. Wallis got in beside him.

Helena was shouting instructions to the butcher's wife.

'Please gather a few more women to help at the schoolhouse.

135

The doctor will need candles and hot water.'

She did as she was bid and a group of four or five women hurried over to the school. Some were already arranging the desks into makeshift beds when we arrived. The butcher's wife and the baker's wife, who were both strong women, came out and helped Edward lift the vicar inside. The man who had gone into the church with James was ushered in by Helena.

'Where's James?' I asked.

'He only had a scratch on his left hand which he bound with his handkerchief, so he insisted on staying to help. However,' she continued, 'Thomas's hands are badly burned. He had to push a burning bench out of the way.' She led him to a chair.

The vicar started coughing again and began to speak.

'Sorry,' was all he could rasp out.

Mrs. Wallis murmured soothingly.

Edward was writing furiously on a piece of paper which he handed to the schoolmistress. 'This is a list of supplies I need from my surgery – do you think you could fetch them for me, please?' he asked, withdrawing a key from his pocket.

'Of course, Doctor,' she replied.

Helena came over to me. 'I am going back out.'

Stealing a last, relieved look at Edward's back, I nodded and followed her.

Robin and I brought back two more injured in the carriage: a man who had sprained his foot and another whose eyes were streaming from the smoke.

With each delivery to the schoolhouse, I checked for Edward, relief still making my heart leap at the sight of him safely working there.

After my last trip it was growing dark and the men in the chain were tiring. Some of the women took their places. Helena was there among them, her face smeared with soot and sweat, her bonnet hanging crookedly down her back. The carriage no longer needed, I ran over and got in line, hefting the heavy buckets with all my might. They were being passed to men just inside the door of the church, the heat and smoke not allowing them any closer now. Before long, my shoulders and arms were aching.

Then someone shouted at the door and the men came running out. 'Get back, get back!' they cried.

I thought I recognised James' voice, but they all looked the same with their blackened faces. They waved their arms, driving everyone back, and just in time.

A moment later, an ear-splitting noise sounded from inside the church as one of the main crossbeams crashed to the floor, blasting out the stained-glass windows. Glass showered the ground only feet away from us. Smoke billowed out.

'The roof is going to go. Stay well back,' someone else shouted.

As one, the crowd retreated further, well back onto the green. Like many others, I sank down onto the grass exhausted and watched, defeated, as the fire claimed the church. The roof collapsed, sending millions of sparks into the night sky. Someone nearby started sobbing and many faces were streaked with tears. I rubbed a shaking hand across the sweat and soot on my own forehead.

I turned to Helena who was sitting beside me. 'There is no more to be done here. Thank the Lord, no one else can get hurt now.' Keen to be back with Edward, I continued, 'I am going to the school to help.'

Without a word she followed me. Others had started to move that way as the inn was just beyond the school, and the proprietor and his wife were bringing out trays of tea and ale.

The school was well lit with candles and lamps when we

arrived and was very full. The men who had been closest to the fire were being treated for burns and coughs and some people had cuts from the flying glass. Edward was moving swiftly and efficiently from person to person. Helena went straight to the vicar and his wife, while I found a bowl of water to wash my hands in.

Edward was turning away from a patient as I approached. He stared hard at me, then picked up a towel and tenderly wiped my face.

'Ah, it is you,' he murmured, 'and safe, thank the Lord.' He leaned towards me as though he would kiss me, but at the last moment remembered where he was and straightened, blinking rapidly.

I released the breath I did not even realise I was holding. 'Oh Edward,' I whispered, 'I thought you were trapped in the church. I could not find you anywhere. I could not live if anything had happened to you.' My voice cracked on the last words.

'Hush, my love,' he whispered back. 'All is well now. We will not be parted that easily.' He smiled. 'You look exhausted. Go home. There are plenty here to help.'

'No, I am fine. I want to stay, be with you, help you. Just tell me what I can do.'

He hesitated but relented when he saw how determined I was. 'Over there, those men,' he nodded to five soot-covered men sitting on the floor, backs against the wall, who were all coughing loudly, 'They each need a spoonful of this.' He reached for a bottle and spoon and handed them to me.

As I gave the third man in the group his medicine, he spoke. 'Thanks, Martha.'

I blinked. It was James. I called Helena over. They embraced in relief, as I continued to spoon the medicine into the others.

Assured that James was okay and just needed to rest for a while, Helena left him and got to work. We helped where we could for another two hours. In that time, relatives came and went, taking their loved ones home as soon as Edward allowed them to go. The carriage was borrowed again so Mrs. Wallis, with the help of some neighbours, could take the vicar home, his head and right leg bandaged. He was still very pale.

It was nearly midnight by the time all the patients had gone. James had gone to the inn for some ale with the other men earlier. Helena, having sent Robin to fetch him, came and linked arms with me, making it impossible for me to have a private word with Edward.

'Time to go home,' she said.

But Edward saw us leaving and came over.

'Thank you both so much. I am very grateful for all your help.' He bowed slightly and smiled at Helena and then did likewise to me, holding my gaze a touch longer.

I prayed no one else was looking at me as I was sure all my love for him was there in my eyes.

It was a tired, aching, and dirty group that dragged itself up the front steps of the house. Higgins had the door open before we got to the top. Cook and Lily came forward to fuss over us, and to announce that there was plenty of hot water ready for baths, and plates of sandwiches and tea.

As the three of us wearily made our way upstairs, James spoke.

'Well done, both of you. You worked very hard. It is such a shame we could not save the church.'

'Everyone will pull together and rebuild it, making it even finer than before,' Helena said.

Exhaustion was setting in and I barely heard her words, and it was not until I was turning out my light later that I recalled James' reply, but was too exhausted to puzzle over it.

'A pity we shall not be here to see its completion.'

Chapter 20

Florence, Italy, 2010

The day following their mountain trip, Juliet spent alone. Logan was catching up on the work he should have done the previous day and she was happy to potter leisurely around Florence, picking up the odd gift here and there for back home.

Pleased with all she'd seen and photographed, she returned to the apartment in the late afternoon. She hoped Logan was finished work and that he might want to join her for dinner. Having stopped at a local market, she was now carrying a shopping bag filled with chicken, vegetables, bread, olives and some white wine. As she unlocked the door she was wondering what recipe she would choose. Elizabeth had an impressive array of herbs and spices she could use.

The moment she stepped into the apartment, she saw a small travel bag on the floor. Logan came hurriedly into the room, frowning. He threw a glance in her direction.

'Good, you're back,' he said. 'I thought I'd have to leave you a note.' Distracted, he looked around before walking to the coffee table to pick up his phone and wallet.

'You're leaving?' Juliet struggled to keep the disappointment from her voice.

'Just for a couple of days,' he replied, checking the contents of the wallet. 'I've an unexpected meeting in Rome with a guy from the UN. He's just passing through and only has a small window. I have to get the train from Santa Maria Novella station in less than an hour, so I'd better get going.'

Juliet had wandered over to put the groceries on the coffee table and turned to watch him put a file into his bag before straightening and looking around to make sure he hadn't forgotten anything.

'See you probably the day after tomorrow,' he said, lifting his bag up. Making eye contact with her for the first time since she had come in, he went still. He drew a long breath. 'I'm sorry about this, but at least you will have the apartment to yourself for a while, like you were supposed to.'

Juliet smiled. 'Yes. Well, enjoy Rome.'

There was a moment's silence before, with a sudden movement, Logan dropped his bag back down on the floor. Covering the distance between them in two long strides, he took Juliet's shoulders in a gentle grip. He pulled her towards him, pressing a brief feather-like kiss on her mouth.

Raising his head, he looked into her eyes and swore softly.

'Damn,' he murmured, 'I wish I didn't have to go.' He studied her for a moment. 'I didn't get half the work done today that I should have. I spent a lot of it thinking back on yesterday. You're one distracting and very beautiful woman.'

Lowering his head, he placed a firmer kiss on her lips which sent her nerve-endings singing.

This time her lids slid shut, but in an instant the touch was gone. When she opened them he had turned away and was grabbing up his bag. She released a breath, not realising she had been holding it.

Logan paused at the door and smiled. 'See you soon, Juliet.' And he was gone.

A smile spread across her face as she picked up the groceries and took them to the kitchen. It might be dinner for one tonight, she thought, but there was promise in that kiss.

Maybe it wasn't such a bad thing that she was alone, she thought. Since returning from her assignment in Africa she had been on the go. Now that she had the apartment to herself, she decided to have a totally relaxing evening. And music was her first priority. Flicking through Elizabeth's collection she found a CD of Argentinean tangos. The vibrant music filled the apartment while she hummed along in the kitchen, preparing a casserole. Her toes tapping, she poured a glass of wine.

As soon as the casserole was in the oven she swopped the tangos for some Ella Fitzgerald, took her glass to the main bathroom and ran a bath. After lighting the candles that were in a row on a shelf, she sank up to her neck in bubbles while Ella crooned 'Dream a Little Dream of Me'.

An hour later, when bringing her dinner into the living room she heard a knock on the door. Wondering who on earth could be there, she went to look through the spy hole only to see Signora Padelli outside.

Opening the door, Juliet saw that she was holding a large bulky envelope.

'Signore Logan?' she asked, lifting up but not holding out the package, and looking around Juliet to see into the room.

'He's not here.'

'Soon?' the woman asked.

'No. He's in Rome.'

'Ah, Roma. He will be back?'

'Yes, in a couple of days. I can take that for him, if you like.'

'No, no, it's okay. I give Signore Logan. *Buona sera.*' She walked away and Juliet, glad the interruption to her evening had been brief, returned to her meal.

As she ate she checked back through the photographs she had taken that day. It certainly was a very photogenic city and for a moment she wondered if her editor might be interested in some of the photographs. It hadn't taken her long to realise how entertaining the Italians could be, and how the slightest thing always came across as a huge drama. She smiled at one particular photograph of three wildly gesticulating men standing around two entangled bicycles. Though her wildlife photography was well complimented by readers of the magazine, she knew she had a talent for capturing people too.

Looking up now at the old photograph on the wall, of the grand old house with the Pershaw family and Martha-of-no-surname in front of it, Juliet reflected on how wonderful photography was for giving a glimpse of other lives. She fixed on a plan to spend the following day wandering the streets of the old town to people-watch for a while and get some more shots.

Juliet spent the following day sightseeing and finished the day with a meal in a restaurant near the apartment. A group of English tourists at a table next to hers invited her to join them for coffee. They were good fun and she stayed late with them. Back at the apartment it was quiet after their hilarity and, though happy with her own company, she had to admit that she was looking forward to Logan being back the following evening.

Chapter 21

Berkshire, England, 1888

To Helena's surprise Mrs. Wallis arrived at the house mid-morning to call on her.

'Alice, how lovely to see you!' Helena said, embracing her friend when she was shown into the morning room.

'I had to come and thank you all for your help last night,' Mrs. Wallis said.

Her daughter was with her, and Beatrice immediately ran out with her to the garden to play, with a warning from me to stay where I could see them.

'Please pass on my thanks to your husband. He and Thomas Stewart saved Henry's life.' She paused to wipe away a tear that slipped down her cheek. She gave a little laugh at herself. 'All is well now, thank the good Lord and all our good neighbours and friends. You and Martha were such a great help. Everyone was marvellous.'

'And how is Henry today?' Helena asked as she passed her a cup of tea.

'His throat is very sore and his leg is going to take a while to heal. But Dr. Adams said that the fact that he is young and fit helps. He is not happy about having to stay in bed for a few days, but those are the doctor's orders. He is very grateful that no one was seriously hurt.' She took a sip of tea.

'He must be upset about the church,' I said.

'Yes, of course, but, as chance would have it, he had removed all church records and documents just last week to his study at home, because he wanted to reorganise them. If he had not, they too would have been lost.'

'That is good fortune,' Helena said.

'To see how everyone came to help last night did my heart good.' Mrs. Wallis sighed.

'And it is that same spirit that will see the church rebuilt in no time, I am sure,' Helena smiled.

They both went on to praise Edward's work the night before. I glowed with pride listening to them.

The door of the room was thrust open and Mother Pershaw joined us, harrumphing as she lowered herself into an armchair opposite Mrs. Wallis.

'How did it start in the first place?' she asked gruffly.

'Henry said that it must have been a candle too near a sheaf of wheat.'

The harvest had been celebrated the previous Sunday and the church would still have been full of sheaves of wheat, and fruit and vegetables displayed on arrangements of cloth, all of which would have provided ample kindling for the wooden pews.

'The wheat caught fire,' she continued, 'and in turn set fire to some cloth nearby. Apparently it was all very sudden.'

'Damned stupid to have a candle anywhere near wheat, I say,' Mother Pershaw sniffed in disdain.

'Mother!' Helena cautioned, as she saw her friend blush. 'This

145

is no time to lay blame anywhere. It was an accident and it has been very upsetting for everyone.'

Mother Pershaw harrumphed again and put her hand out too quickly to take the cup and saucer Helena proffered. She hit the saucer, spilling tea on to it and on to the white tray cloth.

'Accidents happen,' Helena murmured quietly.

Good for you, I thought.

Mother Pershaw seemed to miss the irony of it and tut-tutted. 'Be more careful, girl,' she snapped at Helena.

What had been a pleasant visit now became uncomfortable, resulting in Mrs. Wallis standing to leave shortly afterwards.

'I must be on my way. I have so many other people to visit and to thank. Please come and see us soon, Helena.'

I called the girls in from the garden and Higgins was summoned to show the Wallises out.

'Time to go to the nursery, Beatrice,' I said. 'Come along.'

My duties gave me the excuse to leave the drawing room, whereas poor Cousin Helena was being subjected to a lecture from her mother-in-law on carelessness in general, and by the clergy in particular.

James was coming down the stairs as we crossed the hall. Beatrice ran to meet him. He scooped her up and hugged her.

'Was it very scary at the big fire?' she asked, tugging at his moustache.

'No, not at all,' James replied in a raspy voice, his throat still raw. 'There were lots of us to help.'

'I wish I could have been there too.'

'Martha was there and worked very hard.' James looked at me across the top of her head.

'Thank you,' I mumbled, surprised at his compliment.

'Excuse me, sir,' Higgins, who had been to answer the front door, spoke from behind us. 'There is a letter here for you from London.'

146

Giving Beatrice a quick kiss on the cheek, James put her down. I took her hand and continued up the stairs.

Below us I heard the rustle of paper. A moment later he called out Helena's name in an excited tone before rushing into the morning room. The door closed behind him, so I did not discover at that point the reason for his excitement.

Later that afternoon I took a brief walk in the woods. I had guessed correctly that Edward would not have time to meet me so I did not linger as it was very cold and showery. It made me long all the more for our meeting the following day when we could talk about the night of the fire.

After putting Beatrice to bed that evening I went down to the dining room. Helena was already seated at the table. Her cheeks were flushed and she fiddled with her cutlery. James moved from the fireplace to hold my chair as I sat. Mother Pershaw was absent.

Helena answered my unspoken question. 'Mother Pershaw is not joining us for dinner. She has a headache and I have sent a tray up to her room.' She smiled at James and then at me. 'It gives us the opportunity to speak with you alone.'

My heart pounded. Had they found out about Edward and me? Had my fear and anxiety for him the previous night been noticed after all? In my lap I twisted my napkin round and round my fingers, holding my breath.

'Shall I tell her, dearest, or will you?' James asked.

'You,' she said, smiling happily at him.

'Martha,' he said, 'for a while now, as you know, we have wanted to have a house of our own. Well, that is going to be the case very soon.'

I breathed again.

Helena continued to fiddle with her fork, and her smile

seemed a little nervous. Unease crept up my spine.

'I am having a house built at this very moment,' James said. 'I thought it would be well underway by now, but there was trouble with the labour. Bad weather prevented the delivery of some building materials from Italy. We even had Higgins get the trunks ready as I was going to take Helena to see the location. But I have decided to wait until it is completely finished so that the first time she will see it will be the day she becomes mistress of it.' He smiled proudly at her and she beamed back at him. 'I received a letter this morning telling me that it is back on schedule.' He looked at me, rubbing his palms together.

'Of course,' Helena said, 'we very much want you to come with us and to continue taking care of Beatrice.' She leaned over and squeezed my hand. She smiled, but it was a smile of encouragement and entreaty.

I was confused. Why should she doubt that I would want to go with them?

'Of course I want to go with you,' I assured her.

'The thing is, Martha,' she continued nervously, 'the new house is in Ireland.'

I felt as if I had been hit hard in the stomach.

I looked from one to the other. 'Ireland?'

'County Monaghan in Ireland, to be precise,' James explained. 'It is in a very picturesque part of the country and I have acquired substantial farmland there. The house is being built at present in a beautiful situation overlooking a lake. We are very excited about it.'

'Ireland?' I repeated again like an idiot, staring at Helena.

'It is not like you have any family here in England that we are taking you away from, my dear,' she said. 'You will be happy with us and Beatrice, will you not? And although I have not been to see it myself, James tells me that it is a place of great beauty.'

A lump had formed in my throat. I wanted to tell her there and then that I could not possibly move that far away from Edward. My goodness, across the sea! They might as well have told me they were taking me to China!

My look of shock at the thought of leaving him was misunderstood by Helena.

'I know Ireland is coming out of a very dark time,' she said. 'There is still a lot of poverty there. But James will give employment to local farmers and I shall employ some local staff at the house. Ireland, James assures me, is not half as barbaric as people make it out to be. Is that not so, James?'

'Indeed, my dear. There has been trouble in the West, but Monaghan is a quiet, peaceful place. And one can always find honest, hardworking folk in any country. You just have to know how to find them. And I am certain they are in plentiful supply in Monaghan.'

'Mrs Wallis has a cousin,' Helena continued, 'who has a parish there and in a recent letter he says his parishioners are looking forward to us joining them in the spring.'

The spring! At least that was months away.

There was silence for a moment and I knew they were both waiting for me to say something, to express excitement, even share their joy.

I forced a smile at Helena. 'It will be wonderful, I am sure. But will you not miss England?'

'Of course, but with my own parents passed away, I have no real ties here and I am so looking forward to being mistress of my own house.'

'When will you tell Beatrice?' I asked, amazed at how ordinary my voice sounded despite my aching throat.

'We shall tell her tomorrow,' said James, 'as it will be common knowledge soon and she might hear it spoken of by the servants.'

'We decided not to say anything until the house was well underway,' said Helena. 'My goodness, that day in town when I got that lovely warm cloth for Beatrice, I nearly said that it would be perfect for when we were in Ireland. I just stopped myself in time!'

I nodded absently.

Her joy at becoming mistress of her own home, far, far away from Mother Pershaw was palpable. I might someday be happy for her, but at that moment I could not be.

'How is Mother Pershaw about it?' I asked.

'Mother is disappointed that we shall not be in the same country obviously, but she understands that this is what I want, so she has given us her blessing.' James spoke with the confidence and arrogance of a much-loved son. 'My sisters and their families will visit often to keep her company.'

Obviously she has given the blessing reluctantly, I thought, if she has confined herself to bed with a headache. I envied her the solitude and longed to escape to my own room.

I could not eat and just pushed the food around my plate while the Pershaws talked and planned. I felt Helena's eyes on me more than once, but I could think of nothing to contribute to the conversation. Excusing myself as soon as was polite, I left the room, closing the door gently behind me, before bolting upstairs.

Venting my anguish, I threw myself on my bed, muffling huge sobs in my pillow.

I would have to go. I was obligated to Helena. I could not stay and marry Edward so soon. Yes, I would have to go. Leave him. Those two words brought a fresh bout of weeping.

Chapter 22

The following day I was glad to get to our meeting place before Edward did. I stood outside the cottage garden so I could watch him approach. I did not have to wait long before I saw him in the distance striding along by the river, his head up, looking at the sky through the bare branches, as though he did not have a care in the world. Inhaling deeply, I knew I was about to change all that.

As he got closer, I stepped forward.

'Hello!' he called, increasing his pace.

I am so sorry, my love, I thought, as I turned and went into the garden, where I stood waiting for him.

He gathered me in his arms and I clung tightly to him, squeezing my eyes shut and forbidding myself to cry.

Pulling back, I smiled bravely at him.

'I am sorry that I could not see you yesterday,' he said. 'There were so many patients to visit after the fire.'

Linking hands, we sat down.

'It was quite a night,' I said as brightly as I could.

Edward looked at me more closely. 'Martha? What is it?' He placed a finger under my chin, tilting it upwards until I raised my eyes to his. 'There is something in your voice today and sadness in your eyes. What is the matter?'

I swallowed, but held his gaze. 'I have some bad news, Edward.'

His fingers moved around so that his palm cupped my cheek.

'The Pershaws are going to move to their own house, and they will be taking me with them.'

He was about to speak and I pressed my fingers to his lips, so that I could say it all.

'They are going to live in Ireland —' My voice caught, and I could not finish.

'When?' The word was whispered.

'The spring.' A tear escaped and ran down my cheek. My throat ached.

Edward pulled me into his arms and rocked me from side to side in silence.

We sat that way for minutes on end. Eventually he spoke, his voice rough with emotion.

'Do not go. Stay and marry me.' He kissed my hair.

'You know I cannot do that. Your circumstances have not changed, and I made a promise to stay with Beatrice.' I pushed back from him and looked into his troubled eyes. 'I do not expect you to wait for me. It was one thing to have a secret agreement, and to be able to see each other almost every day, but another not to see each other for a year or more. I will not ask it of you, Edward. I free you of your promise.' I spoke quietly, my outward composure belying the silent cracking of my heart.

He crushed me against his chest.

'Do not talk nonsense,' he said gruffly. 'That is a ridiculous suggestion. Of course I will wait for you.'

He was silent for a long while. When next he spoke, his tone was firm. 'We have until the spring together and perhaps by the following spring I can send for you. Beatrice will be older then and will have more understanding of the way the world works. Our love is strong enough to survive this parting until then.'

I sagged with relief, the fear of never seeing him again melting away. All I could do was nod my head against his chest.

'We will make the most of every moment we have in the coming months,' he continued. 'Hail, rain or snow, I will meet you here each day and you must find excuses to come into town too and drop into the surgery. He paused and leaned back so I looked up at him. A grin began to tug at his mouth. 'We shall fabricate some skin disease on your arm or leg that I shall have to treat every day!'

I laughed, getting caught up in his mood.

'Oh Edward,' I said, 'you are impossible and I love you so much.'

He sobered. 'We are meant to be together.'

We sat for a while longer but it started to get cold. Edward pulled away and looked at the cottage.

'I wonder if we could get inside?' he said. 'It would give us some shelter from the wind.'

Moving to the door, he pulled away some of the climbing rose bush, now without its flowers. Putting his shoulder to the door, he shoved against it. It gave very easily and he disappeared inside.

'Come in, Martha!' he called.

I followed in, allowing my eyes time to adjust to the dimmer light, caused by dirty windows which were mostly covered by plants on the outside. We were standing in the living area, which still contained a table, some chairs and a dresser. Everything was very dusty. But Edward's smile was lighting the room.

'Now we can meet in all weathers,' he said and opened his arms for me. I walked into his embrace, thinking that at least our meetings could continue over the next few months but the impending departure would be there with us all the time. We held on to each other as we tried to come to terms with the change in our future.

An hour flew by too quickly, and it was time for me to return to my duties.

'Do not fret about this, Martha,' Edward said, as he walked me through the cottage garden. 'It will all work out in the end. When we have been married for fifty years this one year's parting will seem like nothing at all. We can tell our grandchildren about it!' Again his words coaxed a smile from me.

'We will never be short of laughter, will we, Edward?'

'Not if I can help it.'

He gave me one last lingering kiss before I left him.

'Try to get into the village in the morning,' he called after me and waved.

I waved back and returned to the house with a much lighter step than I'd thought possible when I had set out.

I was delighted the next morning when Helena asked me to take Beatrice to the village to collect some material she had ordered.

'The tea chests for our packing are being delivered this morning and it is best to keep Beatrice out from under my feet,' she said.

It was a cold, grey morning so we wrapped up well in scarves and gloves. Beatrice had been told about the move to Ireland and she was jittery with excitement.

'Stand still, I will never get this scarf knotted with you jumping around,' I admonished her gently.

She talked incessantly all the way to the village about the ship and the new house and whether her doll would like her new room. I only listened with half an ear, wondering if we would see Edward.

But there was no sign of him as we went about our business. We did however meet the vicar's wife, who said that her husband's condition was improving. Beatrice was still giddy and jumped from one foot to the other while I spoke with Mrs. Wallis. I was mid-sentence when I heard the child say, 'Oh look!' and she pulled her hand out of mine, making to cross the street.

Suddenly a horse and carriage were bearing down on her from the left. Screaming her name, I lunged forward, grabbing her coat and pulling her out of the path of the carriage wheels with only a second to spare.

The momentum knocked us awkwardly down onto the pavement. Beatrice let out a wail and tears streamed down her pale face.

Shaking, I wanted to berate her for running away like that, but the pain in her face stole the words before I could utter them.

'It is her hand, dear, she seems to have hurt it,' Mrs. Wallis said, lifting Beatrice onto her feet.

I got to my feet and took Beatrice's hand gingerly in mine. The wrist was already swelling.

'The doctor will need to take a look at that,' Mrs. Wallis said.

I lifted Beatrice into my arms and she sobbed into my neck, clinging on with her good arm.

'There, there, sweetheart,' I soothed her.

Mrs Wallis ushered us down the street to the surgery.

Edward opened the door.

I had wished to see him, I thought, but I certainly had not wanted to see him under these circumstances. My legs, which were already shaking, now turned weak at the thought of what could have happened to Beatrice if I had not grabbed her in time. I staggered under the weight of her.

Edward's eyes opened wide in alarm and he quickly reached out and steadied me, then lifted Beatrice into his own arms.

'It's her wrist, be careful,' I said as he did so.

Mrs. Wallis put her arm around my waist, lending me welcome support as we followed Edward inside.

'What happened?' he asked, walking ahead of us into the surgery and sitting Beatrice on the examination couch.

'They had stopped to speak to me,' Mrs. Wallis replied, lowering me into a chair, 'and Beatrice made a dash to cross the street. A carriage nearly ran her over, but Miss White's quick reaction saved the little girl from certain death.'

Edward paled, his eyes fixed on my face. 'Were you struck?' he asked.

'No, no,' I said. 'I am fine. Beatrice fell when I pulled her back and she landed on her wrist, I think.'

Reassured by my words and Mrs. Wallis's nodding head, he turned back to Beatrice.

'Well, young lady, first your doll's arm and now yours,' he said softly. 'What an adventurous life you lead! Now, let us take a look.'

'Sore,' Beatrice sobbed.

I got up and sat beside her, putting my arm around her shoulders. 'Let the doctor take a look, sweetheart.'

Her good hand fell onto her lap and she held out the injured one. Edward examined it gently.

'Just a sprain. No broken bones today. I will strap it up and it will be as good as new in a week or so,' he said brightly. 'It might hurt for a few days but you will have to be a brave girl.'

Beatrice, who had stopped sobbing, nodded her head.

Edward glanced at me again.

'And you, Miss White, are you sure you are not hurt?'

'I am not injured, thank you – I just got a terrible fright when I saw the . . .' My words trailed off and I shuddered, hearing again the horse's hooves.

'What you need is a strong cup of sweet tea. Mrs. Wallis, would it be an imposition if I asked you to put the kettle on the stove while I strap up Beatrice's arm?'

'It would be my pleasure, Doctor,' she replied, scurrying off to the kitchen.

'Are you trying to give me heart failure?' Edward whispered as soon as she left. 'I am flattered, but was this not a bit drastic?'

Humour warred with concern in his eyes. He placed his hand on my cheek and I pressed into his palm unthinking until I saw Beatrice tilt her head in curiosity as she watched us. I sprang upright, and Edward quickly withdrew his hand. We cleared our throats simultaneously, then burst out laughing at the absurdity of the situation.

Beatrice had already lost interest and held out her sore hand to him. He began to wrap a bandage around her wrist.

'So, Beatrice,' I asked, 'why did you run off like that?'

'There was a beautiful doll in the shop. She had on a hat and scarf like me.'

'Well, if you see something like that again, you must ask me if we can go together to look at it,' I chided gently. 'You are never to pull your hand out of mine like that and run across the street. It is not safe.'

'I did not see the horse, Martha,' she said, looking at me with big, sad eyes, her bottom lip trembling.

'I know, sweetheart, and I know you will not do it again.' Squeezing her shoulder, I dropped a kiss on the top of her head.

Edward smiled at me and my legs turned weak again.

Just as well Mrs. Wallis chose that moment to return with my sweetened tea. I felt foolish sitting there, sipping it under the strict supervision of both of them, as though I was the patient and not Beatrice. I nearly scalded my tongue in my haste to finish it. But I had to admit that I did feel the better for it.

'You must come to the vicarage and I shall send you home in our carriage.'

'That is very kind of you, Mrs. Wallis. Thank you. Come along, Beatrice.'

Edward relieved me of the cup and saucer before lifting Beatrice off the couch, and I caught a glint in his eyes as he watched me hastily stand up unaided. I hid my smile in the pretence of tightening my scarf.

Mrs. Wallis took charge again and ushered us out without a chance for any further conversation.

We had only gone a few paces down the street when we heard him call after us.

'Miss White, I think you should bring Beatrice back tomorrow, so I can take another look.'

'Yes, of course. Thank you, Doctor.'

I threw a last glance over my shoulder and caught his smile, before Mrs. Wallis moved us on again.

Chapter 23

Florence, Italy, 2010

On the agenda for the day was the Galleria degli Uffizi, which, according to Juliet's guide book, was an art gallery crammed with masterpieces. On the book's advice, Juliet had booked a ticket the day before, so she stopped for a leisurely breakfast, knowing she didn't have to get there early to queue.

'How is the *bella signorina* this morning?'

Juliet looked up at the flirtatious smile on the face of a young waiter.

'Fine, thank you,' she smiled back, not in the least flattered, knowing that smile would be flashed at every female who sat at his tables for the day.

'*Bene*,' he suggested.

'*Bene, grazie,*' she repeated, trying to imitate his accent.

He nodded his approval at her attempt.

'You are going to the Galleria today?' he asked, looking at the open book on the table in front of her.

'Yes, I really want to see this – Lippi's *Madonna with Child and*

Two Angels,' she said, pointing to the painting of a woman and children, which had captured her imagination when she opened the page.

'So much to see!' He rolled his eyes. 'Too much beauty in one day! You look at just a little – *poco* – little, yes? Then go up to the roof. My cousin, Alfredo, he runs the café there. You tell him Nico sent you. You will see all of Florence from up there – *bella* – and clear your head after so many paintings! Then you go again tomorrow, for a little bit more art and then more coffee on the roof!'

'Thank you.'

'Is no problem,' the waiter said with another cheeky grin and went off to get her order.

Juliet smiled to herself, wondering if Cousin Alfredo was giving him a cut for sending him tourists.

However, two hours later she found herself very grateful for his advice. It would have been ridiculous to try to get around all forty-five rooms of the art gallery, each crammed with paintings more beautiful than in the last. So, covering just a small section of the Renaissance era, she took her time and studied the pictures carefully. Finding the Lippi painting she wanted to see, she looked at it for a long time, after reading about the artist himself. There was something very soothing about the painting, in the gentleness of the woman's face and the humorous expressions on the faces of the child angels.

She shook her head in amazement at some other tourists who rushed around and took photographs of the paintings without looking closely at the paintings themselves, then moved off to the next room to do the same thing. For once she had no inclination to take out her own camera. If she wanted to see photographs of paintings she could buy a book, but nothing could replace seeing them up close with her own eyes.

Logan's voice came back to her, telling her to put her camera away at the Ponte Vecchio on their first evening together. But she knew she wasn't like these tourists in the gallery. She always saw fully what she was going to photograph, before she took the shot – she experienced and felt the scene, then captured the moment before it changed. These paintings on the other hand were not going to change in an instant and therefore she felt no urge to preserve them.

After five more paintings Juliet had reached saturation point and, again following the waiter's advice, went to check out the café on the roof. Presuming the large, round man behind the counter was Alfredo, she made her way towards him. As she was practising the word '*buongiorno*' in her head, two other women cut in ahead of her saying: 'Hello, you must be Alfredo. Nico sent us.'

Juliet laughed, deciding Nico must definitely be getting a cut, and veered off to a table with a magnificent view of the city.

Enjoying a café latte and a chocolate slice, she was glad that she was only in Italy for two weeks, or she would be a couple of sizes larger in no time. After a while she took out her phone and texted a few friends, whom she hadn't had a chance to tell that she was away on holiday.

One friend texted back instantly, saying: **'Mad jealous, lucky cow. Raining here. Want all details asap. Rose xxx'**

With her phone Juliet took a photograph of the city spread out below her in the sun and sent it to Rose, just to drive her even more crazy.

Rose replied immediately: **'Wow! Looks fab. Russell with u?'**

'No – I ended it – going nowhere! On lookout for wealthy Italian!!!'

'Bring 1 back 4 me, pleeeeese!!!'

Juliet laughed, but it was Logan's face that came into her head as she texted back a smiley face to Rose. She wondered if he was already on a train back from Rome. To distract her from the sudden dance of a hundred butterflies in her stomach, she took a pen from her bag, pulled a paper napkin towards her and wrote out a shopping list for the meal she was planning for that evening.

Later in the afternoon she took the list from her pocket as she strolled through a market near the apartment, and took her pick from the magnificent range of fresh produce all around her. At the last minute she also bought a bunch of yellow roses for the coffee table in the living room.

Back at the apartment, Juliet emptied her shopping onto the kitchen counter and searched the cupboards for a vase. Finding one of clear glass, she filled it with water and arranged the roses loosely. She was just putting them down on the coffee table when she heard a key in the lock.

Logan came in, grinning at her. 'Hi, I'm back!'

Her heart gave a little jump at the pleasure of seeing him again. She grinned back.

Walking over to her, Logan grabbed her up and swung her around.

'Someone's in a good mood,' she laughed, as he let her feet touch the ground, but did not release her. The strength in his solid body, which had scared her on their first meeting, now thrilled her.

He grinned again. 'Absolutely. I'll tell you all about it, but first I must do this.' With that he lowered his head and kissed her, softly at first but, on feeling her respond, he deepened the kiss.

Juliet's arms went up around his neck. She melted into him, knowing nothing had ever felt more right.

When the kiss ended, he hugged her close.

For the Love of Martha

'All the way to Rome I kept asking myself,' he said, his lips moving against her hair, 'how is it possible to miss someone I've only known a couple of days? What is it about this woman that feels so . . . right?' There was a little hitch of emotion in his soft voice.

Pulling back a little she looked up at him, and saw the genuine puzzlement in his eyes. And she recognised it, for it was exactly what she had been asking herself.

Lifting her hand, she stroked a finger across his lips. 'Maybe fate double-booked us here in your mum's apartment, so maybe we shouldn't try to analyse it, but just go with the flow.'

Beneath her fingers his lips curved into a smile. 'Sounds good to me.' He kissed her fingertips. 'Now, I'd like to take a shower – God, it's hot in Rome – and then I'd like to take you out to dinner to celebrate being back in Florence with you.'

Juliet laughed. 'Well, I have the makings of dinner. Maybe we could eat in,' she suggested, her heart racing at the thought of a cosy evening together.

A light came into his eyes. 'An excellent suggestion.' He narrowed his eyes at her. 'You can cook, I presume? Or do I have to go into the kitchen and show you how it's done?'

She gave him a withering look and pulled away. 'Go shower, and mind your manners or you'll have to ring out for a takeaway for yourself.'

He grabbed her back into his arms and kissed her until she was breathless. 'Just whetting my appetite,' he mumbled.

Juliet couldn't help the laughter from bubbling up in her throat.

'Where have you come from, Juliet Holmes?' he murmured, shaking his head in wonderment, his eyes roving over her face.

'Go,' she ordered, her voice not quite steady, 'while I do my domestic goddess impression.' She gave him a shove towards the door, and went into the kitchen.

About fifteen minutes later Logan was back, freshly shaved, hair still damp, and wearing a navy polo shirt and jeans. And, Juliet discovered when he came and put his arms around her at the sink, he smelled as wonderful as he looked.

He kissed the side of her neck and, aware that she must be smelling of Indian spices, she moved away to put the curry into the oven.

'Why don't you pour the wine, while I go and change? I've been sightseeing in these all day.' She flicked her hands self-consciously down over the T-shirt and three-quarter-length shorts she was wearing. 'If you want to help you can put on the rice.'

'Slave driver!' he called after her.

Juliet showered and then looked through her wardrobe, glad now that her mother had encouraged her to buy some prettier summer clothes. Choosing a long, loose-fitting crimson dress, she slipped it on over a white vest top, and fluffed up her short hair with her fingers to help it dry a little. The style not only suited her, but was very practical for the many occasions on her travels where hair dryers were not available. Now, giving herself a last glance in the mirror, she realised she was smiling.

'You're looking very happy with yourself,' she murmured at her reflection. 'That's because I am happy,' she answered herself, 'and this is going to be a wonderful evening.'

Chapter 24

Logan was pouring the rice into a pot of boiling water when Juliet returned to the kitchen. He turned his head.

'You look lovely,' he said.

After placing the lid on the saucepan, he picked up a glass of wine and passed it to her. He was leaning towards her as though to kiss her but the timer on the oven beeped. Juliet sidestepped him to take the curry from the oven, stir it and put it back in. The rice had come to the boil so she turned it down and set the timer for fifteen minutes.

They took their wine to the living room and sat beside each other on the couch, Logan turned towards her, with his arm along the back. His fingers toyed with her hair as he asked her how she'd spent her day.

After giving him a summary of it, she asked: 'And how was your meeting in Rome?'

'Oh, it was fine, went well in fact. Some information I got will help me with finishing my report. But what was more exciting is the decision I made coming home in the train. I have been toying with it for a while and now I think it's time to go for it.'

Juliet raised her eyes from her wine and found he was looking off into the distance, his eyes bright.

A moment passed.

'Logan?' she prompted.

He looked down at her and smiled, the smile of a kid who has been told he has free rein in a sweetshop.

'I'm going to move back to Ireland,' he said. 'To Carissima – and expand the existing orchards there.' His accent seemed to have thickened as excitement rose in his tone. 'I want to trace several varieties of Irish apple and grow them at Carissima.'

'Ireland?' was all Juliet could say, her hopes of a holiday romance that could grow into something more back in England shredding. But she kept the disappointment out of her voice. 'Is your father still living there?'

'No.' The smile left Logan's eyes, replaced by a frown. 'He died ten years after my mum took me to England.'

'I'm sorry.'

'Oh, you needn't sympathise – there was no love lost between us. I hadn't seen him since we left.' A note of bitterness had crept into his voice.

'What?' Juliet, whose relationship with her own father was wonderful, felt sorry for him.

'It's a long story, which I don't want to go into now. The strange thing is, to my utter amazement, he left me the house and the estate. I thought I would never want to go back, yet I couldn't bring myself to sell it, so since my father's death it has been managed by a farm manager. But now . . .' the light came back into his eyes, 'now, it's perfect for what I want to do.'

Juliet couldn't but respond to his enthusiasm. 'That's

wonderful for you, Logan. It's great when someone has a dream to follow. I hope it all works out for you.'

Lifting her chin with a finger until she looked up at him, he watched her intently for a moment.

'Come with me. I'll hand in my notice to the university and we can be there together in the autumn.'

Juliet didn't reply.

Logan looked expectantly at her.

'Signora Padelli has a package for you,' she said.

'What?' he said, startled. 'Oh, right. I've been waiting for it. It's some computer disks I need. I'll be back in a minute.' He got up and left the apartment.

Juliet stared at the open door, not knowing whether to be pleased or appalled at his suggestion. Then annoyance had her jumping up and moving impatiently to the window.

He's being too presumptuous, she thought, planning a future so soon. It's too much!

The timer rang and she went into the kitchen, where Logan found her a few minutes later when he returned with the package.

'I'm sorry,' he said. 'I may have sprung that on you a little bit too soon.'

'Well, yes, it did come out of the blue.'

'It seems like the right thing to do and I'm sorry if I was getting ahead of myself.'

'On one level I can appreciate your suggestion,' she said, her voice strained. 'On another I'm not sure what you're asking here. It might be an exciting adventure for you, but what about me? Are you asking me to give up my career and move to some farm in Ireland and grow apples with you?'

He looked annoyed. 'Is that what you think? That I'm some old-fashioned fool, who would ask you to do that? This is my dream – I wouldn't force it on anyone else. I never expected for a moment you would give up your career. Dublin airport is less than two hours from Carissima. You could come and go as you please – be a part of Carissima as much or as little as you want. And, by the way,' he said, his voice humming with pride and anger, 'the "farm in Ireland" as you call it, is a huge estate of some of the most glorious countryside you could find anywhere.'

He turned away and started stirring a pot.

Juliet leant against the counter for support, willed herself to breathe and counted to ten.

Suddenly Logan swore loudly and stuck his finger under the running tap.

'Are you okay?'

'I'm fine – just burned my finger off the damn saucepan.'

'Sit down, I'll serve up.'

She drained the rice, tossed it onto some plates and spooned the curry on top. She put the plates on the table. There was silence all the while.

She took a seat opposite him.

'Maybe this is all going a bit too fast – hence the misunderstanding,' he said.

'I was disappointed, you see,' she said, her eyes asking him to understand. 'I hoped that when we both got back to England we could go on seeing each other and we'd see where it took us. I felt as scattered as a bunch of skittles being hit by a bowling ball just now.'

She was encouraged when the corners of his lips lifted slightly at her description.

'In the space of a few minutes,' he drawled, 'I've gone from being a Neanderthal to a bowling ball!'

A smile crept onto her face.

'I didn't know what you were asking,' she finished softly.

Logan sighed and stuck out his bottom lip in concentration, in that distracting way he had. Juliet pulled her eyes away from it to concentrate on what he was saying.

He reached out his hand to rest it on hers for a moment, before picking up his fork. 'I let the excitement of my plan carry me away and, what with the pleasure of seeing you again, the two became tangled in my head and I could see you being a part it. I'm not sure myself what I was asking or offering.'

Juliet nodded. 'I know there's been something very strong between us from the start, but we need time to get to know each other, don't we?'

'You're right, because if we don't, arguments like that will become the norm. Okay, let's be practical.' He huffed out a breath and thought for a second before continuing. 'I hope to be settled in Monaghan by the autumn and maybe you could come over for a visit then? I'll still be over and back to England a lot over the summer so we can keep seeing each other. What do you think?'

'Okay. That sounds good.' Juliet kept her voice light, but she knew Logan's future was going to be in Ireland and that she would have to compromise a lot if this was to go anywhere. She didn't know how she knew it so soon, but she already knew he was going to be part of her future. She'd go with the flow for now and deal with things as they arose.

At the end of the meal, when they were tidying up, Logan leaned over and kissed the back of her neck. She caught her breath and then let it out on a long sigh. Putting his hands on her shoulders, he turned her around, all the while trailing kisses along her jaw until he reached her lips.

Juliet started to tremble, her breath coming in little gasps. Logan continued to explore her lips and, when a low moan sounded in the back of her throat, his kiss gathered heat. Juliet's hands slid around his back and drew him closer to her, pressing her body against his in an attempt to still the trembling.

A few breathless moments later, he lifted his head and looked at her. She opened her eyes, not attempting to conceal from him what she was feeling, and was relieved to see that he wasn't guarding his own expression either. If it was possible for her insides to melt even more, they did at that moment when she saw the tenderness in his look, a tenderness in stark contrast to his laboured breathing.

Her hands moved up and her fingers tangled in his hair. Drawing his head down, she gave him one long kiss, gentle and soft, pouring all her love into it. Crazy as it was, she knew she had fallen completely and utterly in love with a man she had only met a few days before.

Logan gave a shaky sigh, then put an arm under her knees and scooped her up. Carrying her out to the couch, he laid her down and then lay beside her. He kissed her neck again and the sensations it sent rippling over her body made Juliet stretch sensuously beneath his touch. The action made him groan with need and his lips moved around her jaw and up to nibble on her ear. She laughed and opened her eyes. Unfortunately the photograph of Logan with his parents was right in her line of vision. She went still under his hands.

'What is it?' he said, raising his eyes to look into hers.

She was chewing her bottom lip. 'Sorry – the sight of your parents staring at me has brought me right down to earth.'

He laughed. 'We can easily deal with that. Let me pop them in a drawer.' He started to get up.

'No . . . wait . . .' She sighed. 'Logan, do you think we might be moving a bit fast? I don't usually fall into bed with someone I've only known a few days.'

He lifted his head and studied her face. Touching a fingertip to her bottom lip, he looked into her eyes. 'And I don't usually fall in love with someone I've only known a few days,' he said.

Juliet's breath caught and she gave a shaky laugh, while looking at him in wonder. 'I've fallen for you too. I don't understand it but I've never been more certain of anything.'

He looked at her with so much love in his eyes she could have sworn her heart sighed.

'Make love to me, Logan,' she whispered, pulling his head down until his lips touched hers again. She wanted this man, needed him, in a way she had never needed anyone before.

Chapter 25

Berkshire, England, 1888

An empty cart was being driven away from the courtyard when Beatrice and I arrived back. Helena was standing near Higgins as he issued instructions for large tea chests to be taken into the scullery.

Alarmed by our arrival in the Wallises' carriage, she dashed forward. Immediately noticing the white bandage on her little girl's wrist, she put her arms out to lift her down.

'Whatever happened?' she asked, looking from Beatrice's flushed face to mine. 'Martha?'

'I nearly got run over by a horse and carriage,' Beatrice said with relish, buoyed up on the homemade lemonade and cake Mrs. Wallis had plied her with before allowing us home. The morning for her had taken on the hue of a great adventure.

'Her wrist is sprained,' I said. 'I am so sorry, Cousin Helena, but she managed to slip from my grasp.'

'Martha saved me! She pulled me out of the way. I hurt my hand when I fell down.'

Helena's eyes were wide with unanswered questions. She looked from Beatrice to me and back again. 'Well, you're just in time for lunch. Let us go inside and you can tell me all about it.'

I followed her across the cobblestones.

'Higgins,' she turned back to the butler, 'come up to the dining room after lunch and we will discuss what I want you to do with all of these . . .' She waved her arm towards the tea chests.

Following her in through the scullery I worried about what she was going to say.

'Lily,' Helena called into the kitchen, 'take Beatrice up and get her cleaned up for lunch, please, and bring her down to the dining room in fifteen minutes.'

I removed my coat hastily and passed it to Lily, mouthing the words *thank you* before following Helena up the back stairs to the ground floor.

Instead of sitting down in her place at the head of the table, she sat on the chair by the fireplace, her back very straight, her hands clasped in her lap.

I hovered, unsure what to do. There had never been this formality between us before.

'Please sit down, Martha.'

I sat in the chair opposite her, wincing as my left hip hit the arm of the chair, leaving me in no doubt as to what part of me had taken the impact when Beatrice and I had landed on the ground.

'Now, what exactly happened this morning?' Helena asked, a small frown between her brows.

I related the tale as accurately as I could.

'One minute her hand was in mine and the next it was gone. I did not expect her to run off like that. I am so sorry. I should have been holding her more tightly.'

Helena was quiet for a long moment. 'It seems to me that you saved her life.'

I looked up in astonishment at the praise in her tone. For the first time since we arrived home, her face relaxed into a smile.

'Do not look so scared, Martha. You are not in trouble. It could have been a very different story if you had not reacted so quickly. You cannot walk with Beatrice and have her hand constantly in a fierce grip. It seems to me she was a very naughty girl to run off like that, doll or no doll. I will give her a severe talking to over lunch.'

'I am afraid she might not eat much lunch as she is rather full of Mrs. Wallis's sponge cake. She could not have been kinder to us. Nor Dr. Adams,' I added.

'That poor man has had his hands full with you and Beatrice since he came to Mirrow, what with one thing and another.'

Her innocent remark had me blushing. 'I – I will pay for this visit,' I stammered, 'as I feel it was my fault.'

'Nonsense, it was Beatrice's wilfulness.' She dismissed the notion with a wave of her hand. 'James will sort it out at the end of the month. Now,' she said, getting to her feet, 'do you have an appetite? Mother Pershaw will be down shortly. No doubt she will have something to say on the matter, but . . .' she lowered her voice to a whisper, 'I am satisfied with your ability to take care of *my* daughter, so pay no attention to anything she might say if Beatrice tells her what happened.' With a conspiratorial smile she moved to the table.

Lily appeared a minute later to say that Beatrice had fallen asleep.

'Then let her sleep on,' Helena said. 'She must be tired out.'

'Very good, madam.'

My shoulders sagged with relief, especially when Mother Pershaw arrived into the room obviously in very bad humour already. She addressed Helena with a thunderous look on her face.

'What a ridiculous racket out in the courtyard this morning! What was all the fuss?'

'The tea chests were delivered for our packing, Mother,' Helena replied, nodding at Higgins to serve the cold meat.

'Hmm,' she replied, opening her napkin with a snap before laying it across her lap. 'Why James has to run off and be a *farmer*,' she spat out the word as though it was vulgar, 'is beyond me. The merchant business is in his blood. Why can he not stay here, or build his own house near here, and continue with the business?'

Soft as it was, I caught Helena's sigh.

'James has explained all this before, Mother. He wants a place of his own. The estate here is too small for the type of farming he wants to do. He got the land in Monaghan at an excellent price – twice the amount of land he would have got for a fraction of the price here. It will be wonderful for me and Beatrice to have him with us instead of halfway around the world most of the time.'

'It worked for me and his father. I do not see why it could not work for you.'

Helena did not reply. I kept my head bent over my plate.

'He'll get tired of it, mark my words!' Mother Pershaw continued, undeterred by the silence. 'Travelling is in his blood. After a year or two he will long to go back to sea, searching for bargains in the Far East. You just wait and see.' Oblivious to the fact that she was attempting to tear apart Helena's dream of a settled future as easily as she was tearing apart the bread roll in her hands, the insensitive woman continued to mutter to herself, 'Mark my words, mark my words.'

I stole a glance at Helena. A blotch of red scorched each cheek and she very slowly laid her knife and fork down on her plate.

'With all due respect, Mother, James is not his father, and he has decided that this new life *is* for him, and I am behind him completely as it is very much what I want too.' She pushed back her chair. 'Now if you will excuse me, I seem to have lost my appetite.'

I stared hard at my plate as she closed the door very carefully behind her. I wished I could be anywhere else but alone with Mother Pershaw.

'Pure foolish, and utterly delusional! They will be running back here with their tails between their legs in no time. Driven out by the wild Irish – burnt out, most likely!'

My eyes widened in alarm. Did she forget I was going to be there too? I feared I would have nightmares about it if she did not stop saying such things.

'I shall look forward to seeing their faces when they come running back to me for shelter when this hare-brained scheme fails.'

I sat there saying nothing, afraid to draw attention to myself by moving my fork to my mouth.

Several minutes passed.

'Oh for goodness sake, girl,' Mother Pershaw exploded, 'ring the bell and tell Higgins to bring some very strong tea to the drawing room!'

Jumping up, I moved to the fireplace and pressed the bell. To my great relief Mother Pershaw then stalked out of the room, thumping her walking stick hard with each step.

I would have felt sorry for the old woman, losing her grandchild and son to another country, but her bitter attitude prevented any such compassion.

I waited until I heard the door of the drawing room close behind her, then I dashed across the hall and up the stairs to the sanctuary of my room.

Chapter 26

Excitement fluttered in my stomach when I was still only half awake the next morning. Turning on my side brought me fully awake with a groan as my weight rested on my bruised hip. Immediately I remembered the events of yesterday and the cause of the excitement: I was to take Beatrice back to see Edward that morning.

Rising from the bed, I was aware of stiffness after the fall and, before getting dressed, I twisted and turned to see my hip in the mirror. A black-and-blue mark, the size of a small plate, covered my entire left hip. Foolishly I poked it and winced at the tenderness. As I finished putting on my clothes I wondered how sore Beatrice's wrist would be.

She was just stirring when I went through to her room.

'Time to get up, sleepyhead,' I said brightly and threw open her curtains. 'Oh!' The sound whooshed from my lips when I beheld a world glistening with frost in the early sunshine. 'Beatrice, come and look at this!' I held out my hand to her.

She tumbled out of bed, her bandaged arm held out in front

of her, and tiptoed over the cold floor. Throwing a shawl around her I lifted her up and pointed to a jewel-encrusted cobweb hanging outside the window.

'The first frost of winter,' I murmured, very conscious of the passing of time.

'Pretty,' she said, tracing the cobweb with a finger of her good hand.

'How is your wrist?'

Leaning her head to the side, she held her wrist up and tested it with a small movement.

'Still sore,' she replied.

'The nice doctor is going to look at it again this morning, so let me get you dressed quickly and we'll walk to the village before all the lovely frost melts.'

Dressing took longer than usual because of the bandaged wrist, and she was cranky by the time we were finished. I soothed her with a story while we ate breakfast in the nursery and her spirits were brighter by the time we were ready to leave.

Helena met us in the hall and, to my disappointment, I noted she had her coat on too.

'I thought I would join you and get some fresh air before the work of the day gets underway.' Smiling at us both, she finished fastening a glove and then reached her hand out for Beatrice's.

Higgins was opening the door for us when Cook came bustling out of the drawing room, panting a little by the time she reached us.

'I beg your pardon, madam,' she said, 'but Mrs. Pershaw has requested a change in tonight's dinner menu and I don't think I can get the fish she wants at this late stage.'

Helena sighed. 'Martha, will you and Beatrice wait here a moment? Cook, come with me.'

She went into the drawing room to talk to her mother-in-law.

A few minutes later she reappeared, with a red spot staining each cheek. 'This is going to take longer than I thought,' she murmured to me. 'She is in a foul humour and nothing is suiting her.' She stooped down in front of Beatrice. 'I cannot come with you after all to the doctor's, my love. I need to help Cook sort this out for your grandmother.'

She hugged her before straightening up. Shrugging her shoulders at me, we exchanged a look of understanding.

Feeling a little guilty at the relief I felt that we could now go alone, I took Beatrice's hand and we set off.

The air was crisp as we walked, putting colour in our cheeks. Taking our time, we stopped on several occasions to examine other cobwebs and glittering twigs.

'It is good to be alive on a morning like this!' I sighed, turning my face up to the sun.

My steps were light as we arrived into the village, made our way down Main Street and knocked on the door of Edward's surgery.

Opening it, he bowed with a flourish.

'Ladies,' he said, making Beatrice giggle, 'please come in.'

He stepped back and I urged Beatrice in ahead of me. Closing the door behind us, he quickly brushed my lips with his as Beatrice walked ahead of us down the hall. I tried to give him a disapproving look, but my lips curved of their own volition and he gave a soft laugh, low in his throat.

In the surgery he lifted Beatrice up and sat her on the examination couch. It only took a moment for him to examine the wrist and he proclaimed it to be improving 'marvellously'.

All too soon it was time for us to leave again. We discussed the weather and some local news in an attempt to prolong the visit, but soon Beatrice began to tug at my hand. Smiling in resignation, I held Edward's gaze for a long moment.

'Until we meet again,' he said and then above Beatrice's head he mouthed the words *this afternoon.*

I nodded and we went on our way. I had a few other jobs to do in the village, one of which was to buy some handkerchiefs for Edward for Christmas.

Feeling a little self-conscious about purchasing male handkerchiefs, I hoped Mrs. Beckett presumed I was buying them on Helena's behalf for James. I stowed the package carefully in my basket, then quickly asked her to help us choose some ribbon that Beatrice might give her mother as a Christmas gift.

'You must keep the ribbon a secret until Christmas Day,' I told her as we walked home, knowing there was every possibility that she would let it slip.

On arrival at the house, she ran straight to the morning room and flung her arms around her mother's neck, before pulling back and grinning at her.

'We did not buy you anything for Christmas in the village!' she chirped and danced around the room, her curls bouncing.

Helena laughed as she met my eyes. 'You had better tell me what the doctor said about your arm then, instead of the shopping you did not do!'

'He said it is doing mar – mar –' Her nose wrinkled with the effort of remembering.

'Marvellously,' I finished for her. 'It will not take long to heal.'

'That's wonderful,' said Helena.

'Now,' I said to Beatrice, 'time to go and see if you remember the numbers you learnt yesterday.'

I took her upstairs where we made a big fuss of wrapping the ribbons in paper and hiding them.

'I want to draw a picture to give Papa for Christmas,' she said.

'Good idea!' I said, though I knew Helena would be providing another gift for Beatrice to give her father. 'And you can tell me your colours at the same time.'

The rest of the morning went slowly and I glanced at the

clock more than once, willing the hands to move on. The time for Beatrice's lunch and nap eventually came round and I left for my daily walk.

We met three afternoons in a row that week. I had dusted the furniture in the cottage so we would have somewhere to sit, while wishing it was our own home I was looking after. Our meetings were more intense, both of us wanting to learn more about each other, our moments together now feeling even more stolen than they had before. We still planned our life together as if there was not going to be any long separation from each other before it could happen. Therefore we did not discuss the move to Ireland, but instead talked about events in the village and in the house, and shared stories of our childhoods.

At these times I could almost forget about having to leave. But, as soon as I returned to the house, I was thrust painfully back into the world of packing and planning. Helena was constantly preparing lists and some of the trunks were already filled with summer clothes and other items not in use for the winter. The weeks flew by in the business of it all and, before we knew it, Christmas was fast approaching.

One afternoon Mother Pershaw attempted to give Helena even more advice.

'You will have to pack your linens and tableware with extreme caution. If the sea crossing is rough, you do not want everything being spoiled or broken.'

'Yes, Mother. James has advised me very well on all that already. He has transported enough by ship all his life to be able to pass on some helpful advice.'

Helena bent her head over her list and continued writing. Beatrice and I were sitting across the room making a holly bough for the front door.

Mother Pershaw would not leave well alone. 'Still, you cannot be too careful. Put plenty of wrapping around each piece of china and stack the plates vertically not horizontally.'

'Yes, Mother,' Helena replied. Gathering up her lists, she rose. 'I think I will go and check on how Higgins is getting on with the silver. It has been in boxes the whole time we have lived here. It will be nice to see our wedding presents in use in Carissima.'

'Where?' Mother Pershaw boomed, halting Helena who was halfway to the door.

She turned back. 'Carissima,' she replied. 'That is the name James has chosen for our new home and estate.'

'What kind of a ridiculous name is that?'

Helena glanced over in our direction and I saw her crumple the papers in her fist.

'It is not a ridiculous name at all,' she replied, pink staining her cheeks. 'When James was in Italy he learnt that *carissima* means *dearest* and *cara* means *dear* – and then he remembered that *cara* means *friend* in Irish. He loved the sound of it and so,' she lifted her chin and, though the colour in her cheeks had risen even more, she looked her mother-in-law in the eye as she continued, 'he says that since I am his "dearest friend" and since *cara* is part of *carissima*, he is calling it after me – Carissima.'

Mother Pershaw snorted. 'I still think it sounds ridiculous. I do not like it at all!'

'I think it is a very strong name and I like it very well.' Helena whirled around and left the room.

My fingers, which had been busily weaving a decorative bough, slowed now in their work. It was the first time I, too, had heard the name of where I would be living in the spring. It made it seem more real to have it named, and a physical pain passed through me at the inevitability of leaving Edward.

Chapter 27

London 2010

'Well,' Frances Holmes asked her daughter, 'how was Florence?'

'It was wonderful,' Juliet replied.

They were sitting in a restaurant near Frances' G.P. practice two days after Juliet's return to London.

'I'm so thrilled you've hit it off with Elizabeth's son!'

'Me too.'

'So why the glum face?'

'Because Logan was supposed to be coming to London to visit me in two weeks, when he gets back, but I was told this morning by my editor that I'll be in Montana by then!'

'That is disappointing.'

Juliet saw her mother looking intently at her.

'There's something else bothering you, isn't there?' Frances asked.

Shutting the menu, Juliet vented her emotions.

'Is this what it's going to be like now?' she asked crossly. 'Always torn between my work and the man I –' She stopped abruptly.

'Go on, say it,' her mother urged, smiling

'Okay then. The man I'm in love with!' Juliet's shoulders were tense as she snapped a bread stick with restless fingers.

'With the type of job you have, you knew it would be like this with whoever you fell for,' her mother argued gently.

'I know, I know. It's just that I didn't know I'd feel like this.' Juliet absently rubbed a spot low on her ribs – a spot that ached when she thought of being away from Logan. 'And I always imagined that if I did get seriously involved with someone, he would be in London to come home to, not somewhere in Ireland. It's the first time I've resented an assignment and I don't like it.'

'Logan really is "the one", isn't he?'

Juliet heard the concern behind the words. 'Oh, Mum, why did he have to pick now to do his thing over there?'

'You fell in love with a man with a dream. I believe that's part of the attraction. Would you rather be in love with someone who didn't have a dream, or worse someone who had a dream but never bothered to do anything about it?'

Seeing in her mind the way Logan's face lit up when he spoke of apples and harvest time and working with the soil, Juliet smiled.

'Damn it, why do you always have to be right?' she scolded.

'It's a mother's prerogative. Now let's order. I have surgery at two.'

A week later, Juliet and a journalist called Stuart were on a plane to Montana. With her phone on flight mode, she clicked on messages to read Logan's most recent text again.

'Florence not the same without you. Work getting close to completion, but concentration poor! Have a great trip. Email me when you get there. Lx'

Juliet remembered their last morning in Florence. They had

stood in the airport, Logan clasping her hands in a solid grip, as though he never wanted to let go.

'Good luck with finishing your research papers,' she had said. 'I'll see you when you get back.'

'I wish I was going with you. It's going to be a long two weeks.'

She'd dropped a kiss on the back of his hand. 'I'll be thinking of you. Oh and thank your mother for me again.'

'And thank yours for sending you here. These past two weeks have been wonderful. You're a beautiful woman, Juliet, and an amazing lover – gentle, loving, passionate. I didn't know there was this big empty space in my heart until you arrived in Florence and filled it.'

Juliet had thought her own heart would burst at his words. She'd smiled with joy and her eyes had filled with tears.

Logan pulled her into his arms and held her close for a long time.

Now Juliet looked out at the clouds above Montana and sighed. Then she thought about the telephone conversation she'd had with Elizabeth Pershaw on her last evening in the apartment.

'Ah, my dear,' Elizabeth had said, 'I just phoned to thank you for taking the time to look after my apartment for me. I'm so sorry about the confusion at the beginning and I hope Logan hasn't been in your way there.'

'No, not at all,' Juliet replied, knowing Logan hadn't told his mother about their relationship yet. He was planning to tell her after Juliet went back to London.

'I'm glad. I was hoping you two would get along.'

Juliet changed the subject. 'Thank you very much for letting me stay here. You have a lovely home.'

'You're very welcome. But I'm sorry your mother didn't get

a little holiday. I always think she works too hard. The fact that she couldn't make it proves that point. Hopefully she'll come to visit me later in the year, and I'm so glad you've been able to stay there. Did you enjoy Florence, Juliet?'

'Immensely.'

'Well, you're welcome to come back any time you wish. I would like to meet you in person.'

'That's very kind of you, thank you.'

There had been a pause before Elizabeth continued hesitantly. 'Logan told me a couple of days ago about his plans to go back to Ireland, and I know he told you too.'

'Yes, he did.'

'I certainly hope he knows what he's doing. I never thought he would go back there, although when he inherited Carissima and didn't immediately sell, I had my fears. If you have any influence on him, try to make him stay in Cambridge. It would be for the best.'

She had rung off shortly after that with good wishes for a safe journey back to London. Juliet had found the call a little unsettling. The anxiety in Elizabeth's voice had been very obvious.

She'd told Logan that his mother had called to thank her and wish her well, but she didn't say any more than that. She had no intention of trying to dissuade him from pursuing this new career path. He was a grown man and perhaps Elizabeth was just being protective, and therefore anxious about him giving up the security of a good job. Yet she knew that it couldn't be the reason as she'd learned from her mother that Logan's father had left him a wealthy man.

Brought back to the present by the pilot announcing their approach to Billings Logan Airport, the usual adrenaline rush hit

Juliet's stomach. She smiled at the coincidence of the name of the airport. Now that they were there she was focused on the job ahead and she felt this one was going to be good. Her remit was to photograph the wild horses that roamed the Pryor Mountains, and Stuart, who was sitting beside her engrossed in a John Le Carré novel, was to write a feature on the way of life at the ranch and the co-existence between the wild horses and the family he and Juliet would be staying with. They were to immerse themselves in ranch life for two weeks. Rob, their editor, wanted the finished work to be spread over at least three editions.

After collecting their hire car and stowing their luggage and equipment, Stuart drove sixty miles south of Billings across vast farmlands to Blue Meadows Ranch at the foot of the mountains. The cattle ranch was owned by the Davidson Family, who gave them a warm welcome.

After a lively supper, Juliet asked if she could connect up to the internet. Having been given the password, she went to her room and opened up her laptop.

To: Logan
From: Juliet

Hi, Logan,

We arrived safely. I could never have imagined anything as vast as this place. So much open space, so much sky. And the mountains just take your breath away! The Davidsons are lovely and are so welcoming. There is Peg and Nate, and their two teenage sons, Seth and Josh, and one daughter Sue, who's ten, and their grandfather Hughie, who is Nate's father. We are staying in their ranch house, which has a magnificent view of the mountains in the distance. Apparently they are 'a full day's ride away'! That's where we will have to go to see the wild horses.

Since we are behind you, I suppose you've already gone to bed and you're sleeping now. I miss you and can't wait to hear from you.

J x

✉ ✉ ✉

To: Juliet
From: Logan
Hi. Great to get your email. Glad you had a good journey. I'm still working away here. The information on those disks which came through the post has been very helpful in tying up some loose ends in my research. It's all coming together nicely now and I hope to print off the finished paper before leaving Florence on Friday. Hardly getting out, so I'm glad I took some time off to be a tourist with you during those first two weeks. Would love to be there with you.

Logan x

✉ ✉ ✉

To: Logan
From: Juliet
Hughie, the grandfather here, and semi-retired owner of the ranch, insisted today that Stuart and I get in a bit of practice with the horse riding. Both of us are a bit saddle sore tonight. I'm emailing now while sitting on the swing seat on the porch as the sun is setting and cattle lowing somewhere. It's beautiful. Wish you could see it too.

I'll be going to bed soon, as the days start at 6.30 around here! Sleep tight. J x

✉ ✉ ✉

To: Juliet
From: Logan
Sounds wonderful. Paper is finished. Sending copy off to my

contact in the UN tomorrow and then it's back to England on Friday. I know you're having a great time but I can't wait until you get back.

Logan x

⊠   ⊠   ⊠

To: Logan
From: Juliet

We'll be setting off at 7 tomorrow morning for the mountains. Hughie has warned that sightings of the horses are not guaranteed, so keep your fingers crossed for us. I'll be gone for a few days and I'll email as soon as I get back.

J xx

⊠   ⊠   ⊠

To: Juliet
From: Logan

Stay safe up there in the mountains, and good luck. Can't wait to hear all about it.

Logan x

⊠   ⊠   ⊠

To: Logan
From: Juliet

Hi, Logan, we're back and it was amazing. I've never had such a sore butt in my life but it was worth it. We saw the mustangs! Twice! The first time we were just coming out of a valley and startled a herd of about thirty horses which were very close to us. The horses took off at a gallop past us, and the thunder of their hooves pounding the earth vibrated right through my chest. I didn't realise I'd let out a whoop of delight until I saw the ranch owner laughing at me.

The mustangs had kicked a cloud of dust up into the rays of sun streaming between the ridges, and their manes were flying back from their heads. I took shot after shot.

The following day we saw them grazing in the distance and managed to get close enough for a few shots before they took off. We got back to the ranch this evening, tired but elated.

I transferred the photographs to the laptop and showed them to the family. I thought I'd burst with pride when Hughie, who can be a bit gruff sometimes, said: 'Young lady, I didn't think a camera could ever do those wonderful creatures justice, but somehow you got them, got them just right – untamed and free.'

I'm exhausted now, Logan, and need to go to bed. Goodnight.

J xx

P.S. Are you back in Cambridge?

✉   ✉   ✉

To: Juliet
From: Logan

Hi Juliet,

Yeah, I got back yesterday. Today I've been packing up my stuff and getting it ready for shipment to Ireland. I've also made contact with an organisation there called Irish Seed Savers who will be able to give me information on the indigenous species of the Irish apple. I'm getting very excited now at the prospect but I'm anxious about what state the existing orchard at Carissima will be in. I should've paid more attention to the annual reports I was sent!

So are the whales still your favourite shoot? Or have the wild horses kicked them into touch?

Counting off the days.

Logan xx

To: Logan
From: Juliet

You're right, the whales have been relegated. Although they were amazing, I'm totally awestruck by the horses. They were free and proud and I felt they knew it! I can't put it properly into words. I hope my photographs will do that.

We're going to be here for another five days. Stuart is getting some great interviews. It turns out Hughie is a great storyteller, and he's passing on a lot of folklore to him.

Talk soon.

J xx

✉ ✉ ✉

To: Juliet
From: Logan

Going to Ireland for two days to check the place over. See you in London on Friday. My train gets in at 6.20 and I'll go straight to your place.

Logan x

✉ ✉ ✉

To: Logan
From: Juliet

One day left. Everyone here has been wonderful.

Peg is preparing a farewell supper for us tonight. I think Stuart has picked up an American accent, although I think the London Underground is still his preferred mode of transport! I'll be sorry to say goodbye to all this, but long to be back in London with you. See you Friday.

J xx

Chapter 28

Berkshire, England, 1888

It was a cold December that year. Everyone was predicting a white Christmas. I spent the long dark evenings in my room, embroidering the letter 'E' on the corner of each of the handkerchiefs I had bought for Edward. When I got to the last one, a week before Christmas, I added a tiny heart in red thread, and placed that one under the other five. I was also crocheting a new hat for Beatrice and a centrepiece for Helena for her new dining table at Carissima. My heart ached with each stitch but I felt it would mean a lot to her. I knew she sensed my reluctance about moving to Ireland, so I hoped the gift would make it up to her.

It started to snow on the twentieth, and it snowed all day and night. Beatrice was beside herself with excitement, but for me it brought great disappointment as I could not get to the cottage because of drifting snow blocking the path to the woods.

Walks were not possible to the village either, as our feet would have been soaked through and frozen by the time we got there.

I spent some of the time half-heartedly building a snowman with Beatrice and having snowball fights. On the morning of the twenty-third, Helena came out and joined in. Soon my mood picked up and I was laughing as much as the other two, our cheeks glowing from the exertion.

Half an hour later as we all sipped hot cocoa I had to stop myself from hugging Helena with delight when she asked me to go to the village.

'Robin will take you in the trap. He has some errands to do, and I want you to go to the post office and collect a parcel that is waiting there for me.' She smiled and lowered her voice to a whisper. 'It is my present to James. I had to order it from London. Be very careful with it. It will be heavy. Be sure not to drop it as it would break.'

She did not say what it was.

I hurried upstairs to fetch my outdoor clothes. Opening a drawer, I pulled out the neatly wrapped parcel containing Edward's handkerchiefs from their hiding place beneath my own. I folded the parcel into my pocket while hoping the handkerchiefs would not get too creased.

With a lightness in my step I ran back downstairs and out to where Robin was waiting with the pony and trap. The pony blew out great cloudy breaths in the cold, sunny air, and he pawed at the snow. I climbed up beside Robin and we put a blanket over our knees.

In the village we arranged to meet back at the trap after half an hour. I stepped down gingerly to avoid the dirty snow at the side of the road.

When Robin was out of sight, instead of making my way to the post office, I went in the opposite direction, to Edward's door. After knocking I waited, stamping my feet as much with excitement as to ward off the cold. There was no reply. I knocked again, my excitement beginning to waver. I wanted so much for him to be there that I had not entertained the thought that he might not be. But the house remained silent and the door remained closed. I dared not stay there any longer in case I drew attention to myself from passers-by.

Retracing my steps, I scanned the street in the hope of happening upon him as he returned home. My pace grew slower as I neared the post office, allowing myself one last glance back the way I had come. But still there was no sign of him.

Inside there was one customer at the counter ahead of me. I waited, continuing to glance out the window, but to no avail. When it was my turn, the Post Mistress and I exchanged season's greetings. She placed a parcel about one foot by one and a half foot on the counter.

'I do not know what is in it,' said the Post Mistress with a short laugh, 'but it certainly is heavy.'

I thanked her and lifted it up into both arms. I could not imagine what Helena was giving James that could weigh so much.

It was too early to meet Robin so I went into the bookshop and browsed for a few minutes, shifting the parcel from one arm to the other as the need arose. I had bought a book there on the Orient a few weeks before, which was going to be my gift to Mother Pershaw. Finding nothing of interest now, I returned to the street and took my time making my way to where I was to meet Robin.

More greetings were exchanged with people I passed, but not with the one person I wanted to see most. Robin rolled up with the trap as I was berating myself for not thinking of having a note ready which I could have slipped under Edward's door. It was a wasted trip and a lost opportunity.

As we drove home with our parcels stacked between us on

the seat, I mused on how romantic the countryside looked in its layer of snow, gleaming fresh and new in the sunshine, while I sat there feeling lonelier than ever. I touched the parcel in my pocket, wanting so much for Edward to have it for Christmas.

Just then, Robin broke into my thoughts.

'It'll be lovely at the service tomorrow night. You weren't here last year, were you? All the village up together at midnight, singing their hearts out. It'll be magic this year with the snow, but strange for it to be in the schoolhouse.'

Christmas Eve service! I had not given it any thought before now. Beaming I touched the parcel in my pocket again.

'Yes, I am sure it will be wonderful!'

As we pulled up in the courtyard, Beatrice was chatting excitedly to her mother as two farmhands unloaded the fir tree for the drawing room.

'Please be careful of it as you go up the back stairs,' Helena instructed.

'Martha,' she called to me, 'you are just in time to help us decorate it!'

I beamed at them both, their excitement contagious.

Helena thanked me as I handed over the parcel. Her eyebrows rose when she registered its weight, and she smiled mischievously. 'This will be the first thing to go underneath our lovely tree,' she said.

'What is it, Mummy?' Beatrice asked.

'It is a present for your father. But do not tell him.'

'What is it?' Beatrice repeated, lowering her voice to a whisper, delighted to be in on a secret.

'I cannot tell you that. It is a surprise. Come along.'

We followed in the wake of the tree, the waft of pine delighting our nostrils when it brushed off a corner of the stairs.

Helena issued instructions on its arrangement in a large bay window. The two farmhands, still in their outdoor clothes, were sweating from their exertion and from the heat of the fire. James opened the box of decorations and Helena, Beatrice and I helped to decorate the tree. Even Mother Pershaw was caught up in the moment and did not interfere once, but sat in an armchair watching proceedings with a smile tugging at her mouth.

'And it is going to be even prettier,' James said, coming into the room. 'Look what I brought back from Italy.'

He placed a large box on the floor and we peered in.

'Oh . . .' we all breathed in unison, for inside were rows and rows of small porcelain candleholders with a short white candle in each.

'They go on the branches, like so,' James said, taking one out and securing it to a branch.

'Can I put one on, please, Papa?'

'Of course. Let us do it together.'

So with her father's help, Beatrice put on her first candle. Soon we were all helping, James putting them on the tallest branches with the aid of a footstool.

Then he lit the candles.

We stood back and admired our work. It was wonderful.

Mother Pershaw had resumed her seat and was smiling up at the effect. Beatrice ran over and threw her arms around her neck.

'It is beautiful, Grandmama!'

'Indeed it is, child.' She hugged the child to her in an unusual show of affection and I saw the gleam of a tear in the old woman's eyes.

Difficult and all as she could be, I felt immense sympathy for her in that moment, knowing we were kindred spirits in facing a year of unwanted changes. My throat grew tight and, blinking rapidly, I pulled my gaze away from them and back to the splendour of the tree.

Chapter 29

Christmas Eve dawned and it seemed the whole household hummed with excitement. Wonderful aromas wafted up from the kitchen and all the staff scurried around busily. Beatrice awakened early and chattered non-stop all morning. It took two stories to settle her down for her nap after lunch.

While she slept I helped Helena with an arrangement of greenery for the centre of the dining table. The sky had darkened ominously and I watched it anxiously, afraid that another heavy snowfall would prevent our going to the church that night.

'Do you think it might snow again?' I asked, looking towards the window.

'I do hope not,' she replied, following my gaze and my train of thought. 'I am so looking forward to the service. It was quite beautiful last year. Mr. Smythe sang, and truly his voice would open the gates to heaven. Perhaps his Welsh accent has something to do with it. Do you know him?'

I shook my head.

'He and Mrs. Smythe,' she continued, 'had moved here just two months before Christmas last year and someone had heard him sing at a party. Everyone was talking about him, so the vicar asked him to sing at the Christmas service. He was delighted with his discovery, and I believe he has asked him to sing again tonight. You will enjoy it.'

'Yes, I am sure I shall.'

'Of course it will not be the same, having to have the service in the schoolhouse. I know the vicar is concerned about where we shall all fit,' she laughed. 'It will be very cold for anyone who has to stand outside the door!'

We fell silent. It was not the cold that was concerning me but rather how I would manage to give Edward his present without being seen.

At last it was time to go – fortunately the snow had held off. Before leaving I pinched my pale cheeks to get some colour into them, which turned out to be a needless act of vanity, as I am sure they were quite red from the cold by the time we got to the village. Once again, the parcel was nestled safely in my pocket. Mother Pershaw stayed at home because of the snow, and the hour was too late for Beatrice to be up.

Helena looked lovely in a coat of burgundy with matching fur hat and muff. I consoled myself with the thought that, although the leather gloves I wore were a bit worn, they were fur-lined and very warm.

Arriving in the village, we averted our eyes from the burnt-out ruin of the church and looked ahead instead at the candles in the schoolhouse windows. Someone had made a beautiful bough of evergreen and placed it around the door where the vicar was standing to welcome everyone.

When we stepped inside, it was already quite full and I looked about as discreetly as I could for Edward. Then I saw him. He was leaning against the wall at the back, just a little way inside the door. Our eyes met, the warmth in them making up for the smile our lips could not form.

James saw some empty seats and ushered us forward. He then went to stand at the back with some other gentlemen. Once seated, I could no longer see Edward, but it was enough to know he was there. I do not think I heard a word of what the vicar said, I was so preoccupied with how I was going to have a moment alone with Edward afterwards.

My reverie was broken when Helena touched my arm and nodded towards a man making his way up to the front of the schoolroom. Large, with a ruddy face, I presumed him to be the Welsh singer of whom she had spoken earlier. Standing there in the candlelight, he sang in rich, deep, lilting tones the most hauntingly beautiful hymn I had ever heard. When the last note faded, a collective sigh of admiration was breathed into the silence.

The vicar stood and finished the service with a blessing. He invited us to stand and sing 'Now Praise We Christ,' as the final hymn. By the time we had reached the last verse, my heart beat had picked up its pace and my hands had grown damp inside my gloves. As we moved with the crowd towards the door I intentionally kept walking when Helena stopped to talk to a friend.

Edward caught my eye before slipping outside.

At the doorway I exchanged season's greetings with the vicar and his wife. Then I moved slowly down the path, along the edge of the crowd.

It was a gorgeous night. The moon had broken through the clouds and its light gave the snow a magical glow. All was hushed and still. Even conversations seemed muffled and soft.

A quick touch of a hand on my sleeve had me stopping abruptly. I turned to find Edward beside me.

'Season's greetings, Miss White,' he said, bowing.

'And to you, Dr. Adams,' I replied a little breathlessly.

I looked around quickly and saw that the crowd were breaking into similar knots of people to have a few quick words before the cold drove them on their way. No one was paying any attention to us.

I withdrew the parcel from my pocket and slipped it into his hand.

'Happy Christmas,' I whispered.

I wanted dearly to kiss him in that moment, the moon lighting the side of his face and a single snowflake in his hair. I longed to brush it away with my fingertips. I had only just thought it when he caught my gloved hand in his and pressed something into my palm.

'Happy Christmas to you, my love,' he whispered back.

My fingers tightened around the small parcel and quickly I secreted it in my pocket.

'It was my mother's and I want you to have it,' he murmured.

I beamed at him, glad my back was to the crowd as I just knew my eyes were shining with my love for him. At that moment he put his hat on and gave another small, but formal bow of his head.

'Yes, thank you for asking,' he said in a more formal voice, 'I have been invited to the home of Mr. and Mrs. Reeves over at Hazelwood to join their family for their Christmas dinner.'

He turned his head and pretended he had just seen Helena and James approaching.

'Ah, season's greetings to you both! I wish you and yours a very merry Christmas.'

'Thank you, Dr. Adams, and to you,' Helena said. 'I hope all this snow has not made it too difficult for you to get to your patients these past few days.'

'It has been a bit tricky, but my horse is a shrewd enough fellow and has kept me upright so far, thank the Lord.'

'Well, goodnight to you,' Helena said, linking my arm, as well as that of her husband. 'We had all best get along before we catch our death of cold.'

He bowed to them and then to me.

'Miss White.'

'Dr Adams,' I replied, giving him a small smile.

James insisted I join them for a hot port in front of the fire when we got back to the house. Although I was anxious to open my gift from Edward, of course I could not refuse. Helena and I went to our rooms to remove our outdoor clothes and change our shoes, but I only had time to put the gift under my pillow before returning immediately to the drawing room. I am sure I looked quite relaxed there in the firelight, but inside I was burning with impatience while willing my drink to cool.

But the alcohol mellowed my impatience a little and I enjoyed the amusing stories James told us about some of his travels. It was good to hear Helena laughing. She looked so sweet and happy. I loved her dearly, not just because she was the only family I had, but for her own sweet nature. I felt a bit guilty at wanting to dash off earlier, and sipped more slowly at the remainder of my drink.

It was Helena who made the first move and, discreetly hiding a yawn, she pronounced we should get some sleep as Beatrice was bound to have us up early in the morning.

I got ready for bed slowly, the earlier impatience gone, replaced by a delicious sense of anticipation. I had removed the gift from under my pillow and had placed it on my dresser where I could look at it. It was wrapped in blue paper and tied with a tiny ribbon.

In my nightdress, I took the gift and the lamp from the dresser and placed the latter on my bedside table. Getting into bed, I tightened my shawl around my shoulders.

I tugged off the ribbon and the paper. A small navy-blue ring box was revealed. The box was old and worn at the edges. Its hinges creaked as I opened it. The air whooshed into my lungs when I saw what was inside. Nestled there was the most beautiful ring I had ever seen. It was a ruby, with two diamonds on either side of it and set at an angle on a gold band. Reverently I touched the gleaming stones with a fingertip.

A small piece of paper was tucked into the side of the box. I tugged it out and whispered the words written on it: "'*Wear this, with all my love, as a promise of our life together –Edward.*'"

Bittersweet tears of joy and sadness rolled down my cheeks when I took out the ring, for Edward had thought of everything. It was on a chain as he knew the only way I could wear it, for now, was to hang it hidden around my neck.

However, there in the secrecy of my room I removed the chain and slipped the ring onto my finger. It was a little too loose, but looked wonderful. I turned my hand this way and that in the candlelight to see how it glowed.

After a while I reluctantly took it off, replaced it on the chain and fastened it around my neck. It nestled low, between my breasts, close to my heart. Blowing out the candle I snuggled down under the blankets and pressed the ring to my skin, loving Edward deeply, and on that cold Christmas Eve was warmed by his hope for our future.

Chapter 30

Darkness still lingered when Beatrice knocked on my door on Christmas morning. In her excitement she did not wait to be invited in, but instead burst through the door and ran to my bed, her words tumbling over each other. Laughing at her sparkling eyes, I told her to slow down and go back to her room.

'Tell Vicky which day this is, and I will be with you as fast as I can,' I called after her.

My hand went immediately to the ring. I reminded myself not to repeat the action in view of the others.

The rest of the house was stirring as I helped Beatrice to dress. Helena arrived just as we finished.

'Happy Christmas, my darling,' she said, gathering her daughter up in her arms.

'Can I have my presents, Mummy?' Beatrice asked, jiggling up and down.

'Immediately after we have breakfast,' she replied. 'Happy

Christmas, Martha dear.'

'Happy Christmas, Helena.'

'The thaw has arrived,' she said. 'I could hear the melting snow dripping from the eaves when I woke. Our guests will be able to get here for lunch without too much difficulty.'

Reverend and Mrs. Wallis and their children were joining us, which I was pleased about, as it would make the occasion lively.

After a very rushed breakfast Beatrice dragged us all to the drawing room to see if Santa Claus had come. The door was locked. Although I longed to be with Edward, I could not help being happy in that moment as I watched her jump from one foot to the other in excitement as James took the key from his pocket. He opened the door and we all went in.

Beatrice's stocking was hanging from the mantelpiece and a large box lay near the hearth. Running over she knelt in front of the box. Then, reaching out, she lifted off the lid. 'Ooh,' she said as her eyes fell on the exquisite porcelain doll lying there. The face was dark and the doll was dressed in a bright costume.

'It looks like a lady from India,' her father said. 'That is how the ladies dress there. Her gown is called a sari. Santa Claus got it exactly right.'

'She is beautiful,' Beatrice said, lifting the doll out.

Then, jumping up, she ran from person to person, proudly showing off her prize.

James took down her stocking, out of which in great excitement she pulled some small wooden toys, fruit, confectionery, crayons and hair ribbons.

Then she rushed to the tree where she snatched up the little pile of wrapped presents Helena and I had prepared for her. Importantly, she handed one to each of us. Besides the ribbon for Helena, there were some handkerchiefs for James together with the picture she had coloured for him, a pair of lace fingerless gloves for her grandmother, and, for me, a very welcome gift of some crochet hooks and thread.

After we had made a fuss about our presents and thanked her, we all gathered by the Christmas tree, so Mother Pershaw could distribute the gifts to the rest of us.

I was touched to receive a beautiful pair of kid gloves and a scarf from Helena and James.

I thanked them and then opened my gift from Mother Pershaw, which was a book of English verse.

'I have a great love of poetry myself,' she said when I thanked her. 'Everyone should have an appreciation of fine writing.'

She also seemed quite pleased with the book on the Orient from me and the silk shawl from James and Helena.

Beatrice loved the hat I had crocheted for her, and Helena, the centrepiece. For James I had purchased, in the local confectioner's, a box of the mints he favoured after his evening meal. He thanked me warmly.

Helena received a beautiful gold locket from James. Her gift to him was the last to come out from under the tree. He grunted as he pulled it out.

'Good Lord, what could this be?' he asked.

Beatrice giggled.

Helena smiled at him while nervously playing with the new locket at her throat. Mother Pershaw and I looked on with undisguised curiosity.

It was still wrapped in the brown paper from the post office, but Helena had added a pretty bow. He rested it with a thud on the floor in order to remove the wrapping.

'Be careful of it, dear,' Helena urged.

He looked at her inquisitively before turning back to the task in hand.

Ripping off the paper, he revealed a plaque hewn from

granite. Something was written on it, but I could not make it out before he lifted it and tilted it towards himself.

Swallowing hard, he looked at Helena, his voice rough with emotion. 'Thank you, darling, it is magnificent.'

Helena's face relaxed into a huge smile.

James turned the plaque around for us to see. There, engraved in bold, black letters was the word 'Carissima'.

'It will look well, do you not think?' Helena asked her husband.

Fortunately the fact that Mother Pershaw and I had remained silent went unnoticed as they discussed how it would be positioned beside the door of their new house.

It was an unwelcome reminder of the upheaval to come, and once again I found myself at one with the other woman in the room whose heart would be twisted by pain in the near future. Now, more than ever, I was grateful that the Wallis family would be there for lunch as I knew that with my mood so altered I would not be able to contribute much to the conversation.

By mid-afternoon I had a headache and longed for fresh air. The meal had been a great success and now Beatrice and the other children were with me in the nursery and were still full of energy. I thought up a game which kept them busy for a while and which allowed me to sit by the window for a few minutes to gaze longingly at the woods. The thaw had been sudden and already the snow was nearly gone, so the access was open again. I sighed and rubbed my temples.

As if in answer to prayer, Lily came into the nursery.

'Madam says you are to have some time to yourself, miss, as it is Christmas Day after all. I am to stay with the children for an hour and then I'm to take them down to the drawing room to their parents. You are free until Beatrice's supper time at five.'

I had jumped up from the chair before she was halfway through her little speech and was already at the door.

'Thank you, Lily,' I beamed at her. 'Goodbye, children, see you later.' Still absorbed in their game, they hardly noticed my leaving.

Within minutes I was wrapped up warmly in my coat and my new gloves, and striding along the path to the woods. I knew, however, that I could not expect to meet Edward at the cottage as it was later than the time I would normally meet him and this was not an ordinary day anyway. He was probably still visiting Hazelwood, or perhaps he was already home.

My heart raced at the thought and, before I could change my mind, I changed direction and headed to the village. I knew my actions were bold but it was Christmas Day and I wanted to see him, even if only for a few minutes. As was typical of a December day, it was already dusk at this early time of three o'clock and, with the light fading, I reasoned with myself, I would be less recognisable if seen knocking at his door. I had an hour and a half to get there and back before it became fully dark.

Twenty minutes later I arrived in the village, grateful to find the main street deserted. I hurried along the terrace of houses until I reached Edward's door, which I tapped on twice. After a few seconds he opened it, his eyes rapidly registering first surprise, and then delight.

Hastily I stepped inside. Closing the door, he pulled me into the warmth of his arms, then as suddenly leaned back to scrutinise my face.

'How did you get away? Are you ill? Is that why –'

I stopped his questions with a light laugh. 'No, I am not ill, I just had to see you, and I will not be missed for a while so I came by to wish you Happy Christmas.'

'It is now,' he beamed, before gathering me into his arms

again. 'Come into the parlour,' he said then, guiding me past the examination room to a small, cosy room beyond.

There was a small settee to one side of a blazing fire and an armchair on the other. Nestled next to the chair was a table holding a lamp, brandy glass and open book.

I barely had a chance to take it all in before Edward kissed me tenderly.

'So you can stay for a short while?' he asked, his lips continuing to brush mine.

I smiled in agreement.

'Then wait here just a moment – I will light a lamp in the examination room, so that if anyone comes calling, I will put you in there and pretend this is a professional visit.'

He rushed out, a willing accomplice in my afternoon of daring. When he returned, I was unbuttoning my coat.

'Let me take that,' he said, helping me.

As he laid it over the edge of the settee, I moved around the room looking at his bookshelves, noting that the majority of the books were medical, with a few novels interspersed here and there.

'Martha?' He called my name so gently that I felt my heart melt.

Turning, I saw him standing with his back to the fireplace and his arms out to me. I walked straight into them with a wonderful feeling of coming home.

'I would never have thought you could have got away today. I am so happy you are here,' he murmured. 'And so glad I didn't linger at Hazelwood – I felt too restless to stay so I told them I had a patient to visit.'

We moved to the settee.

'I wanted so badly to spend some of Christmas Day with you,' I said.

'Just before you arrived I was trying to concentrate on a book, but I kept thinking about you, wondering what you were doing. When I opened the door I thought I had conjured you up out of the air.'

The tension that had been in my body since I had set out seeped away. I melted against his side.

We stared at the fire for a moment, my head on his shoulder, our fingers linked.

'Edward, thank you so much for the ring. It is so beautiful.'

'It was my mother's. I know she would have been very happy for you to wear it.'

I was too moved to speak.

'Will you put it on now?' he urged. 'Just while you are here with me?'

Sitting forward, I turned my back to him, lowering my head. Sensation spread over my body as his fingers brushed my neck. He undid the clasp, and withdrew the chain from inside the high collar of my dress.

I faced him again as he took the ring from the chain and, in a movement so swift that it made me blink, went down on one knee.

Taking my left hand in his, he held the ring at the tip of my finger and looked into my eyes, his face serious.

'Martha White, will you marry me?'

'Yes, absolutely yes.'

My simple reply had him slipping the ring onto my finger. When he looked up at me again he was smiling.

'My mother's fingers were not as slender as yours,' he said. 'But it suits your hand very well.'

'It is perfect. I love it.'

We raised our eyes from the ring to gaze at each other, both of us grinning foolishly. The fire crackled. Placing his hands on either side of my face, he pulled me towards him until our lips met.

'Happy Christmas,' he said softly.

Resuming his seat beside me, he gathered me close. After all our meetings in the draughty cottage where we sat on rickety old chairs, it was heavenly to be seated on a comfortable settee in a warm room, wrapped in his arms.

'Thank you for the handkerchiefs. I love them.' He pulled one from his pocket and showed me that it was the one with the heart on it.

We kissed then talked for a while, describing our separate Christmas mornings.

'Mrs. Reeves is a great cook,' Edward said, 'and I did justice to each course.' He patted his stomach. 'Mr. Reeves is very passionate about his farming but is also very humorous. He regaled us with many a tale about growing up on his father's farm.'

'I have met his wife a few times. She is a very jolly woman too.'

'Even so it did not stop her from rapping him on the knuckles a few times to make him temper his language and stop sharing gory details while sitting at the dining table.' He smiled at the memory.

'They have a lot of children, do they not?'

'Six and all still at school. Mind, I think the boys would prefer to be at home on the farm all day, judging by some of the stories they told.' Edward laughed at the memory, tightening his arms around me. 'I wish you could have been there with me. I would have proudly shown you off.'

'Maybe we can have them to our house for Christmas sometime,' I suggested.

He brushed his lips against my forehead before tilting my chin upwards so I could meet his eyes.

'I look forward to it.'

I kissed him tenderly.

'There is something else I want you to have,' he said, getting up and going over to his desk.

Opening a small book lying there, he inscribed something inside the cover. Closing it, he brought it over and sat beside me again.

'It's a book of poetry by one of our own Lake poets,' he said. 'William Wordsworth.'

I ran my fingers over the new soft leather before opening it and reading what Edward had just written:

To My Darling Martha,

As you read these poems, think of me as I will be thinking of you.

With all my love,

Edward

'Thank you. I will keep it with me always. You are a kind and thoughtful man, Edward, and I love you.'

'And I you.'

After a while I tapped his waistcoat with a finger. 'Will you check the time? I probably should be getting back.'

He gave a resigned nod, sighed and flicked open his pocket watch, tilting it towards me.

'Oh Lord, it is twenty minutes to five already!' I exclaimed.

In unison, we looked towards the window. To my horror it was pitch black outside.

'I must hurry if I am to make it back by five.'

'I will take you back on my horse.'

'No, Edward, we cannot risk that.'

'You will be late otherwise.' He watched me chew my lip for a moment. 'Well, that's decided then. Make your way to the end of the street. Turn the corner and wait for me there. I will saddle up and bring the horse around, and then,' he smiled mischievously, 'young maiden, I shall carry you off into the night!'

'Well, I have no one to blame but myself, Sir Knight. I started this escapade.' I smiled back at him, while buttoning up my coat.

Edward turned down the lamps and we stood together in the firelight for a moment.

'You are the most beautiful woman I have ever seen. I love you.' He pressed one last, heady kiss to my lips before releasing me. 'Come on, we had best move quickly.'

He opened the front door, glanced up and down the street and nodded at me to go out. Keeping my head lowered, I walked down the street and around the corner as he had instructed. It was dark there – only the main street had lamps burning. I waited in the shadows, feeling like a fugitive.

'Come on, Edward,' I muttered, my breath clouding in the cold evening air. After another minute or two the silence was shattered by the sound of hoofs. I felt sure everyone in the village would hear them and come out to look.

Edward drew level with me and removed his right foot from the stirrup.

'Give me your hand, put your foot in there, and lever yourself up. Ready?'

Pulling me up to sit sideways in front of him, he clamped his left arm around me and urged the horse forward. Luckily there was a moon again that night to guide our way. I pressed tight up against him, both out of fear of falling and to gain some extra warmth.

'Are you comfortable there, Lady Martha?' Edward asked with a laugh.

'Yes, thank you, sir.'

Beneath my hand I felt laughter rumble in his chest.

'Edward, you cannot take me up to the front of the house.

Someone will see or hear us. Can you take me home by the back laneway and leave me at the bottom of the vegetable garden? The view from the house is blocked there by hedges.'

I felt his nod. His concentration was now on the road ahead, so I fell silent too.

I was feeling a mixture of contentment to be there in his arms and nervousness. There were only a few minutes left before Beatrice's supper time.

The moon had gone behind a cloud by the time we reached the lane. Edward encouraged the horse along carefully.

When we got to the vegetable garden, he kissed me quickly and helped me to slide down from the horse.

I stepped back and tried to make out his face in the dark, but could not. But I did catch his whispered words: 'Good night, my love, take care.'

Pulling on the reins, he turned the horse and went back the way we had come. I waited a few moments until the sound of the hooves had retreated, then hurried up the path to the door.

Luckily it led into a passage and not directly into the kitchen. Opening it gingerly, I heard the usual sounds of supper being prepared. Closing it behind me, I crept along the passage to the back stairs. I did not encounter anyone and fled as quickly as I could to my room. Once inside I leant against the door, my heart pounding. I allowed myself a little smile of triumph at the success of my daring plan.

Before the smile had faded, a knock at my door had me jumping away from it.

'Miss, it's Lily. Beatrice wants you to –'

Before she could finish, Beatrice impatiently opened the door herself and pushed it in, dragging Lily in behind her.

'Martha, will you read a story to me and my new doll while I have my supper?' She looked at me and stopped, cocking her head to the side. 'Why are you wearing your coat?'

Flustered, I stammered something about having been outside to take a little air, hastily pulled off my gloves, and started to unbutton my coat.

'That's pretty,' Beatrice said.

To my horror, I saw her looking at my hand and Edward's ring. I thrust my hands behind my back.

Lily was looking curiously at me now too.

'It was my mother's,' I lied. 'I only wear it at Christmas, to remember her. I must put it away now to keep it safe.' I knew I was blushing furiously. I cleared my throat. 'Lily, please take Beatrice back to the nursery and I will be there directly.'

When they had done as I had bid, I finished taking off my coat and, with shaking hands, took the chain from my pocket and replaced the ring on it. It took me another moment to clasp it closed around my neck and tuck it away.

What if Beatrice tells Helena about the ring, I thought. I will have to lie to her, too, if she asks about it. How could I have been so careless?

Going to the mirror, I smoothed my hair, took some deep breaths and went to the nursery.

Dismissing Lily, I read to Beatrice without registering a word. She did not mention the ring and I began to relax. However, a little while later I realised that she had not forgotten it.

'Where is your ring? Can I see it again tomorrow? Will you let me play with it?' she babbled as she snuggled down.

'No, dear, I need to keep it safe because it is all I have to remember my mother by.'

I hated having to lie to her again, but my own carelessness had left me no choice.

With trepidation, I joined the adults downstairs for supper. The Wallis family had long since gone home and the talk was mostly reminiscences of a pleasantly spent day. I, of course, did not add mine and it seemed that my absence from the house had gone unnoticed. The only question Helena asked was to enquire if I had had a nice rest. I thanked her for her consideration in giving me some time to myself. We were walking together into the dining room at the time and, if I blushed, then she did not see it.

Later, as I was brushing my hair before bed, I reflected on the day and knew the lies had been worth it and that I would not undo a minute of the afternoon. Every memory of my time with Edward was so precious to me. Besides, I rationalised, when Edward and I married, his mother would be my mother-in-law, even though she had passed away. So in a way the lies about the origin of the ring were not really lies at all.

As was my habit before getting into bed, I gave a last check on Beatrice. I crept into her room and tucked the blankets up around her. Bending down, I pressed a kiss to her forehead, my hair brushing her cheek. She did not stir.

'Sweet dreams,' I whispered, before returning to my own room.

Chapter 31

London, England, 2010

Juliet stood in front of the mirror. She had arrived back from Montana two days earlier and had been hard at work at the magazine with her editor each day. But now it was Friday evening, Logan was expected in fifteen minutes, and there was a flutter in her stomach. She looked critically at the short black linen dress and admitted that it looked well against her Montana tan and sun-bleached hair. Her legs were bare and she wore flat leather sandals.

Happy that she looked casual but stylish, she brushed on some lip gloss and ruffled her hair one last time before going to light some candles in the sitting room. Her fingers shook slightly as she struck the first match. Her phone rang. It was her friend Rose.

'Hope all goes well,' Rose said.

'I hope it wasn't just the magic of Florence. It was all so fast really, if you think about it.'

'Don't think about it. It's not like you to be nervous.'

216

The doorbell rang.

'There he is. I have to go!'

'Have a great time!'

Replacing the receiver and taking a few calming breaths, she went to open the door.

And there he was, looking as wonderful as she remembered, albeit a bit tired. And she knew immediately it hadn't been a passing thing in Florence. They stood there for a few seconds, staring at each other, until a slow grin spread across both their faces.

'Welcome,' she said.

'Thank you,' he said, stepping over the threshold and pulling a bunch of red roses from behind his back, handing them to her with a flourish.

She clocked the colour instantly and looked at him as she lowered her head to smell them.

'Yes, I chose red deliberately,' he said. 'I didn't want there to be any misunderstandings.'

She put them on a small table next to her and closed the door before going into his arms. She pressed against him, relieved that nothing had changed.

'I've missed you so much,' she said.

'I've missed you too.'

He touched her face with the tip of a finger. 'I love you, Juliet.'

She laughed and slipped her arms around his neck. 'I love you too.'

His own laughter was muffled by her lips. Mirth turned immediately to heat as he kissed her back with all the passion of the weeks of waiting.

After a few moments she heard him whisper: 'I hope you can wait a bit longer for dinner?'

'Absolutely,' she replied.

He scooped her up into his arms and she pointed to the bedroom.

Much later they ordered in Chinese. They sat on cushions in front of her coffee table. He was in a T-shirt and sweatpants and she was in a towelling robe, their hair still damp from the long shower they had just taken together.

'I'm ravenous. I hope you ordered enough for ten!' he said.

Juliet opened the boxes on the coffee table and inhaled the delicious smell that wafted her way. She passed food to Logan, before tucking in with relish.

She felt glorious. Logan was a considerate and very passionate lover. Their lovemaking was even better than it had been in Florence, if that were possible. They seemed to be so in tune with each other and the 'rightness' of it awed her, and now she was more in love than ever.

She studied him.

'I thought you looked tired when you got here,' she said.

'Did I? I've been very busy. I've been over to Ireland this week and I've got a lot of new information to get my head around. I'm going to move over there in two weeks' time.'

They heard a train rumble past in the distance.

'Juliet, when are you able to come to Carissima?'

'I have ten days off around the second week of September. I have to attend a seminar on the Saturday but I could fly over on the Sunday to Dublin, if that suits you.'

'Perfectly. Let me know your flight times and I'll collect you.'

'Do I need to buy a pair of wellingtons?'

'Not at all – there's a load of them in one of the sheds,' Logan replied, concentrating on snagging a noodle with his chopsticks. When he popped it into his mouth, he looked up and saw her teasing grin. 'Ha ha. Well, don't be so smart, woman – a spoiled city girl like you might find country life a little tough.'

It was her turn to raise a sardonic eyebrow. 'Spoiled city girl?'

'Okay – world-travelled famous photographer – same thing.'

She laughed. 'Although you might have a point. I've been a lot of places, some very rough and ready, I'll have you know,' she pushed her shoulder against his, 'some quite exotic, but I've never been to a farm here or in Ireland. So it's a totally new experience. And a ranch in Montana doesn't count as having experience of a farm.'

Logan laughed. 'I can't even imagine the vastness of the ranch you described, but I think you'll like Carissima – acres of land spread over gently rolling hills, called drumlins, and woods and a lake. And the house is lovely. I can't wait for you to see it. The photograph you saw in Florence doesn't really do it justice. It's so quiet there – it'll suit your meditative side.'

Juliet nodded. She thought she would like it too, for a visit, but any longer than that she wasn't so sure. Any time she travelled she enjoyed the new places and people, but she always loved to come home to London and the buzz of the city.

'Although,' Logan continued, glancing around her living room, 'this is very modern in comparison. In Carissima a lot of the furnishings are original.'

Juliet groaned inwardly. Not only was it in the middle of nowhere, but it sounded dreary and old-fashioned. She knew it meant a lot to him, so she was very nervous that she wasn't going to like it.

She changed the subject. 'What condition was the orchard in?'

Logan grimaced. 'Not too bad, but it will need a lot of work. The trees are very old but some are still producing fruit. Luckily there are three different varieties of fruit tree there still – you have to have variety for pollination purposes. But the soil is poor now and needs some decent nurturing. As well as working on that I'm going to start a new orchard and I've already picked out the area. It's sheltered from the easterly winds by a hill and it's south-facing for the sunshine. I got some great information from Irish Seed Savers Association and I'm going down there – there being County Clare by the way – at the end of September, when they have apple tastings. When I find what I like, I'll decide on my rootstock and then on the main body of the tree.'

'Hang on, explain. What are rootstocks?'

'They are the root stumps onto which a bud from another tree is grafted. Apple trees can be propagated by grafting or budding onto rootstock for early fruiting and to control growth and size – the more dwarf the rootstock, the smaller the tree, the shorter the life span. The larger the rootstock the more fruit it produces and it will have a longer life span.'

Juliet nodded, more interested than she thought she'd be. 'Go on.'

'Once you've decided on your rootstock you must then decide on the main body of your apple tree. This is known in the horticultural trade as the 'scion', a graft onto the rootstock. With the rootstock controlling the growth, the grafted 'scion' controls the type of apple produced.'

'I didn't realise it was so complicated. I thought you bought a tree and planted it and that was that.'

'No, and that's not all,' he continued. 'Tremendous care has to go into the soil and you must be on the lookout for diseases and pests, etc, etc.'

Logan's eyes were alive with the challenge of it all. Juliet found his excitement contagious.

'When will you start planting?'

'In the spring. I have so much learning to do before then and the ground will have to be prepared.'

'It'll be great, Logan. Are you looking forward to living there again?'

'I've mixed feelings about it. It wasn't an easy time for us before we left. Mum and Dad were always fighting. My memories of the place are good and bad. Even though I loved it there, at that point I couldn't wait to get away. But in later years I knew it was still in my blood. I think that's why I couldn't bring myself to sell it. So to answer your question, it's a mixture of excitement and dread. I just hope the good memories will prevail, especially when I'm back on the land. ' He gave a huge yawn. 'I need some sleep.'

And he was right. He fell asleep the minute they snuggled down together in Juliet's bed, and slept like a baby. She snuggled up close to him and drifted off to sleep with the pleasant weight of his arm across her.

They had a fantastic weekend together. They took walks in Wandsworth Park near Juliet's apartment and had long talks over leisurely coffees, and since Juliet loved Sunday mornings in Borough Market, they took the Tube and spent a few hours strolling hand in hand and indulging in their shared love of food at some of the many artisan stalls.

'It's so easy to be with you,' Logan commented at one point as they wandered towards the Thames, eating hot falafel from paper bags.

'I know what you mean. I feel the same.'

'What have you lined up, work wise, before you come over to Ireland?' he asked, pressing his shoulder against hers.

'Nothing as amazing as Montana,' she laughed. 'We're going to Cornwall at the end of the week to do a shoot on seagulls and then the assignment after that is at a city school, which has set up

221

its own pet farm and vegetable garden. The editor has been muttering about budgets, so I think the shoots for the rest of the year will be mostly in England and Scotland.'

'But that's great. You'll be able to come to Carissima a lot then.'

Smiling at him, she realised she still felt uneasy at the thought of going there. She was afraid that he would be disappointed if she didn't love the place as much as he seemed to. She was keen for the first visit to happen too, but for different reasons to him. She just wanted to get it over with and hopefully find that she was wrong to be so worried.

Chapter 32

Berkshire, England, 1889

That wonderful visit to Edward's on Christmas Day was savoured in my memory day after day while the cold weather of December gave way to the dark, wet days of January. Walks were rare, and I was so conscious that time was running out.

In the afternoons, I paced with agitation in front of my bedroom window and cursed the rivulets of water that ran down the window pane.

Even Helena's sweet nature was tried as a result of being so confined, as there was nowhere to hide from Mother Pershaw. After the brief interlude of Christmas, she had once again resumed the role of teacher to Helena in all things domestic. Nearly every sentence began with: '*A well-run household must . . .*'

With the help of Mrs. Wallis's friends in Monaghan, two housemaids and a gardener were already in residence in the house in Ireland, preparing it for our arrival. Helena had decided to take a cook and a butler with her. Higgins had a nephew whom he presented to James and Helena as their possible future butler. They were very impressed with him and his previous experience, and much relieved to have that issue settled so easily.

Helen advertised in the London papers for a cook and arranged for several women to come for interview during the last week in January. She had hoped to conduct the interviews with the help of Mrs. Richards, our own cook, but to her dismay but not her surprise, Mother Pershaw insisted on being present too.

After the interviews on the first day, Helena burst into the nursery, wringing her hands.

'We will never have a cook at this rate. I found a couple of the women most pleasing but then Mother Pershaw picked holes in all that they said and sent them on their way before I could have my say. It was so frustrating. What am I going to do?'

I drew her to a chair.

'You must say something to her, Helena. It is Mrs. Richards' opinion and your own instinct you should be going by. You have been firm with Mother Pershaw in the past, you can do it again. Why not go and discuss with Mrs. Richards exactly what you liked most about the women you interviewed, draw up a list and keep to that in the remaining interviews, and do not be swayed.'

She patted my hand. 'You are right, of course. I must take up my own authority on this matter. This new cook is for my home, not Mother Pershaw's. I will speak to Cook now and to Mother after lunch.'

She rose and kissed my cheek.

'Martha, what would I do without you?' she said. 'I do love you dearly.' She smiled brightly and left happier than when she had arrived.

I stayed standing in the middle of the room, thinking sadly that it was her love for me, and mine for her, that was keeping me a prisoner.

She returned to the nursery in the late afternoon, her eyes sparkling.

'I told her, Martha. I told her if she sits in on the other interviews, she may do so to ask questions only, and that after each interview I would take note of everyone's opinion. When we have seen everyone I shall make the final decision.'

'What did she say?' I asked, proud of her.

'Oh, she huffed and puffed a little, but she saw I would not be moved.' Her smile was triumphant.

'Well done.'

'Mrs. Richards is very shrewd and will help me make a very sound choice, I think.'

And so she did. By the end of the week a cook had been chosen and invited to spend a few days in the kitchen before the final decision would be made. She excelled apparently, and Mrs. Richards recommended that she be hired. Helena was very pleased with herself. I met the woman briefly, a Mrs. Dawson, a widow from London, who came with very good references, but also with a kindly face, and a no-nonsense approach. Even Mother Pershaw approved of her.

With that job out of the way, Helena began to speak of our leaving with great enthusiasm, not realising how it pierced my heart every time she mentioned it. Her need to keep herself sane was very nearly driving me out of my mind.

'We shall depart on Friday March 3rd, if the weather permits it,' James announced at dinner on the last day of January.

My grip froze on my knife and fork.

'How will we travel?' was the last I heard Helena say as the words in my head drowned out most of their conversation.

It is happening. It is really happening. March 3rd. Oh God, it is still too soon.

I heard the words *train* and *paddle steamer*. We might as well have been travelling by camel for all I cared, for with all my heart I did not want to go. And a journey that involved trains and ships made our destination seem impossibly far away from Edward.

Helena forced my attention back to her by addressing me directly.

'Martha, we shall be ready by then, will we not? Most of the packing is already done.'

'Yes,' I agreed mechanically.

'Excellent,' James said, wiping his moustache with his napkin. 'We shall ship everything, bar our personal luggage, ahead in advance in the care of two men who used to be in my employ. They are very reliable fellows.'

'It will be such an adventure,' Helena declared. 'And before we go we have several dinner obligations to meet from friends and neighbours who wish to say goodbye. It will be a busy few weeks, James.'

'It is all arranged for the third of March,' I said, as Edward and I sat in the little cottage the next day.

His grip tightened but he did not reply. After a moment he cleared his throat and told me about a patient he had seen that morning. And so it was decided. We did not mention my departure again, although it loomed above us like a shadow from that afternoon on.

Those last few weeks were hard. We managed to meet several afternoons but only for a few short minutes at a time because the light and weather were poor. I did not cry and made every effort to talk normally about day-to-day things, but the joy in being together was slowly suffocating beneath the pain.

Night after night I fell into bed emotionally exhausted. Keeping up the pretence of excitement about the trip in front of the household was becoming a strain.

'You are looking quite peaky again, Martha,' Helena said one morning, frowning at me.

'It is this weather, I suppose,' I said quickly. 'I cannot walk as much as I would wish. But I feel quite well, I assure you.' I smiled to allay her fears.

'I hope you are right, my dear. It would not do at all if you were ill when it is time for us to travel.'

'Please do not worry yourself. I really am perfectly well.'

'Well, if you are certain . . .' She let the words hang as Lily came in with the morning post.

I gratefully used the distraction as an opportunity to leave the room.

Chapter 33

I woke on Monday morning and curled into a ball, not wanting to get up and begin the week, for it would end in Ireland. We were due to leave on Friday. Silently I prayed for storms to prevent our departure, while at the same time I prayed that the weather would not stop me from seeing Edward every day before I left. Four more afternoons was all that remained for us. Groaning, I burrowed further under the covers.

But then I heard excited voices out in the corridor. There was a knock and I heard Helena call my name.

'What is it?' I asked, opening the door quickly, becoming alarmed at seeing her standing there in her nightclothes and in an obvious dither.

'We leave tomorrow. You must get dressed. There is so much to be done.'

'What? But we do not sail until Saturday!'

She had already turned away, replying over her shoulder, 'James has decided to go a few days early because the weather is so settled. He does not want to risk it changing again. So we will sail the morning after next instead.'

'But wait!' I cried.

She turned back.

'Our passage is booked, surely that cannot be changed?' I said.

Helena waved a hand dismissively. 'James will organise all that.'

I grabbed her arm. 'But we cannot go yet!'

She frowned. 'Martha, what is the matter with you?'

'The trains!' I frantically searched for any excuse I could.

'What about the trains?' Helena's voice took on an edge of puzzled impatience.

'Surely James has booked tickets for the trains for Friday and not tomorrow,' I said.

'Martha, I just told you James will sort everything. He would not have suggested an earlier departure if he could not rearrange everything. What has come over you? Now please get dressed – we have enough to do without trying to do James' business as well as our own.'

I continued to stand there.

'Martha, there is packing to be done! Please get ready!'

The finality in her tone brooked no more argument from me. With a last exasperated shake of her head she went into her room.

I returned to mine in a panic. How could this be happening? Leaving without saying goodbye to Edward was unthinkable. But how could I get away to see him?

I could not think straight at the suddenness of it all. My breathing became uneven, forcing me to sit down, where I promptly burst into tears. After a few minutes I jumped up again and paced, thoughts whirring through my head.

I stopped suddenly as a plan began to form. I had said nothing about Edward and me and had made no demands of my own. Well today, I thought, I will demand to have one hour to myself to go to the village. Helena can ask for an explanation but I will not give one! I am giving him up for a year – I deserve the chance to say goodbye.

I washed and dressed, my determination to see him blocking out all other emotions for the moment.

I rushed Beatrice through her morning routine and we joined Helena downstairs.

'Ah, good, there you are. Beatrice, you have to be a good girl this morning and help Mummy and Martha get ready for our trip,' Helena said. 'Do you think you can do that?'

'Yes, Mummy. Can I carry all my dolls?'

'You can carry one. The others will have to be packed in the trunk.'

Helena turned to me, flushed with excitement.

'Oh, Martha, my own home at last! Now, let me see.' She consulted the list in her hand. 'Most of our things are packed already, so can you organise all the last items from the nursery and your own things? Robin will come up and collect the luggage as soon as you have it ready. Keep one small bag separate for your overnight items and Beatrice's, for the hotel at Holyhead tomorrow night. We will be leaving first thing in the morning so make sure Beatrice has a bath this evening.'

'There's something I have to do,' I blurted.

'Pardon?' Helena asked, her head already bent over one of her lists.

'Can Lily make a start on Beatrice's packing? I need to go out for an hour.'

Helena's eyes were wide with puzzlement. 'Go out?' she echoed. 'But what –'

'Please, Helena,' I cut her off. 'Just one hour, and then I will get ready to come to Ireland with you.'

A worried frown creased her brow and I knew she could not possibly understand the significance of the trade-off I was offering.

'Please, Helena,' I repeated quietly but firmly.

She did not say anything,

'I will get everything done when I return, I promise.'

'Well, yes, then, of course.' She sounded as confused as she looked, but to her credit she did not pursue the matter.

'Shall I send Lily to you?' I enquired.

'Yes, yes, do that, please.'

Hesitating at the door, I looked at her. 'Thank you.' It came out as a whisper, but she heard and nodded at me.

After speaking to Lily, I left and walked quickly along the driveway, breaking into a half-run once I was away from the house. Near the village I had to slow down again to catch my breath.

Morning surgery would have started and I did not know what I was going to say when I got there, but I had to see him.

As I rounded the corner he was showing a woman and child out. 'Good day, Mrs. Cauldwell. Goodbye, Peter.' He tousled the young lad's hair.

'Thank you, Doctor. Good day,' the woman replied.

I walked up quickly just as he was about to close the door.

'Mar– Miss White. Please come in.' His eyes searched my face.

My throat was suddenly tight and I could not speak.

'Please take a seat. I will not be long,' he said.

Only then did I see an old man sitting on a chair in the hall. I nodded and took the one next to him.

'Come along, Mr. Reed.' Edward helped the old man up and into the surgery.

They must have been in there for only a few minutes but it seemed like hours. I could hear the muffled sound of the old man's deep gravelly voice behind the door and Edward gently questioning him.

At last, they finished, and Edward showed him out.

He took my hand and led me into the surgery. 'What is it, my love?' he asked softly, holding me by the shoulders, his handsome face filled with concern and love.

I shook my head and burst into tears.

He rocked me in his arms.

'We are leaving in the morning,' I said.

'*What?*'

I nodded against his shoulder.

'No. We have four more days!' he exclaimed.

I clung to him, soaking his waistcoat with my tears. His arms tightened and my sobbing increased, knowing that I would not feel them around me again for a very long time.

'James decided to go early.' I was suddenly angry. 'A few days here or there does not matter to him. But they matter to me. I am going with them, am I not? That should count for something.'

'I do not want to let you go.' Edward's voice shook as he whispered the words.

I pushed back out of his arms and stared at him.

'Then I will not go. They can get another governess. I was insane to think I was duty bound to go with them. I'm sure Beatrice will be so excited about their new home that she will not miss me at all. And yes, I know I owe them for taking me in when I had nothing, but surely Helena will forgive me in time.'

'Oh Martha!' he said, pulling me back into his arms with a fierce grip.

My thoughts began to tumble over each other. I drew back

again slowly and looked into his eyes.

'My darling,' he said, 'I wish with all my heart that you would stay, but –'

'Then that's decided. I will stay and we will get married soon.'

Only then did the word 'but' register with me. His eyes were sad and he spoke gently.

'All the same arguments for you having to go are still there, Martha.'

I thumped my fists against his chest. 'They do not matter any more!' My voice rose. 'I do not want to leave you!'

He pulled me close again. 'Shh, my love,' he soothed. 'You know I do not want you to go either, but we have already looked at this from every possible angle and decided this was our only choice. You know if there was any way we could have arranged it differently we would have.'

Hearing the anguish in his tone I opened my mouth to argue further, but then I remembered the day they had told Beatrice she would be going away and would not be seeing her grandmother for a while. The little girl had been so sad. How would it affect her if I was to be gone out of her life too? I had to keep my promise to Helena. I knew Edward was right and that it was fear and pain that had made me desperate.

I stamped my foot.

A soft chuckle sounded in my ear. 'Oh, how I love that temper of yours. Use it, my darling, to get you through, to get you home to me.'

'Edward!' Fresh tears ran down my face as I held him close.

'It will be a short year, Martha,' he murmured. 'Our wishing it away will make it so. Then we will be together for always.'

After a few precious moments Edward leaned me away from him and dried my face with his handkerchief. His eyes were so sad. I stood on tiptoe and kissed each cheek in turn before he turned his head and captured my lips in a kiss that burned with our mutual pain. It was a long time before we drew apart.

Edward pressed my head into his shoulder and kissed my hair. 'I will wait for you, Martha. Please come home to me.'

I nodded, my cheek moving on his chest. 'I love you,' I whispered.

'I love you too, my darling,' he said, his voice cracking on the last word.

I took a step back in order to see his face properly. With our hands linked I drank in each line and feature.

'You will be my wife before we know it,' he said, laying his hand over the ring beneath my dress.

I placed my hand over his and pressed it hard against my breast, the little stab of the ring a welcome relief from the pain in my heart. Then, wrenching my hand from his, I ran out the door without looking back. Once out on the street I forced myself to walk at a dignified pace, but with my head lowered to hide my tears.

Taking the path back through the woods, I crumpled onto an old log and wept in the privacy of the trees. After a while I started to shiver. Standing up, I dried my eyes, brushed off my coat and straightened my shoulders. I would do him proud by hiding my sadness from the others. That way no questions would be asked to jeopardise things between us. After all, I would be relying on James and Helena to release me from their employ and help me to return to England within the year.

I knew my eyes must have been red and swollen when I returned and Helena looked at me with concern but, to her credit, did not pry. I threw myself into my work, wishing now to be gone as soon as possible, as every day would be one day closer to coming home.

Chapter 34

An early morning fog hung silently all around, and the horses shifted nervously.

'If it does not work out, you will always have a home here,' Mother Pershaw said, embracing her son at the bottom of the steps.

'Goodbye, Mother.'

'Goodbye, my darling boy.' The old lady's voice shook and I swallowed hard against the tears in my throat.

James joined Helena, Beatrice and me in the carriage. Mrs. Dawson, the new cook, and the butler, Mr. Hawkins, were in the second carriage.

The staff stood on the top step to wave us off.

Beatrice called out, 'Bye, Grandmama!' and waved.

The three of us were quiet, lost in our own thoughts. Beatrice sat down and snuggled into me, her eyes still sleepy, holding tightly to her doll. I pulled the rug tighter around us, feeling as though my insides had been completely hollowed out. James and

Helena exchanged a look of excitement, their hands linked tightly.

Robin closed the door and climbed up front. The carriage jolted forward and I blinked hard, knowing that this was it. It was finally happening.

As we moved down the driveway, I could barely make out the pathway to the woods that I had rushed along joyfully so many times to meet Edward. The trees stood bare and motionless now in the fog's befitting cloak of grief. We rolled on, passing the field Edward had watched Beatrice and me play in, now ploughed awaiting spring. I sucked in a shaky breath, trying to suppress the pain.

Our route to Reading train station took us through the village, bleak and hushed at such an early hour. As we neared Edward's surgery I leant forward in the pretext of fussing with Beatrice's blanket, in order to look out the window. As we drew level, the curtain in the surgery window was pulled back and there he was, his eyes burning straight into mine and his hand pressed to the window pane. I almost cried out. In a second the carriage had gone past, but it had been enough to feel his love reach out to warm me.

Sitting back, I closed my eyes to keep his image there. Sniffling from beside me had me opening them again. I looked down to see Beatrice crying.

'Whe-en will we-ee see Grandmama ag-gain?' She hiccupped the question.

James and Helena exchanged a look. Helena leant forward and wiped away her tears. I swallowed against the ache in my throat, trying not to let my own tears fall.

'Oh my darling, before you know it we shall be making a trip back here to see her,' Helena told the child.

Unfortunately I knew her words were only to placate her and I knew it would be some years before they would make a return journey.

'In the meantime you will have so much to see and do in our new home,' Helena continued. 'Is that not so, James?'

'Of course it is. You are going to love it there.'

'Will my dolls like it?'

'Of course they will, sweetheart,' Helena assured her, 'and you will have a lovely room to keep them in.'

This thought seemed to cheer her up and she snuggled in close to me again, while having a whispered conversation with Vicky, the one doll she had been allowed to carry.

It took us only forty minutes to get to the station and Beatrice's loneliness for her grandmother totally evaporated in the excitement of going on the train. As we walked along the platform, she shielded her ears from the hissing of the big black steam engine.

A porter and Mr. Hawkins followed behind with the luggage. Mrs. Dawson carried a picnic basket which Mr. Hawkins offered to take, but which she would not relinquish.

In the carriage it took a moment for James to join us and Helena used the opportunity of his absence to ask me how I was.

'You are very pale, my dear. Are you well?'

'Yes, thank you. I did not sleep very much last night, knowing we were leaving this morning.'

At least there was no lie in that, I thought. She patted my hand and to my relief James joined us, which prevented any further questions. She continued to look quizzically at me as she had done several times since my return from Edward's the previous day, and I knew she could not fathom why I had to go to the village. I smiled brightly and expressed the hope that the fog would lift, to further distract her.

The journey to London took less than an hour and we soon left the sleepy countryside behind and entered the city's sprawling outskirts. I did not care for it. Everything seemed grey and dull in the lingering fog, and just made me feel even lonelier. I was glad to arrive into the hustle and bustle of Paddington Station.

Unfortunately our train for Holyhead did not leave from there and we had to take a cab to Euston Station. The streets were busy, crowded and noisy.

Euston was also crowded and a little overwhelming for Beatrice. She clung tightly to my hand, her eyes huge trying to take it all in. I held one of her hands tightly while Mrs. Dawson held the other, talking cheerily to her.

'Wait 'til you see what I 'ave in my picnic basket for you when we get on our train, dearie. Mrs. Richards told me you like a certain jam sponge cake, and I just might 'ave made one yesterday and slipped it in here!' She winked when Beatrice looked up at her with a huge grin.

I gave Mrs. Dawson a grateful smile, pleased that such a warm-hearted person was going to be with us in Ireland.

Our party made its way slowly along the busy platform for the train to North Wales. Porters bustled past us in both directions, pushing trolleys stacked high with luggage. Helena and James were ahead of us and Helena kept looking over her shoulder, anxiously checking that we were close behind.

James stopped three quarters of the way down the platform and motioned us through the door of a first-class carriage. The peace and quiet inside was in stark contrast to the bedlam that reigned in the station.

Helena unwound her scarf and sighed as she took her seat. 'This is a relief. I am quite exhausted already and we have not yet left London!' But she smiled and the sparkle in her eyes quite belied her words.

James smiled indulgently at her. 'You can have a good rest tonight in the hotel in Holyhead. It is very comfortable, my dear.'

After only ten minutes the train pulled out. Within an hour we were on our way, and were being served scones and cake from the picnic basket by Mrs. Dawson and Mr. Hawkins. Lacking appetite, I only picked at mine, conscious of miles, and more miles, being put between me and Edward.

'Tomorrow,' I heard Helena ask James, 'what time do we sail?'

'Ten – not too early a start.'

'And the crossing? How long will it take?' she asked, a little nervously.

'Just short of four hours.'

She nodded and went back to watching the passing scenery.

The journey seemed to take forever. Though the mountains in North Wales were particularly spectacular I had to force myself to take an interest in them, only so that I could describe them to Edward in my first letter.

I read some stories to Beatrice who was feeling restless and confined. After that she slept for an hour and I could return to my own thoughts.

When we arrived in Holyhead after the eight-hour journey, I was quite weary.

Tangy salt air filled our nostrils the moment we stepped from the train, but it was dark by that time and we could not see the sea. The small station was so much calmer than what we had experienced in London.

On arriving at the hotel Helena exclaimed at its comfort and charm, but as James checked us in I longed for my bed. However, dinner would have to be endured first.

Helena interrupted my gloomy thoughts.

'Would you mind very much if I arranged to have supper sent up for you and Beatrice to the room you are sharing. I would like you to settle her down for an early night. There is still so much travelling to be done tomorrow.'

I was only too thrilled with the suggestion. The strain of making polite conversation over dinner would have just been too much.

'Of course,' I replied. 'That is the most sensible thing to do.'

Beatrice was giddy when we got to the room and kept going to the window and cupping her hands around her face in an effort to see the sea.

'Shall I see it in the morning?' she asked.

'Oh yes, lots of it,' I laughed. 'You will be *on* it, in a big ship.'

I opened the window a crack so she could hear the distant rumble.

Tilting her head to the side like an inquisitive bird, she listened. 'What is that?' she asked.

'The waves on the shore.'

'Shall I see those too?'

I nodded, closing the window again. She jigged around the room.

A knock announced the arrival of our supper, halfway through which, to my relief, Beatrice began to yawn. Twenty minutes later the telling of a short story was enough to have her falling asleep.

I took my time getting myself ready for bed. Leaning my forehead against the window, I imagined the sea out there which would carry me away from England and from Edward. My hand touched the ring, hidden beneath my nightgown, and I blew him a kiss, to travel through the darkness, back to Mirrow.

After getting into bed, I lay staring at the ceiling, willing the rhythm of the waves to put me to sleep, but it was late into the night before the ache of loneliness allowed me to eventually slip into oblivion.

Chapter 35

London 2010

The first Sunday in September arrived, and Juliet was up early to get the underground to Heathrow for her flight to Dublin. Her large suitcase had been packed since the night before. For once she wasn't travelling light. Since Carissima hadn't been lived in for ten years, she was anticipating that it might be a bit damp or cold, or both, so she had packed plenty of warm clothes.

Even though they had seen a lot of each other over the summer, it was three weeks since Logan's last visit. She couldn't wait to see him at Dublin airport. She got on a tube at eight, and even at that time it was very full of people and luggage. Arriving at Heathrow half an hour later, she made her way up to the terminal building and checked in her bag. Her flight was leaving at nine fifty, which gave her time for a browse through the duty free. While buying a bottle of Scottish whisky for Logan, she realised that she had no idea whether he drank whiskey or not. In case he didn't, she also bought a gift box containing a red and a white wine.

Her flight was called ten minutes after she got to the gate and they boarded on time. Juliet picked a window seat. She hadn't done her yoga that morning and, feeling both anxious and excited, she put in her earphones and chose a guided meditation on her iPod. Afterwards, she pulled a book out of her bag and tried to concentrate on the plot.

The hour-and-twenty-minute flight passed quickly. When the captain announced that they would shortly be arriving in Dublin Airport, she glanced out the window. It was a clear morning, and the sea below soon gave way to green fields and mountains. Juliet's lips curved in a smile. It was beautiful and she couldn't wait to see Logan.

Twenty minutes later she was tapping her foot impatiently, watching for her suitcase to appear on the carousel. Spotting it eventually, she hauled it off and silently thanked the inventor of luggage with wheels. Pulling her phone from her pocket with her free hand, she switched it on and made for the '*Arrivals, Nothing to Declare*' sign. Instantly a text message came through from Logan. Juliet's smile faded as she read it. **'So so sorry. Problem with boiler. Awaiting plumber. Don't want ur 1st wkend 2 b without hot water!! Ordered u a taxi. Driver outside with your name. C u soon. L xxx'**

'Damp, cold and no hot water either. Great! I hope the plumber comes, Logan Pershaw, or I'll take your mother's advice and persuade you to go back to Cambridge.'

Juliet only realised she was muttering aloud when she saw a child looking back over her shoulder at her.

Giving herself a shake, she texted back, **'No problem. Jx'**, before scanning the waiting crowd for her taxi driver.

She spotted the cardboard sign with her name on it, held by a burly but friendly-looking, man. Juliet walked up to him and identified herself.

'Welcome, love. I'll take that for you,' he said in a strong accent, reaching for her suitcase. 'We'll have you over to Monaghan in two shakes of a lamb's tail.'

He stopped walking abruptly and Juliet was forced to stop too.

'Actually, it will take us over an hour and a half. Would you like to get yourself a coffee and sandwich? I'm sure you had an early start in London.'

Juliet was surprised at his thoughtfulness. 'Yes, actually, I could do with a coffee. Can I get you one?' she asked as he led her to a coffee bar nearby.

'No thanks, love, you're grand. You just sort yourself there.'

A few minutes later, armed with a latte, Juliet followed him out to the taxi. He put her bag in the boot and held the back door open for her. She hesitated.

'Do you mind if I sit in the front? It's my first time here and I don't want to miss any of the scenery.'

'No problem at all.'

As soon as they set off, John (Juliet read his name on the ID that was hanging from the dashboard) radioed in that he had picked up his fare and they were on their way.

'Have you been to Ireland at all before?'

'No, it's my first time.'

'We're north of Dublin City here and we'll be on the motorway now in just a minute. We turn off it before Monaghan town and head across country. You have a lovely morning for it anyway.'

They were soon driving through some lovely countryside, which looked lush in the September sunshine. Juliet had known many taxi drivers who talked non-stop, but luckily John was not one of them. He allowed her to enjoy the view and answered the odd question she asked.

Juliet could see what Logan had meant when he had described the rolling hills. There was a gentleness to the landscape, as they travelled further northwest, which Juliet found quite attractive. After an hour or so the roads got narrower and they passed through several small towns and villages.

'Nearly there now,' John said.

Juliet's heart beat a little faster. She glanced at her watch. It was nearly one o'clock, five hours since she'd left the apartment. Not bad. But it would eat into a weekend trip. She'd have to take a Friday off too, to make the most of it. When she realised she was already planning the next visit she was amused. I might just like it here after all, if the scenery is anything to go by, she thought.

John got her attention with the words, 'Here we are.'

Ahead she saw two imposing white pillars and an open gate. John drove between them and up a drive that curved around to the right then left for about half a kilometre.

They came out from between a row of trees and there was the house up on their right.

'Oh,' Juliet uttered, 'it's gorgeous.'

The sun flashed off its stone facade, making it look bright and cheerful. The gravel crunched as John pulled the taxi up at the bottom of three steps.

'It's a fine house, all right,' he said, opening his door and going around for her luggage.

Juliet got out, rooting in her bag for her purse, dreading to think how much the long journey would cost.

'That's all right,' John said, taking her suitcase up and putting it on the top step. 'It's already paid for. I hope you enjoy your stay.'

'Thanks, I will,' she said, doing a quick calculation from sterling to euro so that she was sure she was giving him a decent tip.

'Ah, thanks, love,' he said, getting back into the car.

As Juliet put her purse back in her bag, the sound of the taxi died away, leaving her in complete silence.

She gasped when she looked up and saw the beauty of the scene before her. A huge lawn sloped away to a line of trees, beyond which was a lake reflecting the hill beyond. A giant redwood tree dominated one corner of the lawn and the first hint of autumn was beginning to show in the leaves of a group of oaks down to her right. The sun was warm on her face and she took in a few deep breaths of the clear air before turning to look up at the house again.

Juliet's first thought was that Logan was right about the photograph in Florence not doing the house justice. Her second thought was that it was beautiful. The windows of its three storeys glinted in the sun. The top row was comprised of small attic windows, the second floor had bigger windows, while on the ground floor there were four large bay windows, two on either side of a strong, red timber door, complete with brass knocker and bell. All the window frames were of white wood and appeared to be sash in style. Boldly carved into a piece of granite beside the door was the word 'Carissima'.

Juliet went up the steps and rang the bell.

Chapter 36

Wales 1889

The low moaning of a foghorn was the first thing I heard upon waking. It sounded as lonely as I felt and I wondered if this meant our sailing would be delayed. But by the time we had all breakfasted in the dining room, the fog had been blown away by a stiff sea breeze. Although the sky remained clear, the breeze strengthened and whipped the surface of the water up into thousands of small white waves.

Beatrice 'oohed' and 'aahed' as we approached the dock. 'Is that our ship?' she asked, pointing at the berthed paddle steamer.

'That's her,' replied her father. 'The *Olga*.'

'She has a name? Like my dolls?'

James laughed. 'That's right. Every ship has a name.'

We climbed the gangplank to the deck. Helena gave a nervous glance out across the sea.

'James, I do hope we will not have too rough a crossing. Thank goodness you booked us a cabin, dear, even though the journey is short. I think I will go and lie down.'

'There is no need to worry, dearest,' he said. 'This is not a bad sea at all. I have seen a lot worse! It would be best if you stayed on deck for a while.'

She paled, and avoided looking out over the vast expanse of water. 'Thank you, but I would rather go to the cabin and take Beatrice with me.'

'Very well, my dear, I will take you both down immediately.'

As she took his arm, I made to follow, but she turned and said, 'Martha, if you are happy to stay, then do so. We will be fine.'

I was glad to remain on deck. Despite the fact that it would carry me away from Edward, I loved the smell and the sound of sea. Turning my face to the wind, I breathed in great lungfuls of salty air, as though to fill the massive void inside me. I moved to the stern and watched the land slip away.

Unfortunately, twenty minutes after we set sail I was summoned below deck to tend to Helena and Beatrice who had swiftly succumbed to seasickness. And there I stayed for the remainder of the journey, trying to make them as comfortable as possible, with Mrs. Dawson's assistance.

Three hours later I was on deck again looking for a steward when I caught a glimpse of land up ahead. It was what I considered to be my temporary country of exile. I went to the rail and watched for a few minutes. A feeling of inevitability pressed down on my shoulders like a dull, heavy blanket as the sliver of land grew bigger and bigger.

Out of the corner of my eye I saw an approaching steward and with a start remembered my errand.

When it was time to dock, Helena and Beatrice still looked pale. I helped them on with their coats and James came to escort us up onto the deck.

'Look, my dearest, there is Kingstown.' James drew Helena's hand through his arm where we stood by the railing, looking at the harbour ahead. 'And that pretty headland over there is Howth. Welcome to Ireland. Or should I say "Welcome home!"'

She smiled at him, only too glad to be near solid ground again.

I sighed in resignation as I gazed around at the bustling harbour, full of craft of various sizes.

Helena must have heard my sigh for she turned to me and squeezed my hand.

'Thank you for coming with us, Martha. You are a great comfort to me. This is all very new and strange for all of us. It means a lot to have you here.'

I did not know how to respond. I was a little embarrassed by her gratitude in the light of my desire to return immediately to Mirrow. My mixed emotions of loyalty and despair warred with each other. I gave her a genuine smile of affection, for I loved her dearly. Indeed I would not have made the sacrifice I was making for anyone else.

Once again James took charge and shepherded us down the gangplank and on to the train for a short journey to Amien Street Station, where we were to board another train. We had two hours before departure, so James took us for a late lunch in a nearby hotel. We were served by waitresses with soft Irish accents, in black dresses and pristine white aprons. The meal brought the colour back into Helena's and Beatrice's cheeks.

An hour later we returned to the station.

'I do not want to get on another train. I want to see my new room now!' Beatrice whined, tugging on my hand as she dragged her feet.

'You will see your new room when we get to Carissima,' I promised, the name strange on my lips, 'but you have to get on this train to get there.' I refrained from telling her that I had learnt from her father over lunch that we also had to change trains in a place called Portadown. Feeling sorry for her, I swung the tired child up into my arms for the remainder of the walk along the platform. The journey seemed endlessly long to me too. Edward already seemed very, very far away, and yet we had even further to go.

'I will write to Mother Pershaw first thing tomorrow,' Helena announced once we were in the carriage, 'and tell her all about our journey.'

Obviously the distance that now stood between her and her mother-in-law was improving Helena's disposition towards her.

The thought of letter-writing cheered me somewhat, and I began to compose a letter to Edward in my head, describing in detail all that I was seeing. The thought made me feel close to him. He had promised to write to me often and I was already looking forward to receiving his first letter.

As it happened, Beatrice was asleep when we arrived in Portadown and was unaware of the fact that her father carried her from one train to the other in the tiny station. Mr. Hawkins oversaw the transfer of our luggage.

The rest of our party were also travel weary by the time we alighted in Monaghan and there was very little conversation as we took the seven-mile journey, again in two carriages, to the estate. By then it was dark and I could not see anything of the country we were passing through. This added to my sense of displacement, and made me ache for Edward. I missed him so much I had to press my fist hard against my abdomen to try to ease the pain of it.

'We have arrived!' James' excited voice startled me.

We passed between two large pillars and travelled about half a mile up a curved driveway before the carriage came to a stop.

James jumped out and first lifted Beatrice down before holding his hand out to Helena. The three of them gazed up at their new home. I got out slowly and stood beside them. Helena clapped her hands in delight.

'James, it is beautiful!'

Its stone facade rose up before us, all its windows lit from inside in welcome. Three storeys high, it had large windows to the left and right of the front door. In the shadows I could make out a stone bench beneath one window.

'Can I see my room now?' Beatrice asked sleepily, following her request with a huge yawn.

'Of course you can, darling,' Helena answered with a carefree laugh.

The front door was pulled open at that moment and a maid curtsied. 'Good evening. I'm Brigid,' she said in a soft, shy voice, her Irish accent strange on the night air.

The others moved forward and up the three front steps in a babble of greetings. As James drew Helena and Beatrice across the threshold I heard him say proudly, 'Welcome to Carissima!'

Still standing at the bottom of the steps, I felt totally alone. Tears slipped down my cheeks.

Glancing over my shoulder into the night, I whispered. 'I will come home to you, Edward, my love. I promise.'

Chapter 37

Carissima, County Monaghan, Ireland 2010

When no one came to the door, Juliet turned the old-fashioned doorknob and, finding the door unlocked, she pushed it open. She walked in, rolling her suitcase behind her.

Looking around, she gave a delighted laugh. There was nothing dreary about this place at all. The hall she was in was a large square, with white tiles on the floor. There was a door to her left and one to her right, both closed. The sun streamed in above her head through a half-moon-shaped window and through panes on either side of the door. A well-polished wooden staircase rose up at the back of the hall along the left-hand side, before turning right and flattening out onto a landing.

Above her, a crystal chandelier glistened in the sun, and a mahogany table stood against another wall. A huge antique vase with an exotic yellow bird painted on it stood on the floor beside it.

Just then a sound came from behind a door at the back of the hall, under the stairs. It burst open, and Logan strode through, wearing a pair of faded denim jeans and a navy sweatshirt on his broad frame. He was drying his hands on a towel which he tossed onto the banister.

'Juliet! You made it. Welcome to Carissima! I'm so sorry I couldn't pick you up myself.'

He put his arms around her and kissed her soundly.

Juliet beamed up at him. 'It's good to see you,' she said. She was surprised to see dark circles under his eyes but was too happy to comment on it for the moment.

She hugged him, sinking into his familiar warmth and scent.

'I'm glad you're here at last,' he said.

'The house is beautiful!' she exclaimed, pulling away and looking around. 'I don't know why, but I was expecting something dreary and not very lived in.'

'Didn't I mention that it had been rented out a few times since my father died, to different families? But they never stayed very long. I stopped renting it about a year and a half ago, but kept on a housekeeper who comes in every week, cleans it and keeps it aired. The farm manager kept it heated sufficiently in the winter months.'

'I'm dying to see the rest of it.'

'Soon. First I'm going to feed you. Are you hungry?' he said, putting an arm around her waist and taking her through the door under the stairs.

'Starving.'

They were now in another hallway that ran left to right behind the entrance hall.

'Hey, who's this guy with the moustache?' Juliet asked as she paused in front of a portrait of a tall, lean man in tweeds, with a shotgun across his arm.

'That's my great-grandfather, James Pershaw. He built this place.'

Juliet studied the picture. 'Oh, the man in the photograph in Florence,' she said then looked at Logan. 'From what I remember of that photograph, it's a good likeness. But I can't say I see any family resemblance to you.'

'I probably take after my mother's side.' Logan went ahead of her, turned left at the end of the hall, went down two stone steps and held the door open into the kitchen.

'Wow, this is enormous!' Juliet said, swivelling her head this way and that to take in the cavernous kitchen and all its trappings. 'Oh this is impressive!' She walked the length of the scrubbed wooden table. 'You must be able to seat a dozen people at this.' She nodded towards a modern Aga. 'Aw, no big black cauldron over an open fire, to match these old flagstones! I'm disappointed.'

Logan grinned at her before lifting the lid of a saucepan and giving it a stir. 'I'm afraid it's just a tin of soup. The plumber only left about twenty minutes ago so it's all I had time to throw together. But there is some nice homemade soda bread to go with it, which Sheila left in this morning. Sheila is the housekeeper I told you about.'

'Can I help?' Juliet asked.

'Sure. You'll find butter there in the fridge.'

The table was already set for two at a right angle to each other at the end of the table.

Logan brought two steaming bowls over. 'Sit down, please. I hope you like tomato.'

She nodded.

After cutting some bread, he leaned across and kissed her cheek.

'It's great to see you here. Thanks for coming, Juliet.'

'I'm glad to be here. Thanks for organising the taxi. I couldn't believe the house when we came up the driveway. As I said, I was expecting something more austere and cold. But it has a wonderful country charm and elegance to it.'

'Every place looks well in the sun of course.'

'True. But it really is beautiful, Logan. I can understand why you didn't want to sell it.'

'Even if it's in the middle of nowhere?' he teased gently.

'Yeah – it certainly is quite a trip from Dublin. It would have been a four-hour-round trip for you, if you had collected me.' The thought made her frown.

Logan shrugged. 'I enjoy driving.'

'So, are you going to turn me into an apple-growing farmer in a week?'

'There's a challenge.' He winked at her. 'I might just manage it.'

She smiled, watching him eating, relieved to see that some of the tension had eased from his face.

'How has work been?' he asked.

Juliet filled him in and they chatted for a while, lingering over a cup of tea and a slice of cake when the soup was finished.

'You have circles under your eyes, Logan. Are you okay?'

'I'm fine, just finding it a bit hard to sleep lately. Too much going on in my head, I suppose.'

Juliet continued to study him.

'Stop frowning at me,' Logan said, putting a fingertip to her creased forehead. 'Shall I show you around the house now?'

'I thought you'd never ask,' she replied, gathering up the dishes.

'Let's leave all that, we can put it in the dishwasher later. There's a pantry through there,' he pointed to a door at the back of the kitchen, 'and an exit to the yard. I'll show you that later.'

They left the kitchen by the door they had originally come in.

'Off this back hall is my office.' He opened a door into a large study which had a leather inlaid desk, a computer, cupboards, a couple of filing cabinets and overloaded shelves. 'Not the tidiest, I know, but I haven't got around to sorting all my stuff and the existing stuff yet.' He waved a hand at the shelves.

They moved on down the hall.

'There's a toilet in there.' He pointed at another door, before leading her past it.

'Broom cupboard . . .' He indicated another door. 'Dining room . . .' He opened another door to a long room with a large mahogany table and chairs down its centre.

'It's a beautiful room,' Juliet said, noting the fine silk wallpaper and the decorative coving.

'Hasn't been used for years,' Logan commented before moving them to the last door in the corridor. 'This is the drawing room and the room we used most. Though it looks dark now, those windows face west and it's lovely in here in the evenings.'

The walls were covered in wood panelling, with a marble fireplace opposite the windows. There was a leather couch, several armchairs, and a flat-screen television on a low table.

Juliet raised an eyebrow at it.

'A man has to have some modern conveniences,' Logan said with a grin.

'It's cosy, and obviously where you spend your evenings,' Juliet commented, watching him tidy up a newspaper and three books on fruit trees from the end of the couch, then pick a mug up off the floor and put it on the mantelpiece.

They went back into the entrance hall.

'This is the morning room,' he said, opening the door to the right of the front door.

'Oh Logan!' Juliet spoke softly, almost reverently.

Sun streamed in the bay windows at the front, lighting an airy room with a high ceiling. There was a large black marble fireplace, in front of which stood a long couch upholstered in cream, with cream and beige scatter cushions. The floor was polished wood with rugs placed here and there. Behind the couch was a round table, with an arrangement of lilies in its centre. Beyond the table, the wall was curved and inset with another bay window, with a cushioned window seat running its length. A baby grand piano sat in the far corner.

Juliet moved slowly around the room, totally amazed and thrilled with what she was seeing.

Logan spoke. 'I know it's not modern like your apartment, but do you like it?'

'It's beautiful.' She turned to face him where he stood hovering near the door. 'When you said your mother liked the antique furniture here, I was expecting dark, overcrowded rooms, with a mixture of spindly chairs that you couldn't possibly put your weight on or heavy furniture that you would need a bulldozer to move.' She laughed, not without a touch of relief. 'I love it.'

Grinning, he walked over to her and took her in his arms, hugging her close.

'Thank God.'

They kissed.

'Come on, show me the rest.'

Across the hall Logan opened the other door. 'The library,' he announced.

Juliet followed him in and gasped. She was standing in a room of similar size to the morning room, but this one had two walls that were covered from floor to ceiling in glass cabinets, each full of books of all shapes, sizes and ages. Dust motes floated down through the sunlight from the front windows. While the drawing room had a lived-in feeling, this room had an undisturbed air to it, as if no one had used it for a long time. It sat hushed as if waiting for someone to come and read there again.

'You can forget the farming. This is where you'll find me for the week,' Juliet laughed, pointing to an old stuffed leather armchair, positioned to the left of the fireplace.

'Well, there are books here from the 1880's onwards – you should find something you like. I'll have to put some order on them some day, catalogue them, maybe.'

Juliet moved along the cabinets and paused in front of one. '*Beano* and *Dandy* comics? I'm pretty sure they didn't belong to your ancestors.'

'Memories of my misspent youth, I'm afraid.' Logan came to look over her shoulder.

'I nearly did a degree in English, you know.' Juliet continued her perusal. 'I did very well in it in my A levels and did the first year at university, but that summer I was introduced to photography by my then boyfriend, got bitten by the bug. It became my passion and, after a few heated discussions with my parents, changed courses. And the rest, as they say, is history.'

'Aren't you full of surprises?' Logan came and kissed the back of her neck.

Juliet leaned into him for a moment but then her eyes fell on the view from the windows and she moved over for a better look.

'The lake is beautiful. Your great-grandfather certainly understood the premise 'location, location, location'!'

'Do you want to see your room?' Logan asked, leading her back out into the hall, then rolling her suitcase towards the stairs.

Juliet followed him. '*My* room? I thought we'd, eh, be sharing,' she said, feeling a little awkward and a lot surprised.

Logan lifted the suitcase and headed up. 'I'm so restless these nights, it wouldn't be fair on you. You wouldn't get much sleep.'

'That's crazy,' she objected, as he led her through an arch and onto a corridor which ran, she guessed, above the back hall downstairs. Their footsteps were muffled by crimson carpet as Logan took her to the first door on the right. Before he could open it, she caught his hand, looking up at him, puzzled.

'We only have a week before I have to go back to London.'

'It's for the best, Juliet,' he said, taking her face between his two hands and kissing her gently.

'Surely it's not that bad?'

'Of course it's not,' he tried to reassure her, 'but I don't want to disturb your sleep with my restlessness.'

'Naturally you'll ravage me first every night before going to your own room, leaving me all loved-up and starry-eyed?'

A gleam came into his eyes and he kissed her tenderly. 'Of course. Now, your room!' he said, throwing open the door.

'My whole apartment could fit into this,' she said.

Like the morning room, this room too was essentially cream, but this had a more modern feel, with thick carpet, matching cream curtains, duvet cover and pillow cases. A cream armchair sat angled towards the window with its view of the lake. Built-in wardrobes covered one wall and up two steps in the corner was a fully tiled en suite with power shower.

'Mum insisted on some modern plumbing.' Logan said, watching her explore.

'It's like a five-star hotel!' she exclaimed, coming back out of the en suite. 'I feel very spoiled. However, beautiful and all as this is, I'm determined to teach you some relaxation techniques, so that I can sleep in your bed before the week is out.'

Logan opened his arms and she walked into them, feeling extremely puzzled and trying not to be too worried about him.

'That's enough of indoors for now,' he said then. 'Let's take a trip around the farm, unless you'd like to unpack and settle in.'

'No, I'd love some air and to stretch my legs a bit after the journey,' she said, going to her suitcase and taking out a fleece.

She made a snap decision to tell him how much she liked the place and how nervous she had been that she wouldn't. She turned to him.

'I didn't want to come to Ireland,' she started, but the moment she spoke those words the air seem to shift around her. She became lightheaded with a sensation she had never felt before, and the words she had just said echoed in her head.

I didn't want to come to Ireland.

'Juliet?' Logan put his hands on her shoulders, his voice full of concern. 'You've gone pale. Are you okay? Here, sit down.'

He guided her to the bed.

She sat, puzzled at the lingering sensation. As she shook her head, it slowly cleared.

'That was weird. I felt a bit faint or something for a second.'

'Your colour is coming back now though. You scared me. Maybe you're tired – early start, travelling, all that.'

'I'm a seasoned traveller, Logan,' she said dryly. 'It doesn't knock a feather out of me.' She stood up. 'I'm perfect again. It was probably an allergic reaction to your tomato soup,' she joked, trying to brush it off, even though it had been a most peculiar sensation. 'It's fresh air I need. Here, this is for you . . .' She was happy to take the spotlight off herself by passing him the duty free bag she'd carried upstairs. 'Do you drink whiskey?'

'As an occasional treat, yes.' He whistled at the label. 'Mmm, very nice. You shouldn't have. And wine too, thanks.' He kissed her, still watching her carefully. 'We'll enjoy that together later. Now for that air!'

Chapter 38

Out in a yard, which was surrounded by outbuildings, Logan suggested they take the jeep to tour the farm first because of Juliet's earlier light-headedness.

'I'll show you the farm and the orchard, then if you like we can take a walk by the lake.'

Feeling fine again, Juliet belted herself in. Logan drove up a laneway that led away from the back of the house, past yards and barns. He pulled up after only a minute and pointed to a long meadow that stretched ahead of them, first on flat ground and then up the side of a gentle hill.

'That's where I intend to start the new orchard.'

'It's a lovely spot. It has sun most of the day, I'd say,' Juliet said, looking around.

'Yes, it's perfect. I've had the soil analysed too and it's very suitable.'

They drove on.

The farm covered a lot of land. Logan explained that they

kept cattle for beef and grew a lot of crops – feed for the animals and grain for industry.

'There's a farm manager, Michael Cummins,' he said, 'and two farmhands, Peter and Des. The place is run well and profits are good. I leave Cummins to it. He knows what he's doing. His father was manager too, and his father before him. I think they are here almost as long as the Pershaws. See that house down there?' They were parked on a little hill near the far perimeter of Pershaw land and Logan pointed to a small gate lodge at the end of the lane. 'Cummins lives there. You'll meet him in due course. He's a serious kind of chap, but a hard worker.'

'It looks a bit small for a family. Is he married?'

'No, no wife and kids. Too surly and set in his own ways, I'd say.'

'How old is he?'

'Mid-fifties.'

Turning the jeep, Logan took a different route back, stopping beside a field to the left of the house, which had three horses grazing in it.

'Are they yours?' Juliet said, the delight obvious in her voice. Turning in her seat she looked at Logan. 'I know you ride – you told me when I was in Montana. Do you ride these?'

He nodded. 'Yeah, Lucy there, the chestnut. But they're not mine. They're owned by a local man, Seán Hayes. He used to rent the field and stables, but now I let him use them for free, and he lets me ride when I want to.'

'I'm impressed.'

'I think the grey would be right for you, if you want to ride this week. I'm sure Seán won't have a problem with that. I'll give him a ring later. Although he and his son Joe are down here a lot, I don't see much of them. They come and go to the stables via the back lane and rarely come down to the yard or the house.'

Arriving back in the yard, they got out and went around the side of the house. Another courtyard opened up in front of them, with an old glasshouse along one end, facing south. Leaving the courtyard, through an arch, they took a path along by a high wall.

'Is this a walled garden?' Juliet asked, thrilled at the prospect. 'How romantic is that?'

'Sorry, it's the orchard, but it's completely walled in. We get in through this gate up here.'

He opened a very old iron gate, which Juliet expected to creak, but which in fact was well oiled, a sure sign of where Logan's interest really lay.

Juliet felt like she had stepped into the pages of *The Secret Garden*, one of her favourite childhood books. The huge orchard was completely enclosed by the high stone walls. Row after row of trees stretched out in front of them and a path branched off in both directions, running inside the walls. The paths weren't well used and weeds grew in patches. It was sunny and bright, with a few late bees buzzing around, yet Juliet felt cold and gave a little shiver.

'There's actually quite a crop this year,' Logan said, 'which I'm really pleased about. I thought they would have suffered from neglect, but I think we'll manage a very nice harvest.'

Taking his hand in hers, she gave it an encouraging squeeze.

'Your hand is cold,' he said. 'Let's go for that walk to warm you up. I'll save my lecture on apples for another time.' He laughed at himself. 'You know I'm consumed by it at the moment so you'll have to tell me if I'm going on too much about it.'

Juliet put her arm through his as he closed the gate behind them. 'Don't worry, I will.' Her tone was lightly teasing.

She was glad of the heat of the sun on her face as they came around to the front of the house. Turning onto a gravelled path which ran down the left-hand side of the lawn, they walked down to the lake. The air was full of birdsong. Juliet was able to distinguish the song of the blackbird.

Going through a gap in the fence, they crossed a small gravelled beach to the water's edge. The lake spread out in front of them, glistening and bright at their side and dark across the way in the shadow of the wooded hill. Off to their right was a boathouse, its front end reaching out above the water.

'Boats too?' Juliet asked. 'Is there no end to the discoveries here?'

'Two rowing boats. We'll take a turn about the lake some day, m'lady!'

The path continued off to their left. Logan put his arm around her waist and they walked along with the water lapping gently on one side and a wooded area of deciduous trees rising up on their other side, leaves rustling in a very gentle breeze.

'It's so tranquil here,' Juliet murmured.

'We're having an unusual run of nice weather. It'll be stunning in another couple of weeks when all the leaves change colour.'

'Logan, your mother didn't sound Irish. She wasn't from around here, was she?'

'No, she grew up in England. My father got restless with farming in his mid-twenties, did a marketing course and moved to England. He got a job there and met Mum. Remember I told you she lectured in botany? They got married, were very much in love, had me, and when I was five Dad decided he wanted to be a farmer after all. Mum had given up work anyway when I was born, so was very glad to give it a go. So we came back here.'

'I had assumed you were born here.'

'No.'

'Did your mother like it here?'

'Yes, she loved it. She was from the country herself, the Cotswolds. She got on great with everyone here.'

'So what happened? Why did they split up?'

'It was complicated. But all's well that ends well. A couple of years after the divorce when Mum and I were back in England, she met a very nice guy. I liked him, we got on okay. It nearly broke Mum's heart when he passed away four years ago.'

Juliet was quiet. Logan had successfully avoided the subject of the breakup once again, and it puzzled her. Maybe it was still painful for him. She didn't pursue the subject.

The conversation became more light-hearted after that, with Juliet telling him about a comedy she and Rose had been to see at the cinema during the week, and a general discussion about films ensued.

'I brought over my collection of DVDs, so we can watch a movie tonight if you like,' Logan offered.

'I like a good thriller. Do you have any of them?'

'I think so. It's a fairly eclectic mix.'

And that's exactly how they spent the evening, curled up together on the couch in front of the TV, their empty dinner plates and wineglasses on the floor by the fire. Even though it was a mild evening, Logan had lit it anyway, more for effect than heat.

When the movie ended, Logan zapped the TV off with the remote, tightened his arm possessively around Juliet and kissed the top of her head

'It's good to have you here, Juliet,' he said.

She linked her fingers with his, unfurled her legs, and, standing up, pulled him up too.

'Time for bed,' she said softly and led him up to her room.

Later she was so languid and tired that she fell asleep quickly, not even stirring when Logan slipped from under the duvet to return to his own room.

Later that night, Juliet dreamed that someone kissed her on the forehead, whispered goodnight and tucked her in. She slept undisturbed for the whole night.

Chapter 39

'Did you sleep okay?' Logan asked at breakfast the next morning – a little too casually, Juliet thought.

'Great, thanks.'

'I left a small lamp on in your room, just in case you woke during the night. It's pitch dark here compared to your apartment in London with the street lights outside it.'

Juliet didn't think there had been a light on when she was getting up, but it was a bright morning and she hadn't noticed it. She made a mental note to go up after breakfast and switch it off.

'I was thinking,' she said, buttering a slice of toast. 'How would you feel if I was to make a start on cataloguing the books in the library for you? I don't expect you to abandon your work for the week to entertain me, and I'd enjoy it.'

Logan looked speculatively at her. 'Are you sure? That doesn't sound like much fun for you and I'd feel like a bad host.'

She put her hand over his, trying not to focus on the dark circles that were back under his eyes this morning. She'd been disappointed when she'd woken up to find him gone, but she wasn't going to raise the subject again, especially as he seemed a bit preoccupied.

'If truth be told, I'm itching to get my hands on those old books. Besides, you said you were under time pressure to study as much as you could before preparing the ground for the new orchard. This way I wouldn't feel that I was keeping you from that.'

He thought for a moment. 'Okay, if you're sure, then how about we both work in the mornings and then spend the rest of each day together?'

'Perfect. I'd like to take some photographs too.'

To her relief he smiled and leaned over to give her a lingering kiss.

Just as they pulled apart, they heard the door to the yard open and close. A moment later a small, wiry, black-haired woman in her late forties came into the kitchen, carrying two shopping bags.

'Sheila, good morning,' Logan said, standing up. 'This is Juliet Holmes. Juliet, Sheila, my housekeeper.'

The woman put the bags on the counter and came forward with a warm smile, saying good morning in a thick Monaghan accent, making Juliet realise how mild Logan's accent was in comparison. Not surprising, she thought, since he had spent more time in England than he had in Ireland.

'It's lovely to meet you,' Sheila was saying. 'I hope you had a good trip over?'

'Yes, thank you.'

'Is your room all right for you?'

'Yes, it's lovely, thanks.'

Sheila threw a fleeting glance at Logan.

No doubt wondering too why I have a separate room, but knowing it isn't her place to question him, Juliet thought.

'Well, if you need anything, you've only to ask. Leave those dishes now. I'll sort them out.'

'Thanks, Sheila,' Logan said. 'You spoil me rotten.'

'Not too rotten,' she said. 'There are a few bags of groceries out in my car if you'd like to bring them in for me.'

'Sure,' he said and disappeared out the back.

'Where are you from yourself?' Sheila asked, starting to unpack the bags.

'London.'

'Oh, I was there for a weekend with my sister last year. We went to see *Les Misérables*. It was fantastic.'

As Juliet was replying, Logan came back in carrying two bags in each hand.

'I hope to see *Phantom of the Opera* next time,' Sheila said.

Juliet was just opening her mouth to respond when Logan cut in.

'We both have work to do, so if you'll excuse us, Sheila,' he said.

Both women's eyes widened at the abruptness as Logan took Juliet's elbow and turned her towards the door.

'Eh, nice to meet you, Sheila. I'll see you later,' Juliet said over her shoulder, a bit embarrassed at Logan's rudeness.

Sheila smiled faintly but said nothing.

'That wasn't necessary, surely,' Juliet said when they stopped outside his office.

'What?' Logan looked at her blankly.

'You were a bit rude, stopping us from chatting like that.'

'Did I? Sorry, I'm a bit distracted, that's all.' He ran a hand through his hair. 'I apologise and I'll apologise to Sheila later. I have to make a phone call now.' He looked over at his desk.

'Do you have a notebook I can use in the library?' Juliet asked.

'What? Sure. Actually, take my laptop. I've got the computer in here.'

'Okay, but a notebook would be handy too.'

'In the filing cabinet there.'

Juliet pulled open the first drawer, only to find it full of files.

'No, the other one,' Logan snapped impatiently, indicating the second filing cabinet.

Juliet frowned at his tone and was about to make a remark about getting out of the wrong side of the bed but thought better of it, knowing that he must have slept badly again.

Finding a new A4 refill pad she rolled the drawer shut.

'Okay, I'll see you later then,' she said.

He just nodded, already reading something on his screen.

She'd only taken a few steps down the hall when he called her back. Smiling, she came back to the door, expecting an apology, but she was disappointed.

'The password for the laptop is *photosynthesis*,' he said.

She rolled her eyes.

Logan shrugged his shoulders. 'I'm a plant scientist – what can I say?' His face lightened and he smiled at her.

Some of her unease lifted. She moved away, only to hear him call out again.

She came back.

'You're a beautiful woman, Juliet. Do you know that?' he said seriously.

'Get to work,' she said, but she blew him a kiss, feeling a warm glow at his words.

In the library she put the laptop and notebook on the surface of the mahogany table that stood in the middle of the room. Suddenly remembering the lamp in her bedroom, she dashed upstairs to switch it off, but both the lamp beside her bed and the one on a table in the corner were switched off. Shrugging, she went to brush her teeth.

Returning to the library, she looked around the shelves and wondered if she had been wise to make the offer to do the cataloguing – there were so many books. Well, she could make a start anyway and work on it again maybe on her next visit. Although she knew it was going to be hard to leave Logan at the end of the week, she was also excited about her next assignment, which would take her to a seal sanctuary in Scotland.

Deciding to be systematic about the job in hand, she walked over to the first cabinet and opened its doors. Wood creaked against wood. The top shelf was too high for her to reach. Moving a set of wooden steps from the corner under the window she positioned them in front of the open cabinet and climbed up.

A row of identical volumes, all encyclopaedias, marked Vol. I through to Vol. X lined the shelf. They were thick and heavy and Juliet nearly lost her balance pulling out the first one. Climbing down, she placed it on the table. The musty scent of old leather filled her nostrils, a smell she considered to be quite pleasant. The cover creaked open and she searched for the signature of the owner, but to no avail. She made a note of the date of its publication – 1843 – and its title and returned it to the shelf. She repeated the exercise with the other nine.

The shelf below had a range of atlases and books of maps on it. Again she noted down their details. Next to them a large book was bound in faded red leather and contained sheaves of maps of the Far East. James Pershaw's signature and the date April 1881 were inscribed inside the cover, in a long sweeping hand of beautiful penmanship.

Juliet touched the writing with a fingertip, surprised at the thrill she felt at seeing the handwriting of the man in the portrait in the hall – written in the eighteen hundreds. Turning the pages carefully, she found that he had noted other dates on some of the maps. On one of India he had written the words '*magnificent silks*' and an arrow pointing to a town whose name she couldn't pronounce. She put back the book, and added two columns in her notebook, one headed *Signature* and the other *Handwritten Notes*. She put a tick in each. Working on for a couple of hours, she found nothing else as exciting as James' maps. Tedium made her take a break.

For a change, and to rest her arms, she switched on the computer, inputted the data she had already assembled, and made a note to print some labels for each shelf for cross-referencing purposes.

Before leaving the library to get a cup of coffee, she went back to close the glass doors. A small book on the bottom shelf caught her eye. Bound with a piece of ribbon, it had the title *Lyrical Ballads* and was by William Wordsworth. A thrill ran up Juliet's spine. Considering the age of the other books, she dared to hope that it might be an original. She ran her fingers lovingly over the cover. Wordsworth had always been a particular favourite of hers. Slowly opening the first page, her hope was confirmed. It was published in 1800 and had a preface by Wordsworth himself. A grin spread across her face. She looked inside the cover to check for the owner's name. What she found was a handwritten note:

To My Darling Martha,

As you read these poems, think of me as I will be thinking of you.

With all my love,

Edward

The words blurred for a second and she had to shake her head to clear it. Martha, Juliet thought. Now, why is that name familiar? In an instant she remembered the photograph in the apartment in Florence and the young woman who had stood a little apart from the others. She was sure Martha was the name Logan had said.

'So who were Martha and Edward?' she wondered aloud. A faint sound, like a sigh, made her look up from the words, thinking Logan was about to come into the room. But the door didn't open and all was quiet again.

She retied the ribbon and replaced the book. Thoughtfully she wandered to the window to lean on the sill and look out at the lake. It had looked lovely in the morning light earlier when she had got up and done yoga and meditation in front of the bedroom window. Now, with the sun higher, the light was different again.

She was wondering about getting her camera when a tall, thin, grey-haired man in a dark jacket appeared at the window. He stared in at Juliet. She instinctively pulled back with the unexpectedness of it, and from the open hostility in his look. He was gone as quickly as he had appeared.

Discomfited from the brief encounter, she left the library, feeling the need for a caffeine boost.

Chapter 40

On the way to the kitchen Juliet paused in front of James Pershaw's portrait.

'After being a merchant, how did you enjoy being a gentleman farmer?' she said, tilting her head, studying him. 'You're a bit severe-looking, aren't you?'

'Juliet, is that you?' Logan spoke from inside his office, down the hall.

She looked in the door. He was still in front of his computer, clicking the mouse.

'I'm going to make a coffee and sit outside in the sun for a while. Want to join me?' she asked, wondering if his mood had improved.

'Great suggestion. I'll be with you in a few minutes.'

To her relief he smiled at her.

Sheila wasn't in the kitchen, so Juliet rummaged around until she found a packet of ground coffee in the fridge and a cafetière on the counter. When it was ready she poured two mugs, one with milk for herself and a black one for Logan. Carrying them outside to a stone bench beneath the library window, she sat down with a sigh to enjoy the view.

'I thought I'd find this place too quiet after London, but the quiet is so soothing,' she commented when Logan came out to sit next to her.

Passing him his coffee, she saw him rubbing his eyes tiredly. She frowned but, before she could say anything, he asked how her morning was going.

'Great, but I should've spent time in a gym before coming up here. Those books are heavy!'

'Did you find the steps? Be careful on them,' he cautioned. 'Was it boring work?'

'No, quite the opposite actually. It's a bit like a treasure hunt. Yes, some boring stuff, but every now and then a gem!'

Logan's eyebrows shot up. 'Yeah? Like what?'

She told him about James' maps first.

'Yeah, they're great, aren't they?' Logan said.

'He must have travelled a lot.'

'Yes, and made a fortune apparently before investing some of it in this place and making it their home.'

'Did you know that you have an original William Wordsworth book of poetry in there?'

'No. I'd like to see that.'

'That's not all. There was an inscription on the cover from Edward to Martha. I presume she is the Martha from your mum's photograph. Do you know who Edward was?'

He shook his head. 'There was no Edward Pershaw as far as I know. Maybe they visited here, were friends of the family and left it behind or something.'

'Maybe.'

'Are you managing the computer okay?'

274

Juliet sent him a withering look. 'Yes, I can actually spell *photosynthesis*, you know. Though why anyone would use such a pretentious password is beyond me.'

Her teasing didn't illicit a smile, and Logan looked miles away, a frown on his face. Concern for him forced Juliet to speak.

'What's wrong with you, Logan? You're not in the best of form today and you're not looking well, so don't deny it.'

'It's nothing!' he snapped. 'Just drop it, will you? I told you I'm just not getting enough sleep.'

Juliet was shocked at his hostile tone.

He stood up. 'I'm going back in. I've calls to make.'

Without looking at her, he walked away.

'Logan, stop!'

He turned but didn't walk back.

They stared at each other for a moment.

Juliet threw her free hand up in the air. 'You'd better tell me what the hell is going on, Logan. When I got here yesterday I met a nice guy, one who was in love with me, and who was delighted to see me, and today I'm with his hostile half-twin who is angry and keeping his distance.' Walking over to him, she stabbed him in the chest with her finger. 'Do I need to remind you that I'm here on your invitation?'

He continued to glare back at her, but she didn't relent.

Releasing an agitated sigh a moment later, he pushed his hand through his hair. 'You're right. I owe you an explanation and I'm sorry for how I've behaved this morning.' He took her hand and brought her back to the bench. He looked out over the lake for a few moments without saying anything.

Juliet waited.

'It's a longevity thing,' he said quietly, almost as though he was talking to himself.

'What?'

Logan seemed not to hear her.

'They all died young and now I'm next.'

Fear and puzzlement twisted Juliet's stomach.

'What are you talking about?'

'It's crazy.'

'Logan?' She gripped his arm, forcing him to look at her. 'Are you sick? Is that it?'

He stared blankly at her for a moment then gave a humourless laugh. 'That's the joke, isn't it? I'm perfectly healthy, had a complete physical, and everything is fine. *I – just – can't – sleep*.' The four last words were punctuated by him thumping their joined hands on his knee.

'Please try to make some sense to me,' Juliet begged.

His eyes softened. 'Oh Juliet, I'm so sorry to have dragged you into this.'

'Into what?'

'Nothing, nothing. I'm sure it's just all coincidence.'

'Logan, you're not making any sense.'

'Okay.' He blew out a breath. 'You know my father died ten years ago? Well, he was only fifty-seven. His father before him died at fifty-six, and my great-grandfather died at fifty-two. You see? Longevity doesn't feature in the Pershaw male line.'

'What did they all die of? Is there some hereditary thing?' Juliet was very scared now.

'No, I told you,' he snapped. 'I'm healthy as a horse.'

She pulled back. Immediately he looked contrite.

'I'm sorry. It's getting to me now too.'

'What is?' Her frustration and fear were warring with each other.

'They all died of exhaustion.'

'Exhaustion!' She gave a nervous laugh. 'But that's ridiculous.'

'Lack of sleep. It seems to be a problem all the owners of

Carissima had. Well, just the men actually. We can't sleep here.'

'What?' Juliet couldn't believe what she was hearing. 'Did you know that before you came back here?'

'Yes, but I thought it was all nonsense, just an excuse for my father's bad temper.' At her look of puzzlement he explained. 'You know I left here with Mum when I was fifteen. But you don't know that I vowed never to come back.'

'Why?'

'Remember I told you yesterday that my father, Richard Pershaw, brought us to live here when I was five. I have wonderful memories of our family life while we were living in England. But when we came to Carissima, my father seemed to change gradually. He went from being humorous and fun-loving, to being angry all the time. It broke my mother's heart. She said it was like living with a stranger. He would fly into rages and then beg her forgiveness. He used to say that he couldn't sleep, that he didn't have energy for anything any more and the frustration made him angry. Mum tried to get him to go back to England, believing that the responsibility of the farm didn't suit him, but he said his travelling days were over and their life was here now. She put up with it for years and tried to understand, but one day when there was a particularly bad row, he raised his arm as if to hit her. Luckily he didn't, but it was the last straw for her. I witnessed it and hated him for it, and for making her so unhappy. Mum took me to England for good shortly after that. I promised that I would never come back. Later I hated him because I had to leave all this. I never spoke to him again.'

'Oh Logan . . .' Juliet's heart was breaking for him.

'When I thought about growing my own orchards, memories of this place began to filter in. All I loved about it came into sharp relief and I just had to come back. I figured the bad memories could be pushed aside and I could make a go of it here.' He paused and another ragged sigh ripped through him. 'And now I can't sleep.'

'At all?' she asked.

'I get some, but only for brief periods before waking again and in the mornings I'm still so tired. It's damn frustrating.' His voice shook with emotion. Wrenching his hand from hers, he stood up and moved a few steps away, staring into the distance.

Juliet's thoughts raced.

'Are you sure the fear of the same thing happening to you isn't just manifesting itself in the sleep problem?' she asked.

'No. I didn't come here afraid of it, I didn't even think of it. But then it started happening.' He resumed a restless pacing. 'And I'm getting cranky and short-tempered. I've already snapped at you once today, and I was rude to Sheila. Is this the start of it? I'm afraid I'm going to turn into my father.' He swivelled around and burst out with, 'I didn't speak to him for years, not understanding him and what he went through. And now I know it wasn't his fault.'

'God, Logan, you can't blame yourself for that!' Juliet jumped up and put her hand on his arm. He looked so tortured. 'You were only a kid. Even your mother couldn't understand it and had to leave. How could you?' She willed him to forgive himself.

'It's hard not to regret what happened. And I don't want it to happen again.'

Logan took her face between his hands and he kissed her lips gently. When he lifted his head, Juliet was alarmed to see tears in his eyes.

'I love you, Juliet, and it's because I do that I want you to go back to England.'

Juliet's insides turned to ice at his words.

He put a finger against her lips to stop her protest. 'I should never have asked you to come. I don't want to hurt you like my father did my mother.' His voice cracked.

'For God's sake, Logan, couples snap at each other and fight all the time. What we have is stronger than that.' Fear fuelled her anger, and she glared at him.

'My parents didn't survive it.' He gripped her shoulders. 'I want you to leave before it gets worse.' His voice was cold now with determination.

Juliet's anger evaporated and she was scared, knowing that he was deadly serious.

'Sending me away isn't your only choice. You could sell all this, and buy land in England. We could –'

Logan turned and slammed his open palm against the wall of the house. 'A Pershaw built this, and I won't be the one to let it all slip away. The Pershaws are tied to this place. No matter where we go or what we do we're always drawn back. This is where I belong.'

'Well, then, there must be a way of making it work, something must be done to help you. The relaxation techniques I mentioned,' she suggested desperately, 'or if that doesn't work, then sleeping pills, something.'

'I've tried but they just don't work, and I end up walking around like a zombie the following day. You see, the thing is . . .' he hesitated, 'if I'm away from here for a night, I have no problem. It's the house . . .'

'What do you mean?'

'Oh, I don't know. I'm just rambling. Just put it down to lack of sleep.' The attempted joke fell flat.

Juliet tried to think clearly.

Logan went on. 'There are stories handed down locally that my grandfather and great-grandfather just faded away without any obvious cause of death. And I can distinctly remember my father telling my mother that my grandfather was an insomniac.

It was when we were on holiday in France. I couldn't have been more than six years old. We were in a park, and I'd been standing beside a pond watching some ducks. I ran over to where my parents were sitting and heard what he was saying, but when I asked what an insomniac was, I was hushed and sent back to the pond. My grandfather died when my father was only a boy, so I never knew him.' Logan visibly shook himself, coming back to the present. 'Maybe I'm feeling guilty for running out on Dad, and my subconscious is punishing me for that. Perhaps you're right and, if I can forgive myself, I'll be fine.' He pinned on a totally unconvincing smile.

'It might be that simple,' she said, hoping that he had changed his mind about wanting her to leave. 'I'm fine here. I mean, I had no problem sleeping here last night. I felt so cosy. I even dreamed someone tucked me in, like I was a child.'

Logan made a strangled sound.

'Are you okay?'

He nodded, but he had paled. 'I mean it, Juliet. I want you to go home.'

'But . . .'

'No buts!'

'No! The doctor said you were healthy, so there has to be an explanation and I'm going to help you get to the bottom of it.'

He shook his head. 'I'm going to go in and book you on a flight for this evening.' The steely determination was back in his voice.

'No! This is crazy. God, I need to think.' She took a step away from him. 'But one thing is sure. I'm staying out the week here, Logan. I love you too much to just give up on you.'

Bewilderment had her staring at him for a moment longer, before she stormed off down the path to the lake.

Chapter 41

Down by the water the birds sang out cheerfully, in contrast to the turmoil going on inside Juliet. Going around the side of the boathouse, she sat on a rock. Her hands were shaking as she placed them palms upwards in her lap. She couldn't make sense of the conversation she and Logan had just had. Everything had changed so suddenly that she was still reeling.

Closing her eyes, she took two deep breaths before letting her breathing settle into a calmer rhythm, feeling it going in through her nose and down into her abdomen. After a moment she focused her attention on relaxing her stomach muscles, then moved her attention up to her heart area, then mindfully relaxed every muscle in her body.

In her mind she placed the conversation that she'd just had with Logan inside a bubble and placed it on the water in front of her. Then she imagined pricking the bubble with a pin and letting the conversation and all the anxiety that it had raised melt away across the surface of the lake.

Her breathing became deep and calm, her head clearing of all thought. The sound of the birds and the trees sighed through her mind. She stayed like that for fifteen minutes. She was just bringing her awareness back to her body again when she heard a woman whisper so softly that she barely caught the words.

'Help me, Juliet . . .'

Hers eyes flew open and she swivelled around. But there was no one there. At her movement, a squirrel shot up a nearby tree.

Was it some noise it had made that made her think she'd heard a voice, she wondered.

But she could still hear the whispered words in her head. *Help me, Juliet.*

There was something familiar about it. Something tugged at the edge of her mind. Closing her eyes she tried to grasp it. Suddenly, it hit her. The whispered '*Goodnight*' in her dream last night!

She shook her head. That was a ridiculous comparison to make, she thought. Standing up she walked around the other side of the boathouse and paced up and down on the pebbles. Was Logan having strange dreams too? Or maybe he thought he was hearing voices, just like she thought a moment ago. Stress could do strange things to the mind – she must persuade him to get help.

She walked up to the house.

The kitchen was empty, as was the office. Calling out Logan's name she went from room to room on the ground floor, but there was no sign of him.

As she crossed the front hall, Sheila appeared on the landing.

'I think he went out to the yard,' she said.

'Thanks.' Juliet went out through the kitchen. 'Logan?' she called.

'In here!' The muffled reply came from one of the outhouses.

Her footsteps echoed as she crossed the yard. Opening a shed door a bit wider and going in, she saw Logan spreading some seeds out on sheets of paper.

The words she was about to speak froze on her lips when he spoke without looking at her.

'I've booked you on a flight from Dublin at six this evening. We'll leave here at three.'

'I told you, I'm not going,' she said between gritted teeth.

His hands stilled, he stared at the seeds for a moment before turning towards her, his expression completely blank.

'You can't stay. It's over between us, Juliet. I don't want you here.'

'You don't mean it,' she said, shocked.

He just looked at her, still without a trace of emotion.

'I don't believe you,' she said. 'You don't tell someone you love them one day and that you don't the next!'

'We leave at three, Juliet.' He turned back and began sorting the seeds again.

'Logan, talk to me. You can get help for —' Before she could finish what she wanted to say, someone came in behind her. Whirling around angrily at the interruption, the breath whooshed from her lungs when she came face to face with the man who had glared at her through the library window earlier.

Up close he looked even more severe, with pinched features, and thin wispy grey hair. Juliet thought he looked older than mid-fifties. Very tall, in wellingtons and a long wax jacket, he loomed over her and glowered at her, before passing her by and giving an envelope to Logan.

'Here's the vet's report on that bullock,' he said gruffly.

Logan looked up and introduced them, his voice strained.

'Cummins, this is Juliet Holmes. Michael Cummins, my farm manager.'

Cummins looked at her again but didn't offer his hand.

'Hello,' she said, trying to be polite despite the negative vibe he was sending her way. There weren't many people whom she

283

took an instant dislike to but this was one of them. She just wanted him to leave so she could talk to Logan.

But Logan had other ideas.

'I need to discuss the drainage in the east field with you, Cummins,' he said.

When Juliet continued to stand there, they both looked at her. Logan raised his eyebrows. She felt a blush creep up her neck at the obvious dismissal.

Humiliated, she stormed out and marched back across the yard. Taking the stairs two at a time she went to her room, grabbed her suitcase and flung it on the bed.

'How dare he treat me like that!' she said between gritted teeth, stuffing her clothes into the suitcase.

After a moment she stopped and sank down on the side of the bed, gazing out the window.

'This is exactly what he wants, you fool!' she said aloud. 'This is his way of protecting you. This isn't the real Logan, and you know it!'

She unpacked, and stood the empty case against the wall.

A tap at the door made her heart race. Opening it, she wasn't sure if she was relieved or disappointed to find Sheila outside.

'I just wanted to let you know that I'm off now,' Sheila said. 'The tagine is made for dinner and there's homemade vegetable soup and brown bread for your lunch. So just help yourself when you're hungry. I don't think Logan will be joining you for lunch. I just saw him heading off in the jeep with Michael Cummins.'

'Oh,' Juliet said, deflated.

Sheila looked like she was about to say something but changed her mind. 'Well, I'll see you tomorrow then.'

'Wait! Sheila? I met Michael just now down in one of the sheds.'

'Ah,' Sheila said knowingly.

It encouraged Juliet to go on. 'He wasn't very friendly.'

'Don't pay any attention to him. He's not the most sociable of people – doesn't particularly take to blow-ins.'

Juliet nodded. Aware that Sheila was Logan's employee, she left it at that. 'Thanks in advance for the soup and tagine.'

Sheila smiled and left.

Juliet ate a solitary lunch, finding it hard to comprehend the difference twenty-four hours had made. Hurt and confused, she cleared away the dishes and since there was still no sign of Logan she went back to the library.

Feeling the need of a little comforting, she took out the Wordsworth poetry book and sat in the leather armchair, reading for a bit. Every now and then she glanced up to watch the hands of a carriage clock on the mantelpiece move relentlessly forward, nearer and nearer to three o'clock.

With ten minutes to go, she heard the front door bang. Closing the poetry book, she placed it on the arm of the chair beside her and stood up. Her hands were shaking a little, so she stuffed them in her pockets.

Logan came in. 'Are you packed?'

'No.'

They stood staring at each other, a few feet apart.

'I meant it, Juliet. It's over.'

Juliet straightened her spine even more. 'I don't believe that. I just think that you're stressed and that it's playing tricks on your mind, so that you're imagining you can't sleep.'

He remained impassive.

'Either that or the ghosts here are making too much noise at night.'

She had attempted the joke in the hope of getting some reaction from him. But she never expected the colour to drain away from his face the way it did.

285

The book of poetry fell off the arm of the chair onto the floor. Juliet jumped but kept staring at Logan's face.

'Oh my God,' she said as Logan pulled out a chair and sank into it. 'That's it! Isn't it? You think the place is haunted!'

He still said nothing.

'Logan!'

He looked at her wearily. 'I don't think it. I know it.'

'What?'

'Ghost, spirit, force – call it what you like. I don't know, but there's always been talk here of a female ghost who tucks in the women and girls at night and blesses them with a wonderful night's sleep. But she does the opposite for the Pershaw men. As soon as they fall asleep, she wakes them again and again.' He paused. 'I don't know about the others, but for me there's this restless, negative energy that seems to wire my system, making sleep impossible.' He threw an almost apologetic look at Juliet. 'Sometimes I hear sobbing and pleading, and sometimes pacing feet.'

Despite concern for Logan, and the absurdity of what he was saying, a part of Juliet was intrigued. 'What does she say?'

'I can't make out any words, just murmuring.'

'But whose ghost is she supposed to be?'

'I don't know. But since the house has always belonged to the Pershaws, I presume it has to be a Pershaw. God, I can't believe I'm admitting to believing in ghosts.' He rubbed his hands over his face.

Not wanting to increase his resolve to send her away, she refrained from telling him about the whisper she'd heard at the lake.

'What about your mother?' she asked. 'Can Elizabeth shed any light on all of this?'

'No.' The word was a like a pistol shot. 'I'm not involving her. She suffered enough over this with Dad.'

Juliet remembered the telephone conversation with Elizabeth back in Florence and her concern about Logan returning to the house. She figured Elizabeth was well aware of what was going on. Juliet decided to keep quiet about that for now.

'What about your relatives?' she asked. 'Can you ask any of them what they know about this?'

Logan thought about it for a moment. 'There are my American cousins, but I doubt they'll know anything and their mother, my Aunt Ruth, died last year. I might have better luck with the English cousins and Aunt Jane. I suppose I could make a few phone calls, saying I'm looking into the history of Carissima, without giving anything away about my, eh, present predicament.'

'Good, it's a start at least, and in the meantime I'll go on the internet and do a bit of research on paranormal activity.'

Logan grimaced at the term.

'Which means I'm going to stay here at Carissima and help you with this,' she said firmly.

Logan sighed. 'I don't have the energy to fight you but I still don't think it's a good idea.'

Juliet smiled and came to put her arm around his shoulders. He stood up and moved away, but faced her.

'I think it would be best if we kept things casual between us for the moment, Juliet. There is no point in getting more involved if ultimately there's no future for us.'

She thought he was wrong, but was willing to win one battle at a time. But the pain in his eyes helped her to believe in his love for her. That hope would energise her search for answers.

'I'll go and cancel your flight.'

He walked to the door, where he hesitated and turned to look at her.

'Juliet,' he said softly, 'I'm so sorry for all of this. This is a problem going back generations. The solution mightn't even be ours to find.'

He left.

Juliet wanted to curl up and weep at his withdrawal from her, but she hadn't time to indulge in self-pity. Turning on the laptop, she settled down to find out as much as she could about the spirit world.

Within minutes she knew her task wouldn't be easy. The amount of sites available on the subject was endless, from spirit sightings, to poltergeists, to ancient ghost stories, and even movies on the subject. Some of the stuff she read was so far-fetched it had her shaking her head in amazement at the workings of some people's minds.

Sighing, she got up and looked out the window at the lake, trying to think of what to look up next. The water reflected the moving clouds overhead.

'Water!' Juliet exclaimed and rushed back to the laptop.

Sitting down, she typed the words 'water diviner' into the search engine.

'Great!' she said a few moments later when she read how some water diviners are also healers of people, land, animals, *and* houses.

She refined her search for water diviners in County Monaghan, and found that there was only one, by the name of Jack Long. There were some excellent testimonials and reviews of his work, which also included cleansing houses of negative energy. The testimonials seemed legitimate enough to Juliet. She believed in the ancient art of water divining and therefore was willing to believe in their other skills. She made a note of the name and number, hoping Logan would be willing to give the man a call.

Going to the office, she found him fast asleep in his chair. Letting him sleep on, she returned to the library and went back to cataloguing more books to keep herself busy.

Chapter 42

A few hours later Juliet closed the door of the second cabinet, having come across three handwritten letters held between two books. Gingerly removing them, she'd found they were dated 1891 and that they were business correspondence from a merchant colleague of James.

Looking at her watch, she took the letters with her and went to see if Logan was awake. He wasn't, so she went into the kitchen where Sheila had left a pot of potatoes ready for steaming. Juliet put them on and took the casserole dish out of the fridge.

Just as the meal was ready, Logan appeared, yawning.

'Sorry, I must have nodded off.'

Juliet looking up from stirring the casserole and, seeing his frown, tried to sound cheerful as she announced that dinner was ready.

'Thanks for sorting it,' he said, setting the table. 'I should've done that.' He didn't meet her eyes.

'It's not a problem.' Juliet sighed inwardly, hating the awkward politeness between them.

Over dinner, Logan read his great-grandfather's letters, never having seen them before. They seemed to improve his mood a little.

'It's amazing to think he decided to move here after all that travelling,' Juliet said.

'That's just it, I suppose he was tired of being away all the time and wanted to be more of a family man, and travel wasn't very safe in those days.'

'Any luck with contacting your cousins?' she asked.

'The ones in America have to wait until later this evening and the English cousin I'll call after dinner.'

'Logan, do you believe in water diviners?'

'Yes. As a matter of fact one was used to find a location for a well on this land.'

'There's a diviner here in County Monaghan who also has helped to heal houses of negative energy. Do you think it could work here?'

She watched his face while he stared thoughtfully at his plate for a few long moments.

'Is it Jack Long?'

She nodded.

'Okay,' he said. 'I think it's worth a try. A lot of people around here believe in his gift.'

Juliet smiled in relief. 'I can call him now if you like and see if he can come around.'

Logan nodded, but didn't say any more.

'Afterwards I'm going to go out with my camera.' She stood and started to tidy up.

'Good idea,' he replied, getting up to help.

'Some pics of the horses, I think, in the evening light would be good. It looks like there's going to be a nice sunset tonight.'

'Mind if I tag along?' he asked.

'That would be great.' Juliet was surprised at the suggestion and glad he wasn't leaving her alone for the evening, but she wondered how she would stick the casual relationship he was forcing on them. She was longing to be back in his arms, to feel the reassurance of his love, and to love him in return. But for now, she reminded herself, she should be grateful not to be on a plane back to London.

'Meet you in the yard in twenty minutes, after I make those calls to England.'

Juliet went to her room to fetch her camera and, while there, took the diviner's number out of her pocket and rang it on her mobile.

'Hello?' a woman answered.

'Hello. Can I speak to Jack Long, please?' Juliet asked.

'I'm sorry, dear, but he's away at the moment.'

'Oh.' Juliet was disappointed. 'I wanted him to come and check out the energy of a house? When will he be back?'

'He's at a conference in Wales on alternative therapies for the next couple of days and won't be back until Thursday. Will I get him to call you then?'

'Thank you. That would be great.' Juliet said.

She gave the woman her name and number.

'Eh, can you tell him it's urgent, please,' she added on impulse, really wanting him to come to the house during her stay.

'Of course, dear. Goodbye.'

'Thanks, goodbye.'

Down in the yard Juliet asked Logan where the stables were.

'Behind those sheds there.' He pointed beyond the row of

outhouses he had been in that afternoon.

On the way up the track to the horses' field, Juliet told Logan about the call.

'If he's as good as people say he is, he'll be worth the wait, I'm sure,' Logan reassured her, 'especially since I had no luck with my cousins in England. They knew nothing, other than the fact there was a rumour of a ghost, and my aunt is in the early stages of Alzheimer's so can't help either,' he said sadly.

'I'm sorry to hear that. That must be hard for her family.'

Logan nodded.

Arriving at the gate to the field, Logan untied it. The horses looked up from their grazing and when Logan held out some apples they sauntered over to him, nuzzling his hands.

Juliet caressed the neck of the grey Logan said she could ride.

'They are beautiful animals,' she said.

'Seán and Joe take good care of them.'

She moved away and took out her camera. The evening sun setting wispy clouds on fire, Juliet lost herself in her art for about thirty minutes, first taking shots of Logan talking to the horses before he realised what she was doing. He left them and wandered off to sit on the fence. Juliet continued to take shots of the animals on their own, from all angles.

When she was done, she climbed up on the fence beside Logan, and they watched the changing evening sky together.

'I thought it was always supposed to be raining in Ireland,' Juliet commented as they made their way back to the gate. 'Yesterday and today have been beautiful.'

'I love these gentle September days – they're like a special gift before the dark of autumn and winter,' he said.

'Do we need to bring the horses in?'

'No, Seán said he'll be a bit late this evening but he'll be here before dark.'

Logan tied up the gate behind them and they started down the lane.

Juliet slipped her hand into his. He held it for a second, gave it a squeeze, but then, with a sigh, let it go.

'Logan –'

He cut across her. 'No, Juliet.' His voice was soft but firm.

Juliet shoved her hand into the pocket of her jeans, trying not to feel upset and angry at the rebuff.

After a few minutes, Logan spoke, his voice strained. 'I'm trying to do what's best, Juliet. Please cut me some slack.'

She tried to relax her tense shoulders. 'Okay, I'm sorry. I don't agree, but I promise not to push it.'

They walked the rest of the way in silence.

When they got inside, she announced that she was going to go to her room early to read for a while.

'I'll see you in the morning,' she said.

Looking at her across the kitchen, Logan asked: 'Will you be okay? I mean, are you nervous about going to sleep tonight, knowing that we might have our own resident ghost?'

'No. I'm sure she doesn't mean me any harm.'

'Okay then, well, goodnight. Call me if you need me.'

She was pretty sure he could see a very different need in her eyes at that moment, and she could see it reflected in his own.

Shaking her head at the craziness of his decision to keep his distance, she left him standing there, trying not to panic at the thought of losing him.

The house was quiet as she made her way upstairs. On the landing to the right of the arch there was a door. Logan had told her that a stairs to the attic rooms lay behind it, but she hadn't been up there. He'd said it was just used for storage, but she would like to see where the servants had once slept. She made a mental note to go up there before the week was out.

Going into her room, she switched on the main light and a couple of lamps, not feeling quite so brave now. She pottered around for a while, taking her time getting ready for bed. Eventually she turned off all the lights except the one on her locker and got in under the duvet. Picking up the book she'd bought at the airport, she was glad she'd opted for the one on an expedition to Everest instead of the Swedish thriller she had been going to buy. After a while she found the silence oppressive and put in her earphones to listen to some music on her iPod.

After reading for about an hour, her lids grew heavy, the book slid onto her chest and she fell asleep.

Again she dreamed of being kissed on the forehead and being tucked in.

When she woke in the morning, her iPod and book were on the locker and her light was off. Juliet stared across the pillow at them, trying to remember putting them away. She couldn't. Logan must have come in to check on her before he went to bed himself. She wondered if he'd had second thoughts and had hoped to join her after all.

Then she remembered the dream. She wondered if that had anything to do with the energy in the house, causing her to dream the same thing more than once. Slowly she looked around the room, which was dimly lit from the light coming in under the curtain. After rubbing at the goose bumps which were slightly raised on her arms, she got up and opened the curtains. The weather had changed, bringing drizzle and a dreariness to the morning.

Putting on leggings and a top, she ran through her yoga exercises. Then putting on a fleece she sat cross-legged on the soft carpet in front of the window to meditate. But she was restless and half expected to hear another whisper, so she couldn't quieten her mind. After ten minutes she gave up and went for a shower.

When she was dressed she went downstairs. The smell of brewing coffee lured her straight to the kitchen. Logan, looking pale but handsome in a thick wool jumper, was reading a newspaper and nursing a steaming mug.

He looked her over. 'Everything okay?'

'Yes, thanks,' she replied, going to the counter and putting bread into the toaster casually, belying the fact that all she wanted to do was go to him and snuggle into all that woolly softness, and have him hold her tight, kissing her until she couldn't think. To avoid the temptation, she stared out the window at the rain while she waited for the toast to pop up.

'I spoke too soon last night about the sunshine,' she said, bringing the toast to the table.

'Yeah, it's a bit of a dirty day all right, but it might clear later, and I thought we might take the horses out in the afternoon, it you like?'

She smiled. 'I'd love it.'

'I need to do some more work with seeds today.' At her querying look, he continued. 'I'm saving and drying seeds from the existing orchard here, with the hope of growing trees from seed in pots in the old greenhouse in the spring – just an experiment.'

Juliet's face was bright with interest when she asked him to explain a bit more about it. As he was finishing, they heard a car and he looked at this watch.

'That'll be Sheila,' he said. 'I'd better get on. Will you be okay?'

'Yes. I'm going to spend the morning in the library.'

'Good. By the way, I got through to two of my American cousins last night and, like I thought, they don't know anything.'

Sheila came in and, having greeted her, they both left to pursue their separate tasks.

In the library, Juliet pulled the steps over to the third cabinet and opened the doors. Methodically she pulled out the heavy tomes from the top shelf one by one and leafed through them before replacing them. When the top row was done she got down and took the details from their spines. Climbing up again, she started on the second row from the top.

The first three were political reference books from the nineteenth century. They were large red tomes, with thick spines. She checked the first and the second to no avail. She paused to rub her arms which were aching from dragging the heavy books in and out. Reaching for the third and expecting it to be as heavy as the others, she exerted the same pressure to lift it out. But it was lighter and jerked back in her hands, almost unbalancing her on the steps.

'What on earth?' she exclaimed, steadying herself.

On examining it, Juliet saw it was a box made to look like the other books and, from the feel of it, there was something in it. She got down and put it on the table, then unclipped a small catch on the side. Inside was something wrapped in muslin. Lifting it out gingerly, Juliet unwrapped it to reveal a faded brown, leather-bound notebook. It was filled with beautiful handwriting, and there, inside the cover, in the same neat hand, was the name Helena Pershaw. Recognising the name of Logan's great-grandmother, Juliet caught her breath. Turning to the first page, she exhaled very slowly as she read the words '10th April, 1889' and 'Dear Diary'.

Excited at her discovery, she wanted to take it immediately to Logan to find out if this was a treasured heirloom that he was aware of already. But thinking that he probably didn't want to be disturbed, she decided to read a bit and ask him about it later.

Chapter 43

Juliet sat down and started to read the diary, while the air grew still around her.

10ᵗʰ April 1889

Dear Diary,

I have never kept a diary before, but this one was a gift from my friend Alice Wallis, to record my new life in Ireland. So here I am. My name is Helena Pershaw, the first mistress of Carissima! My husband, James, has called it Carissima because it means 'dearest' in Italian and that is what he calls me all the time. I was very touched by his choice. James used to be a merchant, but is now a gentleman farmer, here in Monaghan.

We arrived at our new home a month ago, after an exhausting two-day journey from Berkshire. The sea crossing was rough and both I and our little girl, Beatrice, were very sick. Thank God for Martha, who found her sea legs and was able to take care of us. She is so good with little Beatrice, who loves her dearly.

'Martha,' Juliet whispered. 'That name again.' She read on.

It is wonderful to be mistress of my own home. Although living with Mother Pershaw was fine, James and I have been dreaming of this day for a while now. We have a cook and a butler whom we brought over here with us from England, and two housemaids and a gardener who are from around here.

And, of course, Martha. Martha is the only daughter of my third cousin, who died at the beginning of last year and left her all alone, and I was only too glad to employ her as Beatrice's governess. She has a sweet disposition and is a good influence on Beatrice. Not only is she family, but she has been a dear friend to me.

Juliet realised that Logan mustn't have read the diary before or he would have known who the Martha in the photograph was, and that she was family after all but distant and on his great-grandmother's side. Even though she was feeling guilty now for reading it before him, she read on another bit, her curiosity too much for her.

James has hired some farmhands, and a local man called Cummins as farm manager. I do not bother much with that side of things – that is all for James to deal with. I have enough to do running the house and the gardens. And I must admit I am loving doing so.

Carissima is magnificent. We have seven bedrooms and a nursery, a dining room, drawing room, morning room, study and library. There is also the kitchen and the pantries, and rooms in the attic for the servants. We have acres and acres of green farmland and woods, and our very own lake! James says the first thing he is going to do is build a little boathouse and get a boat so that he can take me out on the water.

Brown, the gardener, has already started preparing flowerbeds and both a vegetable and a herb garden for Cook. He has also planted an orchard, so we will have our own apples and pears.

Juliet paused, now knowing that some of Logan's beloved apple trees had been here since Carissima was built.

We have unpacked all the beautiful linens and silver we received as wedding presents but did not need to use while in Mother Pershaw's house. It is lovely to be surrounded by my own things. James brought back some wonderful floor rugs from his final trip to India, which are perfect here. The colours are quite magnificent and the weaving is of excellent quality.

Juliet looked down at the worn, now faded rug which covered most of the floor, and shook her head in wonder.

The front of the house faces south and, so far, the Irish weather has been kind, giving us plenty of spring sunshine. I know we are going to be very happy here, although I worry about Martha, who seems quieter since our arrival. Perhaps she just needs time to settle in.

We have been made very welcome by the community here and have met some of our new neighbours at Sunday service. We have already received four calling cards. I am sure I shall make some fine new friends soon.
Helena

The sound of the vacuum cleaner out in the hall made Juliet jump. Afraid Sheila might come into the library, she wrapped the diary up in the muslin, returned it to the box and put it back in the cabinet, closing the doors firmly on it.

'I'm going to go out for a little air, Sheila,' she said, passing her on the way upstairs to get her camera and jacket from her room.

Outside, the drizzle had stopped and Juliet took a walk around the lawn. Some raindrops still rested on several cobwebs strung on the shrubs and across the grass. She took photographs of them and of the giant redwood. Going across the lawn she started photographing the oak trees, zooming in on the ripening acorns.

The oaks were old and majestic. Juliet stopped, rested first her palm, then her cheek against the rough bark, breathing in the damp woody scent. Moving around the tree and looking down for any acorns that might have already fallen, her eyes fell on the toes of a pair of green wellingtons.

She gave a little yelp of surprise and just managed to avoid walking headlong into Michael Cummins. He was so close that the pungent smell of his wax jacket assaulted her nostrils.

Rapidly taking a step back, she looked into his face. 'You gave me a fright,' she said, her attempt at a smile failing dismally.

'You should go home, like Pershaw said,' he growled from low in his throat.

Juliet was shocked at the menace in his tone, but was even more shocked when he grabbed her upper arm in a fierce grip, bringing his face close to hers. Stale tobacco breath spread across her face.

'Go back to England and take him with you.'

Juliet, quashing her fear, looked down at his hand and then steadily into his eyes. 'Take your hand off me,' she said through gritted teeth. 'And don't you ever touch me again.'

Cummins narrowed his eyes, obviously surprised at the fight in her. He removed his hand.

'Neither of you belongs at Carissima! The ghost doesn't want you here!'

With that parting shot he turned away and strode off towards the back of the house.

When he was out of sight, she leant against the tree trunk, her legs turning to jelly.

She had been right not to like him. There was something very sinister about him, and it was definitely stronger than a casual dislike for blow-ins.

How could Logan work with the man? She'd have to tell him what happened. But on the way back up to the house, on legs that still weren't quite steady, she changed her mind. He had enough on his plate without adding further worry to it, and it might just give him another reason to send her home, and she certainly wasn't going to risk that. She would just be sure to stay out of Michael Cummins' way. She had no fear of a ghost – Cummins was the one to be wary of.

Wanting to get back to the diary, Juliet hoped Sheila was finished in the library, but before she got there Logan met her in hall.

'I was looking for you. Do you want to have lunch?' He looked closely at her. 'You okay? You look a little pale.'

'Just got a bit cold out there while taking some photographs,' she said, tapping the camera around her neck. Hating that she was lying to him, she turned her face away while taking off her jacket and throwing it on a chair.

'Well, let's get you some hot soup then.'

To Juliet's relief and great comfort, concern for her must have made him forget his own rules, because he put his arm around her shoulder and pulled her against the warmth of his side as they walked to the kitchen. Juliet put an arm around his waist and held on tight while she was afforded the luxury.

The comfort was gone too fast with their arrival in the kitchen and the business of heating up the soup. Sheila had also left out a salad for them. They ate well, though after her run-in with Cummins Juliet was amazed she had any appetite at all.

'Logan, have you ever seen a diary written by your great-grandmother, Helena Pershaw?' she asked.

'No,' he said, eyes widening.

'I'll be back in a minute.'

A moment later she returned with the diary, and handed it to him.

He looked at it in amazement. 'Where did you find it?'

'In the library.'

'You'll see from the first page there that she started writing it as soon as she got here. I've only read a small bit and it's very interesting. I like your great-grandmother. She's got guts.'

He flicked through it before reading a few lines from the first page.

'So that's why he called it Carissima. What a find, Juliet! My great-grandmother's handwriting! I never knew this was here. I wonder if my father knew.'

'It's possible he didn't. It was high up in one of the cabinets, hidden inside a box disguised as a big old tome. She might have hidden it there herself. Maybe no one else has ever read it.' She was thrilled at the possibility. 'And there is a Martha mentioned in there – perhaps the same one in the poetry book and in the photograph.'

'So was she a Pershaw too?' Logan asked.

'No, she was on Helena's side of the family, a third cousin. She lived with them here, as governess to their daughter.'

Seeing the wonder on Logan's face made her smile.

'I'd like to keep reading it if that's okay with you,' she said. 'It will break up the tedium of the book cataloguing.'

'Of course. I'll read it at a later stage when I've a bit more time, but now I need some exercise. You ready to go out on the horses?'

'Sure.'

Before long they were out in the fields, managing a gallop in one or two places. But they came back at a gentle pace via a bridle path through the trees beside the lake. By the time they brought the horses back to the stables, to brush them down, she had a much better sense of the lie of the land and size of the farm. As Juliet gave her horse a drink, she watched Logan's hands stroke his horse's neck. She loved being with him. The afternoon had been wonderful. She prayed the water diviner was going to be of some help to them and that they could then return to normal.

Chapter 44

That evening after dinner, Logan went out and invited Seán and Joe Hayes in for a coffee. They were lovely gentle people and Juliet warmed to them immediately. The four of them sat around the kitchen table, talking horses for a couple of hours.

'Montana? No way!' Joe, the son, who was about fifteen, exclaimed when Logan told them where Juliet had been in July.

'Yes, I was photographing some wild horses there.'

'No way!' Joe said again and his father cuffed him affectionately on the head.

Juliet entertained them for a while with stories from her trip, until Seán looked at his watch and declared it time to go because it was a school night. Joe groaned.

'I'll tell you more another time,' Juliet promised him.

She and Logan waved them off from the back door.

'You'll have Joe's never-ending devotion now,' Logan laughed. 'He lives and breathes horses.'

'I could tell.' Juliet smiled, going back inside.

Logan locked the door behind them.

'I'll say goodnight, then,' Juliet said.

'We can watch a movie if you like,' Logan offered.

She hesitated.

'I've got popcorn!' He pulled a microwavable packet from a cupboard and waved it in front of her.

'Oh, all right then,' she laughed.

It was very different from their first night. This time they sat at either end of the couch, with the bowl of popcorn between them. The movie they had chosen wasn't any good either – one about espionage, which was convoluted and implausible. Halfway through, in frustration, Juliet announced she was going to bed.

'We can start another one if you like.'

'No, thanks – anyway it's getting late. I'll see you in the morning.'

'Want me to walk you up?'

'No,' she said, knowing that if he did, she would make a fool of herself by trying to lure him into her room.

Pausing at the door she looked back at him where he sat on the couch, the remote control still in his hand.

'Did you by any chance come into my room last night and turn off my light?' she asked.

He frowned. 'No, there was no light coming from under your door when I was going to bed.'

'Oh, okay. Goodnight.'

'Juliet?' he questioned.

'It's nothing. I just don't remember turning it off. That's all. Goodnight.'

'Hmmm.' He didn't sound convinced by her casualness so she left the room before he could continue the conversation.

Nothing untoward happened that night, although she dreamed of being tucked in again and slept like a log.

'Hello,' Logan greeted her as she came out of her room the next morning. He had just left his own room and walked along the corridor to fall into step with her. 'The rain has gone.'

'Great. Get any sleep?' Juliet asked, having seen the dark circles beneath his eyes.

'A couple of hours. Are you sure you don't mind doing that work in there?' He nodded his head towards the library as they rounded the end of the stairs.

'No, I'm enjoying it and I'm going to spend the morning at it again.'

They were only halfway through breakfast when Sheila arrived and she joined them for a cup of tea.

'There's a market on in the town on Friday, if you're looking for something to do?' she told Juliet.

Juliet felt a pang of longing for her beloved Borough market, somehow feeling that Sheila's market would be no match for it.

'Thanks, I'll bear it in mind.'

'It starts at ten and runs until two.'

'Thanks.'

Logan gave her a knowing smile and she was sure he was reading her mind.

'Can I have that recipe for the beef tagine, Sheila?' she asked. 'It was divine.'

'Of course you can – I'll write it out for you later.'

Juliet walked with Logan to the office. Instead of walking straight in, he lingered at the door.

'I'm sorry this week isn't what we had planned it to be,' he said, his eyes moving over her face and hair, as if he was memorising them.

'I believe this is just a blip, Logan, and that we'll be okay.' She went up on her toes to kiss him on the cheek, being careful to play by his rules.

But Logan swiftly turned his head and captured her lips hungrily with his own, his arms closing around her and drawing her tightly up against him. Juliet surrendered totally to the kiss, feeling her body almost melting into his, more than pleased to be back where she belonged.

After a few delicious moments, Logan lowered the heat, placing featherlike kisses on her bottom lip and then either side of her mouth, before resting his forehead against hers.

'These last few days have been torture,' he said. 'One minute I am absolutely sure I'm doing the right thing by keeping you at a distance and the next I'm calling myself all kinds of a fool. I'm sorry, Juliet. I'm a mess. You deserve better than this.'

'I know the real Logan. I spent two wonderful weeks with him in Florence. That's why I'm sticking around. It'll be okay, it has to be.'

The phone rang over on the desk. Logan sighed, and kissed her quickly.

'I have to get that.'

Juliet nodded. He still sounded weary, whereas she walked away with her steps light, hope burning brightly again.

In the library she had to pass the armchair to get to the cabinets. She saw something on it out of the corner of her eye. Looking properly, she made a sound, half squeal, half scream. Her body tensing, she stepped backwards rapidly.

A dead mouse was lying in the middle of the seat.

While bolting to the office, she called herself a coward for being afraid of mice, but a sense of revulsion was crawling up her spine.

Logan was still on the call, but when he saw the look of panic on her face, he quickly ended it and came over to her.

'There's a mouse in the library,' she said, pulling him by the hand.

'Is that all? She, who has faced lions and tigers, is afraid of a little mouse? Have I found your Achilles' heel at last?'

'Logan,' she said seriously. 'It's dead. And I think someone deliberately placed it on the armchair I've been using the last few days.'

'What?' He sobered immediately, his voice grim. 'But that's ridiculous.'

By this stage they had reached the library and Logan was looking down at the poor creature. Juliet stayed tucked in behind him, barely allowing herself another quick glance at it.

'I'm pretty sure,' she said, 'that mice don't climb up onto chairs and just curl up and die.'

'But how – correction – *who* would do such a thing?'

Michael Cummins' menacing face flitted into Juliet's mind, but she didn't say anything. She didn't want to accuse the man without any evidence.

'Why don't you go and have a cup of coffee, while I get rid of it?'

'Okay.' She was gone in a flash, needing no more encouragement than that.

Logan passed through the kitchen a few moments later to dispose of the mouse outside. Juliet shuddered.

He came back in via the pantry with a bottle of disinfectant in his hand.

When he returned from the library a few minutes later Juliet was leaning against the counter, both hands wrapped around a mug, watching Sheila mix some ingredients.

Sheila tut-tutted when she saw Logan. 'How on earth did the mouse get there?'

'It's quite possible the little fellow did get a heart attack,' he said, 'and literally dropped dead there on the seat.'

'Well, it's the time of year for them to come into the house. I've already put down some traps.'

Juliet shuddered again.

'He's gone now, if you can face going back in,' Logan said. 'But you don't have to, you know.'

'It's all right. Thanks.'

Taking her coffee with her, Juliet went back but stood for a moment taking a good look around. She didn't like the lingering smell of disinfectant.

Taking Helena Pershaw's diary down from its hiding place, she sat on one of the high-backed chairs by the table. She turned to the second entry, seeing that the entries were not made on a daily basis. The second one was two and half weeks after the first.

27th April, 1889

Dear Diary,

We are settling in nicely here. Although it has been raining on and off for the past week, it has not dampened my spirits. Brown says these April showers will do the garden a world of good. Brigid has been complaining that she was unable to get the linens out to dry, so James has arranged to have a clothesline and a turf-burning stove put into one of the sheds. It will be especially useful come autumn and winter. Turf, which is used like coal, is wonderful and I love the smell of it when the fires are lighting in the evenings.

A letter arrived from Mother Pershaw today. I know she means well but, as with her last two letters, it contained advice on running a household. She still does not trust me to run my own home efficiently. I wish she would leave well alone!

Juliet laughed at the fact that interfering parents were obviously a problem for every generation.

She says that although it is only April I should be already planning a Christmas dinner party! "By then it will be known," she writes, "that James is someone of consequence in the community and you must ensure that you throw a dinner party that reflects this. I am including with my letter the menu I suggest for the event. I know Cook made copies of a lot of my recipes for you before you left but if you are missing any for this particular menu, write and I will forward them. Remember when you are planning, to think about what will be in season." The woman is insufferable! I know full well what will be in season and when. Because we lived with her for two years and she only allowed me a small input into the running of the household, she thinks I have forgotten everything my own mother taught me! I have my own menus and recipes and between me, Brown's vegetable garden, the farm produce and Cook's considerable skill, we will do very well! Besides, does she imagine we shall be entertaining Royalty here – 'roast cygnet' indeed! I will decide when and how I will entertain our new acquaintances here. Even having the Irish Sea between us is not stopping her from interfering.

However, I had better keep her menu in here for the moment, in case she should visit and ask to see it!

Juliet had to turn the page to finish the paragraph and there was a folded piece of paper between the pages. She opened it and saw that it was a piece of stationery with Mother Pershaw's address on the top and a Christmas menu written in large, spidery handwriting underneath it. Juliet's eyes widened at the elaborate menu. There were eight courses and indeed roast cygnet was one of them. Juliet laughed as she read it. Listed also was soup, fish, goose, Lord Russell pudding, two desserts, and cheese toast as the last item.

Replacing the page, Juliet figured that Helena's mother-in-law was a force to be reckoned with and that Helena had made a lucky escape. She also realised how much she, Juliet, took supermarkets and the all-year-round availability of a great variety of foods for granted, but she also marvelled at the variety of produce they were able to get from their own gardens. 'And we thought we were the 'green' generation!' she muttered with a smile. She was fascinated and amused at the peculiar list of dishes, some of which she didn't even recognise. She read on.

I do, however, enjoy her news of society in London. I cannot imagine we shall go to very many grand balls here in County Monaghan!

Beatrice is thriving and getting taller every day. I am a little worried about Martha, however. Her spirits still seem a bit low. Although I recall her being in better form for a while after she received a letter this morning. Unfortunately it did not last, and she was wearing a very long face again shortly afterwards. Now that I think about it, she has been receiving letters regularly and there is always the same pattern of raised then lowered spirits. I do not understand it, for I cannot imagine who is writing to her. We are her only family and I was unaware of any friends she might have had back in England.

If there is no change soon, then I will speak with her.

James is away today with Cummins to purchase a new bull. He is taking very well to the life of a farmer. I feared he would miss his busy life of travelling, but he seems most content.

Helena

29ᵗʰ April 1889

Dear Diary,

James and I went for a long walk today on our land. It is a very large farm we have here. It was wonderful to be out in the fresh air with him, and he seemed so enthusiastic as he told me the plans Cummins has for each field.

When we were nearly back at the house I was not watching where I was going and twisted my ankle in a rut. It was quite tender and I am annoyed with myself for being careless.

Martha made a warm poultice for it, which eased the discomfort very quickly. I have to rest my leg for only a day or two. It is such a pity I hurt it because I felt exhilarated from the exercise and was planning to take a long walk again tomorrow. Well, at least it affords me the opportunity to catch up on my letter-writing, which I have neglected. Mother Pershaw will be impatient for news of us, and I suppose I must thank her for that menu!

Helena

Chapter 45

Juliet turned to the next entry but, just as she read the date, she heard a sound above her head. She knew her room was directly above the library. Thinking perhaps Sheila was cleaning up there, she hoped she'd left it tidy, but just then she heard her humming out in the hall.

Sure enough, when she went to check, Sheila was spraying furniture polish on the hall table.

Juliet went to get Logan.

'I think there's someone in my room,' she whispered when he looked up.

Frowning at the interruption, he suggested that it was probably Sheila.

'No, she's in the hall. Come on, Logan, we need to check it out.'

Sheila had moved into the sitting room, so they went up the stairs as silently as they could and sneaked along the corridor to pause, listening, outside Juliet's door.

'I don't hear anything,' Logan whispered.

With that there was a thump from inside the room. Logan reached for the door handle but Juliet held him back.

'Whoever's in there might be dangerous,' she warned, her heart pounding.

Logan shook her off, thrust the door wide open and marched in. Juliet followed immediately behind him.

The room was empty.

Logan checked the en suite and the wardrobes.

'Nothing,' he said.

'That must have been the noise,' Juliet said, pointing to her suitcase, which had fallen over on its face, away from the wall. 'But that doesn't account for the noises I heard earlier.'

Her breathing began to settle down and she advanced into the room, running her eyes over the locker, checking for her iPod and phone. Everything was there. However, the duvet looked rumpled and she knew she had straightened the bed before leaving her room earlier. Reaching out, she pulled the duvet back and screamed.

A dead rat lay in the middle of the bed, just below her pillow, its dark body stretched out and its tail curled around beneath its claws.

Logan was at her side in a minute, and swore.

'What sick bastard is doing this?' he said, pushing her gently away, before pulling off the pillowslip and scooping the rat up into it.

To distract herself from the urge to vomit, Juliet went to pick up her suitcase, her skin crawling both from what she'd just seen and at the thought of someone being in her room and wanting to do that to her.

Standing the case up against the wall again she noticed something she hadn't seen before, a crack that ran up the skirting board, with one side not quite flush with the other. Her eyes travelled up the panelling above it. The crack reached right up to the dado rail at waist height, with the wood on the left slightly protruding.

'Logan, come and look at this.'

As he crossed the room, Juliet put her fingertips against the crack and pulled. A whole section, including the dado rail and the skirting board, moved towards her like a small door.

Logan swore and put a hand on her shoulder to stop her from opening it further.

'Let me do that,' he said, urging her to the side and pulling it open.

It was dark in there and all they could see was a wall about three feet beyond the gap.

'So that's how he got in,' Juliet said. 'There's obviously another way out of this.'

'Bring the lamp over and plug it in there.' He pointed to a nearby socket.

She did as she was told and he hunkered down, pushing the lamp into the space.

'It's empty,' he said. 'It's a very narrow room, like a cupboard. I'll be damned. I never knew this existed.'

After going in, he was able to stand upright. He moved along to one end, and with a little pressure from his hand the wall in front of him moved outward, allowing him to step out into the corridor. He pushed it shut behind him. From the outside it looked just like the wall in Juliet's room, the joining hidden in the panelling. Juliet came out through the bedroom door. Logan was feeling around for some means of opening it from that side. To the right of the joining was a knot in the wood. He pressed it, causing the panel to pop open.

'That's incredible,' he said in disbelief.

'So who the hell has just been snooping around my bedroom?' Juliet asked.

Logan pushed the panel shut, returned to her room, took out the lamp and closed that panel too.

When he turned to her, angry lines were etched around his mouth.

'Whoever it was could have come in here at any time. God only knows what danger you were in. I'd never forgive myself if anything happened to you.'

She shuddered again at the thought of someone being in her room while she slept. Cummins' face went through her mind again and she took in a sharp breath.

Logan's hands were shaking as he put the lamp back on the locker.

'Someone would have to know this house very well to know about that secret room – know it better than me,' he said. 'My father lived alone here for years. After his death Michael Cummins looked after the house ...' He stopped abruptly, staring at Juliet, the thought taking hold. 'No, Cummins wouldn't ... he would never ...' He left the sentence unfinished, while rubbing his forehead. 'Of course he had the run of the place for those years after my father's death and before I moved in.' Anger and betrayal pushed away the doubt. 'What the hell was he doing in your room? If it was him, and he meant to harm you, I'll kill him.' A vein in his right temple was throbbing.

'I don't think he was going to hurt me. I think he was trying to scare me off.'

'What?'

'I had a run-in with Cummins in the garden yesterday and his attitude was pretty hostile. He said the ghost didn't want us here and that we should go back to England.'

'Why didn't you tell me before now?' His voice shook with

anger. 'I'd have done something about it immediately.'

'I didn't want to give you another reason to worry about me being here. Anyway, now I think he was turning off my lamp at night, which was some risk when you think about it, and then leaving both the mouse and the rat,' she shuddered, 'to scare me.'

'I'm going to look for him. See what he has to say.'

'For God's sake, be careful,' Juliet said, trying to keep up with him as he took the stairs two at a time. She tried to avoid looking at the pillowslip swinging from his hand.

'Stay here!' he ordered before storming out into the yard. Flinging the pillowslip and its grisly contents into a dustbin, he slammed the lid shut. Then, crossing the yard, he roared out Cummins' name.

Juliet stood inside the kitchen window, watching.

Cummins came out of a shed and walked towards Logan, cleaning his hands on a rag.

Opening the window to hear what they were saying, Juliet leaned her head closer to it.

'Are you responsible for the dead rodents?' Logan asked, his voice shaking with rage.

'What the devil are you talking about?' Cummins' response was gruff.

'Have you left a dead mouse and rat in the house to scare Juliet?' Logan pressed.

Cummins gave a cold laugh. 'Don't be ridiculous. Why would I do something like that?'

'Because you don't want her here, or me either for that matter.'

Cummins stared at Logan. 'Whether I do or whether I don't is my business. I get on with my job, don't I? Have you any complaints on that score? I've kept it going well, filling your pockets for you while you were in England having your nose wiped by your mother and going to that posh university.'

Juliet could see Logan's fists clenching and unclenching as if he was dying to take a swing at him. She willed him not to.

'You don't sound very happy about it. I like anyone in my employ to be happy in their work. So perhaps you should consider moving on.'

Cummins poked a finger hard into Logan's chest. 'You won't push me out. This land is more mine than it is yours – you and yours breezing in and out of here as you please, while me and mine have shed blood, sweat and tears to make it what it is.'

'So that's it! You've started to think of this place as yours. But you can think again. Your family has always been well paid for your labour. But that's all it was, Cummins, a job. You have no rights to this place and you are delusional to think so. Consider yourself on notice as and from this minute – notice you needn't bother working out. Pack your things and go. Send me your address and I'll send you what you're owed.'

Cummins' face was thunderous. He stared at Logan with total hatred, spat on the ground beside him and walked off.

Inside the window, Juliet was shaking. She hadn't noticed Sheila coming in, until she was standing right beside her.

'Did you hear all that?' Juliet asked.

'Yes, love, I did.'

'He left a dead rat in my bed.'

'What kind of behaviour is that?' Sheila was outraged. 'The man has become unstable.'

Logan, striding back into the kitchen white with rage, stopped at the sight of the two anxious women standing by the window.

'I've fired him. The man thinks the place should be his! Pershaw land and he thinks I don't belong on it!'

'I knew he felt resentful about you coming back here,' Sheila said, a tremor in her voice. 'I should have said something. I suppose having free rein all these years gave him notions. He had moved in here, to the house, a year ago and warned me not to say anything or he'd get me fired by pretending that I had stolen things.' She took a tentative step towards Logan. 'I'm really sorry for not telling you, but he had me scared. My husband was unemployed at the time and this was one of the part-time jobs I couldn't afford to lose. I was very relieved when I heard you were coming back. Cummins, on the other hand, was very angry at having to move out.'

Logan had listened intently to what she said. 'It's all right, Sheila. I'm just sorry he put you in that position. He certainly is a piece of work. Even when I was a child there was something about him that made me wary of him.' Looking around, he ran a hand through his hair. 'God, I need a strong cup of coffee.' He reached for the kettle. 'Of course, now I'm without a farm manager.' He paused and looked at Sheila who was getting out some mugs. 'What about Des and Peter? Is there anything I should know about them?'

'No, they're good lads. I know their families. They keep their heads down and get on with their work.'

They were all lost in their own thoughts while Logan waited for the kettle to boil. He made coffee for the three of them.

Passing Juliet hers he studied her face. 'You all right, Juliet?'

'It's been some morning,' she replied, smiling weakly.

He reached out and touched her cheek. 'I'm sorry but I have to go and make a few calls.'

She nodded. 'That's okay.'

'I need to put Cummins' dismissal in writing and then I'll have to ring an employment agency, but I'd appreciate if you could spread the word locally too, Sheila, that there is a vacancy for a farm manager. I'll get the farmhands to come up to the house so I can explain the situation.'

'Des has been here three years now – he should be able to step up until you find someone new.'

'Thanks.' He looked at Juliet. 'I'm also going to make inquiries about a barring order in case Mr Cummins decides to pay another visit. Will you be in the library?

'Yes.'

'See you later.' With that he hurried out.

Chapter 46

When Juliet got to the library she didn't feel like staying there, so she retrieved the diary and went to the morning room across the hall. It was bright and cheerful, with the sun streaming in through the windows. She went and sat on the window seat and took up reading where she'd left off earlier.

15th May, 1889

Dear Diary,

I cannot believe how ignorant I have been! Poor Martha has been pining all this while for a man she has left behind in England!

I found her crying this morning in the nursery and was so concerned about her that I asked if she was unhappy with us. "Oh, no," she said, "you have been nothing but kind to me and I love Beatrice very much." Of this I had no doubt. One only has to see how well she cares for her, and I have seen her tuck her in for sleep with such tenderness, laying a kiss on her brow, as if Beatrice were her own.

Juliet sucked in her breath, immediately thinking of the dreams she was having about being tucked in. Could Martha be our ghost, she wondered. Surely not. Her eyes raced on.

I explained that I thought she had not been herself since we came to Carissima. I told her she could tell me anything and it would not change my affection for her. She dried her eyes and to my amazement told me that she was in love with Doctor Edward Adams, the handsome young doctor back home in our village. She first met him when he came to the house in Berkshire to treat Beatrice's fever, about seven months before we came to Ireland. I remember the night well. It was late and, while I watched over my little girl, Martha took him downstairs for a cup of tea before his journey home. She said that they had found it very easy to talk to each other and in the months that followed they became close. They used to meet in the garden of the old abandoned cottage on our land, just beyond the woods. She told me they were in love and that it had broken her heart to move to Ireland.

I was amazed as I thought he was engaged to another. She said that was only a rumour and that in fact he had asked her to be his wife. To my surprise she pulled a chain from inside her collar with the ring he had given her on it. It was a very beautiful ruby and diamond ring, the row of stones angled slightly across the gold band. It was quite unique and I would have thought very expensive for a young doctor. So I was not surprised when she said it had belonged to his mother. I asked her why she had not told me or made her engagement public. She explained that it was partly out of loyalty to me and that also Dr. Adams had not been practising medicine for long, and as yet could not afford to marry her. "And I do not have a dowry that I could bring to the marriage either," she said, "so we have to wait. When Edward – Doctor Adams – has saved a little, he will send for me. But the waiting is so hard." At this point, she started to cry again. I held her in my arms, feeling so bad for taking her away from her love, and assured her that I would facilitate her return to England when Dr. Adams sends for her. It will be very difficult for Beatrice and me to see her go when that time comes, but we are happy here, and in all consciousness I could not ask her to stay with us when she so obviously wants to be back in England.

I am resolved to speak to James. She is family, after all, so surely James can give her a small dowry so that when her beloved doctor sends for her, she will not go empty-handed.

I will speak to him this evening after supper.

Helena

'Juliet!'

'In here, Logan!'

He put his head around the door. 'I've asked Sheila to get a different room ready for you. You're not going back to that one.'

'Thanks.' She smiled, touched by his thoughtfulness. 'Logan, I think I might have found something in here,' she said, holding up the diary.

Logan came in and stood looking down expectantly at her.

'Martha was governess to Beatrice Pershaw, Helena and James' daughter, and it seems she lovingly tucked in her "charge" every night!'

Juliet got great satisfaction from imparting the news, but Logan looked disappointed.

'Well, that's not a whole lot, is it? I'm sure it's what all nannies do, and did. I wouldn't get too excited about it.'

'But it's what I've dreamed every night while here.'

'Yes, but if our ghost was a loving nanny, why the hell would she be ruining my sleep and my father's? Shouldn't she be kind to everyone, for God's sake?'

His irritation had her backing off. He was probably afraid to give himself false hope, but she still felt she was onto something. She just needed more concrete evidence to convince him.

She shrugged. 'Maybe. We'll see. I'll keep reading, but it might be worth mentioning to the water diviner – he's due to ring tomorrow.'

Logan shrugged, and took his car keys out of his pocket.

'I have to go into town to collect something from the garden centre and while there I want to see a friend of mine, Sergeant Ryan, at the Garda Station. I want his advice on Cummins. Come with me. It'll do us good to get out of here for a while.'

'Sure.' Juliet leapt up, delighted with the invitation. She was longing to spend some time with him.

Logan was only a few minutes in the garden centre, and then he drove them across town to the Garda Station. The station looked old.

'Apparently they're building a new one, so I suppose they aren't putting any money into the upkeep of this one,' Logan said as they got out of the car.

Sergeant Ryan was a portly, ginger-haired man in his mid-fifties, who listened patiently as Logan recounted what had happened with Cummins.

'I was wondering if I could get a barring order against him,' Logan asked.

'It's the district court that grants those,' Sergeant Ryan said, 'but to be honest, Logan, you won't get one. You would need evidence of Cummins being violent for that – and while what he did was nasty, you don't have evidence he actually did it.'

'But he verbally threatened Juliet.'

'Still not enough, I'm afraid. My advice would be to change your locks and, if he does show up, give me a shout.'

'There's a locksmith on his way there now,' Logan said, standing up and shaking the sergeant's hand. 'Thanks.'

'No problem. Call any time. Nice to meet you, Juliet.'

'I didn't know you'd arranged for a locksmith. You didn't waste any time,' Juliet commented as they drove home.

'I'm not risking that fellow getting inside my house again,' Logan said through gritted teeth. 'Sheila said she'd stay on to let the locksmith in.'

Back at Carissima, as they drove past the wall of the orchard, Juliet spoke.

'Helena's gardener, Brown, planted some of those apple and pear trees in there. They're as old as the house.'

'You're becoming a right little historian,' Logan teased. 'Let's hope that diary continues to be illuminating.'

Juliet knew he wasn't talking about the gardening.

Chapter 47

Logan had work to do when they got back, so Juliet took the diary into the morning room and this time curled up in an armchair. Feeling quite tired after the day's events, she closed her eyes just for a few moments' relaxation before starting to read. But after a few minutes she fell asleep, dreaming of herself picking pears in an orchard while hearing a woman sobbing.

After a while she woke with a deep sense of sadness like a physical pain in her chest. Remembering what she'd felt the day Logan showed her the orchard, she was curious to see the place again. Taking her jacket from the kitchen she went out into the yard. A fog had come down and the light was fading.

All was still and silent, her footsteps muffled as she made her way across the courtyard in front of the greenhouse and around by the orchard wall. The iron bars of the gate were cold under her hands as she pushed it open.

Instinctively she turned left and followed the weed-covered path along the inside of the wall. The trees in this section were

very old, lichen clinging to the bark and branches. The wall
ahead turned right, as did the path. Juliet followed it for a few
feet and then stopped dead. There in front of her was the exact
scene she had dreamed – the same group of trees standing on
their own section of grass near the wall and to the left of them
an old stone bench. All that was different from the dream scene
was that she wasn't up a tree picking pears.

'How can you dream of a place you've never seen before?' she
wondered. The sadness she'd felt on waking was back. It seemed
to hang in the air, with the echoes of the sobbing she'd heard in
her dream. The recall was so vivid, she thought for a moment she
could actually hear it.

Shivering, she pulled her jacket tighter, crossing her arms for
warmth before retracing her steps. She pulled the gate closed and
peered back in through the bars, a sensation of foreboding hanging
over her. Hearing a door closing in the yard, she walked towards it.

Logan was crossing over to one of the sheds.

'Hello,' she said.

'Oh hi, what are you doing out here?' he asked.

'Just taking a little air,' she said, thinking he looked exhausted.
'Logan, did anything sad happen in that orchard?'

'Not that I know of,' he said, shaking his head. 'Why?

'I got a sad feeling in there, that's all, so I just wondered.'

'It's just the fog. It's enough to dampen anyone's spirits,' he
said, shrugging his shoulders to bring the collar of his jacket up
higher on his neck.

'Yes, I suppose you're right.'

'I have a bit more work to do. Is it okay with you if we have
dinner in about an hour? Sheila has left a stew that I'll heat up
once I'm done here.'

'I'll do it.'

Their eyes held for a moment and Juliet thought he was

going to kiss her, but he just frowned and moved off towards the door of the shed.

With a sigh, she went back in to read more of the diary, turning on lights as she went.

In the morning room she turned to the next entry.

20th May 1889

Dear Diary,

I have wonderful news for you today, dear, dear Diary. I am going to have another baby! I was confident of it but James insisted I see the doctor to be sure, and he confirmed the good news. James is thrilled. I do so hope I will give him a son this time, an heir for Carissima.

Also, Beatrice is learning her alphabet. Martha says she is very fast at learning new things. I hope she will take as well to being a sister.

I could not be happier, and also I spoke to James and he is willing to provide Martha with a dowry. She was overjoyed when I told her and hugged me three times in her excitement. Selfishly, I hope that Doctor Adams does not send for her before the baby is born. Beatrice and I will need her especially at that time.

Helena

Juliet was relieved. The foreboding she'd felt since being in the orchard lifted. She read on.

5th June 1889

Dear Diary,

The weather was glorious yesterday, so James took Beatrice,

Martha and me out in the carriage to see a bog, the place where turf comes from. There is one about five miles from here. It was magnificent. I have never seen such a rich brown colour before. It seemed to stretch for miles. There were men cutting the turf and laying it out to dry. Others were stacking the dry turf into large piles. James says it is a very skilled job. He said one of our sheds will be filled to the roof with turf for our winter fires.

We picked some bog cotton for Beatrice. James tickled her nose with the soft plant. She laughed so much I feared she would be sick.

The fresh air today at last put colour in Martha's cheeks. She proudly wears her engagement ring now and although she confesses to missing Dr. Adams, she is full of hope at the prospect of returning to England eventually.

The air did me good too as I have been feeling unwell in the mornings.

Helena

15th June 1889

Dear Diary,

I received a letter today from Mother Pershaw. It made me laugh. She had been to a ball in London and was scandalised when her neighbour, the rather vivacious Lady Irwin, arrived dressed in, and I use her words: "a deep crimson gown, trimmed with purple velvet. Purple! Whoever heard of putting crimson and purple together! And her neckline was far too low!" I could almost see Mother Pershaw's outraged face as I read. I have always thought Lady Irwin's gowns to be exquisite. Although the colour combination is unusual, I warrant it was stunning on her. Mother Pershaw said the ball was magnificent, "but of course music will never be as glorious as it was at Josef Strauss's concert, four years ago." If I had heard that sentence once, I had heard it a hundred times. Mother Pershaw loves to brag about being invited to that concert of the celebrated Mr. Strauss, his first in London, and how that same evening she had shaken hands with the King. I am relieved we are no longer living with her as Beatrice cannot now be influenced by her snobbery.

Martha received a letter from her young man today also. She seems in better spirits since her relationship is no longer a secret. She often talks about him when we are out for a walk with Beatrice. I approve of her choice – the few times I met him he struck me as a very kind and courteous man, and she will make a good doctor's wife.

Helena

28ᵗʰ June 1889

Dear Diary,
The boathouse is finished and now contains two rowing boats. One is very pretty, made of dark wood, and has a wrought-iron backrest on the stern seat. It reminds me of a Venetian gondola I saw in a book once. James makes it very comfortable with cushions for me when he takes me out in it.

It was a lovely sunny afternoon again today so we spent a couple of hours out on the lake. James has become fond of fishing and I like to sit and read, or just watch him.

Helena

Glancing at her watch, Juliet got up and, taking the diary with her, went to the kitchen to put the stew in the oven. Sitting at the kitchen table she read on.

For the Love of Martha

3rd July 1889

Dear Diary,

There was great fuss here last night. A fox got into the henhouse. Luckily, Cummins was still in the kitchen having a late supper when he was alerted by the noise. He managed to shoot the fox which had already killed four hens.

Apparently there was a small gap in the fencing that the fox had squeezed through. Cummins was very apologetic about it and repaired it right away.

Mrs Dawson was annoyed – she says those hens were some of her best layers. I reassured her that we would have them replaced immediately. She calmed down after a while and, despite the late night, still managed to serve excellent scrambled eggs for breakfast this morning!

Helena

Hearing Logan out in the pantry, Juliet finished reading the entry she was on and got up to set the table.

'How are you getting on with that?' Logan asked as they were eating.

'It's very interesting. Just now, I was reading about your great-grandmother's second pregnancy. And the first Cummins to work here was mentioned too.'

Logan grunted. 'I hope he was a more loyal employee than his descendant! I've been such a trusting fool. Damn naive to leave the care of the place to him without ever checking up on him.'

'Don't be so hard on yourself, Logan. You had a different life going on.'

'Well, the naiveté stops here. I rang my accountant today

331

asking him to check back over the records for the last few years, just in case there is anything I've missed.'

'Like what?'

'I don't know.' He pushed his half-eaten dinner away from him, in exasperation. 'But if the guy was starting to believe the place was more his than mine, maybe there was other stuff going on.'

'Do you think he was stealing money from the farm?'

'I'd believe anything of him at this stage. Do you want some coffee?'

She shook her head, continuing to eat.

Waiting for the kettle to boil, he paced up and down.

'The thing is, I've trusted Cummins all these years with the financial affairs of the farm and now there's every possibility that that trust was abused.' He grimaced. 'By the way, I spent some time this afternoon measuring the rooms upstairs and the corridor, looking for any discrepancies that might indicate another secret passageway. But there was nothing. Sheila has made up the room at the end of the corridor for you, the one beyond mine. I hope you'll be able to sleep okay in there.'

I'd sleep better in your room, she wanted to say, but the look on his face made her hold her tongue. To try to lighten the mood she referred to the diary again.

'I was just reading about Helena and James Pershaw boating on the lake.'

'God, I promised you I'd take you out, didn't I?' He rubbed his forehead. 'What a mess this week is turning out to be.'

Juliet got up. 'Logan, it's fine. It mightn't be the holiday of a lifetime,' she smiled, 'but I wouldn't want to be anywhere else.' Tentatively she put her hand on his arm.

With a sigh that seemed to come up from his boots, he opened his arms and, drawing her into them, rocked her gently from side to side. She felt his lips brush the top of her head and she smiled, her head pressed into his shoulder.

'I don't know how you could say that,' he said. 'I know I've been a nightmare to live with these past few days and that there is no hope of a future for us if I can't resolve these things.'

Juliet's smile faded. Tilting back her head, she looked up at him.

'We're getting closer, Logan. I think Martha is more than likely the ghost and . . .' She hesitated, wondering how much to tell him.

'Go on,' he prompted.

'I think she's trying to connect with me in some way.'

'What?' Taking her by the shoulders, he held her away from him while concern, fear and anger all seemed to flit across his face.

In a split-second decision she decided to hold back, not wanting to worry him. 'It's just that I feel she might have led me to the diary, that's all, and somehow I'll figure it out.'

Logan looked sceptical, but accepted her answer.

'Let's tidy up here,' she suggested. 'And then I think I'll head up to bed early and read for a while.'

When the kitchen was tidy, Logan insisted on going upstairs with her. The new room was as beautiful as the previous one, only this time, being a corner room, it had windows facing east and south.

Her stuff was already in the room, having been moved there earlier by Sheila.

Logan closed the curtains then came and put an arm around her.

'I've put Sheila to a lot of trouble,' she said.

'Not you, but that son of bi–' Logan was silenced by Juliet's finger being pressed to his lips.

'Don't waste your energy on him.'

Logan nodded. 'You're right.' Walking away, he turned on the light in the en suite and glanced around it. 'Hammer on the wall if you need anything,' he said, leaving her standing in the middle of the room. 'And Juliet, lock this door,' he ordered, his hand already on the outside handle. 'Goodnight.'

Standing alone, she wished more than ever that Logan would relent and let her share his room. A shudder shook her body as she thought of Cummins having been in her other room. She went and locked the door, quickly getting ready for bed, all the time feeling uneasy.

She'd brought the diary up to read, but found she just wasn't in the humour for it. Exhausted after the day's happenings, she fell asleep.

Chapter 48

Helena's diary was the first thing Juliet saw when she woke in the morning and, since it was only seven, she stayed in bed and pulled it down onto the pillow.

30th July 1889

Dear Diary,
As I write these words I am aware, as I never was before, of how words can change a person's life forever.

Over two weeks ago I received a letter from Mother Pershaw. It was her usual mix of housekeeping advice and social gossip. However, halfway through, she had written a few sentences, the impact of which on this side of the Irish Sea she could not have foreseen.

She wrote: "Our community is shocked at the death of that very personable young man, Doctor Adams, who was thrown from his horse while returning home two nights ago from visiting a patient. He was found the following morning on the side of the road, his neck broken. There was a storm that night, and it is believed that either the thunder or lightning startled his horse."

My heart began to pound on reading the words. This was Martha's young man she was writing about. How was I to break such news to the poor girl?

Trembling, I went in search of her. Brigid was in the nursery watching over Beatrice as she napped. She said that Martha had gone to the orchard, and that is where I found her. She was sitting on the bench by the east wall reading a book. Before I could say anything, she pointed out the tiny new pears on the trees, remarking how quickly the seasons were passing. She looked so lovely sitting there with a smile on her face, so full of life and hope. And I had to shatter it. I sat beside her and told her what I had learnt.

She jumped up and, wringing her hands, vehemently denied that it could have been Edward who was thrown. "He is an excellent horseman. Mother Pershaw must have made a mistake. Edward is waiting for me – we are going to be married – we have it all planned."

I caught her hands and her eyes met mine. What she saw there made her go still and tears slid down her face. Pulling her gently down on the seat beside me, I took her in my arms. I was unable to hold back my own tears, as she sobbed out her heartbreak.

That night, I had to give her a draught to help her sleep.

She did not have the energy to get up for several days. I was very concerned about her and on the fifth day I insisted that she get dressed and sit outside with me for a little while. There, she cried again, guilt at her neglect of her duties with Beatrice mingling with her grief.

I assured her that Brigid was helping me to take care of Beatrice, but that Beatrice was missing her.

From that day on Martha began looking after Beatrice again,

but I know it takes tremendous effort for her to get up each day. The light has gone out of her eyes, which are constantly red from crying. I can only pray that time will heal.

    Helena

A tear slipped from the corner of Juliet's eye down onto the pillow, and a sob shook her body. Sitting up she reached for a tissue and blew her nose, but the tears kept coming. The scene in the orchard was vivid in her head, both from her dream and Helena's words. The crushing sadness was back in her chest. She was more convinced than ever about being connected to Martha and that somehow she, Juliet, was reliving Martha's feelings as she slowly discovered her story.

With a shaky sigh, she read on.

9th August 1889

Dear Diary,
Beatrice is thriving here. She loves walking by the lake with me. She is a very happy little girl and has been behaving very well for Martha. I think she knows something has happened to her, so she is being especially loving towards her.

    Martha tries very hard not to show her sadness in front of her, for which I am grateful. Beatrice is at such a delicate age. I can only hope that her amusing antics help Martha to recover.

    Helena

16th August 1889

Dear Diary,
James is in great spirits. Our first harvest has begun and he says

the yield will be high. He had to hire extra men and the barns have been filling up steadily.

I shall send Martha into town next week for some warm material for clothing for Beatrice for winter. She is growing so fast. The outing will do Martha good. I need to get as much done as I can before I become too heavy and awkward.

Helena

Juliet flicked through the next few entries. They were full of farm news and details about Beatrice's little milestones.

She was feeling dissatisfied. Had she found what she was looking for in Martha's heartbreak? Was it that heartbreak that had her spirit wandering through Carissima down through the years? If so, would the water diviner be able to soothe her and give her peace?

Her head beginning to throb, she put the diary aside and went for a shower. She knew she should be doing some yoga to calm her restlessness and ease some tension, but she was too eager to talk to Logan.

She was just tying her shoes, when there was a tap on her door.

'Juliet, are you awake?' Logan called.

Unlocking the door, she found him already dressed for the outdoors.

'It's a magnificent morning out there. I thought you might like a spin on the lake.' He smiled from a very pale face.

'No sleep again?' she asked.

He shook his head.

'Well, what do you say?' he pressed.

'Now, before breakfast?'

'If I leave it, the business of the day will take over, so let's just go for it.' He thrust her jacket at her, which he must have brought up from the kitchen. 'It isn't often you see a morning like this.'

They went out by the front door, next to which Logan had already propped a pair of oars and two life jackets. Juliet stood transfixed on the top step. The early morning mist that hovered above the lake surface was still in shadow, and the sun, not yet visible, had turned the sky pink. The air was both damp and fresh and there wasn't a sound – even the birds hadn't started to sing.

'Thank you, Logan. I would've hated to miss this. I love the hush of a morning fog.'

In silence they walked down to the boathouse, the oars over Logan's shoulder and Juliet carrying the life jackets. While Logan unlocked the doors, Juliet went to the water's edge and took in some deep breaths, a smile curving her lips.

The lake surface was like glass and the mist hung above it. Rushes stood tall and still to her left and the top of the hill across the lake was slowly being lit up by the sun. Just then two swans flew in from the east, breaking the silence with the whirring of their wings. Gliding down to the lake, they became one with the mist and disappeared from view.

The pink of the sky intensified and then slowly turned yellow as the sun rose higher. Finally it broke over the hill to the left, as simultaneously the mist melted away before her eyes, rising up into the air until it was no more, leaving the swans visible in the distance, gliding gracefully along.

'Beautiful,' she murmured, just as Logan came to stand beside her.

'Nature is some artist, isn't she?' he said softly. 'Ready?'

He passed her a life jacket and helped her to put it on. Her eyes rested on the top of his head as he snapped the clasp shut.

Longing to touch him, she wishing everything was okay so that he would take her back into his arms, his mind, his life. She sighed.

He looked up. 'What was that for?'

'I miss you, Logan,' she said, knowing her heart was in her eyes.

He laid his forehead against hers. 'You must know this is torture for me too, but I won't wreck your life with all this mess.'

'I understand.' She spoke the simple truth quietly. She stepped back and gave him a bright smile. 'Take me boating. I think I might be getting closer to the truth of our ghost, and I want to update you.'

They went into the boathouse. The air was damp. A narrow concrete pier divided the space inside, with a boat floating on either side. One was made of fibreglass and the other was an elegant wooden one. As Logan pulled on a chain to roll up a metal barrier at the lake-end of the boathouse, light gradually filtered in, allowing Juliet to see the metal backrest on the seat in the stern. She was sure she was looking at Helena and James' rowing boat.

'Logan, is that boat over a hundred years old?' she asked.

'No, about thirty, but still in excellent condition. My father had it made to replace one just like it. As a matter of fact that backrest there came from the original boat.'

'I know,' she said. 'I read about it in the diary.'

'Really?' he asked.

He held Juliet's arm as she got in, then climbed in too, using his hands against the pier to push them out onto the lake. Once outside, he was able to put the oars into the oarlocks and start rowing. A few strokes and the boat was turned around, with Logan's back towards the bow and the middle of the lake.

Juliet loved the rhythmic sound of the oars dipping in and out of the water as they glided further out from the shore. Leaning against the backrest, she marvelled that she was doing what Helena had done countless times in the past.

'You never brought any cushions for me,' she accused Logan.

'What?'

She explained about the diary entry.

'I wouldn't want you getting too comfortable,' Logan said after listening to her account. 'You'd have me rowing you around all day.'

He moved the oar in such a way that a little water splashed her.

'Hey,' she said, wiping her face.

They fell silent for a while.

'You're very quiet, and you look sad,' Logan said after a few minutes.

Juliet dipped her hand in the water and watched the droplets run off her fingertips.

'The doctor Martha was in love with died before he could send for her. He fell from his horse in a storm and broke his neck. The poor girl was heartbroken.' Juliet could feel her throat become thick with tears again and she swallowed hard.

Logan stopped rowing and they drifted for a bit.

'So,' he said, 'you think this Martha is still wandering the corridors, pining for him.'

'It would appear so, although the orchard would be a more likely spot. That's where she heard the news.' Juliet could see again the scene in the orchard. 'Oh Logan, she was devastated. They were going to be married, you see. She was supposed to go back to England to be with him. James was going to give her a dowry.' Her voice caught and she paused, swallowing hard again.

Logan looked at her with concern, but before he could speak she continued. 'The weird thing is, *before* I read that bit, I dreamt about the spot in the orchard where she was sitting when Helena broke the news to her.'

'What?'

'I dreamt I was up a pear tree, picking pears, but the place was really sad and I could hear a woman sobbing.'

'It's probably just some weird coincidence. With all my talk about orchards, it must have been in your subconscious or something.' With a pensive frown, he dipped the oars in the water and started rowing again.

They were moving along the far side of the lake. It was colder there where the hill shaded the water from the sun. Juliet hunched her shoulders, snuggling further into her jacket.

'So, I've been wondering . . .' she said, sitting up straight too suddenly, rocking the boat.

'Steady or you'll have us in the water,' Logan cautioned.

'If Martha is our ghost, which I'm one hundred per cent convinced she is, and if she is pining for her lost love, then what will appease her?'

'What I'd like to know is what she has got against the Pershaw men? Why won't she leave us in peace?'

'Well, presumably she came here against her will if her heart was back in England. Your great-grandfather was her employer, so maybe she was angry at him and then his descendants for taking her away from Edward in the first place.'

'But what the hell can I do about something that happened over a century ago?'

'Maybe you could apologise on behalf of the Pershaws.'

Logan snorted. 'Do you know how ridiculous you sound? Apologise to a ghost!'

Juliet looked angrily at him. 'I thought you wanted a solution to this. You said it was this ghost that was stopping us from being together, from having a future. And now you won't even think about it!'

Her angry voice echoed back off the hills, sending a flock of ducks into flight from the rushes.

'It just sounds crazy, that's all.'

He looked embarrassed, but Juliet pressed on.

'The house being haunted seems crazy too, but yet you know that it's true.'

He looked at her and nodded slowly. 'I know, I know,' he said. 'Why don't we wait and see what the diviner has to say? He's supposed to ring today, isn't he?'

Juliet nodded, feeling hopeful at the thought of it, her anger easing.

Logan rowed on in silence.

'It's time to go back,' he said after a few minutes. 'This is harder than it looks. My arms are getting tired and you look cold.'

Without further conversation he rowed back to the boathouse.

Chapter 49

Hungry after their early-morning expedition, Juliet and Logan worked together to produce a breakfast of scrambled eggs and bacon.

'What's happening about Michael Cummins?' Juliet asked, putting a rack of toast on the table and sitting down.

Logan brought over their plates.

'I'm going down to the lodge after breakfast to see if he has taken me seriously and made plans to move out.'

Juliet was frightened for Logan. 'He makes me nervous. He's a very angry and jealous man.'

'Don't worry. I'm going to take one of the farmhands with me. Probably Des – he's big and strong.' He gave her a teasing smile.

'Just be careful,' she said, not returning the smile.

'I will.'

Their gaze held for a moment.

'Now for a nicer topic of conversation,' Logan said. 'With all that happened yesterday, I didn't get a chance to tell you that, resulting from my report to the UN, I've been invited to give a series of lectures on my findings to two universities in England, early in the New Year.'

'That's great. Any of them near London?' she asked, delighted at the prospect, but immediately regretted the question as a veil seemed to slip down over Logan's face.

'No plans for the future, Juliet,' he warned. 'Not until I know what I can bring to the table.'

She bent her head over her meal, not wanting him to see the hurt in her eyes.

They ate in silence then Logan pushed back his chair and took his plate to the dishwasher.

'I have one or two calls to make before going to the lodge. I'll check in with you when I get back.' He picked up his half-finished mug of coffee and took it with him.

Juliet took her time finishing her own coffee and was loading the dishwasher when Sheila arrived.

'You're supposed to be on your holidays. Leave that and go and enjoy yourself.' Not accepting any protests, she ushered Juliet out of the kitchen.

Up in her room, Juliet made her bed, then sitting on it she opened Helena's diary once more.

21st August 1889

Dear Diary,
It is my birthday today and James has given me the most exquisite sapphire pendant. He got it on his last trip to Africa and kept it as a surprise. He says there will be lots of balls in Dublin next spring to which I can wear it. For now it is hidden away in the safe room upstairs, with my other jewellery. He spoils me.

We are not celebrating my birthday in any other way, for poor Martha is still grieving for Doctor Adams and it would not be right. She keeps her grief very private now and I rarely see evidence of tears, but there is such an air of sadness about her it is heartbreaking. It is wrong to see someone so young and pretty dressed from head to toe in black. But she insists on it and I will not argue with her about it. Luckily Beatrice keeps her very busy and her antics bring an occasional smile to Martha's face.

Helena

Juliet snapped the book shut and hurried down to catch Logan before he left for the gate lodge. To her relief he was still in the office. He looked up when she appeared at the door.

'I found a reference to the secret room upstairs. Listen to this,' she said and read aloud from the diary.

'So I was right, it was used as a safe.' he said.

'And where are the family jewels now?'

'Well, I suppose they were all passed on to Helena's children and so forth. Probably my Great-aunt Beatrice inherited them and they're in that branch of the family. I've definitely seen that sapphire pendant in family photographs. I've a box of photos somewhere. I can pull it out, if you're interested.'

'Okay. But don't you think it strange that the room was completely empty. You didn't know about the existence of that room but Michael Cummins did. Maybe he cleared it out!'

'Careful with the accusations, Juliet. It's one thing to try to scare you away, but quite another to take the family jewellery.'

'Well, you're having the accounts rechecked, so I'm just saying that if you didn't know the safe room was there, maybe your father didn't know it either, but obviously the knowledge *was* passed on through the Cummins generations.'

Logan put his hand through his hair. 'I suppose it's possible, but I've never heard of anything valuable going missing. There's a safe here in the office. Maybe when it was installed, that hidden safe room became obsolete.'

Juliet chewed her bottom lip. 'I suppose you're right.'

Logan stood up. 'Sorry, but I have to go. Des is waiting for me outside in the jeep.'

He was gone before she could reply. Wandering to the front of the house, she turned into the morning room. Now that the mist was completely gone, there was clear blue sky outside and the room was bright and warm. The sun streamed across the couch, so she sat there and put her feet up, enjoying the heat on her legs. Opening the diary, she read on.

29th August 1889

Dear Diary,

I am tired during this confinement, more so than when I was expecting Beatrice. Maybe it is because I am running my own household this time round. James asked me to go boating with him today, but I declined. I have a pain in my lower back which would not be helped by an hour in the boat! I think he was disappointed – the sooner I give him a son who can go on fishing trips with him, the better!

Instead I am sitting here in the morning room with my feet up, and a cup of tea beside me. I have taken to having a little rest in the afternoons while Beatrice is having her nap. It is so pleasant here with the sun slanting in through the west windows. From where I sit, I can see James out on the water.

Helena

Very slowly, Juliet lifted her eyes from the diary. Was she sitting in the exact same spot as Helena had all those years before? This was definitely an antique settee, but was it the same one? She ran her hand over the material. If it was, then it had been re-upholstered in more recent years. At this time of the day, the sun was shining in through the south-facing windows, but she had a perfect view of the lake from where she sat. The fine hairs on her arms rose, despite the warmth of the room. Was it pure coincidence that she had come in and sat in this spot before reading this particular entry?

'You don't believe in coincidences,' she reminded herself. 'Just go with the flow.'

With a smile she resumed reading.

6th September 1889

Dear Diary,
I am very afraid. The pain in my back has become worse. James had to fetch Doctor Murray today as I was bleeding a little. He said there was nothing to worry about but I have to stay in bed for a while. I pray my little baby will be all right.
Helena

Juliet's mobile rang, making her jump and dragging her back to the present. Hoping it was the water diviner, she quickly took the phone from her pocket. But it was her mother's number on the screen.

'Hi, Mum.'

'Hello, love. I hope you don't mind me ringing, but I'm dying to know how it's going there. Is it a nice place? How are you and Logan getting on? Is he with you now, or can you talk?'

Juliet laughed. 'You're like someone on speed. Which question do you want me to answer first?'

Her mother laughed at herself. 'Sorry, I'm between patients

and only have a minute. Give me all your news as quickly as you can.'

'Carissima is beautiful, Logan is beautiful, even this Irish weather is unusually beautiful.'

'Ah love, that's great. Oh dear, the light is flashing here on my office line. Got to go. Come over for dinner next week, when you're back.'

'Lovely. See you then. Give my love to Dad.'

Juliet was relieved her mother had been in a hurry. She didn't want her figuring out that something was wrong.

She returned to the diary, hoping Helena wasn't going to have a problem with the pregnancy. Juliet knew for definite that she'd had another child, a boy, because Logan was a descendant of the male line.

13th September 1889

Dear Diary,

After Martha puts Beatrice down for her nap each afternoon she comes to my room to go over housekeeping matters. Being in bed is so frustrating, but Martha has been so helpful in dealing with everything that I cannot attend to. She has a very gentle way about her and the servants respect her and do not seem to have a problem taking my instructions through her.

But her visit today was different. After our usual housekeeping discussion, she surprised me with a most unusual request. She said that Edward Adams had been the love of her life and she knew there would be no other for her. She wanted me to get James to promise her that, when she dies, he will arrange for her body to be taken back to England and have it buried beside her beloved Edward.

God forgive me, but my immediate thought was that she was

349

going to harm herself. She must have seen that in my face, for she quickly reassured me that she had no intention of taking her own life, saying that Beatrice was too special to her to do something like that and also that her gratitude for my kindness would prevent her doing such a thing.

I pointed out that she was eight years younger than I and could well outlive me and James. She asked that maybe her wishes could be made known to Beatrice and the new baby when they were old enough to understand. I felt I had no choice but to agree, and when I did the light seemed to return to her eyes.

I find it very sad that Martha is going to spend her whole life looking forward to her death. I wept when she left the room.

I told James what had passed between us. He thought it a ridiculous notion, what with the difficulties of getting a body back to England by sea. I stressed how important it was to her peace of mind and after a while he promised to carry out her wishes. He is a kind man, and has not been unmoved by Martha's loss.

Helena

Chapter 50

Juliet's reading was interrupted by Logan coming through the door with a mug of coffee in each hand and a shoebox under one arm.

'A quick coffee break,' he declared.

'You back already?' she asked, looking at her watch and swinging her legs off the couch to make room for him.

He handed her one of the mugs and put the other on a side-table. Then, looking grim, he sat down and put the shoebox in her lap.

Though curiosity was killing her, anxiety about his visit to the lodge took precedence.

'Well, was Cummins there?'

'No. He's gone already and taken all his things with him.'

'Thank God. No confrontation then.'

'Nope. I presume he'll get in touch with a forwarding address for his outstanding wages.'

'So what's this?' she asked, turning her attention to the box.

'The photographs I mentioned.'

Lifting the lid, she could see that there was only a handful inside.

'Is this your entire collection?'

'As a family we're a bit camera shy.'

'Tell me about it,' she said drily.

'Touché.'

'Hey, this one is of your graduation,' she said, lifting the first one, which was very similar to the one in the apartment in Florence. 'Did you send this to your dad?'

'No, I chucked it in there when I got back here. That's me and Mum in a restaurant afterwards.' He pointed to the second photograph. 'That's Mum and Dad on their wedding day and, yes, the embarrassing baby photos.'

Juliet grinned as she leafed through them, pausing at one of him in a party hat with a birthday cake in front of him, with four candles on it.

'You were very cute.'

He snorted.

'Who's this?' she asked, holding up another wedding photo. It was black and white, the groom was in a dark suit and the bride was wearing a high-necked wedding dress from the sixties. 'That's Aunt Jane, one of my father's sisters. She married a British engineer and moved to England.'

He picked up another one.

'This is Aunt Ruth's wedding. She was Dad's eldest sister. She went to America and married an army officer. See the necklace?' He pointed to a pendant inside the lace of her wedding dress.

Juliet looked closer. Because the photograph was in black and white, she couldn't tell if the stone was a sapphire but it certainly looked magnificent.

'This one is of them and their twin boys,' he said, pointing to a photo of the same couple, holding a baby each, the woman now dressed in a neat, seventies-style suit. 'So you can safely assume that the pendant is in some safe in America now. But look, in this old photo, you can see it again.'

He pulled out an aging sepia photo of a woman dressed in clothes of the nineteen twenties. She had an elegant appearance and was perched on a dining chair, her feet neatly crossed at the ankles.

At first Juliet only saw a long string of pearls, as was the fashion of the time. But looking closer she saw the pendant resting on the front of the woman's blouse.

'Who is she?'

'Turn it over.'

In ink on the back was scrawled: *Beatrice, 1922*.

'Wow,' Juliet said, turning it over again. It was strange to be looking at the grown-up version of the child she was reading about.

'And this is her brother, my grandfather David.'

It was a photo of a man who resembled James Pershaw in his portrait, his right hand resting on the head of a gun dog.

'Helena's son. So the baby was okay.'

'What?'

'She had trouble during her pregnancy.'

'Oh. I'll have to read that diary soon. It's weird that you are getting to know my ancestors better than I do.'

Juliet was disappointed there were no more photographs.

'No photo of Helena or Martha, then?'

'No, but at least we have Helena's portrait.'

'What! Where?'

'Haven't you seen it, in the hall opposite James' one?'

'No.'

'Of course, you couldn't, could you? It fell down last month, and I didn't get around to rehanging it. It needs new wire.'

'Where's it now? Was it damaged?'

'No, luckily. It's in the office. C'mon, I'll show you.'

In the office he moved a large cardboard box which had prevented her from seeing the portrait any time she'd been in there. Lifting the old frame off the floor he turned it around so she could look at it.

Juliet drank in the image of the woman she'd been getting to know through her own words.

'She was stunning, wasn't she?' Logan said softly.

She was wearing a gown of sapphire blue, as she posed beside a fireplace. And although she was petite, the liveliness in her eyes, which the skill of the artist had managed to capture, showed a strength and magnetism.

'She couldn't have been much more than twenty in this, I think,' Logan said, putting it back on the floor.

'She's just as I pictured her.' Juliet said. 'Soft but determined. You're correct — you should get to know your great-grandmother.'

'I'm looking forward to it, but I've got to get this new farm manager thing sorted first. I've a meeting with the farmhands in . . .' he checked his watch, 'five minutes. They're pretty experienced and can manage for a while without direction, but I won't relax until I've a new man in place to oversee everything.'

'Or woman.'

'Yeah, I'm open to that. I'm sure the employment agency will send a cross section of applicants.'

'I'll leave you to it then,' she said, trying not to worry about the frown on his face. This business with Michael Cummins was putting more strain on him and, coupled with his lack of sleep, he wasn't looking the better for it.

'I'm going to be pretty tied up here for the rest of the day. I'm sorry. Why don't you get out of the house for a bit?' When he saw her about to protest he read her thoughts. 'The diary can wait another while.'

'Okay. The light looks great out today – I might just take a picture or two.'

'Good. Ah, here are the lads now.'

They heard voices coming through the kitchen, so Juliet made herself scarce.

Having spent a wonderful couple of hours with her camera around the gardens and down by the lake, she returned to the house with her stomach growling for lunch. While up in her room, putting away her camera bag, her phone rang.

'Hello, is that Juliet Holmes?' a woman asked.

'Speaking.'

'Hello, I'm Jack Long's wife. He was supposed to ring you today about visiting your house, but I'm afraid he has decided to stay on for the weekend in Wales to see some relatives before coming back on Monday. He phoned me last night but I was in my sister's and didn't have your number with me. I'm sorry about that, but I did tell him about your call and he said he will ring you first thing on Monday.'

'Okay, thank you for letting me know. I'll look forward to his call. I do urgently need to speak to him.'

'I'll make sure he rings you.'

'Thank you. Goodbye.'

Juliet was very disappointed and went downstairs considering their options now in the light of the delay. She was approaching the kitchen when she heard a scream from beyond the door.

Racing in, she saw a very pale Sheila standing with her hand held under a flowing tap.

Logan must have heard the scream too and ran in behind Juliet.

'What's happened?'

'I cut my hand,' Sheila said, her voice shaking.

'How bad?' Logan rushed to her side.

'It's okay. I'm all right,' she said weakly.

'This looks nasty, Sheila. It'll need stitches. I'm going to take you to the hospital.' He wrapped a clean tea towel tightly around her hand.

'Can I help?' Juliet asked.

'Will you get Sheila's coat from the pantry?'

When Juliet brought it in, he put it gently around Sheila's shoulders.

'Will you be all right here on your own, or do want to come with us?' Logan asked, scooping his car keys off the counter, his arm around Sheila's waist.

'I'll be fine. I've some work to do on the internet. Go on, I'll see you later.'

'There's a casserole in the oven, which will be done in half an hour,' Sheila said.

'I'll sort it. You just look after yourself,' Juliet told her.

'Lock the doors,' Logan called over his shoulder.

Through the kitchen window she watched him help Sheila into the car. Going to the pantry door she locked it like he'd said, feeling a bit foolish doing so in the middle of the day. However, the image of Michael's Cummins face came to mind, and the feeling evaporated. She lost no time going to the front door and locking that too.

She had a solitary lunch at the kitchen table, Googling water diviners in nearby counties. Finding two, she noted their details, but wondered how Logan would feel about using them, when he was already familiar with Jack Long's work and trusted him. Her own impatience had her wanting to call both of them to see if they could come over on Friday or Saturday, but instinctively she knew she had to run it by Logan first. Shutting down the laptop, she removed the casserole from the oven and placed it on the counter to cool.

Noticing that Sheila had left a cookery book open at a recipe for peach cobbler, and that some of the ingredients were already laid out on the counter, she decided to give it a go herself.

Over an hour later, the kitchen was filled with the comforting smell of the freshly baked pie and Juliet mentally patted herself on the back because she thought it looked as good as it smelled.

A text came through from Logan, saying that due to a road traffic accident they had been pushed well down the queue and wouldn't be back for a while yet.

Figuring that Sheila's hand wouldn't be up to much for the next few days, Juliet decided to help out some more. Locating the vacuum cleaner and a duster, she went up and cleaned her own room. When she was done there, she also ran it around the drawing room. She took one look at Logan's office, decided not to disturb anything in there, and put the vacuum cleaner away.

When a few minutes later the phone rang in his office, she went in and answered it. It was the employment agency, wanting him to give them a call. A second call came immediately after she hung up. This time it was his accountant, sounding a bit frazzled, and he asked that Logan ring him urgently.

The sky had clouded over outside, darkening the office. Juliet switched on a desk lamp before texting both phone messages through to Logan at the hospital. While she sat there, the window beside her rattled in a sudden gust of wind and within a minute a squally shower was lashing against the glass.

She went to get the diary, taking it into the wood-panelled sitting room at the back of the house. Again she had to turn on a light as the rain outside was now lashing down, causing the evening to close in early. After closing the curtains on it, she put a match to the fire Sheila had cleaned out and reset earlier.

It was just catching when her mobile rang. She heard Logan's voice, edged with frustration.

'Sheila is still waiting to be seen by the doctor. Luckily she has been given some strong pain relief, and the cut has some temporary adhesive strips on it, but the waiting around is maddening.'

'Did you get something to eat?'

'Sandwiches from the canteen. How are you?'

'I'm fine. I've just lit the fire.'

'Sounds cosy. I wish I was there.'

'I wish you were too.'

She heard his sigh.

'I don't know what time I'll be back.'

'I'll see you later.'

Knowing he wasn't going to be back any time soon she went to the kitchen, heated a portion of casserole and brought it back to eat in front of the fire. Passing back through the hall she could see different shading on the wall opposite James' portrait, where Helena's portrait must have been. As she stood there, she felt her mood changing, becoming sad. Turning away, she hurried back to the warmth of the fire, closing the door behind her. She opened the diary.

For a moment she thought she'd opened the wrong page because the entry was written at the end of October. She flicked back the page, to check. On it was the one she'd just read for the thirteenth of September. That meant Helena hadn't written for about six weeks. The sense of foreboding came back.

28th October 1889

Dear Diary
I have been unable to bring myself to write of my grief. But now I find that if I do not, I will go mad from keeping it all inside.

For the Love of Martha

Two tragedies are more than anyone should have to cope with.

What words can a mother use to describe how she feels when her baby is stillborn? There are none.

The pain I had in my back got steadily worse until September 21ˢᵗ, when I went into labour. The baby wasn't due for another four months. I was terrified.

James fetched the doctor and midwife, but there was no hope for the baby. It was too early in my pregnancy. It was a little boy. They let me see him for a moment. He was perfect, but so tiny. I lost a lot of blood, and felt as though it bled straight from my heart, the ache was so great.

James gave him the name Andrew.

He was buried here on our land. There is a ruin here of an old church with some consecrated ground beside it where the clergy were buried. It is a beautiful spot, not far from the boathouse. James got permission to bury my baby there so he would be near me and I could visit him every day. James and Martha took him there and the local vicar was in attendance. I was too ill to attend.

I was so sad for James too — the son he had wished for was not to be. He was very loving and attentive, promising me that there would be other children, but I could not take it in — a future does not exist in the immediate world of grief.

Juliet's throat ached for Helena. Helena definitely had a son, but it had to be from a later pregnancy.

A few days later, Martha stopped visiting my sick room. I was too weak to notice. I believe Brigid took care of me at that time.

Afterwards, James told me that Martha had fallen ill with a fever. Because I was so weak, the doctor insisted she take to her bed and stay away from me.

Two nights later, again James came to my room and told me

that during the night Martha's coughing had become worse and that the doctor could do nothing more for her. Taking me in his arms, he said that her fever had worsened just after midnight and she had passed away.

I could scarcely believe it and my first thought was that if I had been well I would have been able to nurse her and make her well again. But James told me that the doctor said her lungs were weak from a previous infection and just could not cope.

I wept until I was limp in James' arms. Then suddenly I remembered her request. "You must take her body back to England," I cried to James.

"I cannot," he replied. "The doctor said it all must be taken care of immediately, or we risk the spreading of infection."

I beseeched him to remember our promise to her. I clung to his arm, weeping and begging him to do as she had asked.

He soothed me and said he would speak to the doctor again. He laid me back on the pillows, smoothed the hair from my brow and dried my tears. I was exhausted and fell asleep almost at once.

When I awoke in the morning, my heart hurt with this new grief. I tried to console myself that my little boy had Martha to take care of him now. But I missed them both so much.

I did not see James all day, but was not concerned. I knew he had a lot to organise in order to get Martha's body home to her Edward.

When James came in to see me that evening, he would not let me ask any questions, insisting I should not tire myself out. He said everything had been taken care of.

It took another week for my strength to return. The doctor allowed me to get up for a few hours each day.

I must stop for now. I do not have the strength to write what came next.

Helena

The lump in Juliet's throat dissolved into tears, which silently ran down her cheeks. The sadness Helena conveyed through her words seemed to wrap around her heart. The grief was personal to her now. Feeling cold all of a sudden, she took a rug from the back of a couch and wrapped it around her shoulders before reading on.

Helena took up her story the following day, and at the first sentence an audible gasp escaped from Juliet.

29th October 1889

Dear Diary,

He did not do it. He did not keep the promise. I suppose it was not his fault but surely there was something he could have done? The doctor could have embalmed Martha's body. If only I had been well, I would have insisted on it and then she could have been taken back to England without any danger to anyone.

It was five days after her death that James came to my room, knelt by my bed and broke down in tears. He apologised for letting me believe Martha had been taken back to England, but he had been fearful of telling me the truth in my condition. The doctor, he said, had insisted that Martha's body be buried immediately to stop the spread of whatever infection she had succumbed to. He had put the fear of God in him about Martha's illness spreading to me or Beatrice.

"I had already lost my son," he said. "I could not risk losing you or Beatrice too. Driven by grief and worry I asked the vicar to return immediately and Martha was buried beside our son."

I was appalled.

James could see the disbelief on my face, but did me the courtesy of finishing the story.

He said that now I could visit both of them there. "I knew you wanted me to take her back to England, but I just could not arrange that." Looking embarrassed, he continued, "There is a young oak tree behind her grave and when the vicar left I asked the oak to watch over her since I had not kept my promise." He hung his head.

I could not speak but I reached out and caressed him, my anger at his actions easing in the light of his thoughtfulness and torment.

He continued: "As soon as I stepped away from the tree, the air was shattered by a great wail of grief. For a moment I was terrified, until I realised the sound had come from me. A second wail was torn from deep in my chest and an aching sorrow clings to me constantly since."

I held open my arms to him and he came into them and sobbed like a child.

While my own heart was aching at not keeping our promise to Martha, I told him that he must not torture himself, that the doctor had forced his hand. I felt Martha would surely understand that.

My words seemed to calm him somewhat and he kissed my brow before leaving the room.

I am exhausted and heartsick that Martha has died so young and that I had been unable to tend her in her last days. And now too, in death, we have failed her.

Helena

Juliet swiped away more tears and took a shuddering breath before she could read on.

8th November 1889

Dear Diary,
My strength is returning and I go down every day to the lakeside

to lay flowers for Andrew and Martha. Yesterday James placed a small headstone at each of their graves.

James is still taking their deaths very hard and rarely smiles these days. I hear him losing his temper with the servants and he is even intolerant of Beatrice's childish chatter.

He tosses and turns at night, and seems to be sleeping very little. I am very concerned about him. But he will not talk to me about it.

Helena

Chapter 51

Juliet thought she heard a car and, putting down the diary, she ran down the hall, wiping her eyes as she went. She needed to tell Logan what she had read.

Entering the kitchen she reached out to turn on the light but froze before touching the switch when a movement outside the kitchen window caught her eye.

In the rain she could see a man in riding breeches and a young woman in a long black dress. He was trying to walk away but she was holding on tightly to his arm. Her words came clearly to Juliet even though the windows and doors were shut.

'Please, James, please, take me back to England!' she cried. 'Take me back to Edward!'

'Leave me be, for pity's sake,' he growled, shaking her off and striding away.

'*You promised!*' she cried, collapsing to the ground, sobbing.

Car lights came up the drive and swept over that piece of lawn, but now it was empty. However, the heart-wrenching sobs continued.

Juliet only realised it was she that was making the noise when moments later Logan switched on the light and rushed towards her, helping her up off the floor.

'Oh, my god, what's happened? Are you all right?'

Too dazed to speak, she just stared at him for a moment, the sobbing easing. He held her by the shoulders, peering into her face.

'Juliet, for God's sake, answer me! Has someone hurt you?'

'No, I'm fine. I saw ... I mean I think I saw ...' she mumbled as Logan helped her onto a chair.

'You're as pale as a sheet, and you're shivering.' He took off his jacket and put it around her shoulders.

'It's Martha. They promised to take her back but didn't, and she's been haunting the Pershaws ever since.'

'What? What are you talking about?'

She lunged forward and grabbed his jumper in both of her fists. 'Listen, you've got to help her. You've got to take her back.'

The wildness in her eyes made him lean away from her in shock.

'Juliet,' he said firmly, 'you've had some sort of fright. You need to calm down a little.'

'She won't give any of you any rest, don't you see? Any of the Pershaws! She blames you all. You'll never rest until she rests.'

Logan gripped her wrists, pushing at them gently, easing her back down in the chair. She still didn't let go, so he had to squat down in front of her. Juliet looked at her hands, only just becoming aware that she was holding on to him. She released him, blinking rapidly and taking quick, shaky breaths.

'I saw her, Logan,' she said, calmer now, 'out there on the side lawn, begging James to take her back to England.'

Logan stood and, bringing over a glass and the whiskey she'd brought him, insisted she take a drink.

Grimacing on swallowing, she refused to take another sip. 'I'm fine, just a little shaky. Maybe I could have a cup of coffee?'

'Sure.' Logan made a cup of instant and upended the whisky into it. 'Now, drink it,' he ordered.

'That's better,' she said. 'Thanks.'

Pulling a chair up close to hers, he brushed the hair back from her face and rubbed the tear stains on her cheeks. The drink began to warm her a little.

'What happened?' he asked gently.

'Martha died of a fever, and James broke his promise to take her body back to England to be buried with Edward Adams. Martha had asked James Pershaw to take her body back to England when she died. James made a promise to do so, while believing that her death was so far in the future that the promise was of no consequence to him. He was totally taken by surprise at her early demise, only months after she lost Edward. The doctor said because of the risk of infection it was too dangerous and insisted that transporting her to England was out of the question and that James had to bury her body immediately.'

'But if the doctor gave him no choice, then technically it wasn't his fault.'

'But, if he never thought he'd have to fulfil the promise, maybe it hadn't been genuine in the first place.'

'And you think she has been haunting the Pershaws ever since?' He shook his head. 'God, it's all a bit hard to believe, isn't it?'

'I don't think so, especially after what I just saw out there.'

'Or imagined?'

'No way!' She got up and paced.

'Well, it's dark, a wild night, you were here alone. It's a bit spooky – you'd just read a very emotional piece in the diary –'

'I didn't imagine it,' she said, stopping in front of him. 'It's just like the dreams. I didn't imagine them either. And you aren't imagining your sleepless nights, are you?'

He stared up at her, his fingers tapping restlessly on his knees.

'You've been looking for an answer,' she pressed. 'Now accept it.'

'And what if I do? All we know now is why she is haunting us, but how do we stop her? Apologise, like you said. Apologise for a broken promise.'

Juliet paced again. 'I don't know. It doesn't seem enough somehow. God, I can't think straight.'

'And I'm too hungry to think straight. Is there some food left?'

'Yeah.' Juliet sank down onto a chair, suddenly drained.

'Did Jack Long ring? Maybe if we tell him all of this, he'll have some suggestions.'

'He's not coming, well, not until Monday at least. He's still in Wales. But I found the name of some other diviners we could try.'

'We'll wait,' Logan said firmly. 'I know of Jack's reputation. I'd prefer it to be him.'

Juliet was disappointed but suddenly remembered Sheila and changed the subject. 'Oh, I forgot about poor Sheila! How's her hand?'

'It was a deep cut and needed several stitches, but it should heal nicely, the doctor thinks. It's bandaged up for the moment and she will be on painkillers for a few days. I asked if she wanted to stay here, but she says she can manage fine at home.' He plated up his food. 'Is that fire still lighting in the sitting room?'

Juliet nodded.

'Good. Let's take this in there. Do you want anything?'

'No, thanks.'

They were silent while he ate. Juliet stared into the flames, curled up on the opposite end of the couch to him, her feet against his thigh. Soon the heat and the effects of the whiskey took hold and her eyes drifted shut. She vaguely remembered Logan putting the rug over her before falling asleep. In her dreams, the scene she'd witnessed in the garden was repeated over and over again, but it took place in different rooms in the house. Twice Logan had to shake her awake because she was moaning. Each time, she fell asleep again quickly and he sat with her until the morning, dozing on and off.

Chapter 52

It took Juliet a second to remember where she was when she woke up at eight the next morning. Blinking at the ashes in the grate, she stretched her cramped legs. She was alone and the memories of the previous evening came rushing back. She felt an urgency to find Martha's grave.

Running upstairs she took a quick shower and changed her clothes. When she came down there was a note on the kitchen table from Logan, saying he was gone out on the farm with Des.

The coffee was still hot so Juliet poured a cup and had a hastily buttered slice of toast before putting on her jacket.

A cool breeze hit her the minute she stepped outside the front door, and a flurry of leaves blew down from the nearby trees. Zipping her jacket up, she headed down the path to the edge of the lake.

She searched along the water's edge on either side of the boathouse, but could not find an old ruined church or graves anywhere.

Suddenly recalling the words in the diary about the young oak tree, she looked up at the trees around her. Not a distinctive oak leaf or acorn was in sight.

'Ash trees, all ash,' she said. 'Damn!'

Returning to the boathouse, she leant her back against its wall. Slowly she straightened up and turned around.

'You great big idiot!' she said, putting out her hand to touch the concrete breeze blocks that made up the wall. Then she looked up at the roof of corrugated sheeting. 'This is too modern!'

With a glimmer of fresh hope she returned to the house, veering off to go to the back yard when she heard the jeep.

Logan and Des were passing through the kitchen when she came in.

'You go ahead to the office, Des. I'll be with you in a moment,' Logan said.

'That boathouse isn't the original, is it?'

'Good morning, and no.'

She waved her hand in dismissal of the greeting. 'Was it built in the same place as the original? I was searching for oak trees there and then I copped on to the fact that that wasn't the first boathouse, and mightn't be the same location as the original one.'

'Why were you looking for oak trees?'

'The diary mentions that there was a young oak next to Martha's grave on consecrated ground here, on the estate, near the boathouse.'

'Yeah, those ruins and the original boathouse were further along the shore. You were right in your deductions, dear Watson. Of course the boat house was made of wood and is long gone. But the church ruins are still there.'

'How do I find it?'

'Instead of taking the path to the left of the front lawn, take the lane to the right. At the bottom turn right and about two hundred metres along you'll find a gap in the hedge. A tall holly bush stands just next to it. From there, a path leads down to a small clearing and a stony inlet. That's where the boathouse was. The ruins are in amongst the trees to the left of that. The path is probably overgrown so take a stick with you for the brambles. You'll get one in the front hall. Or maybe you'd like me to go with you?'

She saw him glance towards the door Des had gone through.

'No, Des is waiting for you. I don't mind going on my own. I just want a look at the place, that's all.'

'Have you had any breakfast?' he asked.

She smiled, loving that he was still looking out for her despite all his preoccupations.

'Yes, thanks. See you later.' She paused. 'And by the way, with a surname like Holmes, shouldn't you call me Sherlock instead of Watson?'

She was glad to see the quip bringing a smile to his face.

In the hall, she pulled a blackthorn walking stick out of the umbrella stand and followed the directions Logan had given her.

She was glad of the stick. Having found the holly bush that marked the start of the path, she had to fight her way through the brambles. 'Path' was a generous term, she thought. She couldn't make out a trail to follow, but could see the lake through the trees and shrubs and headed for it.

Coming out into a small clearing a few minutes later, she stopped and looked around. Her heart was beating a little faster and she knew it wasn't from exertion. The breeze had become stronger and danced the trees into noisy movement. The sky was grey and the lake surface was ruffled by scurrying ripples, driving them onto the shore. Despite the sounds, there was an underlying silence, the silence that comes with the absence of people-noise – the sense that she was the first person to come here in a very long time.

Walking to the water's edge, she imagined Helena stepping gingerly into a boat here, mindful of not getting her gown wet, and then she and James setting off for a serene afternoon in their gondola-like boat.

Juliet moved into the trees to the left of her which were a mixture of ash and oak, again whacking brambles out of her way. The trees thinned and walking on a little she found herself in another clearing with its own gravelled shoreline. Towards the back of the clearing was a stone ruin only about two feet high and overgrown with ivy. It was small and only covered an area of about thirty feet by twenty feet.

Her heart started to beat faster. There were a lot of oak trees bordering the area. The ground here was moss-covered and full of lumps and hollows. At first glance she couldn't see any gravestones. Going to the left of the ruin, she checked in semicircles away from it, pushing any growth aside with the stick, but she found nothing. Going to the right of it, she repeated the action. Just three feet away from the wall of the ruin, the stick connected with stone beneath the moss.

She bent to examine it but it was just a small rock with no markings. She moved on nearer to the line of trees and there she saw two small headstones covered in ivy, each only a foot high. Falling to her knees, Juliet ripped the ivy from the first headstone and with some difficulty read the carving that was there.

It said:

Andrew Pershaw, born and died on 21st September, 1889.

Juliet felt her throat tighten with emotion.

Getting up, she moved to the right and tore the ivy away.

And there it was . . . Martha's headstone.

Juliet hunkered down.

On the stone was engraved the name Martha White and the dates 1870–1889.

The wind died away abruptly. All was absolutely still.

Juliet put her hand on the cold stone. The light-headed feeling she'd had on her first day in Carissima came back. She bowed her head until it passed. A feeling of sadness and despair nearly overwhelmed her. She gasped with the pain of it.

'Oh Martha, this isn't where you want to be at all,' she whispered.

From her vision the previous night she remembered the plaintive cry of Martha begging to be taken home to England, and she knew with certainty what had to be done. She just hoped Logan would agree to it.

The wind returned and sound filled the air again. Juliet was relieved to hear the birds singing cheerfully in the trees. She sat there for a while, as she knew Helena had done many times before her.

Reluctantly she returned to the house, but was prevented from going into Logan's office by the sound of him talking to Des behind the closed door. Divulging her idea to Logan would have to wait a while longer. She fetched the diary and brought it to read while sitting in the kitchen so that she'd be aware of Des leaving.

She read the next entry.

3rd December 1889

Dear Diary,
We have a new nursemaid for Beatrice, called Gwen. She came highly recommended by the friend of the local vicar's wife. She is from Dublin. Beatrice likes her and is content, thank the Lord, despite the loss of Martha. I was so worried that she would be

distraught. She makes up stories about Martha still tucking her in every night, and that seems to comfort her.

I am in full health again, but I cannot say the same for James. He is grieving the loss of our son. The doctor said it would be safe for me to try again in the spring. I so much want to give James a son. Maybe it would turn him back into the happy person Beatrice and I knew.

Helena

12th December 1889

Dear Diary,
Beatrice has so filled my head with her stories, that I now dream too, every night, that Martha tucks me in!

Would that James might know the peaceful sleep that I have! He still sleeps little and is more cantankerous than ever. I have asked him to forgive himself about the broken promise to Martha. But he denies that it bothers him, saying that what is done is done. But the change in him belies his words. I found him asleep in his study at three in the afternoon today!

Our first Christmas is fast approaching, but I know it will not be the happy affair I would have imagined it to be when we first moved here. How much has changed since then. Maybe I should stop writing for a while – maybe this diary has brought bad luck.

Helena

The next page was blank and Juliet couldn't believe it when she flicked through the remainder of the notebook and found it empty. Even the arrival of Helena's son the following year hadn't prompted another entry, much to Juliet's disappointment.

She was roused from her frustrated ruminations when she heard Des coming out of the office.

'I'll check in with you later,' he said to Logan before passing through the kitchen with a nod in her direction.

She went to the office.

Logan looked up, his face once more grey and tired.

'Colm, my accountant, just called, looking for some more figures. He thinks there might be some discrepancies after all.' He swore, and rubbed a hand over his face. 'I'll have to spend the rest of the morning at it, I'm afraid. And there are three candidates coming in this afternoon to be interviewed for the manager's position. Thank God Des has agreed to sit in on the interviews with me. We've drawn up a very good list of questions between us.'

'That's great. I'll let you get on, but can I tell you something before I go?'

'Sure.'

'I found the burial place, and I feel sure I know what needs to be done.'

She paused, biting her lip, afraid he was going to resist.

'Tell me,' he prompted, but his voice was wary and she saw him flick a glance at the clock.

'I think *you* need to lay Martha to rest and not a water diviner.'

He gave a humourless laugh. 'And how do you propose that I do that?'

'Now don't be so cynical. You know you wanted to solve the mystery of this ghost, but finding out who she is isn't enough, and apologising isn't enough. She needs to be laid to rest ...' She hesitated.

He urged her on with a quirk of his eyebrows.

'. . . in England,' she finished, her eyes fixed on his.

'Oh, I see. Go on,' he said drily, throwing his pen onto the desk.

She knew she was going to sound crazy but she went on anyway.

'James Pershaw was tormented from the moment he broke his promise to Martha and, like you, couldn't sleep. By Helena's account he became quite miserable. The similarity to what his descendants went through is obvious. So I think you need to exhume Martha's remains and take her back to England, to the graveyard Dr. Edward Adams was buried in, thereby keeping the promise.'

'Just like that.'

'It's worth a try, isn't it?'

'And how on earth are we supposed to get her exhumed and back to England?'

'I need to think about that.'

'And where exactly in England am I supposed to find this graveyard?'

'Berkshire of course – where your ancestors came from. A doctor was a significant member of the community, so I'm sure there will be a record of his death in the local church.'

'I'm sure there are a lot of churches in Berkshire, Juliet.'

'The one near where the Pershaws lived would be a good start. Have you never gone looking for your ancestral home?'

'No, I don't know where it is, and I never bothered to find out.'

'Well, I know where it is.'

'How?'

'James' mother wrote regularly to Helena and her address is on the top of her stationery. There is a sheet of it in the diary, with a menu written on it.'

'You're wasted in photography. You should've become a detective,' he said dryly.

'I'll put your sarcasm down to lack of sleep,' she shot back.

There was an uneasy silence.

Eventually, Logan sighed, and lowered his eyes to the work on his desk.

'Sorry, you're right. I'm under pressure. Anxious about these interviews, I suppose.'

'Well, will you at least think about it?'

'Yeah, later, if I get a minute.'

Juliet fisted her hands by her sides at his distracted reply, but knew she had no choice for now but to wait.

Too restless to sit around, she took her camera down to the lake, very conscious that it was already Friday and that she had only a few more days left.

After lunch, while Logan and Des spent the afternoon interviewing prospective farm managers, Juliet went into the library. Since she had nothing better to do, she decided to search through the remaining books just in case there was another diary hidden there that Helena had started at a later date.

She spent over two hours lifting books in and out, but found nothing. It seemed they were to have only a snapshot of Helena's life after all.

Cars came and went outside, and she heard each interviewee being greeted at the front door by Des and let out by Logan or vice versa.

It was only when she heard the jeep starting up outside that she went to see if it was Logan or Des, and saw it was both of them. Sighing, she closed the last cabinet, knowing she would have to wait a while longer for Logan's decision.

Taking her laptop and camera to the kitchen, she worked on her photographs for a while. She was relieved an hour later to hear the jeep returning.

Logan came in through the pantry, said 'Hi', tossed his keys onto the table and put on the kettle.

'Was there a suitable candidate?' Juliet asked.

'Yeah,' he said, his voice weary. 'Luckily we were both impressed with the same guy. I'll ring him tonight and offer him the position. Unfortunately he won't be available for another month, but he's my first choice.'

'Have you decided what to do about Martha?'

'I haven't had time to think about it, really. I went to see how Sheila was and wasted my breath trying to persuade her to take a few days off. She said she was already bored out of her mind and insists on coming back to work on Monday.'

'That's great. Now about Martha –'

'Not now, I'm hungry. What would you like to eat?' he asked, casually looking into the fridge.

Juliet snapped her laptop shut, and stood up, her temper flaring. 'God, Logan, you'd swear this wasn't important! At the start of the week, you seemed desperate to find a solution and now that one's offered you're dragging your heels.'

He whirled around. 'Dragging my heels!' His eyes flashing hot anger. 'I don't have a farm manager, my housekeeper is off sick, my accountant is hassling me for information, so excuse me if I can't find time to consider your little game plan right now. And even if I did consider it, I'd wait and get Jack Long's opinion first before doing anything crazy!'

His voice had risen steadily, but Juliet didn't flinch.

'I'm sorry the timing is so bad, but you're not just fighting for your sanity here, Logan, you're fighting for us!'

With shaking hands she grabbed up her laptop and camera and left.

'Juliet!' he called after her.

She kept walking, not wanting him to see the angry tears in her eyes. In her room, she dumped the equipment on the bed and went to stare out the window. She looked in the direction of the old ruin and laid her forehead against the cold glass. It was nearly dark out, the trees black against the hills beyond.

'I'm doing my best, Martha, for you and me.'

The room seemed to sigh around her, and her anger melted away, leaving a warm comforting feeling in her chest. Minutes later her stomach rumbled but she ignored it. She didn't want to be in Logan's company tonight. He was battling with his own demons right now. She felt they both needed some space. She spent the evening in her room, surfing the net for information on exhumation, only succeeding in depressing herself with the technicalities it would involve like relatives' permission, and deeds to the grave, etc. It would be a long and protracted affair, which would not help Logan or their relationship. She gave up Googling and caught up on her emails instead.

Just after ten, she heard Logan coming upstairs. His footsteps stopped outside in the hallway and she held her breath, but after a moment he continued on to his own room.

Hunger was getting to Juliet and she knew she wouldn't be able to sleep if she didn't eat something.

As quietly as she could she sneaked down to the kitchen, made a sandwich and brought it back up to her room, making sure to turn off all the lights as she went. She could hear the hum from Logan's shower as she passed his room. This time she paused, wanting to go to him, but knowing that the time wasn't right. She moved on and closed her door behind her.

After eating, she got ready for bed, turned off the light and lay staring at the ceiling.

She didn't know what else to say to Logan to make him agree to her plan. Maybe he needed to read the diary himself to get a proper feel for those people's lives. Just telling him about them wasn't allowing him to have enough empathy with Martha.

Eventually, to the sound of him moving around in his room, she fell asleep. She dreamed again of Martha tucking her in and whispering '*Goodnight*'.

Chapter 53

What seemed like just minutes after she fell asleep, Juliet was woken by the sound of knocking. A look at her watch showed that it was six o'clock.

'Juliet, Juliet, wake up!' Logan called.

'Just a minute,' she mumbled.

When she unlocked the door, he was standing in the corridor, fully dressed and wearing an outdoor jacket. In his left hand he held a torch. 'Get dressed! We're going to do it, damn it – exhume her, so she'll let me be.'

'What?'

'She's been crying in my room all night and begging me to take her home.' He shuddered. 'I thought I was going to go mad.'

'You saw her?'

'No, I just heard her repeating it over and over again. Half an hour ago I sat up, thumped my two fists on the bed and said, 'All right, all right, I'll do it!' and she fell silent. I don't need a water diviner to spell it out any more clearly than that, do I? We just need to go ahead and do it!' But he grimaced as he said it.

'Logan, it's still dark outside!'

'It'll be bright shortly.'

'But you can't just go and dig up her body! I looked it up – you need documents and permission and –'

'To hell with all that. I can't take any more of this and this is my land so I can do what I like. Martha is of no consequence to any officials after all this time, and they would never believe our reason for doing it anyway. Are you in or not?'

'Of course!' she said, pulling her clothes on over her pyjamas.

When she was ready, they went downstairs together.

Juliet put on her jacket, her mind racing.

'Have you thought about how we're going to transport her remains?' she asked as Logan opened the front door.

'By ferry. It's our only hope. Cars go to England all the time without their contents being checked.'

'I'm a little scared, Logan,' Juliet said, taking his hand.

He rubbed his thumb over her knuckles.

'But you believe we're doing the right thing, don't you?' he asked.

'Yes, yes, we are.' She took a calming breath. 'Okay, let's go then.'

He had a spade ready by the front door and picked it up, passing her the stick she had used the day before.

'Wait,' Juliet said. 'What are we going to put the bones in?' A shiver ran down her spine.

Logan looked at her for a moment, thinking. 'Well, for now, would a sports holdall do?'

'I suppose so.' She grimaced. It seemed so undignified.

He passed her the spade, walked back through the hall and rooted in a cupboard under the stairs. Retrieving a large blue kitbag, he brought it over and held it up.

Juliet could only nod.

Taking back the spade, he ushered her out the door.

They stepped out into the dark. There wasn't a sound. A fog hung around them and Juliet shivered.

The torch beam lit their way. At the holly bush they turned onto the path Juliet had beaten through the brambles. She followed blindly behind Logan, holding onto the back of his jacket.

They crossed the first clearing and made their way to the second one.

'Why does there have to be a fog?' Juliet said. 'It's making this very eerie.'

'I used to play here,' Logan said, looking around, 'but I never knew there were graves here. Where are they?'

Juliet pointed to the spot beyond the ruin.

When they got closer, Juliet took the torch and led him to the exact spot.

They studied both headstones in silence as morning light began to filter through the fog. Juliet switched off the torch.

'Logan, this won't be an easy job – it could take hours.'

'I know. I suppose I didn't really think this through. But we're committed now so I think we should make a start at least,' he replied, putting the tip of the spade against the ground

'Wait!' Juliet said.

'What?'

'Your great-grandfather asked the oak tree to watch over Martha. It was a young oak then so I presume this is it,' she said, laying her hand on the trunk of a huge oak a few feet beyond Martha's headstone. 'Maybe you should ask permission to take her away?'

Logan stared at her, but then stepped over to the tree and laid his hand on the trunk, thinking for a moment.

'I thank you for sheltering Martha, and now I ask your permission to take her from your care, so I can take her to her rightful resting place.'

There was silence.

He looked back at Juliet. She nodded.

He pressed the tip of the spade into the soil.

'Fortunately the soil is soft here,' he said as he tossed the first shovelful to the side.

Juliet watched him work for half an hour. At which point he took off his jacket.

'Here, let me do some?' she said.

He handed her the spade. They worked alternately, with Logan taking longer turns than Juliet.

'I've got blisters,' she said, as he took over once more.

'Me too. I was stupid not to bring gloves.'

He dug on and eventually stopped.

'We're only down about three feet,' he said. 'I think we should take a break and come back after breakfast.'

'Suits me. Every muscle is aching,'

They went up to the house and returned an hour later armed with a second spade, a trowel and work gloves for both of them. Having had a little time to think, they also brought with them plastic freezer bags in different sizes and a roll of sticky labels.

When they had dug down four feet Logan's spade hit something. They both froze.

Juliet swallowed, her stomach suddenly tense. Logan bent and smoothed away the soil with his glove, uncovering a shin bone.

'It looks like James Pershaw didn't dig down the requisite six feet. We need to be very careful now.'

'I think you'd be better off working on your own in there now,' Juliet said, climbing out of the grave, to stand and watch as Logan gingerly cleared the area, one foot square at a time, until the surface of Martha's remains were visible.

Juliet was silent as she gazed at the skeleton which was about five foot four in length. The solemnity of the moment stole any words that Juliet might have spoken. She felt an overwhelming tenderness for the woman they were trying to help. Logan reached up and squeezed her hand.

She looked out over the lake. The fog was finally lifting and the sun was visible above the hill across the lake. The birds began to sing.

'Pass me the trowel,' Logan said softly.

Starting at the feet, he dug very carefully around each bone and passed them one by one to Juliet. Reverently she placed them in the plastic bags, labelling them as she went, the toes in one, the longer foot bones in another. There would then, at least, be some hope of laying her out properly when they got to England.

Eventually he reached the skull. This he placed in the sports bag himself.

'I'll come back later and fill this in,' he said, climbing out of the grave. He gathered up all the implements and Juliet carried the bag. Exhausted, they made their way back up to the house.

Once in the hall, Logan turned to her and said, 'I'll see if I can book us on a ferry to Holyhead this evening. Can you go online and find us a place to stay in Berkshire? Somewhere near the old ancestral pile?'

'Okay.' So her stay at Carissima was coming to an end four days early.

They kicked off their damp, muddy shoes. Logan took the bag to his office while Juliet ran upstairs in her socks to get her laptop, and to copy down the old address of Mother Pershaw in Berkshire.

Logan joined her there later. 'I've booked us on a ferry for tonight at nine thirty. How are you getting on with accommodation?'

'Helena and James lived with James' mother near the village of Mirrow, in Berkshire,' Juliet said. 'There's an inn there that does bed and breakfast.'

'The ferry gets into Holyhead just after midnight, so we'll drive through the night when the roads are quiet. We should get to Berkshire by early morning. I hope the inn will be open at that time and we can get a few hours' sleep. We'll have to stay Sunday night too. Will you book us a room for two nights then?'

A jolt shot through Juliet at his use of the singular. Her eyes shot to his.

He shrugged. 'I hope you don't mind sharing.'

Juliet laughed, some of the tension of the previous twenty-four hours leaving her shoulders.

'It's just that I have no intention of letting you, or Martha, out of my sight until this is done,' he said. 'But it's not over yet, Juliet, and we aren't even sure this'll work.'

'It'll work,' she said, going up on her toes to steal a quick kiss before returning to her laptop. She was gratified to hear his shaky breath behind her. *The man has a will of iron*, she thought, *but even iron melts with heat.*

'You'll come back with me on the ferry on Monday, won't you?'

Juliet was touched by the insecurity in his voice and was relieved that he had asked. She had presumed that, since they would be near London, he would expect her to go straight home after the visit to Berkshire.

'I mean,' he continued, 'your flight home is booked for Tuesday evening, and you'll want to know if all this works for Martha . . . and us.'

'Of course,' she said, smiling.

'Good.' He returned the smile, and her heart tripped with hope.

'I'll ring Sheila to let her know we'll be away until Monday evening. And I think it would be best if I ring the inn rather than trying to do it over the internet at this late stage.' She noted down the number.

'I've thought of something else,' Logan said. 'I'll be back in a moment.'

He went out through the pantry and she saw him crossing the yard to the seed workshop.

She looked up from her laptop when he returned. He placed a Styrofoam box about two by three feet on the table.

'I get seeds and plants delivered in boxes like this,' he said. 'They also use them in labs at the university. So I thought we could put the bones in here. That way if we are stopped, they will see the container and the very obviously old bones, and I'll flash my Cambridge professor credentials, murmur something about archaeology and hopefully they'll jump to the wrong conclusion!'

He flashed her a grin, the likes of which she hadn't seen since his last visit to London.

She grinned back. 'May I say, you are frighteningly good at this!'

'But now I have to get back to work if we are to get away on time tonight. Will you transfer the bones from the sports bag into this?'

She nodded.

'Good. Can you come and take them from the office now before I start on some phone calls?'

Juliet collected the bag and took it and the empty box into the morning room and placed them on the floor. She knelt in front of them and zipped the bag open.

'I hope we're doing the right thing, Martha,' she murmured, 'and that we haven't disturbed you for nothing.'

The air seemed to vibrate around her but, instead of feeling chilled, she felt comforted as though she had received an embrace.

She pondered on the empty box for a moment before getting up and taking a silk throw from the back of an armchair nearby. It was brightly coloured with the picture of a peacock on it. 'I'm sure Elizabeth won't object if ultimately this helps Logan,' she said aloud, as she lined the bottom of the box with the gorgeous silk and let it hang out over the sides. Then slowly she transferred Martha's remains into it, leaving the skull until last. She lifted it up but instead of bare bone she saw clearly the face of Martha as it was in the photograph in Florence. She stared, then blinked, only to find herself seeing the skull again. With a smile and a huge tenderness, she put it into the box and folded the silk in on top. Pressing the lid on securely, she sat back on her heels and sighed with satisfaction.

Chapter 54

Later that evening they brought their bags down to the hall and put them next to the box.

'Just a second,' Juliet said and dashed into the library, returning a moment later with the Wordsworth book of poetry and the diary. 'Something to read on the ferry,' she said, putting them into her bag.

He gave a low chuckle. 'Once a romantic, always a romantic. I should have guessed it by the way you looked at those locks on the bridge in Florence.'

She grinned unapologetically at him.

'I'll just make sure the place is locked up and we'll be on our way,' he said.

They made good time on the journey to Dublin and drove into their place in the queue with half an hour to spare. A port authority official passed by their car, but didn't stop.

'I think I know how a drug smuggler must feel, and I'm

pretty sure I have guilt written all over my face,' Juliet said.

Logan looked over at her. With a suddenness that didn't even allow her to take a breath he swooped across and kissed her practically senseless.

'That's better,' he murmured, sitting back and studying her. 'Now you look like you've been thoroughly kissed, and not like a guilty drug smuggler at all.'

He laughed low in his throat at her speechlessness, turned on the engine and inched forward in the queue.

They drove on board without incident and left the car deck. Finding two comfortable chairs in the corner of one of the lounge areas they settled down for the journey. What looked like the tail-end of a stag party passed through but fortunately didn't stay in the lounge, searching, no doubt, for a bar.

'You know, I'm glad we couldn't fly over,' Juliet said. 'Martha went to Ireland by boat. I think it's appropriate that she's returning by boat too.'

Logan just nodded. Juliet could see that he was settling himself for sleep so she took out the poetry book. Within minutes of departure, he fell asleep. Juliet read for a while before she too fell asleep.

At midnight they were awoken by an announcement inviting passengers to return to their cars for disembarking.

Juliet groaned as she stood up. 'Every muscle is aching after all that digging.'

Logan stretched. 'I know the feeling,' he said, rubbing his lower back.

On the dock, an official from Customs shone a torch into the car, before waving them on.

'We're on our way,' Juliet said with relief.

Logan handed her some pages. 'I don't have Sat Nav so I

printed off the route. I know the way until we need to turn off the M40 in Berkshire, but that's about five hours or more from now. Why don't you get some sleep while you can?'

Juliet studied the route before tucking the directions into the glove compartment.

'Okay,' she said, 'but if you get sleepy let me know and I can take over.'

'Sure,' Logan said, turning up the heater a little.

Juliet fell asleep shortly afterwards, and they stopped for coffee some time later at a service station.

Back in the car, Juliet talked about everything and anything to help keep Logan awake. They even swopped stories from their college days.

The car's clock read ten minutes past five when Juliet gave Logan the instruction to leave the motorway. For the following forty-five minutes she concentrated on giving directions. They drove through Reading town.

'Look, we've only a mile to go,' she said, a short while later, pointing to a left-hand turn and a signpost illuminated by the headlights, which read 'Mirrow, 1 Mile'.

They drove up over a small hill before descending towards a village, empty that hour of the morning. Logan drove slowly through its main street which was illuminated by pretty street lamps.

'Nice little place,' he commented.

'It's beautiful. Look, it has some of those old shop fronts with bow windows. Aren't they pretty? I can't wait to see it in daylight. I was afraid the place would have been overdeveloped and ugly by now.'

'It's great that a lot of the old English villages have remained unchanged and still retain their charm.'

Juliet looked around, wondering if Edward Adam's surgery had been in one of those buildings.

They arrived at the corner of a large village green.

'Well, I presume that's where we're staying,' Logan said, looking across the green at the inn. 'That wasn't hard to find.'

'What?' Juliet said. Her eyes had gone straight to the church on their left, straining her neck to look beyond the gate for any sign of headstones. But the car had gone past and she couldn't see over the wall. Looking across the green she saw a two-storey building painted in white with large wooden beams framing the doors and window, and a sign saying '*The Golden Cup Tavern*'.

'Yes, that's it. The owner said she'd leave a key under the flowerpot to the right of the front door and she'd leave our room key on the desk behind the counter.'

Logan parked the car and took out the bags while Juliet fetched the key. They went in quietly. Juliet reached over the counter and picked up a key with the room-number six on it. They went upstairs, glad it was carpeted so their footsteps didn't make any noise. Room six was at the end of the corridor. Unlocking the door, Juliet switched on the light. The room had wooden beams on the ceiling, and was tidy and clean.

'A bit too flowery,' Juliet said, 'but it has charm.'

'I don't care, as long as the bed is comfortable,' Logan said, putting down their bags, his eyes owl-like in his face after driving through the night.

'It's got a good en suite,' Juliet said, going in to check it out.

In the time it took to come back out, Logan had stripped to his boxers and was getting in under the duvet.

Juliet laughed. 'That was fast.'

'If you're going to make love to me, please do it quietly – I'd hate you to wake me.' He chuckled and smiled.

Laughing again, she took her wash bag into the bathroom. When she came out a few minutes later, he was already fast asleep.

She set the alarm on her phone for nine, turned off the light and got in beside him. He didn't stir. A little disappointed, although exhausted too, she lay her head next to his shoulder, and put her arm across him. Pressing her lips to his arm, she whispered 'Goodnight'.

A small amount of light from a street lamp came in through a crack in the curtains, illuminating the dressing table where Logan had placed the box. Juliet looked at it until her eyes became heavy. The lids drifted almost closed but she opened them again, thinking she'd seen something.

A mere shadow of a woman seemed to be standing there, wringing her hands. Juliet knew she was looking at Martha, but she felt no fear.

'It won't be much longer now, Martha,' she whispered.

The shadow stilled and faced her. Juliet heard a barely audible sigh, before the form melted away.

Chapter 55

When the alarm went on the phone Juliet woke up with her back curled into Logan, his arm wrapped around her. Moving away from him, she reached out and switched off the alarm. Logan pulled her back against him, murmuring into her hair.

'What time is it?'

'Nine.'

She turned to face him. 'You slept.'

He lifted heavy lids. 'I'm not in Carissima, so no proven theory yet, Detective Holmes.'

She remembered her vision, not sure now if she had dreamt it.

'This will work, Logan. I feel it.' Her voice held conviction, but she was nervous too.

'God, you're beautiful,' he said, 'especially when your eyes are big and scared like that.'

She blinked at him, hoping she wasn't going to cry.

His hand caressed her back. 'Two things – first, I do not hold you responsible for my decision to bring Martha back here and, second, I also believe that it's going to work. It has to, because I don't want to lose you.' His tone was husky and he gathered her to him, pressing her face to his shoulder.

Out in the corridor, some children ran up and down, calling to each other.

'I think we'd better get up or I'll keep you here all day and I think Martha would have something to say about that,' Logan said with regret.

Juliet raised herself up on one elbow and looked down at him. Leaning over, she kissed the tip of his nose before getting out of bed to go for a shower.

Twenty minutes later they were down in the lobby, having put the '*Do not disturb*' sign on the door. They didn't want anyone going in to tidy and coming across Martha. They thanked the owner for leaving out the key for them. She was a young, thin woman, with a warm smile, who introduced herself as Amy.

'We were wondering,' Logan asked, 'do you know how we would go about seeing the church records?'

'You'll need to see the verger – Mr. Nye.' She looked at her watch. 'Service is at eleven, so he should be there in half an hour. That will give you time for some breakfast.' She smiled and led them to the dining room. 'It looks like rain, so help yourself to an umbrella from the stand when you're going out after.'

All through breakfast, Juliet's eyes kept darting to the church across the green. She didn't even notice what she was eating.

At ten thirty they walked across, Logan holding a large golf umbrella over both of them.

'My stomach is doing somersaults,' Juliet declared.

'Mine's out in sympathy,' Logan replied, taking her hand in his.

'I thought you'd have asked the landlady about your ancestral home?'

For the Love of Martha

'She looked too young to know the history of this place and her accent had a hint of Cornwall, I think. She's probably a blow-in. No, I'll ask the verger about it.'

When they went in through the church gate they saw a grey-haired man unlocking the church door.

'Good morning.' Logan called, when they were halfway up the path.

He turned around.

'Good morning. Can I help you?'

'I hope so,' Logan said. 'Are you Mr. Nye?'

'That's right.'

Logan released Juliet's hand and put his out to the verger.

'I'm Logan and this is Juliet.'

'Hello,' Juliet said.

He shook hands with them. 'What can I do for you?' he asked.

'We're trying to trace a grave,' Logan said, 'and the home of my ancestors, the Pershaw family.'

'Well, well, are you a Pershaw then?'

'Yes, Logan Pershaw, great-great-grandson of Sigmund and Eve Pershaw.'

Juliet hadn't known that the 'Mother Pershaw' Helena had referred to was called Eve.

'Very pleased to meet you. It's a long time since a Pershaw lived here,' he mused.

'Yes, early 1900s, I think,' Logan said. 'Yet you're familiar with the name?'

'I'm in the historical society,' he explained. 'There'll be no problem finding the graves of your great-great-grandparents. Why don't you come inside?' He turned to push open the door.

Logan raised his eyebrows at Juliet. 'I've been so preoccupied with all the Martha stuff that I never thought of that,' he said, closing and shaking the umbrella before following the verger inside.

Immediately they were enveloped in the rich scent of flowers and candles. There wasn't an inch of space that wasn't decorated in sheaves of barley, flowers and vegetables.

'Harvest Festival,' the verger explained, when he saw them looking around.

'My great-grandparents might have been married here,' Logan mused.

'You're correct,' the verger said, leading them up the aisle and through a door beside the altar. 'I've seen the record of their marriage.' He led them past a high cupboard, with its door slightly ajar. The edge of a long white vestment was visible through the crack. 'This is the vestry,' he commented.

Juliet barely glanced at it before turning her attention to an old metal filing cabinet in a row of three, which the verger was inserting a key into. Her palms were damp. She nudged Logan.

'It's not actually my family that I'm enquiring about,' Logan said.

'Oh, well, I hope it's a record from 1889 onwards. That's when this church was built – in 1889 after the original burnt down in '88. It was in the original church that your great-grandparents would have been married. All records prior to the fire were sent off to the archive office in Reading five years ago. You'll have to go there for their marriage records. All we have here are the new ones, those dating from April 1889 when the new church was built, I'm afraid.'

Hope had waned at the start of his speech but waxed again by the time he was finished.

Juliet spoke up. 'This person died sometime between May and September 1889.'

'Ah,' he said, moving to the first filing cabinet. He lifted out a worn register and placed it on the table. 'What name are we looking for?'

'Doctor Edward Adams,' Juliet replied, moving in closer in the hope of being able to scan the pages too.

Logan moved to the verger's other side.

'Right then, let's see,' Mr. Nye mumbled, as he took out a pair of reading glasses and put them on – painfully slowly, Juliet felt.

Her heart started to pound as he turned the pages and moved his finger down a list of names. This is too easy, she thought. I just know he isn't going to find him.

'Ah, here we are. Doctor Edward Adams, died 7th July, 1889 – a broken neck, dear, dear, dear.'

'That's him – he fell from his horse!' Juliet exclaimed.

She and Logan exchanged a look of excitement.

'And his grave?' Logan prompted.

'That might be a little trickier. The new graveyard has a very explicit grid reference. The old section however, was just divided into quarters. It seems that Dr. Adams was buried in the lower left quarter. I'm afraid you will literally have to start in the far corner and work your way out until you find it.'

He glanced from one to the other then pointed to an area of the map.

Juliet nodded to show that she was following. She was itching to start the search.

'Great, thank you so much,' she said, already moving towards the door.

'Wait, Juliet,' Logan said. He turned to the verger. 'We don't want to just find this man's grave – we were hoping that we could bury his fiancée's remains there with him.'

'Excuse me?' The verger looked at him in puzzlement.

Juliet came back to stand beside Logan. 'You see, she was a governess here at the Pershaws' house and she fell in love with Dr.

Adams. They were engaged when the Pershaws moved to Ireland.'

Juliet paused. She could hear people arriving in the church for the service. Her palms began to sweat. She rushed on, encouraged by the intrigued look on the verger's face.

'The Pershaws took her with them, but she promised to return. But,' she glanced at the records, 'Dr. Adams died, then shortly after, she died too, of a fever, and was buried in Ireland. We want to reunite them. We have her bones with us and we want to bury them in his grave.'

'My, my, that is some story.'

Juliet smiled hopefully.

'But,' the verger continued, 'it's the vicar who will have to give you permission, I'm afraid. Not me. Do you have the deeds to Dr Adam's grave?'

Juliet's stomach sank. She shook her head.

The verger looked from one to the other. 'Look, why don't you go out and see if you can find his grave and then come back and talk to the vicar straight after the service. He'll be done at about a quarter to twelve.'

'Okay,' Logan said. 'Thank you very much.' He shook the verger's hand.

Juliet did the same, said thank you, and moved towards the door.

'Hang on a second, Juliet,' Logan said, staying where he was. 'Mr. Nye, would you have time to tell me briefly a little about the Pershaws? And where my great-great-grandparents are buried?'

The verger glanced up at the clock on the wall. 'Yes, I can spare another minute or two. The historical society has done extensive research on all the large estates in the area.'

'Logan, I'll take a look outside while you talk, okay?' Juliet said.

'Of course. I'll be there in a minute.'

Rushing out of the vestry and down the aisle to the main door, she got some curious looks from those arriving for the service. She grabbed up the umbrella from where Logan had left it inside the door and dashed out into the rain. Going around the side of the building, she passed the rather sterile 'new' graveyard, with its neat rows of gleaming marble headstones of all shapes and sizes, and rectangles of marble chippings marking out each grave.

Turning the corner at the back of the church, she came to an abrupt stop and the word 'Oh' sighed from her lips. It was as if she had stepped into a totally different world. She had left behind a place of black and white marble with sharp angles and was now standing on the edge of a place of natural beauty and greenery. The old graveyard spread out before her, rich in character, with lichen-covered gravestones at odd angles in the grass and huge, ancient yew trees keeping watch over them. Clusters of fuchsia bushes grew here and there and the ground rose and fell unevenly to eventually slope away to a drenched hedgerow at the bottom. The gravestones all faced a magnificent view of the fields of Berkshire and the hills beyond.

What a lovely place to be laid to rest, she thought.

The peace there was palpable and she was reluctant to intrude.

A movement to her right caught her attention and to her delight she saw a red squirrel foraging in some twigs.

Smiling she walked forward and the squirrel scampered up a nearby tree. Birds were singing and the peacefulness calmed her excited nerves. She made her way to the bottom corner, drinking in the beauty.

Rain pattered off the umbrella and her shoes were wet, but she didn't notice as she tried to read the date on the first headstone in the corner. She thought it looked like 1865, but it was very worn and she had to feel the grooves with her fingers to be sure.

She was able to read the next few headstones and was struck by the number of graves that had young children buried in them.

Cautiously, she moved along the rows, afraid of missing the grave she was looking for. Her back was aching from bending over by the time she was about five rows up, and her fingers were cold and wet. She was trying to rub them warm around the handle of the umbrella when her eyes fell on the next gravestone. She went still, not believing that she had actually found it. But there is was, a simple headstone leaning forward, with the words: *Edward Adams M.D., Born 1861. Died 7 July 1889.*

Juliet's heart pounded. She was thrilled that she had found him, but suddenly her throat ached with grief. This is stupid, she thought, I didn't even know the man. But despite herself, tears ran down her face and a great sob shook her body. Realising it was Martha's grief she was feeling, she let it flow through her.

She stood there for several minutes, eventually remembering that Logan didn't have an umbrella. Wiping her face with her sleeve, and clearing her throat, she noted the exact location of the grave and ran back to the shelter of the church door where Logan was standing in from the rain.

He looked at her expectantly, his eyebrows raised at her red eyes.

She gave a shaky laugh. 'It's okay. I've found him.'

'Excellent.' He took her arm and turned her in the direction she had just come. The rain had eased a little, and Logan held the umbrella while they walked back to Edward's grave.

Logan looked at it in silence.

After a moment Juliet spoke. 'What if the vicar won't let us do this, Logan?' Frustration and anxiety that it might all have been for nothing had her voice cracking.

Logan put his arm around her waist and pulled her in to his side. She rested her head on his shoulder, looking at Edward's name on the gravestone.

'I don't see why he should object,' Logan said. 'They both died such a long time ago.'

The congregation began singing the opening hymn inside the church and Juliet and Logan stood by the grave until the song was finished.

'Do you want to go in to the service while we're waiting for the vicar?' Logan asked.

'Okay, but can I go and get the diary first? I think it would help to strengthen our case. It's all there in Helena's writing.'

'I'll get it.'

Juliet went in and sat in the back row. Logan joined her a few minutes later.

All through the service, Juliet observed the vicar, a tall man in his sixties, and hoped he would be sympathetic to their request. In his sermon he spoke of compassion, so surely he would understand why they needed to do this?

They stayed seated as the congregation filed out and exchanged greetings with the vicar at the door. A small round lady, also in her sixties, bustled around, extinguishing candles and removing books from the lectern and altar.

The vicar came back in after a few minutes. They rose to their feet and went to meet him, but he asked them to give him a moment and went into the vestry. A few moments later the verger emerged and called them in.

Inside the vicar was putting on his jacket. The verger introduced them to him.

'And this is Mr. Thompson, our vicar.'

'Pleased to meet you,' Logan and Juliet said together.

'How can I help you today?' he asked, smiling kindly at them.

Juliet felt herself relax a little.

She repeated what she had told the verger.

'I see,' said the vicar. 'But you don't have the deeds to the grave or even the relatives' written permission?'

'There are no relatives that we are aware of. It was such a long time ago and no one else has been buried in Edward's grave – it has been untouched since 1889.'

The vicar was frowning. 'I don't know. It's all a bit strange.'

Juliet put the diary down on the table. 'Look, this is Helena Pershaw's diary.'

The verger gave an audible gasp and Juliet knew he would love to get his hands on it for his historical society.

'Listen,' she said, flicking through the pages and stopping at the entry for the 30th of July 1889. She read aloud.

'"*Our community is shocked at the death of that very personable young man, Doctor Adams, who was thrown from his horse while returning home two nights ago from visiting a patient. He was found the following morning on the side of the road, his neck broken. There was a storm that night, and it is believed that either the thunder or lightning startled his horse.*"'

The vicar had slipped on his glasses and was peering at the text. 'Hmm,' was all he said.

Juliet was feeling desperate. 'And this,' she said, moving on to a later point in that entry. Again she read aloud. '"*My heart began to pound on reading the words. This was Martha's young man she was writing about. How was I to break such news to the poor girl? Trembling, I went in search of her. Brigid was in the nursery watching over Beatrice as she napped. She said that Martha had gone to the orchard, and that is where I found her. She was sitting on the bench by the east wall, reading a book. Before I could say anything, she pointed out the tiny new pears on the trees, remarking how quickly the seasons were passing. She looked so lovely sitting there with a smile on her face, so full of life and* hope. *And I had to shatter all that. I sat beside her and told her what I had learnt. She jumped up and, wringing her hands, vehemently denied that it could have been Edward who was thrown. "He is an excellent horseman. Mother Pershaw must have made a mistake. Edward is waiting for me, we are going to be married. We have it all planned." I caught her hands and her eyes met mine. What she saw there made her go still and tears slid down her face. Pulling her gently down on the seat beside me, I took her in my arms. I was unable to hold back my own tears, as she sobbed out her heartbreak.'"*

There was a loud sniff from behind them and they all turned around to find the woman who had blown out the candles standing there, dabbing her eyes with a tissue.

'Oh Jeffrey, you have to let these people reunite that poor couple – it's only right!'

'This is my wife, Betty,' the vicar said, shaking his head at her tears but then smiling tenderly at her as he drew her forward. 'My dear, this is Juliet Holmes and Logan Pershaw.'

'Hello,' she said, giving them a watery smile. 'I'm so sorry for eavesdropping but I couldn't help it. I was taking down a flower arrangement just outside the door and I must confess once I started listening I didn't want to stop!'

Juliet smiled at her.

The vicar's wife looked at him hopefully.

The verger cleared his throat. 'It does all tally with what we know of the Pershaws, Vicar.'

'Come on, dear,' the vicar's wife coaxed.

Juliet held her breath as the vicar looked down at the diary again.

He sighed. 'Oh, very well. It can't do any harm, I suppose.'

'Oh, *thank* you!' Juliet exclaimed. She threw her arms around Logan and then, laughing, hugged the vicar's wife and then the vicar himself. They were all laughing at that point.

'When did you hope to do this interring?' the vicar asked, getting down to business.

'As soon as possible?' Logan suggested. 'We're booked to go back on the ferry in the morning.'

The vicar's eyebrows shot up.

'I know it's all a bit rushed . . .' Logan said.

'Well, we can't have her lying about now, can we?' the vicar said. 'If I can get hold of the gravedigger and if he can spend the afternoon opening the grave, we can bury her remains at five o'clock this evening.'

The vicar's wife clapped her hands in delight. He sent her a warning look, but Juliet grinned along with her.

'Can you arrange to have the coffin here by then?' the vicar asked.

'Eh . . .' Logan looked at Juliet who looked at him in panic. 'You see, there isn't a coffin. When the bones were exhumed they were put in a box.'

The vicar was frowning again.

Juliet jumped in. 'We knew that Dr. Adam's coffin would have disintegrated by now and that it would be so much better to lay Martha's bones right next to his. We wanted nothing to separate them after all this time.'

The vicar was silent.

Juliet looked desperately at Mrs. Thompson.

'Now, dear,' she said to her husband, 'that is such a beautiful thought. And I know what you're thinking – that you must make sure there is nothing sinister going on here and these people aren't just using this as a means to dispose of someone's remains. But Logan here, I'm sure, will let you examine the bones carefully and see that they are quite old, isn't that right, Logan?'

'Absolutely, Mrs. Thompson!'

'And I'm sure also that you will show the vicar your passport to prove that you are who you say you are.'

'Yes, of course.'

'Then I don't see any problem. Do you, dear?' she said, looking at her husband.

The vicar rolled his eyes to heaven. 'I haven't a hope against such logic, now do I?'

She patted him on the arm and beamed at Juliet and Logan. 'That's settled then. We'll go home immediately so Jeffrey can call the gravedigger.'

'How can I contact you?' the vicar asked, taking a pen from his pocket.

Logan gave him his mobile phone number.

They all went outside. Juliet walked with Mrs. Thompson and thanked her again for helping them

'Nothing should stand in the way of true love, my dear. I've been married to Jeffrey for forty years, and each year happier than the last, despite my mother having a fit when I told her I was marrying a vicar and I having been raised as a Catholic!' She gave Juliet's arm a squeeze. 'Love happens where it's meant to. Now you two go off and have a nice lunch while you're waiting. I know just the place you can go.'

She gave Juliet the directions to an inn a few miles away.

'It would be lovely if you would come to the burial too this afternoon,' Juliet said.

'Oh, I would be honoured, dear, thank you.'

They said their goodbyes but, instead of leaving, Logan guided Juliet back into the graveyard. They went to a section near Edward's grave.

Logan spent a few minutes looking for the grave of his great-great-grandparents, Eve and Sigmund. Having found it, Juliet calculated from the inscription that 'Mother Pershaw', as she thought of her, had died fourteen years after the others had moved to Ireland.

After a few moments, Logan tightened his arm around Juliet's waist and they moved away. She told him about Mrs. Thompson's suggestion for lunch.

'That's out beyond where the Pershaws lived, so we can stop there on the way,' she said.

They crossed over the green to the car.

Chapter 56

A mile from Mirrow village Logan took a right at a crossroads, coming to a stop two hundred yards along at a set of closed electric gates.

'I think this is it,' he said, leaning on the steering wheel and looking up at the grand pillars.

'*View Manor*,' Juliet read on the left pillar. 'Yes, this is it. That's the name on your great-great-grandmother's letter head.'

'Mr. Nye said the owners are away at the moment, but that we'll be able to see the house from the road further on.'

He drove up a hill and after rounding a bend, stopped where they had a clear view across parkland to a sprawling manor house. Logan pulled up on the grass verge and they got out. It had stopped raining and the sun had come out.

Logan whistled. 'It's much bigger than I expected,' he said. 'It's twice the size of Carissima.'

'It's huge! How come it's not still in the family?'

'We were a family of wanderers. No one wanted to settle

there, so when my great-great-grandmother died, it was sold and the money was divided between her children.'

'I wonder if Mother Pershaw, as Helena called her, ever visited Carissima.'

'She may well have.'

'Are you sorry you didn't inherit it?' Juliet asked.

'God, no! It would cost a fortune to keep a place like that running.'

'So, who owns it now?'

'Mr. Nye says it's some footballer and his wife.'

'Ah, nouveaux riches! Logan, see the woods there to the right of the house?'

'Yeah?'

'There was an old empty cottage beyond it by the river. That's where Martha used to meet Edward when they were courting.'

Logan slipped his arm around her waist, shielding his eyes from the sun as he continued to look around.

Juliet's stomach gave a loud rumble.

'Come on, let's find that inn!' Logan said.

'Sure,' she said, taking a last look at the house.

As she got into the car, Logan's phone rang.

'Hello. Yes, Vicar?' He smiled and gave a thumbs-up to Juliet. 'That's wonderful news. Yes, we'll see you at five. Thank you so much.'

He disconnected and grabbed Juliet in a hug. They drove on to the inn in high spirits.

It was beside a river and was in typical old English style, with signs outside for different varieties of ale, and a blackboard with the menu on it. A row of muddy walking boots were lined up outside and sure enough the pub was busy with groups of walkers slaking their thirst and appetite.

Juliet and Logan got a table near a roaring fire and took their time over laden plates of fresh bread, cheese and pickles.

'Your eyes are sparkling,' Logan said, placing his scrunched-up napkin on his empty plate, pushing it to the side.

Juliet gave a contented sigh. 'It all seems to be working out. It's an amazing day – one I could say I'd tell my grandchildren about, but I don't think they'd believe it. I'm not sure I would believe it myself.' She gave a light-hearted laugh.

Logan, reaching across, pressed his palm to her cheek, his eyes warm in the firelight. 'Thank you for suggesting that I come here,' he said. 'I feel good that I'm about to honour the promise my great-grandfather made to Martha.'

'You're a good man, Logan,' Juliet said, placing her hand over his.

After a moment his hand and eyes slipped away and he stared into the fire. Juliet watched him, wondering what he was thinking.

Turning his gaze back to her, he reached across the table and took her hands in both of his.

'I've decided that if this doesn't work, despite what we're doing, I'm going to do as you suggested . . . sell Carissima and look for land to buy in England.'

A small gasp escaped past Juliet's lips and she gripped his hands hard. 'What?' she whispered.

'I love you more than the house and the land at Carissima, and I've been a fool.'

'Thank you, Logan. That means everything to me. But I know it won't come to that. This has to work so that you can be happy in Carissima, where you need to be.'

He gripped her hands harder. 'You're right. Remember I said "if" our plan doesn't work. I don't know why I'm doubting it. I just wanted you to know that if there is a choice to be made, I choose you. But it won't come down to choosing. We will lay Martha to rest today.'

She smiled bravely at him, but they both knew the last seed of doubt still had a grip on them, and she was so afraid that if he had to sell Carissima he wouldn't be happy anywhere else.

Logan leant across the table and brushed his lips against hers before getting up to pay the bill. She was putting on her jacket when he came back to the table.

'The waiter was just telling me that there's a lovely path along the river that flows behind the inn. Fancy a walk?'

'Great.'

They walked for a long time, saying very little, nerves and hope preoccupying both of them. At four they returned to the car.

Back at the inn in Mirrow, they collected Martha's remains and went across to the church. Mr. Nye was already there and told them to take the box into the vestry.

'The grave is ready. Tim has dug right down close to the young man's remains, but the vicar insisted that he wasn't to be disturbed.'

'We understand,' Logan said.

The vicar and his wife arrived shortly afterwards. He examined the contents of the box and pronounced himself satisfied.

'Please give the verger Martha's details,' he said, 'so we can update our records.'

When the paperwork was done they went in solemn procession to Edward's grave.

They gathered around the open grave and they could make out the shape of Edward's skeleton just below the surface of the soil at the bottom.

'I think you had better get in, Logan,' the vicar suggested, 'and we will pass you – eh – everything in due course.'

Juliet took out the skull and passed that to Logan first. He laid it very carefully in the space next to Edward's.

The vicar, his wife and Juliet began opening the labelled bags and passing the bones in to Logan. Slowly Martha's skeleton began to take shape. He laid her left hand over Edward's right.

The tears began to roll down Juliet's cheeks as all the nervous tension left her body.

At last Martha was lying beside Edward and the vicar began the prayers.

When he was done, Juliet hugged him and his wife and Logan shook their hands.

They left Juliet and Logan alone at the graveside.

Standing side by side, they held hands and looked down into the grave.

After a few moments Logan spoke.

'Martha,' he said, 'I atone for the actions of my great-grandfather, James Pershaw, by returning you to your loved one, Edward Adams, as promised. May you both rest in peace.'

'Rest in peace,' Juliet echoed, moved by his gentle and very sincere words. The grief she had felt earlier was gone and she waited for joy or elation to take its place, but there was nothing. Disappointed, she clung tighter to Logan's hand.

'Well, that's it, I suppose,' he said.

She was silent.

Taking one look at her face, he put his arm around her shoulders and pulled her in close. 'It will work, Juliet, I'm sure. But we can't have our proof until we get home to Carissima.'

They walked back up to the church. When they got to the door, Juliet stopped. 'Would you mind if I went back and said goodbye to her on my own?'

'Of course not.'

She kissed his cheek and hurried back to the grave.

'Goodbye, Martha,' she whispered. 'Thank you for choosing me to help you. Be happy.'

The gravedigger approached then so she moved away and started back up the path.

Then, hearing a light laugh behind her, she whirled around, and saw a couple walking away towards the fields, hand in hand. The woman wore a long blue summer gown, cinched at the waist, with a long skirt and bustle, and he wore a fitted black frock coat and a top hat. The woman looked back over her shoulder, smiled at Juliet, and then they disappeared.

Juliet blinked rapidly, but the graveyard remained empty except for the gravedigger who continued his work. A bubble of laughter rose up into her throat and made her laugh out loud. She ran back to Logan.

'I saw her,' she said breathlessly. 'She was with Edward. He was wearing a top hat and she was wearing a long pale-blue dress. I saw them just for a moment.'

'Are you sure?' Logan asked, scrutinising her face.

'Absolutely, and they looked so happy.'

'That's incredible, but wonderful.' He smiled, gathering her into his arms. 'Thank God,' he murmured.

Later that night, back at the inn Juliet wondered if Logan was going to stick to his resolve until they knew for sure if the plan had worked. She wished they had separate rooms because she didn't think she could handle another night in his bed without begging him to make love to her.

But once inside the room, Logan gave her a look so full of love and longing that she walked straight into his arms.

They made love slowly and with the solemnity of a ritual, each moment precious with the joy of discovery and the depth of their love.

Chapter 57

The car journey to Holyhead the next morning was uneventful, and they boarded at two thirty in the afternoon. The crossing was calm and they docked in Dublin shortly after six.

They were sitting in their car, waiting to disembark, when Logan took out his phone.

'I forgot to turn it on this morning. Oh God, I've had three missed calls from Colm, my accountant! That doesn't bode well.'

He listened to his messages. 'He wants me to call him back urgently.' Keying in Colm's number, he got the office answer phone. 'Damn, I've missed him. It'll have to wait until the morning.'

Arriving in Carissima, tired and anxious, they were met by the welcome sight of Sheila's car in the yard and lights on in the kitchen.

'That woman is a saint,' Logan said, getting out of the car. 'I'll bet she's made us dinner.'

To prove him right, they were greeted by a wonderful aroma when they went in through the pantry.

'Ah, there you are. How was your trip?' Sheila bustled over, scrutinising their faces. 'You look worn out. I can't understand why you didn't fly for such a short trip.' Tut-tutting, she moved over to the stove. 'I presumed you'd be hungry, so I've made a beef goulash and some rice.' She stirred a pot with a heavily bandage hand.

'You're an awful woman, Sheila. You are supposed to be at home getting that hand better.' Logan went over and put his hand on her shoulder. 'But I'm very glad you're here – that smells delicious.'

'The fire is lighting in the back sitting room, so why don't I serve this up and you can take it in there and relax, and I'll be off home.'

'Thanks, Sheila,' Juliet said, getting the warmed plates from the oven and putting them on the counter. 'I've been so spoiled while I'm here.'

An hour later, toes stretched to the fire and empty plates on the floor beside them, Logan and Juliet watched the flames, her head on his shoulder and their hands joined.

'Can I presume now that I'll be staying in your room tonight?' she asked.

He squeezed her hand. 'No. I think it best that I'm on my own, to see what happens.'

'But she's gone, Logan. I can feel it. Can't you? The house feels different.'

'I don't know what I feel. I'm tired, I'm worried about the calls from my accountant, I'm anxious in case we were on a wild goose chase in England.' He gave a shuddering sigh.

Juliet didn't press the issue. She knew he had to do this alone, needed to find out by himself whether their scheme had worked.

She could wait one more day.

'Okay, well, at least let's go up together.'

Logan put up the fireguard and, after putting their dishes back in the kitchen, they went upstairs.

Outside Juliet's door he brought her hand to his lips. 'Wish me luck.'

Going up on her toes, she pressed her lips to his. 'I'll see you in the morning,' she said, her voice full of hope. Their eyes held for a moment longer and then she slipped into her room.

When she turned out her light a few minutes later and lay back on her pillow, she could hear Logan slowly walking up and down in the room next door. She knew that he was delaying going to bed in case sleep eluded him. She prayed hard to God, and to Martha and Edward, to bless him with peace. After a while she fell asleep herself, and slept dreamlessly until morning.

A knock on her door woke her, and Logan walked into the room, a grin splitting his face.

'I slept!' he shouted. 'It's morning and I slept all night long!' He laughed and launched himself onto the bed, gathering her in his arms, rolling her on top of him, the duvet caught between them.

Looking down into his relieved face, she laughed with him. 'Thank God!' she exclaimed, burying her face in his neck.

Placing his hands on the sides of her face, he raised it up so he could look into her eyes. 'It's going to be all right now. I'm going to be happy here, Juliet. It's going to be so different from what it was for my father and his father before him.' He sobered. 'I want to ask you something.'

Juliet's heart did a flip but, before he could finish, his mobile phone rang in the room next door.

He groaned. 'I'm sorry. It'll have to wait. I'll have to get that in case it's Colm.'

Only then did Juliet look at the clock. 'It nine o'clock already!' she exclaimed in amazement.

Logan moved from under her and hurried to his room.

A moment later, he appeared at the door again, this time looking very serious.

'Colm's on the way over. You were right again. Michael Cummins hasn't been up to any good. Colm said he'd tell me all about it when he gets here. I'm sorry all this is happening on your last morning. I will make it up to you, I promise.' He gave her a smile that melted her bones, before going back to his room.

An hour later, knowing that Logan hadn't had breakfast, she knocked on the office door and took in coffee and toast for him and his accountant. Colm was a bit older than Logan, with a friendly face and a head of wavy brown hair. Logan introduced her, a grave expression on his face. After shaking hands she turned to leave, but Logan stopped her.

'Juliet, your hunch was correct that Michael Cummins was stealing from Carissima, but it wasn't jewels. Apparently he had submitted receipts for a new tractor and a combined harvester two years running after my father's death and before I moved here. Colm wasn't aware of it because they had some trainee accountant in at the time of the second purchase who didn't think anything of it. But when I asked Colm to look through everything again, he came across the order and thought it odd that we would need a second tractor so soon, and another combine, so he looked into it further, only to discover that the receipts were from a farm-machinery depot owned by Michael Cummins' brother! We've been quizzing the farmhands here, and the second tractor and combine don't exist! Colm will be putting the Gardaí onto it straight away. It seems Cummins' brother issued a false invoice, I paid it presuming more farm

416

equipment was necessary, and Michael and his brother divided the money, which ran to well over a hundred thousand euro, between them. They'll both be up on charges of theft and fraud.'

'I'm sorry, Logan,' she said. 'It's sickening to have your trust, and your father's, betrayed like that.'

Logan nodded. 'I'm indebted to your intuition, once again,' he said. Their eyes locked for several seconds, until Colm coughed.

'I'll let you get on,' she said.

'It was nice to meet you,' Colm said.

Smiling, she closed the door behind her. Wondering how she would spend the morning, she idled her way along the back hall.

Stopping in front of James Pershaw's portrait, she looked at his eyes.

'The promise has been kept after all this time, James. Martha is at peace now, and I think you are too.' She continued out into the front hall.

Remembering that there had been a missed call on her phone from the water diviner when they'd got back from England, she strolled into the morning room, perched on the window seat and keyed in his number.

Mrs Long answered and Juliet briefly explained that they didn't need the water diviner's services after all. With a feeling of contentment, she told the woman that the problem had been resolved. Juliet thanked her for her time and hung up.

Deciding to take some photographs of the rooms of the house, Juliet went back out into the hall and headed up the stairs. On the first landing, instead of going through to the corridor, she hesitated in front of the door that led up to attic rooms on the third floor, which she hadn't yet explored.

'Why not? I have the time now,' she said, glancing at her watch then reaching for the door handle.

417

The hinges creaked as she pulled it towards her. She was immediately met by the smell of musty air. In front of her was a set of narrow wooden stairs. Juliet felt around for a light switch, snapped it on and went up. After a few steps the stairs turned right and she continued to another door at the top. This led onto a corridor, narrower and less grand than the one on the first floor, with bare floorboards and painted walls. Off the corridor were a series of doors, some open, some closed. Going into the first room, she turned on the light. It was a small box room with nothing in it, not even a window.

Moving on to the next she found it to be a bit bigger and had a small window. There were several boxes on the floor, with the words 'Christmas Decorations' written on the sides in black marker. Going to the window, she cleaned a space in the dust and found there was a wonderful view of the lake from that height. She wondered if the servants of higher ranking would have slept in these rooms at the front of the house. She didn't think for a moment that Martha had slept up there. Not only was she family, but as governess she would have slept in a room next to Beatrice's probably.

The next room was an eclectic mix of discarded equipment. There were old mountain boots, rucksacks, ropes and a canvas bag which held a folded tent. A couple of warped tennis rackets were propped in the corner, along with a shredded green net and some poles.

The next two rooms were empty and Juliet followed the corridor when it turned left. The rooms to the right now looked out over the orchard and she figured she was two storeys above the kitchen. Some of the attic rooms still had their single iron bed and old chests of drawers. She pulled out the top drawer in the first room, but it was empty.

She turned and worked her way up the other side of the

corridor, finding more empty rooms. In the third room along were two huge travelling trunks. Juliet's heart rate picked up. Surely there was something exciting in them, she thought. An old wedding dress or ball gown?

She heaved open the lid of the first, only to find it empty. Doing the same with the second, she was disappointed to find only some broken wooden toys and some Lego. Beyond the trunks were two large cardboard boxes full of comics and magazines from the sixties. Juliet got down on her knees and poked through them. Some were music magazines, one with a picture of the Beatles on the front cover.

'You could probably make a fortune from these, Logan,' she muttered out loud.

Moving on to the next room she found it was full of old furniture: two wardrobes, four chairs, a chest of drawers, a baby's crib and a very worn rocking horse with a broken leg. Juliet ran her hand over the dusty mane. She liked being surrounded by things from another world, another time. She liked to think that seeing and touching these things meant that those who had lived with them day after day were remembered again.

Hearing a door slam in the yard below, she squeezed between a wardrobe and a chest of drawers to get to the window. Wiping a cobweb out of the way, she saw that Sheila had arrived. Juliet raised her hand to knock and wave at her but, laughing, she stopped herself, realising that she would probably scare Sheila to death, since she didn't know she was up there.

Turning back to the room, she noticed that she must have dislodged the door of the wardrobe, as it was now open a crack. She was able to open it a small bit more before it hit off the chest of drawers. It was enough to allow her to see that there were clothes hanging up in it. Wanting to see more, she moved the crib and rocking horse into the corridor to make some space, sneezing a couple of times from the raised dust. She pulled and pushed alternately at the chest of drawers until she could open the wardrobe doors properly.

It was full, and the smell of moth balls wafted out. There were some dresses in pale blue, dark-blue and grey, a fancier gown in peach, a light blue coat, and two full-length plain black dresses. Noting the boned bodices, cinched waists and high buttoned collars, Juliet was pretty sure the style was that of the late nineteenth century and she just knew she was looking at Martha's mourning dresses – the black dresses Helena had written about in the diary – the ones Martha had insisted on wearing after Edward's death.

Juliet touched a sleeve, finding it sad to imagine a woman younger than herself knowing so much grief and wearing these clothes as the outward sign of it.

Letting the sleeve slip from her fingers, Juliet bent down and looked closer at the neat pairs of black shoes and laced boots lined along a shelf near the bottom of the wardrobe.

Beneath the shelf was a row of small drawers. She slid out the first. It held pairs of rolled-up stockings, but she was afraid to touch them in case they fell apart. They lay on top of some corsets. Juliet grimaced at the thought of being held in by one of those all day.

The next drawer held white handkerchiefs with flowers embroidered on them. Juliet lifted one out to examine the neat stitching which she presumed had been done by Martha herself. The linen material was still beautiful. On returning it to the drawer her finger hit off something hard beneath another handkerchief. She moved the handkerchief aside and saw, lying there, a ring box and a bundle of envelopes tied with ribbon.

Drawing them out carefully, and scarcely breathing, Juliet put them on her lap. The lid of the little velvet box creaked as she opened it and inside lay a ruby and diamond ring. Juliet recognised it instantly from the description in the diary.

'Oh my God, it's Martha's engagement ring,' she breathed, touching the stones reverently with a fingertip and gazing at it for a long time.

Carefully, she closed the lid and looked at the bundle on her lap. The envelope on top was addressed to Miss Martha White, at Carissima. There were about thirty envelopes there. Untying the ribbon gently, she removed the pages from the first one. The letter began, '*My darling Martha*', in that same handwriting that was in the poetry book. Juliet turned to the signature. It was signed '*Yours always, Edward.*'

Smiling, she slid the letter, unread, back into the envelope, joy welling up in her chest. 'We did the right thing,' she whispered, 'in getting you back together. It was where you were meant to be.'

Closing the drawer and then the heavy wardrobe doors, she left the chest of drawers where it was, thinking it too heavy to move a second time. The crib and rocking horse she put into an empty room. Then taking the ring box and letters, she left the attic and returned to the ground floor

She went into the library, took down the secret box to which she had returned the diary when they'd got back from England and placed the letters inside with it. She hoped she and Logan could read them together sometime. Then, pulling a sheet of paper and a pen towards her she wrote a letter to the future generations of Pershaws, explaining how Logan Pershaw had laid Martha's spirit to rest, and how she had seen her and Edward together at last.

When she was finished, her hand ached, but she was filled with a wonderful sense of peace as she placed her letter in on top of the others. 'Thanks for your help, Helena,' she said, as she ran a fingertip over the diary.

She didn't put in the ring because she needed to show it to Logan. So for the moment she closed the box, replacing it inside the glass cabinet and, taking the ring box, she went out the front door and stood on the top step.

It was a mild day and the sun was breaking through the clouds. The two swans were gliding across the rippled surface of the lake.

Juliet smiled, remembering her dread at coming here to Carissima, thinking she would hate it. And how now, on the contrary, she loved it and understood Logan's passion for the place. Her holiday was coming to a close but she was already looking forward to coming back. Carissima had got under her skin.

She heard Logan saying her name as he crossed the hall towards her.

She smiled over her shoulder at him and, coming out, he stood behind her looking at the view, his arms around her waist and his face against her hair.

'I must be the worst host in the world. I've given you so little time. I'm sorry.'

'It's not your fault,' she said, nestling back against his chest. 'Is everything going to be okay now? With the farm, I mean?'

He nodded. 'Colm has gone to talk to the Gardaí, the new manager starts in a month, and I can get on with my orchard project, *and*,' he drew the word out, 'with wooing my girl in the couple of hours I have left before I take her to the airport.'

Juliet turned in the circle of his arms, and looked up into his face, relieved to see the tension gone from it at last and a soft smile curving his wonderful lips.

'Were you very bored this morning?' he asked.

'Absolutely not. Wait until I tell you what I found.'

She described her morning's accidental treasure hunt, then opened her hand to display the ring box.

'It's the engagement ring Edward gave to Martha, going on

the description in the diary and the fact that it was with his letters.'

Edward took the box and opened it.

'Isn't it beautiful?' Juliet asked, enjoying looking at it again. 'The twist in the setting makes it very pretty.'

'To think it was there all these years.'

'How come it was never found before?'

'I never played up in those rooms – it was always just a place for storage. Maybe if I'd had brothers and sister we'd have played hide and seek up there, or dress up or something, but being an only child . . .' He let his sentence trail off.

'And the furniture was packed in there pretty tight. That room was just ignored all through the generations, it seems.'

Juliet told him about the letter she'd written.

'I hope you don't mind, but if anyone else finds the diary I want them to know that there was a happy ending for them.'

'It's perfect. I'm glad you did it.'

'So do you think the ring would be safe in there too?'

He thought for a second.

'No, I have a better idea. Come with me.' Taking her hand he drew her along behind him, down the steps.

'Where are we going?' Juliet asked, lengthening her stride to keep up with him.

'You'll see,' he said with a mischievous smile.

Rounding the corner of the house, he led her through the courtyard and along the orchard wall until they reached the little gate. Pushing it open he led her inside. A blackbird was singing high in one of the trees, his song pure and sweet.

'This place feels so much lighter than the last time I was in here,' Juliet said, looking about her and smiling, lifting her face to the warmth of the autumn sun.

'Well, I thought,' he said, 'in case there was any lingering sadness here, that we should turn it into a happy place again.' As he spoke he walked her along the path to the stone bench against the east wall.

Taking her shoulders, he turned her around and sat her down, and then sat beside her.

Holding the ring box up between them, he opened it.

'I don't think this should be hidden away. I think it should be out in the open where it can be seen as a reminder of the great love between Martha and Edward. I think Martha would want you to wear it –'

Juliet gasped.

'In appreciation of what you have done for her.'

'Oh Logan, I couldn't. That's a Pershaw heirloom. It should stay in the family.'

'Well, then maybe you should join the family and take the Pershaw name.'

Logan moved off the bench and down onto one knee.

Juliet laughed, while at the same time her eyes filled with tears.

Logan took the ring from the box.

'I think Martha would want this only to be worn as an engagement ring, don't you?'

He looked into her eyes, holding the ring at her fingertip.

'So, Juliet Holmes, will you marry me? You can come and go as you please, follow your own career, but please be my wife, come home here to Carissima when you can, and let me love you.'

The sun set the ruby on fire as Juliet answered.

'Yes,' she said, her love burning in her eyes as she looked into his. 'Yes, with all my heart.'

Logan slipped the ring onto her finger.

'It fits,' she whispered, moving into his arms, while the blackbird continued to sing.

The End